Steve Wheeler was given the choice at age eighteen of becoming either a Catholic priest or a policeman — he chose the latter. He has served in the military and, since 1987, has worked as a bronze sculptor, knifesmith and swordsmith. He lives with his wife, Elizabeth, and their two children on their twenty-acre lifestyle block in Hawkes Bay, New Zealand.

Also by Steve Wheeler
Burnt Ice
Crystal Venom

ONYX JAVELIN

A FURY OF ACES 3

steve wheeler

HARPER
Voyager

Harper *Voyager*
An imprint of HarperCollins *Publishers*

First published in Australia in 2015
by HarperCollins *Publishers* Australia Pty Limited
ABN 36 009 913 517
harpercollins.com.au

HarperCollins *Publishers*
Level 13, 201 Elizabeth Street, Sydney NSW 2000, Australia
Unit D1, 63 Apollo Drive, Rosedale, Auckland 0632, New Zealand
A 53, Sector 57, Noida, UP, India
77–85 Fulham Palace Road, London W6 8JB, United Kingdom
2 Bloor Street East, 20th floor, Toronto, Ontario M4W 1A8, Canada
195 Broadway, New York NY 10007, USA

National Library of Australia Cataloguing-in-Publication entry:

Wheeler, Steve, author.
  Onyx javelin / Steve Wheeler.
  ISBN: 978 0 7322 9375 8 (paperback)
  ISBN: 978 0 7304 9648 9 (ebook)
  Wheeler, Steve. Fury of aces ; 3.
  Science fiction.
  Interplanetary voyages—Fiction.
  Outer space—Exploration—Fiction.
A823.4

Cover design by HarperCollins Design Studio
Cover illustration by Al Brady
Author photograph by Tim Watson (Studio 62)
Typeset in Palatino 11/18pt by Kirby Jones
Printed and bound in Australia by Griffin Press
The papers used by HarperCollins in the manufacture of this book
are a natural, recyclable product made from wood grown in sustainable
plantation forests. The fibre source and manufacturing processes meet
recognised international environmental standards, and carry certification.

This story is for those who work with their hands and their souls: those who make, those who create, those who quietly bring into existence that which did not exist before

ONYX
JAVELIN

Ayana

Haulers Territory on Storfisk

The snow tigress ACE sat high on the rocky prominence overlooking the vast bowl-shaped territory, which the Haulers' Collective — hundreds of years ago — had put under her stewardship.

She watched over the tussocky land with its vast areas of Earth-type grasses, low bush and scrubby broom-like native shrubs that was liberally dotted with modified trees from distant Earth. Each tree was a foodstuff of some sort for the animals Haulers had introduced to this area, from bioengineered Earth stock.

No normal standard human was allowed to visit the great northern continent. She, and thousands of other ACEs, looked after this enormous biosphere populated by some of Earth's extinct species.

She knew it was a great joy for the Haulers to be able to recreate a type of normality for the animals. The planet had only ever had insect life, none of the higher orders of life having ever evolved. Sometimes, she personally thought that the insects, in all their forms and huge sizes, were little more than a necessary evil in that they were an excellent food source for many of the bioengineered animals of Old Earth.

She took a deep breath, holding it for a few moments as her own systems carried out an analysis of the air's chemistry, noting that the oxygen levels had decreased once again by the tiniest of percentages from her measurements the week before. She also saw that the ash levels from the latest volcanic eruption thousands of kilometres to the east were dropping. With a little sadness she shook her head and opened a link to one of her closest friends, a magnificent ACE panther, whose area of control was fifty kilometres to her west.

'Morning, Sven. The ash levels are falling. No more magnificent sunrises or sunsets soon. I shall miss them.'

Sven's deep voice rang inside her head and, even after all these years, it still made her smile as she knew that he had altered it from its original higher tone.

'Ayana! My love. Yes, it is true. But maybe you will not have to wait longer than a few more years, as another in that chain will erupt soon enough. A few of them appear to be coming back to life. My greetings to you. My charges are well, although I shall have to formally request an extension to the foraging area further north as the herds are growing quickly. My predator groups are not keeping them in check. How about you?'

Ayana nodded and quickly brought up the live births to kill ratio for her own area in her head. She smiled to herself, knowing that Sven was a little bit soft and would shelter some of the older animals, when he should allow the predators to kill them off.

'Mine are well within acceptable limits, Sven. You grow soft, my beautiful friend!'

There were a few seconds before the reply came. He softly said, 'Yes, it is true. Ever wondered what it would be like to walk amongst humanity again, Ayana?'

A little pang of longing shot through her as she let out a long sigh. 'I do dream of sipping vodka martinis from a tall, stemmed glass and eating a meal with a knife and fork. But this life as a guardian is a sacred one … it has its moments. And, one day, I want to ply the stars as a Hauler, so I am happy to do this until I get the call-up.'

Ayana imagined her friend nodding, considering his reply before he said, 'A long draught of chilled ruby beer in a pewter tankard would do it for me. And a celery and walnut salad with real mayonnaise. The olives do not grow that well here and, besides, it would be against the Haulers' protocols to start making my own olive oil! Just imagine what the Games Board nature program monitors would make of it if they found a panther crushing olive oil in a home-made press!'

Ayana giggled at the image in her mind. 'Might almost be worthwhile doing it, Sven! Wonder how they would explain it?'

Sven's laughter boomed inside her head as he replied. 'I actually spoke with ACE Jaffray about getting some furniture made by the chimpanzees for me. I fancied a woven lounger. He really liked my ideas but wondered if it would interfere with their natural evolution. Said that they are a tricky enough bunch to control at the best of times, especially when any of the stone fruits are ripe. Says the latest is a group who gather the fruit and crush it into the tree hollows, wait a few days, guarding it, and then get pissed on the fermenting brew.'

Ayana barked out a short laugh. 'That's good! Pleased that no-one has showed them how to build a still!'

Sven growled with laughter, adding, 'Just as well the *Basalt* ACEs have gone. Having spent time with Glint and Nail, they would think it so funny that they'd insist it should be done!'

Ayana nodded, feeling the joy that the *Basalt* ACEs had brought, and grinned, thinking of how they had smuggled the genius Fritz down with them so he could listen to the songbirds for himself. She sighed, suddenly missing them and their uncontrolled humour and their need to know everything quickly.

She stood up and stretched then silently padded the thirty or more metres down the rocky outcrop and into her home inside the tree. Looking at the screens which showed her a random selection of vistas across the vast area that was her domain, a slowly flashing icon caught her eye. She frowned, looking at the message from a flock of her swallows that some of the local bison herd had eye infections again. She placed a paw up against one of the consoles. The hard interfaces locked together and seconds later the biological computer, that made up part of the tree, directly linked the little swooping birds to her conscious mind. Noting the flock numbers were low, meaning its collective mind would not be fully sentient, she gently wished for the birds to have a closer look at the eye infections.

She used the few minutes it took for the flock to return to the bison to go through the various infections which had occurred in the previous fifteen years, wondering which one it would be. One of the birds deftly landed on the head of one of the huge herbivores and looked down at the runny eye. It sniffed the air around the eye and the information came back to Ayana, who processed it herself, seeing what the bacteria was. Sighing with the knowledge that it was one of the more difficult to treat bacteria, she quietly told the whole flock that their favourite food was flying above her tree. A quick calculation showed her that the flight time would be eleven minutes so she recalled the other two closer flocks as well, giving them the same gentle suggestion.

While she waited she brought hundreds of modified cattle ticks up to room temperature and flooded their enclosures with the medical nanotes which had been successful against the eye infections in other herds. The nanotes swarmed over the ticks, coating them and also forcing their way inside the parasitic insects. The first thing that they did was change the feeding preference in the insects from blood to the highly infectious discharge from the bison's eyes. The next modification was to change the tissue-dissolving fluid that the ticks would normally inject into the host animal to one of the many powerful insect-based antibiotics that had been developed by one of the first settlers to the planet hundreds of years before. Finally, the nanotes programmed the destruction of the ticks by internal overheating as soon as their jobs had been completed. When the nanotes were well on the way to having the ticks readied, and the three flocks were nearby, she released thousands of mayflies above the tree. Moments later, as the birds came close together to feed, their collective mind rose to just at the level of instructable sentience. She let them feed then asked the birds to collect the ticks, that the tree itself was transporting up to its top branches in small gel packages through its internal plumbing, and go out and place them around the infected bison's eyes.

Harold

Human Settlement on Storfisk

'Mum! I don't want oats and muesli for breakfast with just milk! I want it with fruit juice like Glint had, and Jenna is having toast, eggs and fruit as well so why can't I have that?'

Marie looked down at her ten-year-old green-eyed, olive-skinned child, with her long, gleaming chestnut hair, and smiled. She thought of the whirlwind visit of *Basalt* and its eclectic crew, who had stayed with the large Spitz family a few weeks earlier. She had known the effects would be felt by the family for a long time to come and frowned a little at her daughter.

'Because, Rebecca, I know that you will only eat a half of each and leave the rest to be fed to the house tree. You know how I feel about that. It's a waste.'

Rebecca looked up, cheerfully saying, 'OK, then just give me what I will eat, Mum. I wish Glint was still here though. He was so funny. But at least I have Harold so I suppose it's all right.'

Jenna, Marie's other daughter, whose lighter skin and blonde hair reflected her father's strong Old Earth Nordic origins, spoke from the other side of the table. 'So where is that dragon? I bet he's high up the tree stalking the winged rodents again. I wish he wouldn't do that, his breath just so stinks afterwards. And he is so gross when he has killed one, being so pleased with himself. And besides, Marko and Topaz are very good at creating the ACEs, but I will be much better. Everyone says so.'

Marie looked at the fifteen-year-old and silently agreed she would be very good at the family business, as some of her creations were already held in high regard throughout the region. However, she did not agree that Jenna's builds would be as good as Marko's, because even though he was a media star, had a simply superb self-propelled, self-repairing midi design and fabrication computer called Topaz (which she did not believe was a sub-Augmented Intelligence as Marko asserted, but a full AI), and she loved him as her little brother, it was a fact that the cat, Nail, the mechanical spider, Flint, and the creature, Glint — together with the one that they had created by themselves called Spike — were a fabulous group of Artificially Created Entities the likes of which she had rarely seen before.

As she served the children their breakfasts, the large dining room slowly filled with the other members of the Spitz family, including her two husbands and their other two wives together with the remaining younger children. Catlike creatures strolled in to check the contents of their feed bowls, as the watchbirds — originally kea from Old Earth stock — also checked in to pick up their breakfasts before flying back out to their posts high in the huge, altered tree that had been the generational family home for hundreds of years.

Just as Marie had finished making toast, the metre-long dragon that Marko had bought for the family as a special gift arrived in his usual style by flying in through one of the open window ports and gliding quickly around the large high-ceilinged space, cheerfully barking each name of the family members. Finishing his circuit, he landed amongst the cats, bustling them out of their feeding bowls to growled and hissed insults ... their intellect was on a par with petulant four-year-old humans.

Harold dismissively yawned at each of them in turn and announced that they had nothing in their feed bowls which interested him anyway. After folding his four wings snugly down against his body, the dragon walked upright on his two rear legs, swishing his long tail from side to side, across to the main table to quickly climb up the back of the senior husband's intricately carved high-backed chair.

He placed his two small true hands on Peter's shoulder while grasping the back of the chair with the long toes on his more powerful rear hands-feet, then peered around in front of Peter's face as the large solidly built man quietly shovelled large spoonfuls of oats, muesli and finely chopped dried fruit steeped in milk into his mouth.

Peter looked into the eyes of the exquisitely beautiful, almost classic ancient-Chinese, dragon's head. 'Your breath stinks again, Harold. I need you to go brush your teeth, and floss, please, then come back, as you have flying-rat fragments in your teeth. And walk, please. No flying inside, OK!'

Harold nodded. 'Oh, yes, that would be sensible.'

He leapt down to the floor, ignoring the insults from the cats concerning his oral hygiene, and scampered across to the nearest ablutions on all fours. He pushed the screen open, then jumped up onto the nearest basin before reaching out to pull some floss from the toothbrush branch with his small hands. He carefully flossed between his teeth, smiling wide into the mirror to check he had removed all the scales and meat fragments that came from his night-time encounters with the vicious little gliding rodents which constantly tried to gain access to the family tree. Satisfied, he snapped off one of the numerous quick-growing toothbrushes from the scented branch above the basin, vigorously brushed his teeth and tongue then dropped the used brush into the basin, which had already absorbed the discarded floss.

He washed his hands for good measure, wiped them dry on the long, slowly moving soft fibre by the screen door then walked back to the table where his chair had been moved to be between the two husbands. Clambering up, he looked down into his food bowl, with its dried fruits, processed meats, cereal cakes and pot of yoghurt, and reflected that since he had been woken by Marko, some months before while onboard *Basalt*, and told of his special tasks, his life had been very good. Judy, another of the wives, handed him a glass of fruit juice which he gratefully accepted, drinking deep of the delicious nectar that he knew, from his data files, was that of white nectarines.

The tall dignified man on his other side spoke. 'So how many of the little bastards did you get last night, Harold?'

'Six more confirmed dead, John, and ripped up a few more, so I don't actually know how many more will succumb to their injuries. But their numbers are increasing every night. I am intrigued that they appear to be communicating more between themselves. They also seem to be using diversionary tactics as well.'

He saw the look that passed between the men. He cocked his head, then opened a laser link from one of his eyes across to the house comms and memory hub, querying all known behaviour of the creatures. After processing the information he looked up at John and dropped his voice to a low murmur.

'So we may have something more than just an ordinary seasonal infestation?'

Peter smiled down at this latest family member, resisting the urge to pat his sleek, beautiful black-pearl-coloured head. 'Marko, Topaz and Stephine, plus Patrick, certainly made you well, Harold. They created in you a creature of considerable potential. I aspire to someday make one as special as you. Yes, we need to have further discussions about this. But first we need you to guard Rebecca and Jenna well. You know about the Games Board visit to their school today. The Board know who we are and they take a great interest in your makers.'

Harold nodded and wondered if he should share with the men what Fritz had given him to force on the Games Board by whatever means available to him, but decided that it was best not to complicate matters further as he knew that the whole family was agitated over the visit of the Games Board recruiter. Instead, he nodded.

'Yes, it should prove to be an interesting day.'

Peter looked across at Harold, then said, 'Um, Harold ... it might be a good idea to be nice to the cats. They are a tricky lot at the best of times and are good at finding and killing the rats. I think that you should be nice to them as you never know when you will need backup.'

Harold pondered the comment for a few seconds, then nodded and looked at John, who had a small smile on his face, then across at Peter.

'Yes, you are right. I shall try to befriend them, but I find them such a moaning lot!'

The two men chuckled in agreement.

The family finished its breakfast, leaving their plates and bowls on the table. Harold quickly cleaned his teeth again, then, after everyone had left to get ready for the day ahead, he perched on the back of Peter's chair to watch the large dining table clean up. Small, dark green shoots grew, with a slow and dignified motion, up out of the living table's surface to find, then slowly wipe, the insides of the wooden platters and bowls clean. Large leaflike segments of the table opened as the rootlike shoots gathered then gently took the clean tableware down into the table itself, storing them until needed again.

Finally, the last few crumbs and debris from the family's breakfast were absorbed down into the tabletop as the shoots themselves also slowly vanished. Harold smiled and looked across to the stoves and benchtops, seeing the same processes being repeated and also finishing with the ceramic pots being cleaned by spongy pads on the ends of more substantial vinelike shoots. Moments later, Harold wondered if he detected the softest of sighs and smiled again, wondering if it was one of contentment from their living home.

He jumped off the chair and ran up the nearest spiral staircase. He'd noticed the largest of the cats sitting on a step, waiting and watching a large slater-type insect creeping across the ceiling. Harold knew that it was relatively harmless, but flew up and swatted it down to the cat anyway. The cat, who was called Bing, seized it then looked at Harold as he landed and favoured him with a toothy smile. Harold nodded and carried on up the stairway, stopping for a second outside one of the open entrances to a large bedroom to watch Peter and Marie embracing, kissing deeply as Peter cupped one of her breasts and she stroked the inside of his thigh. Harold chuckled to himself, wondering that the true biological members of the human race seemed to have an eternal fascination with their sexual needs.

He quietly moved further up the great tree until he came into Rebecca's room where he hopped up on the bed to watch her. She was slowly gathering her slates, checking her stylus and placing the items in her backpack. She checked her mail on the large wall-mounted screen and replied to a few messages before entering a chat room of her friends. While she was engrossed in chatting, Harold ran a full internal check, the exotic software of his own soul looking carefully into his being. He noted an odd piece of script in his system, which he compared with the household database that Fritz Vinken, from the *Basalt* crew, had rebuilt and massively augmented. The system destroyed the script and downloaded a hunter-killer for any more of the identified unwanted Administration spyware. Harold checked his onboard weapons, which none of the family members knew about, then used his own links to open comms into the planetary web and connect with some of the other ACEs spread around and above the planet and catch up on any news and swap gossip, covering in minutes what normal humans would take hours to do. He uploaded the images of his nocturnal encounters with the flying rats to his new friends, then broke the link as he could see that Rebecca was ready to go.

'Harold!'

'Yes, Rebecca.'

'Call me Bex! I am Bex to my friends, Harold. I've told you that.'

'Yes, I know, but the family calls you Rebecca.'

'Bex, Harold, Bex! Anyway, Marty's hamburgers is coming through here tonight and Pa has ordered for the whole family, including you, of course! Even the cats will have something special for dinner. This is so exciting!'

Harold looked at her and flashed a query to the comms node to be answered an instant later with the information that Marty was a famous itinerant chef whose hamburgers were held in almost legendary awe. The man and his companion travelled the Sphere of Humankind, going from planet to planet with a large, red and wonderfully ramshackle caravan towed by an equally ramshackle housebus.

'I shall look forward to eating one of his fat oversized sandwiches, Bex.'

The girl rolled her eyes, placed one hand on a hip and remonstrated with him. 'Must I tell you everything at least twice, Harold! They are called hamburgers. Our mums will spend ages trying to work out what ingredients are in his latest sauce recipes. They *never* do … and we think it's very funny.'

He thought that any reasonably equipped ACE or AI would be able to identify the ingredients quickly and also work out how they had been prepared. He was about to comment, then remembered a discussion he had had with the ACEs on *Basalt* that biological humans enjoyed secrets. It seemed to give them a little extra zest in their lives, so he just nodded.

Harold looked at Rebecca dressed in her tall, highly polished black boots — everyone wore them to keep most of the native bugs off their legs — black leatherlike pants, which he knew the house tree had grown for her, topped with a long burgundy silk shirt and a subtly pinstriped black waistcoat, thinking that she would make a strikingly beautiful woman one day. She was looking in her jewellery box and he decided that the moment was perfect.

'I made you something, Bex.'

He slid open one of the bedroom's drawers, where he had hidden the dragon-shaped torc, and lifted the silk-wrapped carving up to her. She unwrapped it and squealed with delight, bending down to quickly kiss him on the top of his head.

'Oh, this is just so great! Thanks, Harri! Can't wait until my friends see this!'

She rolled it around in her hands for a few seconds before finding and touching the magnetic release studs. The piece popped apart and she placed it around her neck with the catches reactivating as each end came close together. She rotated it until the head rested at her front then, seizing her bag, she ran from the room, yelling at the rest of the family to look at what she had been given. Harold had to run to keep up with her as they said their goodbyes to the family members, quickly moved down the spiralling central staircase, through the great buttressed, arched entranceway and out onto the paved street which meandered from one massive housetree to the next through short grass and low, flowering gardens. Native multi-winged birds, and just as many introduced ones from the twelve other main planets which humankind inhabited, flew above them or hopped about looking for insects to eat.

Looking up through the massive branches — some of the larger ones reaching across to join with the neighbouring trees — Harold saw additional rooms in the process of being grown, or rooms being absorbed back into the wood. They passed one of the largest trees, which Peter had told him housed three extended families so they were not the wealthiest of the locals. Harold considered it a strange statement as anyone privileged to live in the village was very wealthy by most standards he was aware of. Walking further, mottled light shining through the canopy a hundred metres above them, they came to the centre of the village. Here, the trees not only had people living inside them, but their colossally wide flattened surface roots housed workshops for the local trades and had shops tiered above them on wide leaf-shaded walkways.

Harold was observing a group of domestic-sized cats, as they intently watched a flowerbed, wondering what they were looking at, when Rebecca grabbed his hand and pulled him towards one of the workshops that serviced antigravity motorbikes. He spotted Jenna and a group of the older village girls surrounding a well-built young man, who was sitting on a stool, working on a single-seater. Harold recognised it as a good-quality older model, which, judging by its fairings neatly stacked to one side, must have been configured as a racer. They walked up to the group and Rebecca pulled Harold through the older girls to stand right beside the mechanic. Harold looked over the group, smiling to himself when he realised there was considerable tension and rivalry between the girls for the young man's attention; most of them were now glaring at the back of Rebecca's head. He looked at Rebecca and smiled even wider, seeing that she was only interested in the antigravity unit itself.

The young man looked up at Rebecca and Harold. 'Gidday, Bex mate. And how you keeping, Harold? Haven't seen you down here for a week or so. Finding everything OK?'

Harold nodded as Rebecca replied. 'Yeah, Harri is settling in just great, thanks, Jerry. So this is the old racer you bought at auction? I like it. But what's wrong with it? My dads always say that there will be something wrong with anything you buy at auction.'

Jerry nodded and smiled. 'It arrived late yesterday. Uncle says I can have a couple of hours to work on it this morning. Pulled badly to the left when I picked it up from the airfield and drove it up here. Bloody good for everything else, but I can't find anything obvious on the AG housing. Replaced a couple of damaged modules but it made little difference. Can you have a look, please, Harold?'

Harold leaned forwards as probes and comms units extended from his fingertips. He linked into the control unit on the side of the antigravity sphere and then reached across to one of the workshop diagnostic units. Above them, the screen changed when some of Harold's more specialist software came into play: relative time sped up for him and it was as if he was within the space that the antigravity unit took up.

He looked through the levels of hard titanium on the outside of the machine and down through the sub-surface control units. He moved deeper into the sphere as the metal slowly changed from its solid state through the cold intermediate state, where it was neither solid material nor energy, then down through the energy until he perceived the two, still rapidly spinning, orbiting minuscule nodes of packed neutrons that gave the unit weight, but when spun to a major percentage of the speed of light, and then given momentum, allowed the antigravity effect to take place. He withdrew his perception and allowed himself to slow down mentally to biological-human norm.

'This machine took a large impact sometime recently, Jerry. One part of the inner housing is intruding a few microns into the next level of intermediate state. It will require a powerful adjustment from a magnetic puller to rectify it.'

The curly red-headed young man pressed his lips together, frowning. 'Yeah, I suspected as much. Thanks, Harold. Will have to work a couple of days for my uncle to pay for it. Right, I shall go see him.'

Rebecca was touching the outer casing with a fingertip. 'So is it right under here? The damage, that is.'

Harold nodded. 'Yes! I am impressed, Rebecca. There is an almost imperceptible mark and you found it. Very happy to help out in the rebuild if you like, Jerry. Want to see this machine racing again.'

Jerry smiled and nodded, but before he could say anything Bex said, 'Good! OK, see ya, Jerry. We had better be going to school.'

One of the older girls behind them sneered. 'So who died and made you king, Rebecca? We will go when we feel like it, as school sucks, anyway.'

Rebecca fixed the speaker, who Harold recalled as a friend of Jenna's but not what Jenna described as a 'good one', with a glare and taking Harold by the hand walked away from the workshop.

'I should feel sorry for her, Harold, but I don't. She is horrible. Her little brother is one of the four who is going to be a monitor with the Games Board. And Jenna is going to be late if she does not catch up soon.'

A few minutes later Jenna came running up behind them. 'Hey, you did not wait for me!'

They walked in silence for a few moments, then Harold stopped as he heard an approaching airship. He looked to the north, through the trees, as a huge lifter, with a stretched-disc shape, slid quietly overhead.

The girls both looked up.

'All-environment system capable, so it can operate in just about any conditions, even vacuum,' Jenna said. 'Now *that* we will not see often, unless there is something really interesting happening. Wonder why it is here? When the Games Board recruited one of the boys from my class it was just a small lifter that came to pick him up.'

Harold, they all agreed, was somewhat fanatical about keeping well informed.

'There is a medium-sized conflict due to take place around the local moon in two days' time. They are touting it as a good earner, according to the financial reports. Two corporations want control of the same massive, almost pure nickel meteoroid which is in orbit around this system's outermost planet. So, the Games Board is going to make the most of it. Will be interesting, as all the combat craft must use turbine engines and mechanical lift mechanisms.'

Rebecca's eyes gleamed. 'Old tech! Yeah, I like old tech. So much nicer to look at.'

Harold grinned then said, 'Oops! Almost forgot, Jenna. Have a carving for you, too! Check in your bag.'

Jenna hastily wrenched the bag off her shoulder to find the piece he had placed in her bag earlier that morning.

A few moments later with the ivory carving around her neck, she gathered up Harold and hugged him.

'We are so pleased that you are with us, Harold. You are kind of small, but very cute! Thank you. See you later, guys. Have a good day.'

As she walked away, Harold flashed a signal to the nanotes clinging on the outside of her bag to activate them.

The school was a wing of the local Administration complex, on the southern side of the village overlooking the wide valley that sloped towards the large estuary opening to the sea six or so kilometres away. Harold looked at the long sweeping curves of the school and appreciated the lack of a single straight line in the bioengineered-fungi structure. They passed the daycare centres, then the kindergarten, before arriving at the entrance to the junior school. Arched gates were flanked by two heavily carved, growth-retarded totara trees, which had been gifted and planted by the local Maori leaders many decades before.

Rebecca walked quickly towards a gaggle of her friends and classmates. Each of them patted one of the carved totems as they made their way into the wide play area covered in the same tough grass that grew between the trees in the village. Harold walked over the grass, knowing that it would never need cutting, nor grow past its borders, and could be programmed by the local biological control systems to change colour with the seasons if required. He decided that wild grasses were much more interesting.

He looked at the fence which separated the schools and took a few moments to watch the huge, light-bronze parasol leaves slowly opening and erecting themselves to form large living sunshades around the sides of the play area. Harold took a few running strides and flew up onto the leaves, as much to have a close look at them as to get away from the inquisitive closeness of some of the younger children. He liked them, but sometimes the attention was a little overwhelming.

He walked along the insides of the leaves against the fence, then out onto one of the larger leaves so he could sit on his tail and look over the play areas. The surface was tough and fibrous and he could not see if he was leaving any marks so he walked carefully. He sat and looked south to see that the airship had stopped its slow sightseeing and was descending towards the local airfield, behind the trees, kilometres away.

Sitting in full sunlight, he extended his wings and darkened them as the photosensitive outer layers started to produce delicious system sugars to supplement his digestion, giving him a slightly euphoric feeling of wellbeing. He also felt slightly raised radio wave levels on his skin. He extended his wings to their maximum and orientated them, feeling the energy. Intrigued by the radio waves he looked for the local communication node in the playground and flashed a query across to it. An instant later, he received images of the local star showing a large active sunspot which, to his delight, was producing a sizeable coronal mass ejection. The information scrolling down the side of the image showed that the planet would have a good aurora within forty-eight hours.

Sitting, enjoying the playing children and the sunlight, Harold slowly became aware of a burning sensation on the underside of his tail and on the soles of his feet. He stood up and looked back under his tail to see that little round areas of his skin were irritated. Looking down, he swore at himself for not being more knowledgeable about his environment as he could see thousands of little insect traps, which also oozed attractants, dotted all over the top surfaces of the leaves. Balancing on the outer edge of the huge leaf he looked around to see where he could go as someone started yelling at him.

'Hey, hey, hey, Harold! You look like a dork! Come down here as I hate bending my neck to look up at you, you evil-looking bastard!'

Harold looked down at the grinning face of the pug dog called Reg, who lived in the tree next to theirs and who had been the first ACE he had met when he had arrived those few weeks before.

Harold laughed and leapt off to fly down and land beside the dog. 'Just soaking up the rays, Reg, very tasty. All good? Have not seen you for a couple of days.'

The pug looked at him closely before answering. 'So you can photosynthesise as well, Harold! Impressive. That could come in handy sometime. Yeah, went up country with some of my family seniors. Nice it was. So the Games Board are here today. Wonder what bollocks they will feed the children this time. They had better be off quickly mid-afternoon. Big thunderstorm forecast. Going to come right over the top of us and it will be a cracking good one.'

Harold linked back to the comms node and downloaded the forecast for himself. 'So it's going to be much bigger than the one a few days ago. I will be interested to watch the village trees in operation again.'

'Yeah, always nice to watch when they go into protective mode. Now, my young friend, you may or may not be aware that the director who is coming here has an ACE with him. The information from our data net indicates it could be the one called Tengu. I see from the look on your face you know who I am speaking of. If it is, in fact, the same Tengu who was created around ten standard years ago for the then very young and foolish Baron Willie der Boltz, commander of the Gjomvik mercenary Leopard Strike forces, then we are in trouble as Tengu openly loathes other ACEs.'

'Yes, I am aware of him, Reg. So we watch out for each other, eh?'

The little dog nodded. 'Yes, and if he is now with the Games Board I will bet that any action he takes against us will be a sanctioned one, as far as those money grubbing pricks are concerned. Open season on us, as believe it or not there are biologicals who just don't like our kind. Racist bastards! OK, Harold, I had better get moving. There is a nice big nest of vermin to dig up for the house cats and it's always good to curry favour with them. Watch your back. See you soon.'

Harold watched the little dog trot off towards the gate before suddenly veering off to grab a small ball in his mouth and break into a sprint before spitting it out, laughing at one of his own family members who was shouting insults at him. Harold smiled, having been told by the *Basalt* crew how, sometimes, the basic animal template of the ACE would influence behaviour. He wondered what instincts had been built into himself, not knowing of any naturally evolved creature that was like him. Noting the time, he walked across to Rebecca and her friends just as the school bell sounded. He walked in the middle of the girls, trying to remain inconspicuous as they entered the building, went through the corridors and finally into Rebecca's classroom. After the children placed their bags in the cubbyholes lining one curved wall of the classroom, then went to their desks, Harold suddenly found himself confronted by a severe angular-looking woman he had only seen at a distance in the past. Looking at her skin, the underlying bone structure and the wrinkles on her face Harold could only conjecture that he was in the presence of a biologically deteriorating 'one lifer', someone whose beliefs determined they would live one normal life, and grow old and die without any augmentation or life extension treatments. Or, if they possessed a Soul Saver, they would not be 'tanked' to grow a new body and so live indefinitely in any one of the dozens of body configurations that biological humans could choose from. He was about to ask her questions about her choices and why, when she interrupted his thoughts.

'You!' she said tersely. 'Yes, you, live thing not! You know that you are not welcome inside the school, thing. I presume that you are made and owned by the Spitz family, as you have their look about you. Out, go on, out, out, out, now! Shoo! Before I take a broom to you.'

Harold was completely taken aback by the woman's hostility, but after looking at Rebecca and noting her fear of the woman, and not wanting to make matters worse, he nodded at the woman, apologised and extended his hand to shake hers. She just looked at it in obvious disgust. Harold quickly looked across at Rebecca's bag and lasered deployment instructions to the clusters of tiny nanote insects, nodded goodbye to Rebecca, then beat a hasty retreat from the unpleasant woman who had now started to advance upon him.

He walked out through the corridors and past students and teachers, most of whom smiled or greeted him, and left the building. Affected by the woman's attitude and so feeling a little out of sorts, he had to spend a few moments calming down before he slowly walked across the road. As he approached near an ornamental tree, he carefully focused on a seemingly insignificant large stone and flashed a tight laser signal across to it. Seconds later, three of the flying rats that he had captured, caged and then pushed down an abandoned burrow, nights before, erupted out of the ground and raced to get to the shelter of the trees.

One burst into flight as Harold himself took off, extending his claws from his hands and feet and effortlessly slashing it from the air. The other two raced up the trunk and into the thick foliage just as he had planned. He dived into the thick leaves after them, then created a great commotion as if in a fight. He dropped another carcass out of the tree, then settled down to wait for a few more minutes. In his mind, he unlocked a panel in the flank of one of his legs and opened the containment. He carefully took out the little electronics package and adhered it to the tree bark over a nice thick branch and activated it. He read the tiny signal as it gave off his own bio-signal, then switched his one off and powered up the superb adaptive camouflage system which covered him; his creator Marko and other members of the *Basalt* crew had spent a long time developing it for him.

With great care and deliberation he made his way to the ground and crept across the 200 metres to the tree he had selected as being a good observation post for the classrooms that Rebecca and Jenna were in, plus the outside areas of the schools. Spending two hours creeping across and up the tree seemed extremely tedious, but he knew that the Administration and the Games Board would be watching the area carefully. When he was being prepared for this mission, *Basalt*'s AI, Patrick, had confided that Harold himself would be just as big a target for them as the girls. Also, knowing that Tengu was possibly on the way here meant it was sensible to make a serious effort.

Eventually arriving on the wide sturdy branch, he continued to watch as the village's other ACEs seemed to be planning something of their own as well. Harold was intrigued that the two panthers of the Dine family — who he knew well because the Dines were the Spitz family's best friends — appeared to be playing the same game as he was, but from what he could tell they were using highly sophisticated electronic body doubles: he could see them lying under a tree, by the school, but had also sensed them going past him as he had crept along. The pug, Reg, and two of his ruffian mates, a German shepherd called Zittau and a huge black Labrador called Sailor, wandered down the footpath as if they owned everything around them, then lay down under another tree and appeared to go to sleep.

Harold sighted his eyes to where he had hidden the transponder days earlier, high in the tree above his decoy, which was receiving information directly from the classrooms. Using as tight a laser beam as he could create, he opened a link to the transponder, checking that his micro-spies were still in existence. He sighed when he discovered that over sixty per cent had succumbed to the countermeasures that the Administration, and probably the Games Board, had deployed in the rooms.

He listened for a few seconds to a young teacher giving her lesson to the class. She had piqued his interest shortly after he and the *Basalt* crew had arrived in the village; he had noticed her discreetly watching Marko when they had all been in the marketplace one morning. Harold had seen, from his own hidden vantage point, that she had appeared to have tears welling up in her eyes when Marko walked past. Harold considered approaching her and asking why, but then thought that, as Marko was very famous, perhaps it was simply an infatuation.

Harold opened another link that tapped into public overview channels from the orbitals high overhead, and passively watched as vehicles rolled out of the Games Board dirigible. The antigravity ground vehicles, with large single-drive wheels at their rear, moved along the road, climbing towards the village through the tall, black foliage of the enhanced fennel plants. The fennel was one of the ingredients in the local licorice, which was considered a luxury Spherewide.

Games Board

Human Settlement on Storfisk

The three elegant gold and black vehicles swung into the vehicle park in front of the school just as the senior staff, the local heads of the Administration and members of the Parent Board of Governors assembled at the entranceway to greet them. Harold watched as the director, a smallish man dressed in the latest contemporary clothes, together with a tall woman who he identified as the Games Board system recruiter, climbed out of the first vehicle, along with a male monitor who slid from the rear of the vehicle on his antigravity unit. The four new child recruits, dressed in Games Board livery, got out of the second vehicle in an excited state, guided by a youngish-looking woman and a female monitor.

Some minutes later, Harold cringed a little when the long sinuous figure of the wingless dragon Tengu emerged from the vehicle, stretched, yawned and, looking thoroughly bored, glanced around, staring at the dogs for long seconds before slowly licking his lips. Then he walked on all fours to be beside the director. Once beside the man he stood up so as to be a full metre taller, nodding to the assembled people when he was introduced. No-one emerged from the third vehicle, so Harold assumed that a security detail would be inside.

As they were escorted in through the gates, the director spent a few moments looking at, and appeared to Harold to be enthusing about, the carved trees. As he turned, Harold was able to lipread the director's instructions to the monitors to take images of them for the files, something which appeared to irritate Tengu as he flicked his tail in disrespect at a carving of a long lizard-like creature. Harold could not work out what was said, but judging from the body language of the locals, they did not appreciate it. They all walked into the school to appear some minutes later inside Rebecca's class.

Harold immersed himself in the datastream coming from his nanote spies. The recruiter, upon entering the classroom, had fixed a smile upon her face and looked carefully at each of the children. The recruits followed her in and were directed by her to sit on seats at the front of the room, facing their ex-classmates. Seeing Rebecca, she casually walked over to the seated child, bending down and introducing herself as Svenna. She looked very closely at the carving around Rebecca's neck. She spoke very quickly in a language that Harold understood as high-caste Games Board executive, but he doubted any local understood a single word. Games Board personnel, like any wealthy individual, had augments which controlled their voice boxes. Harold knew this meant such people could think and mentally speak in their native language and, when it came to vocalising, it could come out as any language they wished.

'Monitors, this is the younger Spitz child. Is the carving she is wearing of any interest or threat to us?'

Seconds later, the male monitor slid up beside Rebecca, smiled and nodded at her before replying in the same language. 'I perceive only inert, aquatic origin ivory, high-quality aquamarines, emeralds and fibre optics throughout the body of the carving. I suggest that it is of excellent quality and carved by a sentient, not by a machine.'

The recruiter switched to the local language. 'That is an exquisitely carved piece, Rebecca. Should you ever consider selling it, please make contact as I shall give you a very generous price.'

Rebecca summoned all her self-assurance, which was wavering, and said, 'Thank you, Recruiter Svenna. It was a gift, but if I ever want to sell it I shall send you a note.'

The recruiter smiled down at the girl, turned on her heel and walked to the front of the class.

Once everyone was seated, the young teacher introduced each of the visitors to the class, then walked to the window bench seat and, after looking directly at where Harold was sitting, turned and sat down. Harold continued to listen to the interactions in the class, noting that as the minutes passed fewer and fewer of his nanotes were responding.

The director stood to speak. 'Hello, children. My thanks to your teacher, Claire, for introducing us. As you know, I am Director Francis John. I am here today to answer any of your questions, as it is unusual for us, the Games Board, to recruit so many from one class in one year. We are growing rapidly and so, to be able to bring to you the programs you enjoy, we need more help.'

He looked around at the sombre faces of the children. 'OK. For you to best understand what we are doing, I need you to ask your questions. Just put up your hand and ask at any time. Is that a good thing?'

The children nodded at him.

'Right. You know that we make all the programs that are transported by the Haulers to the places they visit throughout the Sphere. We can't transmit the programs because it would take many many years, in some cases up to fifty years, for a transmission to get across the Sphere and that would be no fun at all, would it?'

Again, heads nodded.

'And, as you also probably know, we are here to help the Gjomvik Corporations and anyone else, if they are about to fight over a resource that a number of them may want. They come to us and if we like them we will buy the rights to the fight and then supply the best people to both sides. We then choose the most interesting places and the right machines and weapons for them to fight with. And we all really like the sounds of those old — in some cases, ancient — war machines, don't we? Then we put our monitors with the fighters, so they can make the programs for us.'

Heads nodded and the children smiled. One of the girls put up her hand.

'Yes, you have a question for me?'

One of Rebecca's best friends, Mary, said, 'So why do the monitors have to be changed so much? Can't ordinary people do the same job?'

'Yes, ordinary people could do the job and a long time ago they did, but we have advanced since then. We ask our people to go into very dangerous places and put themselves at risk in order for you to see the action up close. The Games Board agreed that it is much better to give them good tools and protection, so we supply the best equipment and training for them to film all the action, make it into a finished program and bring it to us. Do any of you know why the Games Board came into being?'

Most of the children put up their hands. The director pointed to one boy.

'Yes, young man, what do you know?'

'It's because once there was a very bad war and billions of people died and whole planets were wrecked forever and we really don't want that to happen any more. Now people sell you the wars so you can make them small and good for us to watch.'

The director smiled. 'I could not have said it better myself, well done!'

He looked around the smiling faces, wondering who else outside the room was watching and listening to what he was saying. Both monitors had reported to him that nanotes were still being found and destroyed by their own countermeasures, but it would take hours to be certain that they had all been destroyed.

He continued: 'And you also know that those people who fight the battles for us to watch and decide who is the better group to win, don't really die! Isn't that a great thing. They have Soul Savers and just go into a tank and remake themselves, with even more money paid to them if their death was heroic. Oh, and think of those really good series of programs we make for you about the frigate, *Basalt*, and its great crew. They were here a few weeks ago, weren't they, for a visit. I really like them and I know that you do too! And Sergeant Major Marko Spitz was born and raised here and his niece Rebecca is in this class. Let's hear it for Rebecca!'

Led by the director everyone, except Tengu who looked at her and stifled a yawn, burst into applause, while the embarrassed Rebecca fervently wished that the floor would melt under her so she could disappear.

After the clapping died down, the smallest boy in the class who the smiling recruiter had looked at earlier and obviously pitied because his family could not afford better gene splices for him, raised his hand slowly.

The director smiled and asked him what his query was. The boy pointed at the figure of Tengu, who was leaning against the doorjamb slowly picking his sharp teeth with a needlelike probe, which had been extended from a fingertip.

In a small quavering voice the boy said, 'Is he, is he … is he with you?'

The director looked across at Tengu and smiled a tight little smile back at the boy. 'Yes, Tengu is with me. He is an advisor and is really not as fierce a dragon as he looks. He was with the famous leader of one of the Gjomvik Corporation mercenary groups, Baron Willie der Boltz. I employed Tengu some months ago when he returned from a long journey. Does he frighten you?'

Most of the class nodded.

'Ah, I see,' said the director, then continued directing his comment at Tengu, who was looking indolently at him. 'Perhaps, Tengu, you would like to go and expedite that little matter we discussed earlier?'

The three-and-a-half-metre-long, powerfully built ACE did not say a word, just pushed his way out through the door and walked away.

The director, who was inwardly seething at Tengu's behaviour, did not let it show and turned smiling to the class to say, 'Now, children. Who can tell me about the Haulers?'

The director selected another boy from the class full of raised arms.

'The Haulers are the huge ships that take everything, and other ships and people, from all the worlds in the Sphere. They also map and guard the Lagrange navigation points everywhere.'

The director nodded, smiled and thanked the boy, before adding, 'Yes, and as we all know the Haulers only take a cargo, even if it is an Administration battleship, between worlds if they believe that it is the right thing to do. They are not like your local Police and none of us have any power over them, so we always try to be friends with the Haulers' Collective, don't we?'

Everyone nodded again.

'OK, so who can tell me what the Administration does and how we work together? Yes, you, young lady. What can you tell us, please?'

The one girl in the class who was Rebecca's academic rival, her friend Rosa, spoke. 'Well, as everyone knows, the Administration does a lot of stuff that allows us to have good lives. They take the taxes and look after everything to take care of people, but it's different here because the home trees get everything for us that we need to live, so our families don't pay as much tax like on other worlds that don't have trees like ours. But they do look after the roads and the airport and the schools and the military and all that other stuff that the grown-ups like.'

The director had winced ever so slightly at the mention of taxes, but smiled brightly as Rosa sat, and thanked her.

'Yes, and they also keep everyone safe so that we can all enjoy long lives. They coordinate shipping with the Haulers, arrange for the Gjomvik Corporations to export their technologies to everyone and, most importantly, they watch out for any dangerous native or engineered species, or any privateers who want to steal from us which is why you have a local Administration-supported militia.'

He looked around the sombre faces, knowing that they were really not that interested, but pressed on regardless.

'We of the Games Board also work closely with the Administration right across the worlds and outposts of humankind to help make sure that the right information and the correct messages get from the Administration to the people. Oh, and of course they also look after the great wilderness areas and reserves which are safe places for all of those animals and plants which were destroyed when Old Earth was devastated by the great solar flare.'

Harold

Human Settlement on Storfisk

High in the tree, Harold was growing agitated, not knowing where Tengu was. He heard the tiniest of sounds behind him and spun his head around to find himself looking into the eyes of the large, deep grey cat, Bing. Before he had time to react, the cat spoke very softly to him.

'Don't be afraid, Harold. It took all our resources and considerable effort to locate you. I am here to help as Tengu is our enemy too. We know where he is and have broken his camouflage code with the help of a few planetary AIs. I can give it to you now if you want?'

Harold looked at the cat for a long second before answering. 'So I suspect that you can see me as well, Bing. And you are no longer acting like the semi-intelligent cat you portray when at home? Who gave you those codes?'

'Fritz Vinken from *Basalt*. He also said to tell you this, Harold. Apple, cliff, bread, trout, Ernst, seventy-two, cabbage tree, Veg, penny. And I shall now laser the appended colours and shapes. Yeah, I so like it when you treat us as of inhibited intellect. We found that condescending to say the least as our job as ACEs is to protect the family as well. But you are new and learning still.'

The dragon nodded and the cat fired a tiny laser burst into one of Harold's eyes and, after matching the codes against his own, Harold let out his breath slowly, knowing that he could at least trust the cat. He nodded and extended one of his hands and opened a fingertip, while the cat did the same, interfacing with him and sending the remaining codes, plus everything that was known about Tengu. His own systems checked and verified the data source codes then allowed it into his conscious mind. He sped himself up, quickly read everything and uploaded the recognition software into the tactical part of his brain. He then looked back towards the school, at the same time maintaining the link to Bing so they could send silent undetectable messages between them.

'So, Bing, are Reg the pug, the dogs, the panthers and the other cats around us all with you?'

Bing chuckled. 'Reg thinks of himself as our leader and we let him. And, yes, we are of the one mind in that we love this existence as a member of each of our families and we have no desire to see that balance upset. Tengu is in for a very tough time of things today. Even if he had been replicated — and there may be more of him here today — we will teach him and the Games Board a salient lesson. You do realise that you are the bait in this trap, don't you, Harold?'

Harold nodded, still passively scanning the area around him. 'Yes, I was warned that that may be the case and I should have suspected that the ACEs would combine. I had thought that the humans would have done the hunting. I don't like it, but I will do what is needed. So if there *are* more of Tengu, what is the plan, Bing?'

'We like you, Harold, but you have only been amongst us for three weeks. Let us say that we will send only one back intact. He will be damaged and messed up, but intact.'

Harold quickly looked at the cat, noting a smug look on his face. 'So, I am to presume that this is a little side play by the Games Board as possible payback for what *Basalt* and crew did to them over the last few years, considering that this village is Marko's home? A little reminder that they can do anything they like with impunity.'

Bing nodded and agreed. Then added: 'But of course we look after our own, so I would not worry too much. What weapons do you have at your disposal, Harold?'

This time Harold allowed himself a little smile as he said, 'Well, Bing, you don't know me and I don't know you, so how about we both see what the day brings us?'

Bing laughed in a tone that relayed acceptance and companionship. 'Well said, Harold. You catch on fast. Now, Tengu, or at least one of them, is about to appear. Watch the fence on the far side of the senior school.'

Harold gasped suddenly. 'I did not see if he was in Jenna's class! I will kill that bastard if he touched her!'

'Yes, he did and all of your nanotes in that class have been compromised or destroyed. They sent you no information that he was in the classroom just as the Games Board wanted it. Don't worry, we have a sophisticated clean-up team in place to remove whatever he put on her. She is safe. Don't concern yourself as I think that this day is only just beginning. Behold a bad-tempered little monster!'

They could both now see Tengu climbing up through the leaves on the fence. Emerging at the top, he walked quickly across the surface just as the leaf suddenly enfolded him and smashed him into the trunk again and again until the obviously enraged Tengu finally tore through the thin, tough plant structure. He rolled on the ground as another leaf shot downwards, smashing him into the grass which promptly fired thousands of silica shards into his skin. He then lost control of his camouflage system, becoming plainly visible to the dozens of children in the senior school who were pressed up against the windows, wondering what the commotion was about. A fraction of a second later, the windows armoured themselves and the screeching Tengu launched himself into the air, leaping from plant to plant as each one tried very hard to damage or entangle him.

Harold looked on in wonder when the parking area surface seemed to explode upwards, with fine roots grasping at Tengu as he exploded with anger: blades flashed open along his arms and legs, slashing and stabbing at every plant that attacked him. Finally, he made it onto the top of one of the Games Board's vehicles where he sat for a few long moments, obviously gathering his wits.

'Wow! Bing! What was that about? How come I have never been attacked that way while here? And why did the grass not react against him when he first arrived?'

Bing laughed. 'We requested a suppression of the standard reaction to a dangerous predator from the village AI and her biohazards systems when he first arrived. We wanted a nasty surprise for him when he thought himself safe, arrogant prick that he is! Do you remember being given a series of odd but quite pleasant drinks when you first arrived?'

Bing was sitting right next to Harold, having moved as soon as Tengu had appeared.

'Yes, Bing. Marie said that they would help my adjustment to the local environment. Did not understand that they were really bio-inoculations. So what else do you have in store?'

The large cat smiled in a merciless way and Harold felt a tiny bit sorry for Tengu.

'Look, Harold. He is not very bright, is he? Almost feel like shouting a warning but the dogs are having too much fun!'

Harold could not make out what the dogs were yelling at Tengu but they were holding his attention as a large snakelike series of roots pushed up through the ground and slithered soundlessly towards the bright red and black dragon. Just as Tengu leapt towards the dogs, the roots struck with the ends parting to entangle him while hundreds of others with hair-fine ends probed fiercely all over his skin, plucking out the hard silica shards and using the pinholes to burrow deeply inside him, shutting down his muscles. In seconds he was completely captive and at the village AI's mercy.

Bing pointed at the bound Tengu and said, 'You have not met the local AI yet, have you, Harold? *There* is an excellent example of what she can do and why it is such a bad idea to piss her off.'

Harold allowed a grimace to show and nodded. 'Yes, I hear you on that, Bing. So why did the security detail in the other vehicle not respond?'

'They can't. While everyone else was watching Tengu, they were locked inside their vehicle. The wonders of bioengineered spider types and their web material! And now we have the director and crew wondering what they are going to do. OK, let's tie you into the alternative local network, shall we, Harold? That way you can listen in on the commotion. Oh, and no doubt, being who you are, you probably have a gift for Tengu?'

Harold smiled at the cat and nodded.

'So I am to presume that you would like Tengu's eyes open, with the intrusion fail-safes removed, so you can laser some interesting software into him?'

Harold nodded again, wondering how the cat knew so much.

'Very well, Harold, give me a second or two.'

Harold looked across to see the director staring helplessly at the prone form of Tengu held above the vehicles. The man had opened his wrist unit and was conversing and gesticulating with his free hand. The third vehicle started to move backwards to find itself blocked by more of the rapid-moving roots, which jammed the wheel. The vehicle's turbine sounded shrilly as it then tried to lift off the ground, but was restrained. Harold heard the machine slow down to an idle. Seconds later, the local Administration heads arrived looking more than a little peeved and demanding to know what was happening, and why an obviously hostile ACE was in the company of the Games Board and why had they not been informed of its presence.

Harold then saw Tengu's eyes being uncovered and opened. Harold sped up his mind to its maximum, made all his protective systems fully operational, then isolated a disposable part of his brain from the rest of himself. He magnified his vision a thousandfold to find a tiny part of Tengu's left eye and fired a laser query signal into it. Almost immediately he received the reply and a fraction of a second later lasered back a three terabit block of data directly into Tengu's operating system. He saw that the data had been received, carefully searched the disposable unit in his brain for any back contamination, then reintegrated himself.

Once he had mentally slowed down again he looked at Bing. 'That part of my mission is completed. I just need a few more seconds to get at one of the monitors to muddy up the waters a little, and I am done.'

'OK, Harold, we will have Games Board combat aircraft over us in about two minutes maximum. Whatever you need to do, do it quickly!'

Harold focused back into the classroom to see that the female monitor was talking to the children about her latest mission. It had been on a distant rocky asteroid, where the two opposing forces had had a daylong battle, wearing spacesuits and firing at each other with rifles and other kinetic weapons, while in almost zero gravity. If Harold had not been so busy, he would have stopped to watch … the battle looked fantastically chaotic and entertaining with the weapons' recoil tumbling the firers. Instead, he focused on the monitor's personal device — which was outputting an audiovisual signal to the wall screen — and looked for the best reflective segment on her eye camera's surface.

At the same time, he used an eye laser to broadcast seemingly innocuous music into the room, which was absorbed by Rebecca's necklace; it energised a tiny gnat-sized craft to rapidly assemble from the components on the torc's surface. The craft lifted off and flew undetected to the monitor. It landed on the lens of one of her eye cameras where it dissolved, changing the camera's data-protection filter. Access was then enabled for a large data file to be lasered across by Harold directly into her central primary subconscious. Her systems recognised the incoming information only as normal feedback from what she herself was transmitting to the screen and, together with the music — which her system recognised only as radio waves originating from the local Games Board station — the monitor had a growing appreciation that music, in all its forms, was a wonderful sensation that she should indulge herself in. A minute later the nanote material on the lens reassembled itself as the gnat and flew off, returning to the carving and leaving no trace of itself on the monitor.

In the few moments that Harold had taken to complete his mission for *Basalt* and its crew, the director, the recruiter and the male monitor who was recording everything, together with a crowd of school and Administration staff were arguing about what had happened to Tengu. The village AI, seeing the whole performance as just the first act, withdrew the entangling roots and allowed a badly bruised and confused Tengu to move freely on the ground once again. He got up and climbed as quickly as he could manage into the nearest Games Board vehicle and closed the door. Two compact, single-seater, open-cockpit fighters slowly and tightly orbited the Games Board group, their weapons deployed.

'That was an interesting result, Harold. Unexpected. So what did you give Tengu?'

Harold glanced at the cat, saying, 'A very beautiful piece of music composed by Fritz Vinken and designed to soothe what can only be described as a deeply troubled mind. The rest is up to him now. In time it will give Tengu a conscience of sorts. Time will tell.'

Looking to the east, both ACEs could see the front edge of the approaching storm roiling over the horizon.

'About to get a whole lot more exciting for everyone, Harold,' said Bing with a smile. 'See how the locals are looking anxiously at the sky, then at the bases of the native trees and vegetation? Oh, and just to make things more interesting, Petal, the district AI, says that there are definitely two more of Tengu and she has strong indications that one is still in the third vehicle and the other is trying to sneak up the road. Fat chance. The stupid bastard is going to get a hell of a fright in a few minutes!'

Harold was staring intently at the third vehicle as its doors opened. Four individuals in light armour suits quickly clambered out, followed by two spherical black monitors that had no discernible features connecting them with their human origin. They immediately rose up above the Administration buildings on their antigravity units, being propelled skywards by their small swivel-mounted turbofans.

Harold switched his attention to the cat beside him. 'Hey, the birds have all vanished! Even those big raptors have headed to their roosts. What is about to emerge? The only data I have is the emergence of a swarm of crab beetle types. Aha! I see, Bing. Although it is a bit early for their seasonal mating flights, nevertheless the conditions right now are optimum! Are we safe here?'

The cat shook his head. 'No, but I would say we have only ten or so minutes before we should move back into our home trees. See, they are starting to seal themselves. But we have contingency plans, so if we have to go to ground out here, we will be OK.'

Harold looked up at the canopy of the giant trees. The uppermost leaves were slowly expanding to link to each other and form a tough, flexible cover over the village. He looked at the fungi-formed Administration structure and saw that it too was reconfiguring to shrug off the worst the weather could deliver.

The school bells chimed and over the course of the next five minutes the daycare, kindergarten and other schools emptied, with the children being marched back to the village by their carers. As they passed the Games Board group, the children chorused goodbye. The Administration officials were verging on being rude in their attempt to get the director and his charges to leave as quickly as possible, but the director was insisting on staying to view what was about to happen. Finally the officials nodded, wished them well and walked inside, leaving the Games Board staff to their own devices.

The four child recruits were ushered into one of the vehicles, which left quickly and headed back to the airfield. Minutes later, a large crablike Games Board lifter arrived overhead with ten more monitors being deployed from its sides before it hovered over the car park area to drop an Event Management Centre onto the hardened surface. The director and the recruiter waited for the centre to unfold and anchor itself before entering. The four-person armoured security detail took up their stations at its entrances. The two monitors who had been the first to arrive with the director, changed their upper body clothing from formal attire to the semi-armoured field clothing, then also left to go to their appointed areas.

The cat shook his head. 'Dummies! Yes, this might be a rare opportunity to witness the crab beetle flight in daylight, but they are going to get their arses chewed off! Those native insects: first they fly, then they screw and then, and then, my friend Harold, they eat! They eat anything that will deliver protein and will go a long way through what is no good to them to get it.'

Harold looked closely at Bing. 'I dare not query the local database, Bing. Please send me the knowledge.'

An instant later, he started to learn about the creature as Bing lasered the information into his eyes. In its initial grub-like stages it will burrow into any form of native foliage, tunnelling its way down, consuming the living tissue, until it reached the roots where it would emerge into the soil to eat anything smaller than itself until it reached an intermediate stage as a medium-sized beetle that could exist on the surface. It would continue to grow for several seasons as it foraged through the undergrowth and waited for the optimum conditions for the mating flights. Tens of millions of the creatures would take to the sky at once, right before a thunderstorm that would assist in spreading the next generation.

'So, Bing, the storm is only a few kilometres away. The beetles will be taking to the air very soon?'

'Yes, Harold. Now, remain very still, they are already climbing the trees and that includes this one!'

Harold opened the sensitivity of all his faculties to the maximum, and could hear thousands of small claws being driven into the tree bark as the 100-millimetre-long creatures climbed the tree and started to fly up into the increasingly strong winds which drove them towards the storm.

'So they must have smelt us surely, Bing?'

'Yes, but they are not interested in us just yet. Being true hermaphrodites they just want to mate — to screw and be screwed, some might say! But as soon as the last of them are airborne, we had better be gone. And that's the last of them from this tree.'

Harold looked out from the tree to see the GB monitors orbiting vast dense swarms of the creatures. A movement caught his eye and he turned to see the GB airship lifting off and heading quickly out to sea to avoid the storm. He looked curiously at what appeared to be a violent mini-sandstorm occurring hundreds of metres down the road which was producing explosive sprays of sand and grit in strange patterns.

Bing saw what he was looking at and laughed hard. Further recognition codes suddenly arrived in Harold's brain and a fraction of a second after he activated them he watched as the two local panthers, whom he had only briefly met a few times, giving one of the Tengu a very hard time of it. The action was blindingly fast, even by his standards, but for every action the Tengu dragon took, exhibiting extraordinary martial arts skills, the two panthers worked in coordination to match and better him. Within a few minutes, the fight was over as a limp and beaten Tengu was dragged by the neck into the bushes from where he had obviously been ambushed.

'Are they going to kill him, Bing?'

'No, Harold, that one goes back to its creator so we can re-educate him. The big cats will have him sedated and underground in a few moments. The one who is just about to leave the third vehicle, that one we kill. Care to join me? The dogs and cats are audibly tracking him. I presume that you are equipped with Master Marko's garottes?'

The dogs were barking in order to paint the opening door with acoustic vibrations, which the surrounding ACEs could map. Harold looked at the sound-generated images of the camouflaged Tengu as he emerged from the vehicle, stretching and then pulling various pieces of equipment from the vehicle and attaching them to himself, seemingly unaware that he was being watched.

A large and very beautiful owl called Owen, who Harold had met on many occasions while hunting the winged rats, suddenly appeared flying at full speed from the home trees to swoop down above the Tengu and neatly defecate on him, much to the dragon's tremendous indignation. The Tengu tried to leap into the air so that he could see the rapidly departing pearl-white bird, but found himself entangled by fine tree roots. Furious, he brought his weapons online, firing his arm-mounted multiple lasers down into the ground. Freeing himself, he jumped onto the car roof, trying to wipe the bird faeces off himself. He shrieked loudly in frustration when he realised that, with every wipe, he allowed the thick fluid to destroy more of his chameleon camouflage.

High above him several of the monitors started to record his actions which made him even more furious with the situation. In a state of killing fury, the Tengu leapt up into the air using the small pulse jet engines attached to his antigravity backpack and, screeching his rage, went looking for the now silent dogs who had slunk back into the undergrowth and were heading towards the tree that Harold and Bing were in.

'Look after the dogs, Bing. I am going to mess up this Tengu a little.'

Bing spun around. 'Wait, Harold, just wait!'

But he ignored the plea and jumped from the branch, extending his wings and climbing hard until he was a few hundred metres above the Tengu. Below him, Bing shook his head and muttered to himself about 'impetuous, impatient youth!' before climbing quickly down the tree to join the dogs and cats moving underground into their toughened shelters.

Harold flew until he was in the perfect position below a swarming cloud of beetles, tucked his wings in so he could still effect good control and, using his tail to steer, dived down towards the much larger dragon. Travelling at high speed, he attached one end of his long diamond garotte to one anchoring finger and extended it out from his other hand. As he flashed past the still unaware Tengu, he reached out, slicing away one of the jet units, parts of the power supply for the lasers and part of the antigravity unit, rendering them mostly uncontrollable. The antigravity's control system instantly went into an emergency default mode, lifting the Tengu clear of any ground dangers and taking him straight up until he was 250 metres above the ground, screaming and impotent as the wind blew him towards the storm.

Harold climbed again, taking great care that he was not producing any sound, scent or visual signal that the insects could detect. He watched the Tengu as he turned his upper torso around, quickly swapping modules of what remained viable, not seeing the cloud of rapidly mating beetles hovering ahead of him. He drifted below them with dozens of beetles, who had now had their spawn fertilised, seeing the prospect of protein almost amongst them. The first few that the Tengu saw were swatted away, but there was an increasing number paying him their closest attention and they were starting to land on him and bite through his armoured skin. He smashed a number of them, unintentionally. The shattered remains then released attack pheromones and exotic acids which started to dissolve their way through his hide.

The Tengu suddenly understood his predicament and hit the release to drop out of his equipment harness, falling towards the ground with Harold silently gliding away to one side of him. The Tengu built up velocity, then extended all four of his limbs, pulling a membrane tightly between them, and gliding down towards the thick undergrowth pursued by thousands of hungry beetles. He soared above the foliage, obviously looking for a suitable place to land, then tightly orbited a deep, clear pool of water, which he dived headfirst into.

Harold could make out his movements by watching the disturbances in the water as the Tengu settled onto the bottom with his head looking up at the beetles hovering above the pool surface. Harold raced through his biological threats data files as everyone knew that swimming in the pools outside of the village was a very stupid thing to do. He landed very quietly and carefully in a tall tree, keeping the pool in view, knowing that the beetles were bad, but the nymphs that made their homes in the pools were much worse.

Back towards the village he could see that the monitors who had taken flight to record the mating of the beetles were now in trouble as literally thousands of beetles had descended on them to try and work their way in through the armoured suits and antigravity units to the protein they scented inside. Harold felt a wave of intense sorrow for the Games Board personnel, knowing that in spite of their director's stupidity they were just doing their jobs. The two defence aircraft were trying to assist their colleagues, but the sheer volume of insects and the reality that they did not have any weapons able to inflict mass damage on the beetles meant they were not effective.

He watched and approved as one of the craft slowly flew up against one of the monitors and reached through the insects with one of its waldo arms to latch onto it, then towed the unit seaward, grabbing another as well, slowly moving away from the storm. The other fighter tried the same manoeuvre, but was having difficulty with its flight controls due to the huge amount of insects holding onto it. The pilot did the only sensible thing and went straight up as the other monitors did the same, abandoning any effort to record the behaviour of the ravenous beetles.

More and more beetles were crash-landing in the foliage to hunt, then tear apart and eat, anything that they could find, including forcing their way into the flying rats' warrens and the deep burrows of the native birds. They ate any animal, native or introduced, which had not found shelter or buried itself deep. As Harold watched, he sent a signal out to the other ACEs, sharing with them what he was seeing, and asking advice as he was very alone and worried that he would also be caught and eaten by the marauding insects. And to make life slightly worse it was raining hard, with lightning smashing into the tops of the trees around him.

Reg the pug was the first to answer. 'Well, Harold, pleased and amazed you are not stripped down to the non-edible parts of you. Stay right where you are! The beetles that find something to eat will then fly up into the thunderstorm, where they will burst and shower the storm with hatchlings which will then be carried further inland from the sea. They will be gone within the next fifteen minutes as that is all the time they have before the storm moves away from us. Those that can't find something to eat will attack each other. Only a small percentage of those then get to fly a second time. The hail will be with you in a few moments; it normally makes things tougher for the beetles as well.'

Harold acknowledged the advice and slowly pushed himself further into the thick foliage of the tree, making his way up the trunk. He generated a low energy radar pulse, looking for a hollow in which to hide. He saw one lower in the tree halfway around the trunk. He slowly opened a compartment on his flank to take out and put in place a small camera unit so he could keep watch on the pool, and its feeder stream, while he hid. He crept down and around the trunk, finding the empty deep hole which, with a serious contortion, he was able to slip into. Feeling a little more secure, he watched the Tengu silently battling with a nymph which had latched onto his belly.

The Tengu rolled and seized the nymph, ripping it apart as another latched onto his neck. He tore that one to pieces as more of the 600-millimetre-long denizens of the pool slipped out of their hiding places around the pool or rose out of the rocky bottom to attack this intruder smelling of anxiety and meat. The fight became more and more ferocious with smashed and bloody parts of nymph being thrown from the pool to be snatched and eaten by the beetles who were gathering in steadily greater numbers. Over the next five minutes the frantic activity in the pool, which Harold could no longer see due to the muddying of the water and the thick

49

cover of beetles above, died down. He surmised that the Tengu had either succumbed, which he thought unlikely, or all the nymphs had been killed.

'Harold, this is Bing. Don't reply or broadcast any type of signal. We can't get to you for a while longer so stay calm and safe. Our sensors show the Tengu is alive and still in the water, and he will be listening for you and us. If he is sensible, he will just slink away back to his Games Board masters, but he is a stupid, very angry dragon, so we expect to have to teach him manners!'

Harold groaned silently to himself, knowing that the Tengu would indeed be listening and that the other ACEs were goading him to come out and fight. He silently shook his head at his own stupidity, realising that the Tengu probably knew exactly where he was hiding because of his earlier plea for help. He checked through his weapon systems and brought them online, deploying his nastiest biovenoms and neural poisons; the brutally sharp molecular chain-link diamond claws pushed out through the ends of his fingers and toes. He also charged the linear rifle that ran the full length of his spine, loaded the magazines for the rifle with flechettes of brittle high-carbon steel — which were coated with toxins and tailored hormones — and settled down to wait for the inevitable while watching the pool, stream and surrounding area as if he was still sitting out on the branch.

The beetles were furiously killing and eating each other with fewer and fewer launching themselves into the overhead storm. The hail had started smashing down, shredding the softer foliage and turning the open areas white with pebble-sized pieces of ice. Harold saw movement in the small stream, through the hail, and wondered what it could be. His processors gleaned as many parts of the images he was seeing as they could and cross-referenced it with his biological data banks and found one of the giant native aquatic centipede creatures was slowly advancing towards the pool. He also saw fragments of beetles falling with the hail and heavy rain. The beetles that had made it high into the storm were blowing themselves apart, scattering the next generation. He could also see that the storm itself was only minutes away from passing overhead as it moved further inland, and sensed the steady gathering of scavengers of all types moving into the area to feed on the beetles.

The four-metre-long centipede climbed out of the stream to snatch and eat the carcasses and injured beetles as the sun slowly came out and the whole area started to steam. Harold anxiously watched the dirty pool for any sign of the Tengu, wondering if he should continue hiding as he probably held a better advantage if he was in the air. He gingerly uncoiled himself from the deep hole and slowly pushed his head outside, trying to look everywhere at once. The wind was slowly dying down although the tree still moved in the occasional gusts. Looking down, Harold saw the centipede being joined by another moving quickly against the side of the furthest bank.

Suddenly the water exploded as the wet shape of the Tengu vaulted out of the pool to land metres away from the first centipede which turned and bit the Tengu on his tail in a blinding blur of motion. The Tengu slashed its head open as the creature coiled itself around the dragon seemingly uncaring about the mortal damage which had been inflicted upon it. The other centipede struck the Tengu in his flank knocking them all back into the pool which boiled in a frenzy of motion. Harold gave up trying to extricate himself from the hole slowly and hastened his struggles to exit. The Tengu ripped up out of the pool again leaving the smashed remains of the centipedes floating in the pool. The Tengu saw Harold trying to get out of his hiding place and raced across to the tree and flashed up its side.

Harold swore as he finally twisted his hips out of the hole just in time to see the Tengu leaping at him. On Harold's head, a nostril-like aperture popped open as his head also widened. In his mind he sped himself up to the maximum, fixed his sight on a damaged area on the Tengu's neck and fired a burst of the needle-thin seven-millimetre-long flechettes into him. As the Tengu closed to within metres of Harold, he suddenly stopped, frozen, clinging to the side of the tree. His head dropped, then he breathed deeply of the oxygen-enriched air and slowly lifted his head to look into Harold's eyes with hatred. The Tengu opened his mouth, threw back his head and screamed in great pain. Choking it off, he looked at Harold hovering in the air above him.

'You fucking bastard slime,' he croaked. 'Come closer, so I can kill you quickly. You evil little prick. So I am now not able to control the pain from whatever you fired into me; that is nasty, very nasty. You will pay for this, creation of Marko.'

Harold took the seconds he needed and pounced, clinging to his enemy's neck, knowing the Tengu's systems would soon counter the neural toxins he had fired into him. He stabbed a specially adapted finger into the Tengu's neck, drew off a blood and tissue sample, and leapt off again as the larger dragon slowly regained control.

Harold was unsure of what he should do while his systems analysed the Tengu's chemistry in order for him to create a more virulent poison. He knew that he did not have the ability to kill the Tengu outright, so he fired again, directly into the creature's eyes, realising instantly that it was a waste of ammunition as the flechettes shattered against the toughened orbs. As the Tengu reached out to try and grasp him, Harold flew higher and identified dozens of other patches of damaged skin, so he fired bursts into the wounds closest to major joints, trying to jam them.

The Tengu bellowed in pain and rage and launched himself from the tree in an attempt to glide back to the ground. However, one of his rear legs was no longer working properly, so he was not able to pull his gliding membrane out to its fullest extent. He crashed into the ground, rolled and immediately spun his head around; his spine locked into a perfectly straight line as he brought an older generation of linear rifle to bear on Harold, whose up-to-date linear weapon could be fired in a bent or contorted configuration.

Because of his damaged leg joint, the Tengu could not react swiftly to Harold's evasive actions, but still Harold felt the projectiles getting very close. Realising his adversary was a difficult target, the Tengu started to command detonate the rounds as they came close to Harold, spraying stinging, white-hot shards of metal outwards, which punched holes in Harold's wing membranes and then hundreds of smaller holes down his flanks when the Tengu switched ammunition types. Harold, knowing he was in deep trouble, put his head down and tried to get as far away as possible, but the Tengu changed ammunition again and sent tiny homing missiles to explode around him, slowing him down further.

Reg's voice suddenly sounded in his head. 'Harold, we see what is happening. Move towards us! We are coming! Here is the meeting point. Be as quick as you can. The Games Board wants the Tengu to win and are dropping another antigravity unit to him!'

Harold swore to himself again as he heard the booming of the linear rifle, then smiled when it became clear that the rounds were going in the opposite direction, past him and towards the Tengu. His sensors showed him the firing position as he noted the fuzzy outline of a woman, high in the air on a chameleon-camouflaged combat antigravity sled. His software recognised the camouflage codes and he saw that it was the young teacher, Claire. He did not have time to further investigate, because an emerald-green and black antigravity bike flashed out of the heavy undergrowth towards the Tengu, who had donned the antigravity harness and was climbing skywards towards the woman.

From Harold's viewpoint the bike's rider possessed extraordinary skill as the bike raced underneath the Tengu and fired a shining black, two-metre-long spear from the side of the bike which hurtled upwards, piercing the dragon through the harness and right through his body. The Tengu rolled over and plummeted towards the ground, regaining control after smashing off the ends of the spear to head towards a large tree and seek cover, near where Harold was. The black bike came close as its rider tried to force the Tengu to the ground. The dragon reached up, slicing away one of the weapons pods on the bike with his arm blades and trying to grasp the machine with his hands. The rider booted him in the face, then fired an automatic carbine into his jaw. The Tengu responded by grasping the rider's right hand, shredding it and crushing the weapon and ripping off three of his fingers. The rider was screaming when Harold pounced on the Tengu's neck and buried his claws deeply into the dragon's neck, pumping the biotoxins deep into him as the Tengu brushed him off, slashing at his wings. Harold tumbled off, trying to regain control as the black rider seized him by the neck and pulled him up, placing him on the bike close to the controls.

The Tengu kept flying down towards the trees as the black rider chased after him.

A familiar voice was shouting … Harold suddenly recognised the voice of the mechanic, Jerry. 'Harri, we need to nail that shit to the tree as we don't want him escaping. Jack yourself into the control system. We only have two of the javelins left. Make them count.'

Harold nodded quickly, extending a datalink from one of his wrists into the bike's controls. Quickly searching through the systems, he found the controls and firing mechanism, then aimed and sent a rocket-propelled javelin at the fleeing Tengu, through his spine, which shattered inside him, taking the linear rifle out of action. He waited a few seconds then fired again as the Tengu quickly decelerated as he came close to the tree. The onyx javelin flashed across the space between them, entering the Tengu's neck and impaling him firmly against the tree trunk.

Jerry landed the bike and looked across at the hanging, twitching dragon. He accessed the first-aid kit, gingerly placing the remains of his hand against it, wincing as it opened up and sprayed the damaged hand with a rapid setting fluid. It then deployed a protective sleeve to flow around his hand, sealing off the wounds, allowing his little finger and his thumb to remain usable. Looking across at Harold, Jerry wanly smiled and said, 'Harold, you need a serious amount of work done on you too.'

Harold nodded as his bio-software showed him the extensive damage to most of his digestive tract, lungs, his wings and a lot of his skin. He shrugged and agreed, feeling suddenly tired and sadly looked up at the wreck that had once been a proud ACE hanging from the tree. Minutes later, the rest of the ACEs arrived. Bing quickly climbed the tree to remove the Tengu's Soul Saver from the back of the dragon's skull before the Games Board arrived to claim the body.

Harold looked around at the cats, panthers and dogs, and flying overhead the owl, with a flock of keas. They all nodded at him, called their greetings and congratulations and started to disperse. He looked upwards, trying to locate the teacher who had distracted the Tengu long enough for Jerry to get in close, but could not see her. He looked across at the young man who was climbing back onto his bike.

'Who was the shooter, Jerry? And who told you what was happening here?'

The youth, who was obviously in great pain, said, 'Time to go, Harold mate. We need to find that javelin launcher pod and get away before all the scavengers arrive. Climb up here and I'll tell you on the way.'

They lifted off with Harold directing Jerry to the precise spot where the neatly severed javelin pod lay in the top of the thick undergrowth. As Jerry hovered the bike over it, he activated a mechanical waldo arm-hand from under the front of the machine that grasped the pod and they then climbed away. They headed back to the village where the trees were opening up again in the late afternoon sunshine. Looking back, Harold saw a small Games Board recovery craft and also a local Administration police craft landing beside the Tengu. He smiled to himself, wondering what the discussion was going to be like between the two groups as one tried to explain to the other what had happened and why.

'I don't know who the shooter was, Harold. And I got the call from the village AI who told me that you were in real trouble. I was asked to run interference while a more substantial force of our militia was being readied. I am a territorial soldier for the Administration, so I grabbed my carbine and armour.

When I was told that the enemy was a dragon I decided to take the tournament bike with its javelins as I thought it would do the most damage. They worked well, eh!'

Harold nodded slowly in agreement, feeling very sick.

They quietly moved up the main road leading past the Administration building where they could see the picked-clean skeletons of two of the Games Board security staff being gently lifted into body bags. The Games Board Event Management Centre looked like it had been chewed on severely as well, with parts of its surface appearing to be heavily acid-eaten. Harold wondered if any beetles had got inside.

Looking behind it, he saw that the Administration building showed only superficial damage and was slowly opening its living shields, the tens of thousands of dead beetles sliding off the unfolding leaves to the delight of the flocks of feasting birds. A few minutes later, they passed under the lowest branches of the giant village trees. The leaves were gradually lifting off the ground as they unlocked themselves from their neighbours, leaving tall piles of slowly melting hail, mixed with beetle parts and carcasses, in a great oval shape right around the village.

Jerry stopped the bike just beside his uncle's workshops with a crowd of locals quickly gathering. They climbed off the bike to be greeted with beaming smiles, then concerned comments when the villagers saw what injuries they had. Harold only had enough time to murmur his thanks to Jerry before the young soldier was rapidly escorted away to the medical centre.

Rebecca and Jenna, followed by the rest of the Spitz family, pushed their way through the crowd, all of them grimacing at the state of his injuries. Peter placed a biohazard blanket on the ground beside Harold, telling him to walk onto it. The little dragon wearily walked into its centre as it activated, folding up and sealing him inside. Peter then picked him up and cradled him in his arms and Harold snuggled down, feeling safe at last. Peter started to walk back towards their home tree when he was stopped by the local senior Administration officer.

'We need to interview him as to what the hell is going on, Peter.'

Peter looked at his longtime friend and shook his head. 'Nope. Not yet, Rob. This little guy is seriously beaten up. You can review his internal recordings of the entire event as soon as I have him hooked up in the tank. Follow me if you want to.'

He started taking long strides towards the home tree, with Rob Patu trotting to keep up.

'But, Peter, the Games Board is most insistent they know immediately what happened!'

Peter Spitz spat out angrily, 'Screw the bloody Games Board, Rob! Those bastards brought three combat grade ACEs here without any of us being advised and they hunted us! And the bloody things were that aberration, Tengu. They owe *us* explanations not the other way around!'

With the family and neighbours following, they walked in silence to the great tree then down into its base and through the high vaulted foyer of one of the ACE workshops.

Peter turned to everyone. 'Family adults, Jenna and Rebecca only from here. Full biohazard suits, everyone, before we go into the white room.'

They pushed themselves up against panels in the walls as the suits reached out and formed themselves around each of them, including their footwear and hands, before helmets flowed up out of the collars and sealed them in. They entered the compact, smooth room with its low ceiling, and sealed the doors behind them as the equipment and lights activated.

Peter placed Harold on a soft table inside a transparent tank, while the blanket unfurled, and asked him to open his access panels and extend his datalinks. The little dragon opened himself up as Peter slid the main molecular level scanner over the top of him and activated it. Around them the screens came alive, showing just how bad the damage was. A brave-faced Rebecca was standing silently, stroking Harold's head with gloves through the tank's wall. He smiled gently at her, but was too tired to reach out. He just wanted to sleep. The majority of his internal threat alarms were going off as one by one his systems slipped into emergency default mode.

Rebecca started to quietly cry, saying between the sobs, 'Dad, you are not allowed to let him die. Not today, Dad. I promised that he could have a Marty-burger.'

Peter looked around at the rest of the family and nodded. The adults were readying systems, or viewing what was happening inside Harold's body as it rapidly succumbed to the powerful ACE-tailored toxins with which he had been infected when the Tengu slashed his wings.

'Decision time, family. Hard-freeze or hold? Just how long do we have before total failure?'

One by one the adults answered that Harold had an hour, at most, if they could not identify and neutralise the toxins.

Peter looked down at Harold, who was trying to speak. Peter reached into the tank and plugged in a few comms links, but said, 'Don't talk, Harold, just think, and while you are at it, upload everything that happened.'

Harold changed the image of the teacher, allowing it to blur, and shunted the original file deep behind his personal firewalls. He then passed on the recording and said: 'Talk with Reg the pug. They captured one of the Tengu.'

Peter smiled as Marie immediately contacted the dog then the panthers, explaining what was happening. Minutes later the DNA of the toxins captured from that Tengu hours earlier was sent planetwide as all the Augmented Intelligences and other ACE builders worked feverishly to identify and counter its effects. Harold slipped into unconsciousness.

'John,' Peter said, 'start preps for absolute-zero freeze. We may not have time!'

John started to clip additional datalinks into the little dragon. 'The damage will be much worse in the long run, Pete, but I can't see a lot of alternatives.'

He then began pulling on armoured, thermal protective gear as Jenna, who was sitting at one of the screens on the other side of the room, said, 'Dads! There's a weird e-file here from a non-disclosed Games Board official! Arrived hours ago.'

There were murmurings of 'junk requests for interviews most likely' between those adults not working on Harold. Jenna spoke again. 'I've scanned it. It's clean. It's a formula of some sort?'

John looked hard at Jenna, then raised his eyebrows at Peter.

'Put the formula up on the main screens, Jen,' said Marie.

Everyone then gazed at the formula for a few seconds before Marie ran across to the comms link unit, instructing it to send the formula out to the rest of the planet for assessment. Within minutes the answers flooded back: it was what they needed. Marie shunted the file across to their main computers and switched on the pumps flooding Harold's tank in gel. She started the regenerative and rebuilding programs as the bioprocessors created the toxin neutralisers and as soon as they started to become available had them injected directly into him.

Over the next few hours most of the adults left the room, going through the decontamination protocols, until just Rebecca and her mother were left watching Harold.

'Will he be OK, Mum?'

'I think so, Bex. Will be a week or so before he is fully recovered. His wing membranes will have to be regrown as will his entire digestive tract and probably both lungs, but yes, I'm sure he will be his old self in time.'

'So he won't get to eat a Marty-burger for a while.'

'No, Bex, but it's OK, as the dads are getting the burgers and are taking a container of liquid nitrogen to preserve some for when he can eat again.'

Rebecca nodded and smiled as one of Harold's eyelids flickered.

Games Board

Human Settlement on Storfisk

The Games Board director was in the airship's front lounge sipping what he considered an eminently acceptable local rosé wine, while leafing through the paper reports of the previous day. He looked across at the other senior officers and smiled at each in turn. He pulled out his seal, examined it, pressed it onto the inkpad then stamped the cover of the report which was titled *The Redemption of the Tengu*. He added his signature with his ancient fountain pen, then looked at his colleagues with considerable delight.

'So, an excellent outcome. Wonderful audiovisual programs of violent and fascinating native life thankfully only found on this planet: a village coping admirably with the threats; giant insects; battles between monsters that humankind created and those of this world; a nice piece on recruiting and a most welcome, unusual gift piece on the mating and propagation of crab beetles. A superb David and Goliath piece, ending with the nasty beast — the loathed Tengu — being impaled by a rocket-propelled semi-precious gemstone spear, a weapon normally used as a tournament antigravity racing bike points scorer! That was outstanding and we did not have to pay for it! Bonus all around. And, finally, yet another program about the grieving family tending to their critically ill ACE and who should come to the rescue? Why us, of course! And the icing on the cake is that we get to return a redeemed, considerably nicer Tengu, to his original tenure holder, the one and only Baron Willie der Boltz! For a nice little fee, of course.'

The attending officers all smiled and raised their glasses to the director. Then the commander of the dirigible spoke. 'Congratulations, director, a masterful manipulation, but what of the missing Tengu? And also of the complaints that the Administration have made about us?'

'That Tengu I am not concerned about. I should imagine its carcass is rotting in some creature's guts as we relax here, safe. And the Administration, commander? Do not concern yourself. After all, we are the ones who control the public mind and soul, not them.'

The commander nodded and snapped his head forwards in salute. 'We shall climb up into orbit, Director John. By your leave, I need to be on the bridge.'

The director smiled and nodded as the commander departed, knowing that he had only been voicing what the others present had been thinking.

Privately, he wondered about the third Tengu and fervently hoped that it was, indeed, dead.

Harold

Human Settlement on Storfisk

Harold decided that being a recuperating hero had many unexpected and pleasurable benefits.

Everyone was kind and considerate, constantly asked after his wellbeing, and most brought tasty, but tiny, portions of food and drink whenever they visited, since his digestive system was only just coming back online. The family had given him his own room high in the great tree, with a wide window and a generous balcony leading out into the top canopy so the cats and the birds who were always about could keep him informed and share tales of their latest exploits.

Bing was sitting on the end of his bed, cleaning himself like a non-ACE cat. Harold watched his friend's quick, fastidious movements, and asked, 'Does your fur not self-clean, Bing? Having to clean yourself is a bit last year tech, isn't it?'

Bing looked at Harold, grimaced, favoured him with a scornful look, replying, 'Of course it does! But I like to do this. It is cathartic for my mind. I find peace in these actions. Don't you?'

Harold looked out through the open double doors into the foliage of the great tree. 'I don't know yet, Bing. I am not of any one particular biological stock. One day I will notice how I do things, and that may show which component of my make-up is the stronger.'

He looked at the cat then around the room before quietly continuing. 'I wonder what it would be like to never wake up. John told me that a part of the chemical weapon that Tengu used on me had started to attack my Soul Saver.'

Bing stopped what he was doing with one of his hind legs still high in the air. He slowly straightened it and sat up, wrapping his tail around his legs. He looked at Harold for a long moment.

'Shit! That is horrible. That is real death. Well, I suppose it would be. Without your Soul Saver being in a continuous conscious state how would we know if the rebuild was really us? That is terrifying, Harold. No wonder the biological humans so fear the Soul Savers. I have known a few killed who went through what they called the darkness when they were in the tank: no sleeping, no distractions, being isolated and focusing only on regrowing yourself. And always the doubt that the new you is actually a new entity with another's memories.'

Bing slowly turned his head and looked to see what Harold was watching. One of the Kahu harrier hawks was high in the sky, slowly circling, watching the ground around the village trees.

Harold looked quickly back at Bing. 'What do you mean, Bing? That because there is not continuation of consciousness the original is dead!' He had a look of horror on his face as he continued. 'No, no, no, that could not be, could it? That would not be true! Would it? The memories would all be there, the spirit of the person would be there. We would see, listen and know that person as they had always been.'

The cat looked unwaveringly at Harold. 'Yes, but would the person? Or is it like sleep? You awaken as a new entity each day with only the memories of another person to assure you of who you are. But what if your memories were changed while you slept? How would you know any different? Nail told me that they believed the Administration was killing people to change their personalities and memories to better suit Administration causes while people were in the tank regrowing themselves. He also said that the Games Board was actively helping them. And remember, only the very wealthy or those who make money for the Games Board have Soul Savers.'

Harold looked shocked. He shook his head, saying, 'So our girls Jenna and Rebecca don't have Soul Savers yet?'

'No, the casings have been grown into the bases of their skulls, but they are empty. Nail says the crew on *Basalt* know how to make them, but it would be very dangerous. The Administration and the Games Board, who hold all the copies, would destroy us if they knew that non-sanctioned Soul Savers were in use.'

Harold stretched his shoulders, trying to relieve the dreadful itch of healing skin. 'So this is all about control, then? The Administration and the Games Board can manipulate people through the Soul Savers? That is a horrible thing. Everyone wants them, I have seen the weekly lotteries, the pleading for life long beyond the normal span. But really it is all about the status quo. To maintain the power of the Administration and the Games Board, so they can assure their future plans.'

Bing showed Harold a tight little smile, gave a sharp nod and answered, 'Welcome to the Sphere of Humankind, Harold. Nothing is what it should be.'

Ayana

Haulers Territory on Storfisk

The alien-designed scoutship sliced into the target system space far to one side of a Lagrange point with its sensors watching the Hauler sentinel at the Lagrange point's centre.

The collective mind of the ship's crew waited for any orbital changes in the watching sentinel's drones to indicate that they had been seen. Nothing changed so they assumed that they were undetected.

Using the ship's existing high speed and precise trajectory, the minds did not have to use any of the ship's propulsion systems while the perfectly visually and electronically camouflaged ship slid past the nightside of the planet closest to the LP.

When they were at the closest point to the vast northern continent of the world, three linked eight-metre-long ovoid units detached and, as the scoutship slipped away starwards towards the asteroid belt, slowly decelerated using their antigravity systems to spin against each other. It took the ovoid units two days to decelerate against the gravitational pull of the Earth-type planet until they were able to drop down through the atmosphere, towards a huge thunderstorm, undetected by any of the orbiting satellites or the single large orbital. As they fell through the air and uncoupled, the ovoids changed their shape into aerodynamically clean lifting bodies which extruded long, slim double wings allowing them to catch the massive air currents of the thunderstorm. With their sensors watching the ground far below, they glided for thousands of kilometres, mapping the area.

Over the next day, one by one the three alien aircraft glided down to land high in the native trees. Large purposefully designed praying mantis and lizard-like creatures — eyeless, six-legged hybrids — then clambered out and climbed down the huge trees to head in different directions as soon as they were on the ground. Each had been tasked to locate and sample a particular species of the large mammalian animals which, the octopoids knew, had originally come from humanity's Earth before it was partially destroyed by a solar flare.

A powerful Bengal tiger sensed one of the alien ships land in the massive bioengineered baobab tree on the edge of the grassed plains. He felt confused, knowing that something large was way above him but could not see it in the moonlight. He heard it moving away from him as it lifted off, pushing aside some of the branches as it did so, and then heard something large slowly climbing down the tree using what sounded like claws driven into the bark to give purchase. He crept closer, through the undergrowth, and after placing himself downwind of the creature he felt confusion at not smelling anything of it. He silently hunkered down, waiting to see what was almost noiselessly moving in front of him towards a herd of Cape buffalo. In the moonlight, the tiger soon saw a long creature whose skin shimmered, becoming almost invisible — what was behind it could be seen through its body — moving towards the buffalo.

The tiger saw the creature walk, undetected by the herd, until it was beside one of the sleeping bulls. It then seemed to gently bite the bull, step back and do the same to a few of the other bovines before moving from sight, heading out into the plain. The tiger waited for it to return, but seeing nothing further crept back into the heavy undergrowth and made his way through the darkness to where the tiger matriarch had her lair, under another of the huge trees, kilometres away.

Ayana was in a partially powered-down state and suddenly awoke as one of her favourites clawed at the entrance to her lair in the huge barrel-shaped tree. She checked the local time, seeing 3.00 a.m. of the twenty-hour day. She unplugged the direct data feeds and power cables which had been recharging her systems and padded out from the centre of the hollowed-out tree into one of the antechambers.

As she came out of the tree and rubbed up against the Bengal tiger, she sensed his extreme unease. She brushed past his head with her systems activating the micro-sensors attached to his head hairs, so she could see what he had experienced.

She sat still for a few long moments watching, absorbing the images, sounds and lack of smells. Her onboard systems uplinked to the local Haulers hub as she compared what she was seeing with the known threats from humanity and, in particular, the Games Board, from the predators that were known in other star systems and from the octopoids.

Not finding any matches, she sent out a planetwide alert to all the other ACEs, including those that were in the sea amongst the dolphins, whales and seals. She then sent a formal alert to the Haulers hub and instructed it to pass on the message immediately.

She turned back to the huge male tiger, preparing within herself a cocktail of chemicals, and then blew it into his face. It calmed him, wiped his fear and also identified the alien creature as a threat to be investigated further.

As he disappeared back into the night, she switched on a series of batlike drones which, minutes later, swept out of the tree, flying away in different directions, and with their biological radar started looking for any other aliens in her area. Knowing that the other ACEs would be doing the same searches, she settled down to wait.

Basalt

Urchin Star System

Two star systems away from Storfisk, the *Basalt* crew were settling back into the routine of doing what they did best: solving problems.

Major Michael Longbow sat in his command pod on *Basalt*'s bridge, ran a hand over his hairless head, sighed once and said, 'OK. So here we go again. Doing dumb shit because someone's decided that we are the best ones for the job. Can someone please remind me why we are here?'

Stephine smiled across at her lifelong companion Veg who looked back at her with a slight smile and raised eyebrows as she replied: 'Because, darling major, I convinced the Administration that it would be a good idea to study the Urchins' life cycle. I mean, we know that they will do anything for antimatter, that they hunt in the upper atmospheres of some of the gas giants, that the adults can jump from star system to star system and that as a species they are on the verge of sentience as we know it, but we know very little of their breeding or their genome. We need to know a lot more about them, their initial stages, their chemistry and how we may be able to better avoid them.'

Below them, slowly orbiting a massive gas giant, which had huge, fierce-looking storms moving around its equator, the primarily liquid-covered blue planet gathered energy from its local star and also electromagnetic energy from the energetic gas giant.

The major sighed again, wishing he was relaxing on a beach and wondering how long he could keep up the frenetic pace of life that he and his crew seemed to be cursed with. Then he allowed himself a tight, private little smile, knowing he was at his happiest when burning the candle at both ends. He smiled again, realising what a gloriously archaic item a candle actually was. He looked at the disposition of the drones that they had placed in orbit days before. He nodded, tapped several of the screens and gave an order.

'Very well. Let the show begin. Games Board monitors, you have clearance to descend into the atmosphere. Fritz, drop the drones when ready. Optimum warm ocean areas are identified. Let's go have a look.'

The heavily armoured black spheres of the specially constructed monitors started their slow descent from their lander, which was holding station on antigravity over the mid-latitude shallow sea.

The drones, which resembled the huge dragonflies of Old Earth, also dropped away, straight down from *Basalt* as it continued on its fast orbit. The semi-intelligent robots descended at a cruise speed of 200 kilometres per hour into the nitrogen- and methane-rich, yellowish heavily clouded atmosphere.

The crew watched the drones' telemetry, noticing the wings slowly extended when the atmospheric density supported lift and slowed down to glide in great circles above the icy-cold ocean, riding the high-speed winds which encircled the moon.

'Lily, you have a "go" to deploy the relay Fast Movers,' the major ordered.

Lily smiled in her beautiful way at the major onscreen, which elicited a wry smile from him as she said, 'First Fast Mover, with twin combat drones, astronomical and comms package is deployed.'

She watched as the unit dropped away from *Basalt* and slowed gently with its rockets firing to take up a slower orbit. An hour later, after the final Fast Mover had been deployed, they had total comms coverage of the moon.

Over the next few hours, the dragonfly drones gathered greater amounts of information about the local environment as they descended below the thick clouds showing the dark sometimes shallow seas at the moon's equator.

Once she decided that she had enough interesting information to pass on to the rest of the crew, who were going about their usual duties, Stephine said in a cheerful schoolmarmish voice, 'Right, this is for you lot who are interested and paying attention.'

Most of the crew just smiled, except Glint and Nail who were plugged directly into the data feeds, absorbing everything and ignoring the slower-mind true humans.

Stephine continued: 'The equatorial area that we are most interested in is only moderately cold. Average surface temperature is a balmy minus three. We have a band of moderately shallow fluid. It's only 350 metres to the sea floor, black smoker volcanic vents where the temperature at the surface gets up over fifteen degrees Celsius, so in those areas we have liquid water. We have a whole group of surface-breaking reef-type formations which appear to be some type of coral. From those we can also see towering masses of what appears to be tree-type structures. They are either very light and strong, or are truly massive at their origin, as the single supported tips reach on average four kilometres up.'

On hearing that, Marko grunted, sliding out from under the Skua combat craft he had been working on and opening his wristscreen. He allowed himself to speed up, linked the external feeds into his cybernetics and opened his consciousness to the datastreams, seeing the spirit images of Glint and Nail as they too gathered information. Their conscious minds slid over next to his as they could see, hear, smell and taste everything the dragonfly drones were experiencing.

The atmosphere was hazy and it smelt horrible and it was also cold. Marko edited those data feeds away as he observed the massive living structure of the treelike growths.

He shared a comment with the two ACEs. 'Not so much trees, but more like an open fungal structure, don't you think?' The ACEs agreed and both said that they wished they were controlling the drones themselves so they could get much closer.

Marko smiled to himself and switched feeds to one of the high flying drones as it circled the knobbly surfaced, mottled dull-red prominence. Looking at the radar signature and at the scanning laser signals between two of the drones, he saw that the internal mass of the plant was honeycombed carbon tube. Intrigued, he looked closer at the exterior, zooming in the image until he could see the metre-long slow-moving worms with their carbon fibre, tubular skeletal structures. They had hundreds of hair-fine netlike structures coming from their spines which waved slowly backwards and forwards in the thick, cold atmosphere.

He smiled, seeing a similarity of structure to corals found on many of the worlds he had visited.

He drew the attention of the ACEs to the worms. They shrugged as Nail sent across another piece of information showing tiny, flylike insects in their tens of millions which crawled or flew amongst the larger open spaces of the massive structure. He looked at the insects as part of the local biosphere showed itself as steadily larger insects revealed themselves to be engaged in the timeless battle for survival of eat or be eaten.

He also saw what he could only presume to be the local equivalent of flowering plants dotted throughout the worms and, in many cases, living on them, which had little, iridescent dark blue blooms opened towards the local star, shining dully through the cloud cover.

He watched as one of the three monitors hovered within touching distance of the coral mass with its cameras and sensors closely examining the creatures and plants. Wanting to examine the surface plant diversity more closely, he tried to jack into one of the Games Board monitors' feeds, but their system rejected his electronic requests.

At Glint's insistence, they switched their attention to the drone closest to the sea's surface.

It was flying five metres above the highest of the waves that were washing through the huge buttresses of the massive coral growth.

Nail slowed a part of himself down to normal human standards and opened a link to Fritz. 'Hey, Fritz. We are in conscious comms with the number 12 drone. Can I have control?'

To Marko and Glint he seemed to take a long time to respond, finally saying with glacial slowness, 'Sure, Nail, switching control to you. Please don't smash it up, OK?'

The other two saw a fast mental picture that Nail generated of the drone doing loops and rolls through the coral structure, and laughed.

'Promise. Thanks, Fritz.'

Nail took control of the drone, slowing it and rotating its cameras and sensors down to the surface of the sea. He slowed it further, increasing its wingbeat and bringing its little antigravity unit online so it could comfortably hover above the rolling waves. He activated the drone's small torpedo-like probe and lowered it on its tether into the brutally cold water.

Below the surface they could see the gradually shelving base of the coral-like structure teeming with life. Fishlike creatures of bloated elongated shapes with numerous fins moved in small schools down amongst dozens of different varieties of sea anemones whose long tendrils slowly moved, sieving the liquid for anything edible. Moving through their bases were hundreds of different shrimplike crustacea: from those that were as long as Marko's hand, right up to the ones at a greater depth that appeared to be metres long.

Stephine interrupted their watching. 'OK, crew. We know a bit more about this planet. We have determined that the local star has been very slowly decreasing in energy output, so this is why we are seeing higher life forms which would not naturally evolve in such a cold sea. They have had enough time to adapt to their environments and prosper. Also this particular area with its shallow sea black smokers, and other sub-sea volcanic activity, is warmer by up to fifteen degrees than other parts of the equator.'

A high-speed message flashed to them from Fritz. 'You have incoming. Get to altitude as quickly as you can. A group of flying creatures is headed your way and we can only presume that they may be Urchin larvae.'

Nail did not wait, but simply lifted the nose of the dragonfly drone and started to fly skywards, towing the probe up through the sea as it was simultaneously winched in. Just as it was about to break the surface they all saw the image of a creature launching itself off the reef to hurtle upwards, moving far faster than anything they had seen.

'What the hell is that?' Glint exclaimed.

Marko's recognition files instantly mapped the creature as he replied. 'Looks like a massive version of a mantis shrimplike creature. Should not be surprised to find them here. Find similar animal layouts to fit that biological niche on most other water planets. Very quick. Nicely streamlined. Don't think we have a problem unless it can fly.'

As the probe was lifted some metres above the sea and the dragonfly drone increased speed, the mantis darted out of the sea and rocketed upwards. Wings flashed open as twin blasts of fluid were rapidly ejected from the creature's abdomen, powering it easily through the air to grasp the probe with claws that opened a fraction of a second before impact. The drone dipped, struggling with the additional weight, and was only able to maintain its altitude by flying in a wide circle. Nail halted the winch, then reversed it, lowering it away from the main body of the drone.

'Should I jettison the probe?' he called out.

Glint answered: 'No. Not yet, just hold. See, the shrimp is trying to see if it is edible. It's feeling it all over and it probably tastes bad anyway. Be surprised if it wasted much more energy. See! Told ya!'

The two-metre shrimp dropped away from the probe, extending its wings to fly towards the sea and seconds later retracting its wings as it plunged into the water.

The drone winched the probe back against itself and continued to climb as Marko switched his conscious to the other drones' cameras to watch the Urchins.

A flight of seven of them were bounding across the surface of the sea, slapping dozens of long winglike tendrils against the surface. From altitude, the watchers on *Basalt* could see they were driving a large school of fish creatures towards the base of the coral towers.

Marko could see from his scales that the creatures were on average twenty-five metres across and up to fifty metres long. They had the same diaphanous structure as their much larger adult Urchin relatives, including the long spiked tail trailing behind them.

He slowed himself down to standard human speed. 'Stephine. How far do you think these Urchins are into their growth cycle?'

Nestled inside her comms and control unit the tall, statuesque woman replied, 'Hmm, I would say that they are ready to climb up into vacuum soon. They are about the size of the one we captured when *Basalt* was inside the ice-ball. Whatever happened to that particular animal? Became quite tame around us.'

They all heard a growling cough coming from the major as he interjected. 'Bloody good that the thing is nowhere around us if it's all the same to you, Stephine. That thing gave me the shits.'

Marko silently agreed, giving his artificial shoulder and left arm a stretch, remembering what had taken the piece of his flesh and blood arm some years ago. They looked back at the datastreams as the school of fish were suddenly pushed against a small amphitheatre in the coral whose rear walls lifted up out of the sea.

Harry grunted. 'Well, they are smart enough to know their killing zones in the area. Perfectly executed drive so far.'

The Urchins fanned out, slowing and slapping the surface harder, and then slashing their long spiked, barbed tails deep into the sea as well. The fish became even more tightly balled together until one of the larger Urchins suddenly flew upwards, contracted down into itself, then dived straight into the ball of fish. The remaining Urchins slowed even further, almost touching each other, furiously agitating the water, pushing the fish closer to the rapidly shelving shore and, as *Basalt*'s crew watched, they took turns to fly up out of the formation and dive through the slowly diminishing ball of fish. As soon as an Urchin touched the outside of the ball, the Urchin's shape changed, reshaping itself to resemble a funnel gathering its fill of fish. Minutes after it had gathered its fill the Urchin would then erupt out of the sea and spew the dying fish high up on the flanks of the coral tower before returning to the other Urchins.

Tiny pieces of destroyed fish discoloured the sea in the area as the watchers saw other predators and scavengers slowly move closer, creeping along the sea floor.

'The behaviour of the other predators is interesting,' Veg quietly commented. 'Wonder why they are not having a feast at the same time? Would really like to see what is happening inside those tubes the Urchins turn themselves into. Not a lot escapes and they all come out mostly intact, but quickly dying.'

As if on cue, dozens of the mantis shrimplike creatures lifted off the sea floor a hundred metres behind the Urchins, propelled themselves up through the surface, climbed fifty metres above the Urchins and dived down towards the ball of fish.

Marko called out. 'Spoke too soon, Veg! This will be interesting.'

The Urchins twitched, as if linked, when the first of the giant shrimps curved above them. Everyone held their breath in anticipation as the Urchins suddenly reared up, their long spearlike tentacles hurtling up to impale, then slash, the shrimps into pieces that fell amongst the remaining fish. Those Urchins that were close to the fallen pieces of the shrimp seized them and threw the dripping remains high up onto the coral to lie amongst the growing pile of dead sea creatures.

Stephine, thinking aloud, said, 'I am wondering if this is just the beginning of something larger. It would be logical if the Urchins were going to attempt to get into space that they would build up as great a body reserve as possible.'

Veg, sitting beside her in his own comms pod, smiled across at his companion of 800 years, feeling a great love and affinity. He nodded. 'Been wondering when you would work that out! Those buggers would not survive on a few little fish. I don't! Hey, anyone want a sandwich? I am heading down to the galley. Have a feeling this feeding is going to go on for a while.'

As he walked past, Stephine reached out and pinched him on the closest buttock.

He laughed, slapping her hand away. 'Is that the best retort you have today?'

Stephine smiled and raised her eyebrows, pursing a kiss at him.

He grinned and walked towards the spiral staircase that wound its way around the central munitions accelerator tube which ran almost the entire length of the mainly organic, living ship. As he walked down the steps, he patted the deep mahogany hues of the wooden structure in admiration of humanity finally acknowledging that working with environments and living structures was so much better than forcing them to be subjected to the collective will. He knew that the ship *Basalt* did not have a conscious entity, but smiled, wondering, as he saw one of the exquisite, deep purple-blue flowers with its emerald-green leaves growing high up one of the walls. The crew had all seen them on and off over the years, interspersed with regular rose varieties, with sweet-scented blooms lasting months before being absorbed back into the wooden structure.

In the galley, he was met by Marko and the two ACEs who were also making sandwiches and hot drinks to take back to wherever they were working.

On one of the main galley-length screens they watched more and more creatures join in the slaughter as the blood of thousands dropped into the water, spreading out and creating a frenzy of feeding desire.

Marko watched, holding a sandwich, as some of the creatures they had suspected were there, started to arrive. Huge eel-like animals slithered up out of the depths, nosing around. Most, on seeing the Urchins, backed off to wait as a few of the smaller ones slipped up onto the coral to try and get at the increasing piles of protein. One ventured just a few metres too close and an Urchin leapt up to seize its head and sever it from its body, then reached down into its thrashing remains, cutting away its three spinal columns.

Glint watched, leaning against one of the galley tables, munching on a roast pork sandwich.

Flint stood on the table with a datalink from one of his front legs attached to Glint's head, also savouring the sandwich. He shook his small head, complaining. 'You never put enough pepper in the apple sauce for me, Glint!'

Glint swallowed and looked at his friend sternly. 'So get your own digestive system, Flint. You know how to make one. Hey, Marko. How about we give Flint some more abilities? He should be able to eat stuff, you know. Unnatural, this linking to us to get his jollies while I or Nail am eating something. What do you reckon?'

Veg and Marko chuckled as Marko replied. 'You better go talk with Harry. Actually, it's about time for some more ACE upgrades anyway. Yeah, I am OK with it. You happy about getting a bit larger, Flint?'

The mechanical spider harrumphed. 'Finally, I get asked!'

He pulled a face at all of them as he withdrew his link to Glint and leapt off the table, heading out the door and talking over his shoulder, 'I shall go talk with Harry. He will advise me best.'

Glint shrugged as Marko raised his eyebrows at him in question. 'It's not as if we have not talked about this, Marko. You always said he could not have the augments as it would make him too big for most of his engineering work. And he's a bit grumpy lately. What's with that?'

Veg looked across at the sleek gunmetal-grey ACE and frowned. 'Have a think about that, Glint. Thought about the date recently? When Flint was made the indenture was for a specific time. That time is due. Harry has not told Flint yet if he wants him to stay, or for Flint to start his own journey through life. I suspect Harry wants him to stay, we all do, but I know that it is troubling Flint.'

Glint frowned with his frill standing up behind his head. He looked at his front hands, nodded, then looked at Veg and Marko, saying in a small voice, 'You are right, you are quite right. That was not kind of me. Think I'll get Nail, Ngoc and Spike and go have a talk with him. Had not thought about that, or what we will do with Spike. We just made him. We did not consider sending him off on his own. Is this something all parents go through?'

Veg and Marko both nodded as Glint walked out, then came trotting back to make another pork sandwich with extra pepper on the apple sauce. When he left a few moments later, Veg lightly punched Marko on the arm.

'You did well with that one, Marko. Great guy. And you never did indenture him, did you?'

Marko smiled a tiny smile and then had a touch of sadness, missing Jan. He took in a long breath and sighed it out, shaking his head. 'No. He is not indentured. We all made him. He belongs to himself. I know that you feel the same about Nail, Harry feels it about Flint and Minh the same about Ngoc. Tough business this being a parent to a created.'

He turned to Veg, who he considered to be one of his best friends, and added, 'That is one thing I do not know about you, Veg. You ever had children?'

The huge man gave Marko the saddest of smiles as tears welled up in his eyes. He nodded. 'Yes. Yes, I did. Two of the most beautiful people I ever had the pleasure of knowing. I buried them so long ago … a hundred or so years after I finally made it back to Earth as a part of Stephine. I knew them for the first twenty-five and twenty-three years of their wonderful lives and then saw them as old people who had never given up hope of seeing me alive again.'

He sobbed once, as Marko hugged him. 'Thank you, Marko. I am OK. I just miss them a lot. Stephine would not allow me to take their souls. She could have, but said that it would not have been fair. And, yes, to answer your question: I still look after the great-great-grandchildren and their kin from afar. Some of them have Soul Savers and have been regenerated many times. They are great people, but none can replace your own children.'

He took a large silk handkerchief from his pocket and loudly blew his nose. He wiped his eyes, gathered the drinks and sandwiches he had made for the others, smiled wanly at Marko and walked out of the mess. Marko stood and watched him go and wondered again if he would ever learn of Veg's story. He made a large pot of tea, gathered a few mugs, tucked a large tin of biscuits under his arm and slowly walked down a few decks thinking of Veg and Stephine.

In one of the engineering bays he met Jasmine, Minh Pham and Julie, who were stripping out one of the four turbine pods from a Maul, one of the three they had onboard. They all had their heads up inside various parts of the brute of a machine, as he called out. 'Cuppa tea, guys!'

They stopped what they were doing to accept the steaming mugs of tea and proffered biscuits. As they sat on the workbenches, they watched the unfolding drama on the planet moon below them.

The Urchins had tightened their barricade of the reef area, waiting for more and more creatures inflamed with bloodlust to try and take the steadily growing stockpile of food behind them.

Minh shook his head. 'There is much more food than they could possibly ingest. May I suggest that this is more than simple food gathering as even they could not eat that much.'

Jasmine nodded. 'This has had me wondering from the onset. Oh! Look, more Urchins, all much smaller. A later hatching maybe? Maybe they are what the food is being gathered for?'

'No, I think not, Jasmine,' said Minh. 'Look, they are acting as an outer cordon.' He paused, tapped his wrist and spoke

84

again. 'Fritz, are your gravity monitors showing anything inside the tree structure, close to the Urchins, moving about?'

They all heard Fritz's adolescent voice. 'Yeah. We have been sensing something slowly coming down the inside of the structure for the last couple of hours. Pretty big. Easily out-mass any of those suckers and everything they have killed so far. Holy shit! Look at this! What the fuck is that? On the five-kilometre screen.'

They all quickly looked at one of the smaller screens to see four dart-shaped aircraft moving quickly, just above the wave tops, aimed directly at the Urchins. The darts, which had been flying abreast, changed their formation to the front two flying almost nose to tail with the other two holding station to their left and right. Two of the smaller Urchins sprang up from the sea's surface to intercept them. The lead dart suddenly flashed open dozens of bladelike fins and went straight through the Urchin, slicing it to pieces, and carried on accelerating towards the larger Urchin which started to scatter. One of the trailing darts sliced the other, smaller, Urchin in half then climbed to chase one of the larger Urchins which was rocketing up the side of the coral wall. The dart did not slow down as it severed away the tail of the Urchin with long blades, then with an almost nonchalant gesture, flicked out another set of blades to cut the Urchin into three pieces.

It then landed high up on the curving wall of the coral tower and opened out its streamlining to resemble an eight-metre-long beetle-type creature. Fritz zoomed the watching cameras onto it and they were just starting to make out the smallest details when it suddenly puffed into thousands of tiny pieces. Simultaneously, the other dart beetles disappeared in the same way with the resulting fragments gently raining down towards the sea, excepting for some tube-shaped pieces which appeared from the clouds of debris, then vanished again. All creatures except the Urchins rapidly fled from sight.

There was silence for a few seconds, then the major was yelling. 'Get the drones away! Quickly, before we lose them!'

Nail started to boost his drone hard away from the coral tower when it flashed out of existence. Glint was right beside his friend who let out a terrible mewing sound and collapsed.

On the bridge, Stephine yelled at Fritz as she ripped the data cables connecting her helmet from her control boards. 'Sever, sever, sever the link!'

He was not quite quick enough and after letting out a tiny moan slid down in his seat.

Seconds passed as Stephine first checked that Fritz was still breathing, then she called out, 'Topaz to the bridge! We have an immersion feedback emergency!'

The major called across. 'Lily. Did any of the drones make it out? Any other injuries?'

Lily nodded. 'Just one drone. Have it high above the tower, orbiting. Nail is down. Nil cerebral function according to Glint and Marko. They are isolating him. Patrick is preparing an isolated cybernetic unit so an in-depth investigation can be carried out. He says it is an hour away from initialisation. The only surviving Games Board monitor is two kilometres away from the coral tower. It is still in datalink with their lander.'

She turned and looked at Stephine, who was holding Fritz's head. 'I am sorry, Stephine. Glint did everything he could, but Nail's upper conscious mind is gone. He says there is no trace of it. He thinks that whatever destroyed the drone may have snatched his mind from it. That's one of the risks of total immersion, but it should not have happened. We have fail-safes and buffers.'

Stephine nodded in answer, still stroking Fritz's large bald head. 'Oh, that is not good, that is bloody awful, actually. Poor darling boy is probably down there with beautiful Fritz. Isolate the comms links that were associated with the drones, please, Lily. We will need to examine them carefully in case whatever took them left surprises behind.'

A minute later Topaz, the AI designer, fabricator and medical unit, arrived on the bridge and immediately placed a soft helm over Fritz's head with large leads running from the back of it into her own head unit. No-one spoke, waiting for Topaz to report.

Ten long minutes later, the ovoid AI settled down towards the floor with her sturdy little legs folding out beneath her. Topaz turned her head unit to face the major.

'My preliminary thoughts are that Fritz is now the equivalent of an intellectually handicapped human. The memories will all be intact, the personality operating on a basic level. He will be able to perform most of the tasks of human existence, but his higher levels of cognitive thought are a jumbled mess. It is as if the cumulative parts that make him Fritz are no longer communicating either with themselves or with us.'

The major nodded, answering, 'OK. So we won't have to place him in a tank, or intensively care for him. Right. Prognosis, Topaz?'

The AI expanded its head unit a little higher with her elegant humanoid face frowning. 'With Patrick's help to operate some of the more esoteric software that Ernst left for our use, we should be able to rebuild those non-connecting parts of his mind within seventy standard hours. We can simultaneously do the same for Nail. It is of course still a risk that we will not get a 100 per cent success.'

The major nodded again, letting out a long sigh. 'There is always that risk in immersion trauma. The question really is: are the parts of their conscious minds down on that tower with whatever destroyed the drones and monitors? Oh, and what the fuck was that, anyway?'

Patrick was the first to answer. 'I am looking through all the datastreams and as part of emergency protocols I have been allowed access to the Games Board feeds as well. Observe the nearest video screens to you.'

They all looked at the nearest screen as Patrick showed them a hazy image of what could only be an enormous Urchin who was a part of the outer structure of the coral tower.

He spoke about the image. 'I have assembled this image from the gravity sensors that were in operation in the seconds leading up to the drone destructions. I believe what is in the middle of the tower is actually part of its tail. We could see it moving, but had no idea what it was.'

After a few seconds, once they had all absorbed the information, the major said slowly: 'Crap! So this thing is enormous. Much bigger than any Urchin we have seen before.'

Stephine was quick to answer that one. 'It would stand to reason. Any queen, and I do believe that that is what we are dealing with here, is always much bigger than its offspring. We have initiated the mind recoveries for Fritz and Nail. Don't worry, Patrick, I am sure that we will get 100 per cent of them back. In fact, I can assure you that we will.'

Marko, who along with other members of the crew were at their workstations, looked across his screens to prioritise what things he needed to be doing and what he was responsible for. He looked at the water fuel levels that he had available to him and sent a quick message to Harry stating that they needed more. The 'message acknowledged' icon came up on his comms screen and a moment later Harry spoke.

'I wonder if it would be a good idea to go hide somewhere for a few days. Let things settle down as we have no idea of how that queen, or whatever we should be calling it, will react to us parked in geosynchronous orbit. Would not surprise me if she sent someone to come have a poke at us.'

No-one said anything for a few moments, as everyone looked at the possible scenarios and of how they would be affected.

Stephine was the first to speak. 'I concur, Michael. It would be a logical course of action to take.'

The heads of the crew members seen in Marko's screens nodded with Lily, who then quietly spoke. 'The astronomical drones identified a whole group of high-value large asteroids in the belt, two Lagrange points further out from here. We could resupply our water reserves while we wait.'

The major, who was sitting inside his command unit, scratched his head, nodded and then, in a slightly frustrated voice, said, 'OK. That's a smart move. But ... we do not know what happened to the conscious minds of Fritz and Nail. What if they exist within that Urchin? Is there any way of finding out?'

There was a prolonged silence as they all thought about the ramifications of that scenario: if their friends' minds, or even just parts of their minds, were within the Urchin. Veg was heard to clear his throat before he said, with deliberation, 'It is possible. Some examples of cross-transference of consciousness do exist in history. However, it was a short-lived thing before self-recognition of soul was then absorbed back into the capturing host completely. The host's behaviour was modified, of course, with the new information, but I have to stress the separate mind states were short-lived.'

The major cut across Jasmine, who had started to speak. 'OK, how about we get moving and carry on this conversation as we move away? Lily, lay in the jumps to those asteroids. Stephine, please get a message to the Games Board stating our intentions. Everyone else start prepping *Basalt* for probable conflict.'

Marko, who was shunting energy around the ship in readiness for the jumps, was keen to hear what Jasmine had to say. 'Jasmine. You and Lily are of the Haulers. What do you know about this?'

Jasmine sent him a quick kissing icon and then said, 'Mind transference is one of the fields that the Hauler, *Chrysanthemum*, who created us, studied for tens of standard years. He came up with very simple nanote technologies. The nanotes would infest a host body and gather all the minute pieces of information. When assembled this information would create a conscious mind post-transference. Amongst the data blocks we brought with us, when we joined *Basalt*, is how they are made.'

Stephine, who Marko could see was furiously busy recalling the orbital drones — while Minh Pham directed those closest to *Basalt* to dock and refuel themselves — and at the same time was dealing with the Games Board's officials arguing the perceived dangers from the Urchins, also excitedly asked Jasmine, 'This is most interesting, Jasmine. If our dear Fritz and Nail are in the Urchin, and, even if by some remote possibility are conscious of their surroundings, we could invigorate their proxy minds further, to a degree that they could pass on information about the Urchins. Is that possible?'

They felt *Basalt* starting to move out of orbit and felt surges of acceleration as the ship hurried to the first jump point.

The major, somewhat belatedly, gave orders. 'All crew: to

your stations please and strap in. This is going to be fast and furious.'

Marko gave Lily and Jasmine a wry smile as he activated his seat, which extended itself and enfolded him. They both blew him a kiss and got about the business of preparing the ship for the first jump with Jasmine replying as she worked.

'Yes, Stephine. We think that that may be possible. The faster we can deliver a nanote package down into the Urchin queen the better, though. The specifications are available now. It is a simple add-on to our existing microsurgical nerve nanotes.'

The major quickly gave a briefing. 'Crew. Do anything that can be done right away to aid the remnants of Fritz's and Nail's minds if they do exist within the queen. We would need to launch a delivery as soon as possible.'

Veg equally quickly said, 'Good. Shunt the files to me, please, Jasmine. I shall prepare them.'

A few moments later Veg had the files in his own sub-systems and started programming the tens of thousands of reserve nanotes they held in storage for medical use. While he was busy doing that, Patrick prepared one of the limited number of fully camouflaged sub-AI controlled Fast Movers that they carried onboard.

The acceleration continued until the precise capture speed of the target asteroid was reached.

When they were still two hours away from the first Lagrange point, Stephine spoke. 'The Games Board frigate has recovered its personnel and equipment and is following. They report adult Urchins are swinging around the planet to be above the target queen's tower.'

Patrick then reported: 'The Fast Mover is loaded with the nanotes and will be deploying in ten seconds.'

The long, slim missile-shaped machine, with a bulky high-acceleration module fitted, lifted away from outside *Basalt*'s engineering deck. When the unit was 100 metres away its engines ignited and it started to accelerate using the velocity that *Basalt* had imparted to it, describing a long curved arc eventually heading back to the planet.

Once the necessary velocity had been achieved the propulsion unit detached and the missile became almost totally invisible on every spectra as its mind began looking towards the planet and laying out the optimum navigation and deployment course.

It took the information that *Basalt* was feeding to it and also the information supplied by the Games Board ship and plotted where the spaceborne Urchins were.

Hours later, it dropped down amongst the adult Urchins. As it approached them, it precisely ejected away the thousands of packages of nanotes which behaved just like a small meteor shower, flashing through the Urchins down towards the planet. As they decelerated in the upper atmosphere, tiny petal-like wings popped out, steering each package down towards the coral tower of the Urchin queen.

By the time they were close to the tower the atmospheric pressure had slowed the packages further, to terminal velocity. The packages then split into hundreds of tiny pieces of icelike material which splattered downwards, sticking onto the tower just like in any other wet weather event on the planet.

Most of the nanotes assembled themselves into the little gnatlike, or beetle-like, creatures that the crew had seen early in their investigations of the tower. The remainder dispersed and hid amongst the native fauna to wait until they were needed.

In their thousands, the little machines rapidly moved into the central structure of the great coral clump until they identified the queen's tail mass. As soon as they were on her outer surface, they disassembled and reformed into minuscule worms that burrowed into her skin.

Over the next hours the nanotes found, then dropped into, the massive creature's bloodstream after they had coated themselves with material identifying them as benevolent protein blocks which the creature's antibodies ignored. When they finally arrived at the Urchin's core, they dissolved again and spun microscopic threads of datalink between each of them and started to search for the tastes of Fritz's and Nail's minds.

High above them the Fast Mover had slipped into orbit and settled down to wait for any information from the miniature invasion force.

Basalt had jumped, then hours later, jumped again to slowly overhaul the asteroid they needed.

As the information on it came through, Patrick gave a report. He had fired lasers at it and analysed the spectral signatures.

'Interesting lump of rock and ice. I am launching the astronomical drones, plus deploying weapon drones. I am seeing plenty of useful volatiles including phosphorus and sodium. Oh, and we now have caesium to add to the mix. Explosives, anyone?'

'Good!' Harry grinned. 'Nothing quite like having a few extra things that go bang and throw bits about!'

Marko chuckled. 'Hey, Harry! Thought that you had left the ship. You've been a bit quiet of late.'

Harry's image showed on Marko's comms screen. The older-looking man nodded, adding, 'Yeah, I suppose that you are right, Marko. Sometimes pays to just listen than have to make a bundle of intelligent-sounding noises.'

Julie burst out laughing. 'That will be the day the cosmos fails completely, Harry! You, listening? I do love you and you make me laugh!'

Everyone smiled, then laughed, as Harry replied, 'And that's what you get for taking a much younger, beautiful engine builder into your bed! Public abuse!

'Marko, I am seeing some relatively clean deep ice a third of the way around the asteroid from where we are now. Major, I suggest we top up our water fuel reserves before anything else.'

'OK. Works for me. Let's hang off by ten k first and give it a full survey then, yeah, water first and any other goodies can follow.'

Basalt slowed as it came up on the five-kilometre-long knucklebone-shaped asteroid which was very slowly tumbling through space. Everyone who was at their workstation was watching the rock for any possible threats.

Veg and Stephine, who were inside *Blackjack* watching all the data feeds, were the first to see the tunnel entrances in one of the stony outcrops. Veg pointed them out to everyone else.

'Interesting. All exactly the same size; all curve sharply to the right twenty or so metres in. We can't suggest anything non-biological that would make them. Good idea that we stand off a greater distance until we know a little more about what we are looking at.'

'I concur,' the major said. 'Patrick, move us away at speed, please. Lily, Jasmine. Take a combat drone each and go have a close look. Oh, and no sublimation into the machines, please. We have had enough of that. Screens only. Marko, I note that the main ice areas are a kilometre away from the tunnels. How about you investigate that area as well with another drone? Same rules apply.'

Patrick fired the nose-manoeuvring thrusters in a long burn as he then fired the main engines, taking them away from the rock. As they were moving, three combat drones dropped away with two starting towards the hundreds of holes. The other drone Marko had rapidly programmed to search the ice area and report back to him only if it found something unusual.

The imaging was mapped, which showed all the holes to be precisely the same shape and two metres plus in diameter. Lily spoke first.

'We are two kilometres out. Holes are very similar. Showing indents around them plus what appear to be scratches, with the same spacings around the holes. Looking like biological in origin. We are moving in closer and deploying the swarm micros.'

Ten small drones lifted away from each of the large combat drones and moved towards the rock until they were fifty metres away from the holes. One from each group then slid up to a hole entrance and fired a small tethered camera and sensor unit inside.

Back on *Basalt* the crew watched as the camera units extended little legs and started walking inside the tunnels.

'Looking at the walls, I would agree that these are biological in origin,' said Veg. 'Both have subtle variations, but they definitely seem to have been bored with tooth or claws. Wish we had some way of aging the marks. Oh, this is interesting. Now seeing outgassing from the tunnels. Mixture of gases. We have seen this once before. Twenty or so years ago, Stephine and I saw these same readings from where something had consumed an Urchin.'

Everyone started talking at once, until the major called for quiet.

'Something ate an Urchin, Veg! I don't want to be anywhere around something that eats Urchins! Patrick, back us off another fifty klicks right away, please. OK, Veg, Stephine … what do you know?'

The ship started to move again as Stephine, sounding a little exasperated, said, 'Michael. The information is in the reports we made available to you all years ago. Right, well, if none of you has read them I shall tell you. For every predator, there is always another. Some are much bigger than the Urchins and they are remarkably bad news for everything and everyone. These, if they are the same, are at the other end of the scale. They are a swarm creature, thousands of them, and from everything we know are only interested in the Urchins and any creatures that are similar to the Urchins.'

Everyone watched the major furiously scratching his bald head which they knew was a sign of agitation.

'Right, sorry, I was not aware of those reports. I will get into them as soon as time allows. So please, Stephine, show us all just what these things are and what they can do.'

A few seconds later images and schematics of the creatures were displayed on the screens that everyone was looking at.

Marko looked at them intently, seeing basic plate-scaled two-metre-diameter spheres. He touched the icons beside the display as the image turned and opened up, forming a parabolic dish-shaped creature with tendrils that folded out from its edges. As he rotated the image further, it showed a series of interlocking plates forming an armour on one side with numerous rotating hooked pads and a central mouth part. He also noted the layers of insulation over every exposed part of the animal. He tapped the icon on his comms unit for Topaz to ask, 'Hey, buddy, you having a look at this critter?'

The AI design and ACE manufacturing unit replied, sounding slightly scornful. 'Of course, Marko. I know everything there is available to know about these creatures. They are of great interest to me and it would be beneficial if we could have one to examine more closely. I wonder if you could arrange that? If not, then samples would be welcome.'

Marko smiled, thinking that Topaz was constantly gathering information on all creatures wherever they went. Topaz then added: 'We consider this predator probably evolved, or was created, alongside the Urchin. It would be logical that they came from the same planet. Note the various sea creature-like characteristics. The things that I would most like to investigate further are the parasites that exist on these predators. They really are alien.'

Seconds later more data files arrived on Marko's screens showing segmented, armoured, winged, wormlike creatures which appeared to be 100 millimetres long. He looked at them briefly then went back to the predator files.

He told the image to peel away the outer layers and saw three independent digestive systems, plus numerous small hearts which pumped blood, which he could see from its chemistry was remarkable: it could still fuel the needs of the body no matter how hot or how cold the creature was.

What really interested him were its gas generator propulsion systems that seemed far too meagre for the animal's requirements for manoeuvring in space.

He keyed his microphone. 'Fascinating creatures, Stephine. They have small propulsion and manoeuvring capability. So how do they go up against Urchins?'

Her image appeared on his main screen. 'They hold hands, Marko. Well, shall we say, they hold tentacles. In fact, they plug themselves into each other. They layer themselves in sphere-shaped shells with the innermost shell covering a ball of ice which they heat, producing steam which is then vented producing a constant thrust. They can vector it through holes that the numerous shells create, so the whole ball, with sometimes thousands of individuals in communication, can easily keep up with Urchins.'

She paused for a few seconds as more images came up on everyone's screens, now showing hundreds of individuals forming great disc-shaped nets that folded away from the ball and captured an Urchin. While consuming it, it slid down inside the ball as the next shell deployed to envelop and consume another Urchin.

'As you can see, they are very efficient at hunting and consuming Urchins. Of course, a percentage of them are killed or maimed by the Urchins, but as they are the swarm equivalent of an insect, the losses are acceptable. Because they are coupled, even if the ball only consumes a few Urchins they all get fed. And because they are linked their natural chameleon abilities are excellent. What is seen by one individual on one side of the ball is communicated to its opposite number who displays that image on its armoured plates.'

Harry spoke up, curious about something. 'What happens with the antimatter the adult Urchins hold, Stephine, when this predator consumes them?'

She nodded, answering, 'It would seem that they also know how to manipulate the containments that the Urchins use for the antimatter. They store it, and from what we know, use it in minuscule reactions to heat their shelters in the icy asteroids they use as their homes.'

Harry nodded and cocked his head to ask, 'So they are intelligent?'

Stephine paused for a few seconds before replying. 'Not sure. There are lots of parallels amongst other swarm creatures. As individuals, they don't demonstrate much intelligence, but it seems to build with numbers. My thoughts are that as more and more link together the processing power also increases, and as a collective they start doing smart things.'

The major, at his station, looked closely at the predators and asked, 'So what happens if we disturb them?'

Stephine allowed a twitch of a smile on her face as she answered. 'Nothing. We do not represent meat to them, nor does anything on *Basalt*. But if we still had an Urchin here they would be onboard by now, consuming it.'

Lily frowned, saying, 'Unusual for a predator to have only one food source.'

Stephine shrugged. 'Perhaps so, Lily, but then again we only have a very basic knowledge of this creature's breeding cycle. Who knows. They may also be down on that planet right beside the Urchin queen. That would be interesting, would it not?'

Marko slowly nodded, tapping his chin. 'Could we capture one? We could find out soon enough if it is also down on the planet by cross-referencing parasites, maybe?'

Spike, the little mechanical spider who was with his constant companion, the once-Games Board advanced monitor Jim, spoke up. 'We could get in there. Jim could reconfigure himself to slip inside that place and I could get samples of one of them, maybe? You and Topaz only need samples, don't you, Marko? We are a good team. As long as I can keep a laser link to Jim, my mind would remain fully sentient. I should get bigger, I know, so I would not have to rely on everyone to store my complete mind, but I like being small and am best that way.'

Everyone smiled, as they all loved the little spider. Flint, the much larger engineering spider, gave his opinion.

'It is a good plan. Ngoc and I would be best to escort them and we can quickly extract them if something goes wrong. And besides, our zero gravity manoeuvring units are much more compact than anyone else's.'

'OK, I like it,' the major said. 'Get yourselves sorted. Lily, can you have a combat drone standing by outside the small port-side airlock on engineering deck two to transport the guys across? Marko, Lily, to your Skuas, please. I want you as close support. Jasmine, Minh, to your Hangers, you fly outer cordon. Harry, go fit the *Albatross* with heavy weapons, and stay on standby. Julie, I am switching all *Basalt*'s weapons to your board. Stephine, Veg, keep a close watch over everything with Patrick. Glint, you are with me. OK, go to it, people.'

The three mechanical spiders scuttled away down the central spiral staircase with Jim the red-coloured ovoid machine. Jim housed an augmented human brain and spinal cord which controlled all his machine functions, following on his antigravity unit. As soon as they were on the second engineering deck, the two spiders clipped on their manoeuvring units with Flint climbing up onto Jim's outer casing and locking himself on. They cycled through the airlock and then pushed out from *Basalt*'s hull to the waiting double teardrop-shape, combat drone. As soon as the drone sensed that they were onboard, its computer flew the machine out through the huge treelike outer skeletal structure of the frigate and then down towards the asteroid.

Minutes later, the Skuas and the Hangers were overhead holding positions that covered the ACEs as they all moved towards the looming lump of ice and rock.

Ayana

Haulers Territory on Storfisk

'Sven, have you had any reports come in of these creatures in your sector?'

'No, not yet. Cannot find any reference to them in any database. What are you going to do?'

Ayana swished her tail, a little irritated at this unwelcome intrusion into her orderly life, wondering if the creature was a scout from an unknown alien race examining the animals on the planet, or something else.

'Could be a first contact, could be a nasty, could be a created creature from Administration, Gjomvik or Games Board. Need to front one and ask some questions, I suppose. Can almost certainly eliminate it being a native as there is nothing that matches its body configuration. The obvious lack of eyes bothers me. Everything here has eyes; even the deepest sea creatures and deep cave dwellers have vestiges of eyes.'

Sven's voice in her head agreed. 'Don't think that it is a first contact scout. The standard human settlements on the southern island chains are fairly obvious and the Haulers said that there is nothing they are aware of for twenty-one light years further out.'

'Yeah, you are right,' Ayana sighed. 'Leaves Administration, Gjomvik, Games Board or a nasty from someone else.'

'If it is Admin or GB or Gjomvik, then it is totally newly created. Quite unlike anything the Haulers are aware of. I would suggest we treat it with great caution until we know more. Have you a plan?'

Ayana had a sinking feeling in her heart, as a chilling sense of dread seeped through her. 'Oh, hell, I hope it is not another of the Infant monsters.'

Sven grimaced, saying, 'Has all the hallmarks of a designed extreme bioweapon. Plan, Ayana?'

'I will go have a close look at the buffaloes it touched, Sven. I have one of the tigers out tracking it now, so I know where to go for a closer look. I am waking up, and launching, the recon drones.'

High in the tree, metre-long artificial dragonflies were powered up and given their orders. Ayana shunted the recognition images of the alien to the pair as they flew up out of the tree and quickly flew out towards the tiger who was stealthily tracking the creature.

Ayana loped across the fields to where the buffaloes were still resting. She altered her scent to that of a cow and she slowed down to quietly walk amongst them. She recognised the bull the alien had touched, and moments later saw the other three it had also touched, all of whom appeared more restless than the remainder of the mob. She stopped, sensing that something was not quite right, so rather than approaching them swung around until she could see it all. A flap opened in her side and a small disposable flying drone, which looked identical to one of the native moths, flew across to the bull, gently alighting on its back. The moth bit down through the hair, taking samples of the animal's skin and a tiny blood sample and compared the results with its own database which Ayana had loaded into it moments before. Minutes later, it lasered the results into a large beetle comms unit which Ayana had unloaded from another of her internal storage units onto the ground beside her. The comms unit uplinked the data to the Haulers' AI orbital, Angelito, tens of thousands of kilometres above them, shielding Ayana from any possible data intrusion.

The AI received the data into one of its secure units and quickly looked over the alien proteins that it could see in the buffalo's bloodstream. It dispatched another fast picket, with the information, to the nearest Hauler base and sent a confirmation to Ayana, and the hundreds of other ACEs on the continent, that the alien was to be treated with the utmost caution and to be acknowledged as probably hostile. After a moment's consideration of the consequences, it sent a message to all the other ACEs who lived amongst the standard humans on the planet, giving them a warning of what was happening.

The voice of the Hauler AI sounded in Ayana's mind. 'You were right to treat this with caution, Ayana. There is a protein that I cannot identify in the bull's blood. I would suggest that you remove yourself from the area immediately. Warning messages have been propagated. Whatever it is, this alien is new to us. I am receiving information from other ACEs and it would appear that there are six of these creatures spread over a 9000-square-kilometre area. Gather every piece of information that you can on the alien and report your findings immediately. You are authorised to use any individuals and systems at your disposal. That is all.'

Ayana did not even have time to acknowledge the message before the AI Angelito removed itself from her mind. Looking at the map the AI had given her of where the aliens were, she saw that one was also in the sea to the south of where she was. In her mind, she opened a comms link to Sven.

'Sven, there are none seen in your area. Please make your way over here as soon as possible. I am also calling Fenyang down here to help.'

She changed frequencies in her mind and placed a call to the huge baboon.

He answered with his usual abruptness. 'Yes, Ayana. You have a situation of which I am aware. I have already started preparations to move to you. Expect me within a few standard hours.'

'My thanks, Fenyang.'

He abruptly cut off, but she knew that that sort of behaviour was normal for the sentient as he hated anything interfering with his studies of the native insects. She moved south, away from the mob of buffalo, and seeing that the dawn was not far away switched her attention to the beetle that she had left behind, instructing it to climb onto the buffalo bull and conceal itself. She then switched datastreams to see that the silent high-flying dragonflies had found the alien and were watching it from a kilometre up.

The alien moved amongst a small herd of bluebuck antelope which were resting beside a great marshland.

Ayana took control of one of the dragonfly's eyes, zooming in on the creature while her own processing power started to map the alien. As soon as she had composited an external body map, she uploaded it to the orbital AI, then, deciding that a tissue sample would be useful, launched a pair of artificial wasps from under one of the dragonflies. Following established protocols, she instructed one of the dragonflies to follow the wasps while the second one went totally passive, switched on its camouflage systems and climbed much higher.

In the time that it took the wasps to close upon the alien, it had slid up to one of the bluebucks and appeared to briefly touch the antelope's neck with its lips. It crossed to another animal and did the same. And as it was about to do the same to a third, the first of the wasps alighted on the animal's shoulder and was able to see the alien slightly open its mouth; a pair of fine needles flashed into the bluebuck's neck, which seconds later were withdrawn into the alien's mouth.

The other wasp flew over the alien's head and down its back, taking samples of the air, as the first wasp slowly walked along the bluebuck's neck. The alien hesitated for a second, then simultaneously snatched the first of the wasps from the bluebuck with its mouth as one of its forearms twisted around, snatching the other wasp from the air and deftly depositing that drone wasp also in its mouth.

Ayana instantly realised that she could be compromised and cut the datalinks to the dragonfly the wasp information was being relayed through, and sent a message about what she had learned to the orbital AI. A few moments later she saw the descending dragonfly do a slow barrel roll then shut down to fall into the marsh a hundred metres away from the bluebuck herd.

Swearing to herself, she flashed a brief message to the orbital and, just before the alien got to the crashed drone, it disintegrated into thousands of nanotes which rapidly dispersed into the watery bog as its hostile takeover protocols overcame whatever the alien's commands had told it. The alien sloshed around for a few moments with its mouth parts sucking in the water, obviously searching for the remains of the dragonfly. It then returned to firm ground and stood still for a few moments, then slowly disappeared from every spectrum that Ayana was observing.

The orbital AI spoke. 'Ayana. In my isolated comms and analytical units I have discovered that the wasps were being dismantled within seconds of being taken into the alien. Before they ceased, I learned that it is a construct of the highest order and not of humankind. Nothing the wasps detected is anything remotely resembling known natural or constructed biological material from our worlds. However, there are octopoid proteins present so I can only conclude it may be of that race. We will observe it and attempt to learn of its plans before I will allow any action against it. There is a most interesting group of software packages that I shall investigate further as well. The Administration created the despicable destruction of the octopoids on Cygnus 5, just to allow the Administration to help themselves to their technologies. We must not allow ourselves to do the same here.'

Ayana wanted to destroy the alien quickly, as all her instincts and intuitive feelings screamed out that the alien was hostile, but mentally acknowledging what she ultimately wanted from the Haulers' Collective she grudgingly agreed.

Seeing that the first light of the approaching sunrise was now obvious on the horizon, Ayana wondered what the day was going to bring her.

Gjomvik Carrier *Haast*

Human Settlement on Storfisk

Lieutenant Colonel Jeremy 'Bob' Thompson looked at his screens while sitting in his command pod and groaned, wondering why he had so readily accepted a promotion from the Baron to command one of the latest versions of Leopard Strike's light combat carriers.

It was not that he did not like the ship, because he did very much and, as a junior flight officer, had cut his teeth flying earlier versions for the Administration. And it was not that he had not always wanted an independent command, it was more that he had underestimated one major thing: the continual admin relating to eighteen operational Mauls, plus four spares; a close protection squadron of Chrysops; a Heron; three battlefield salvage craft; four Hawks; and three Aurora recon aircraft. Until taking command, what was involved in maintaining, arming and fuelling all this hardware, their transportation, plus the feeding, watering and housing of 110 mostly human crew, and a few ACEs, had not really registered.

He stood up, stretched, thought about another cup of coffee, but decided that any more and he would have to switch on part of his biosystems and start shunting it directly to his bladder.

He vigorously ran his fingers through his close-cropped blond hair, then sat back down and started prioritising what was needed as he looked at the latest intelligence reports which the Baron had sent him. After an hour, he nodded to himself and tapped his comms screen, then the icons for the flight leaders, the admin-logistics officer, the workshops commander and the security officer.

'OK, here it is,' he advised them. 'Movement order. We are heading up to Hauler 19 *Rose Foxtrot* in about twelve hours time at 2100. The basic engagement orders remain the same. The other Gjomvik Corporation outfit that we are up against is the same. There is, however, a change in the area of the fight. We will have an orders group at 1600. Go to it, people.'

In the workshops, Captain Paul Black stuck his head around the corner of his office and yelled the movement order at his crew of techs and mechanics.

They looked up from their workstations and nodded or gave him a thumbs up. Most went back to working on their own private little projects as all the Mauls, Chrysops, Hawks and Auroras had been checked and rechecked while they had waited the six days for the Games Board to finally decide the best terrain for the set battles to take place. They had also done every piece of preventive maintenance possible on their carrier in the previous weeks. The Maul crews had flown all their training missions in the simulators, only launching and flying the Mauls and other aircraft as a goodwill gesture to entertain the local planetary settlements when the carrier visited them.

Paul looked at the two individuals who had not acknowledged him and grimaced, wondering if he should yell at them or not, but then shrugged, knowing that it was not worth the effort. Both were effectively freeloaders who, because of family connections, had their jobs and he in turn had to put up with them.

He heard a sound behind him and knew who it would be, turning with a fixed smile on his face to greet Major Nick Warne.

Nick Warne looked down the long symmetrically tapering workshop, noticing the two individuals who were not actively engaged in making something, then looked up at the taller Paul Black to comment quietly in his soft, nasal voice: 'You know, we could just leave them behind. I am sure that I could arrange to be looking the other way, but then again, who would brew your beer for you, eh, Paul?'

Paul looked at the major, who was sporting a small smile that showed an overlong canine tooth jutting out and down to the side of an otherwise perfect denture. Paul had always wondered if it was a natural affliction, or an augment of the perfectly mannered, but generally overbearing little man. But, although he did not like him, he respected his abilities as an engineer, a pilot and a man who would always get the job done, no matter the odds.

After gazing at the other man for a few seconds, Paul finally answered. 'Yeah, true. Our leader does not mind either, so I suppose we will just live with it. And what brings you to see me?'

Nick smiled again. 'Force of habit, I suppose, Paul, force of habit. Just spending my time working my way through the ship. Wonder how long it will be before we are yelling at each other again, eh? Me demanding why my aircraft are not flightworthy and you coming up with all sorts of excuses. Let the good times roll.'

With that Nick turned on his heel and marched towards the closest stairway which would take him up through the rest of the 145-metre-tall carrier. His comms softly chimed and seeing the colonel's icon appear in his vision he answered it immediately. 'Nick. We good?'

'Yes, just working my way around the ship doing a bit of a check, but I would say that we are OK. You got anything of interest for me?'

Bob smiled at his old friend and wondered for the hundredth time why Nick had not taken the command of *Haast* when he had been offered it first.

'Not really, apart from now knowing what the *Aquila* are going to throw at us.'

Nick grunted and said, 'OK, be with you in twenty minutes. Your tea selection had better be up to speed.'

He carried on walking up one of the spiral staircases at the centre of the Gjomvik Light All Systems Carrier *Haast*. As he walked between the decks, he could see the lifts were moving, but preferred the exercise. Finally, he made his way onto the command deck and walked through the bridge and into Bob's ready room.

The colonel called out a greeting and gestured to Nick to make his own brew as he was known to be notoriously fussy and almost on a par with the Baron in his pursuit of the perfect pot of tea.

Nick looked through the teas available, then fixed the younger man with a sour look. 'Your tea selection is crap, Bob Thompson. I thought I had trained you better than this.'

Bob laughed at his old commander and mentor. 'Battered-looking tin at the back of the cupboard, Nick. Something especially for you.'

Nick reached in and gingerly lifted out the well-travelled tin. He rolled it around in his hands dubiously, thinking that maybe he should have one of the hazardous materials drones take a look at it first. Judging by its weight, he thought it probably was tea, but gave a little shrug of resignation as he prised off the lid, believing that it would be another of Bob's practical jokes. The aroma of one of the rarest of all teas rose up into his nostrils as he took a long breath. He put the lid back on and looked across at a grinning Bob to say, 'By all that is holy, Bob. This is the Baron's finest Jun Shan Golden Needles! How the hell did you get this? And it's in one of his favourite tins as well. You know he will hang you for that alone!'

Bob nodded with a serious look on his face. 'Yeah, I flogged it for you, Nick. Know that you love your tea. Go on, be bad for once. He can afford it. He stamped around *Lynx* for a whole day searching for that tin, getting progressively more and more angry. I thought it bloody funny.'

Nick looked very uncomfortable, then Bob burst out laughing. Nick smiled with some relief as Bob added, 'Nah, it's all OK, Nick. Our fearless leader gave it to me to give to you. There is another kilo in storage, plus a whole bunch of other teas he sent for you. Said to bring the tin back, though.'

Nick busied himself for a few minutes making the pot of tea, then finally gathered up two tall glasses with handles and walked over to the low table where Bob was sitting, looking out of the ship through the curved multi-layered graphene windows.

They both sat in silence as the tea brewed then Nick poured both glasses and handed one across to his commander.

'So, how are you finding it, Bob?'

'Yeah, not too bad, Nick. Not too bad really. The admin drives me nuts and I wish we had an AI onboard. Smart computers are great, but an Augmented Intelligence would be so much better. Bit archaic of our Gjomvik Corporations not to have them, but those in control fear them, and they pay the bills plus our wages so there you go. But yeah, it's nice to be the slightly bigger boss. And besides, you are here to help me out.'

Nick gave Bob a wry smile. 'Yeah, and when you stuff up I shall say that I told you so and give you a good kicking. And speaking of which, I note that you have not been keeping up your required simulator time. You need to lead from the front, Bob. The whole crew likes you, but they are all cheerful enthusiasts so need to see that you can still foot it with them.'

Bob looked down at the crops of black fennel far below them as the battle carrier hung vertically in the sky, its atmospheric turbofan engines just ticking over. The ship moved sedately over the landscape, the navigation staff actually sailing the great structure downwind through the sky; with tens of thousands of linked graphene-covered one-micron-thick titanium spheres — within each a perfect vacuum — making up the skeletal structure, the whole wing-shaped ship was almost neutrally buoyant in the late morning sunshine. The external surface of the ship was also covered in graphene solar panels, producing an abundance of electricity available to power the thruster units as needed. They could also power the ship's systems, including the catalytic crackers taking the water moisture from the air and breaking it down into oxygen and hydrogen to be used as the fuel for the Mauls, the protective fighters and the drones.

Bob looked up from his reverie, nodded and took a long drink of tea. 'Damn, but that is good tea! OK, so where are we at? Anything more we need to do this afternoon?'

Nick poured himself another glass and leaned across to top up Bob's. 'Just pick up a container of the local produce to which this crew has become accustomed while we have been training here, have a final meeting with the Games Board director which is set down for 1500 hours local time, then your orders' group at 1600 and then we are off to leisurely climb up to meet the Hauler *Rose* 19. So are you going to let me in on what the *Aquila* have in store for us?'

Bob looked up slowly. 'Oh, yeah, almost forgot to tell you. We are going up against mid-21st century Saluki. Nice machines. Want to capture one as it is a helicopter that I have not flown for real.'

Nick put down his glass as a screen unfolded from his battledress sleeve. He tapped the screen a few times and looked over the other Gjomvik outfit's choice of aerial combat machine for a few minutes, then had the screen fold away.

'OK,' he mused. 'They have gone with old tech contra-rotating helicopters. So they are a lot lighter than the Mauls, not as much punch, more manoeuvrable, better battlefield flight time and they are single-seaters. So, based on the Games Board articles and rules they will be able to field fifty per cent more craft than us. That's going to be interesting AV, is it not?'

Bob looked out of the windows and agreed. 'Yeah, going to be a right royal punch-up this one. Wonder where the Games Board are going to take us?'

'Hmm, well we are not staying here. Looking at what this system has to offer, the choices are too great to give us any idea … there are three gas giants and over thirty large moons, most with an atmosphere that will oxygenate fuel and give us plenty of lift. So we will just have to wait and see, Bob.'

Bob nodded then looked over his tea at his old friend. 'So what do you think of this latest class of carrier, Nick?'

Nick made a show of slowly looking around the spacious lounge, then back at Bob. He shrugged, then quietly replied. 'Well, we will see if it's any good in combat soon enough. Flash piece of hardware and every convenience that we could wish for, but it's just one enormous wing and I will be really interested to see how it performs in lousy weather. At least we have Mauls and I like them. Tough, brutish, without any redeeming aesthetic features, so yeah, we will wait and see, eh, Bob.'

Bob drained his cup and nodded. 'Yeah. We'll find out soon enough. The Baron's corporation are knocking these carriers out by the dozen as they tick so many of the Games Board's boxes. I think we will take a few good hits but reckon that we will be able to dish it out as well. I was on the evaluation board of the original and we gave it a good beating, then had the Scimitars knock the crap out of it. Lost half of its capabilities, but got the majority of the crew home still breathing.'

'OK, if we are going up against Saluki that would mean the *Aquila* are going to deploy one of their massive carrier airships?'

'Yeah, would stand to reason. You going to run another defence drill this afternoon?'

Nick frowned then shook his head, looking into his empty tea glass then back at Bob. 'No, don't think it's really necessary, do you? We have had plenty of drills of late and I judge everyone is good to go. No, let's not. Within a couple of days we will be in the thick of things anyway. Leave it be, Bob.'

Bob pursed his lips, looking up at Nick. 'Last time,' he said sternly, 'the bridge crew were bloody slow getting their shit together for close aerial support of this carrier. Would not mind if they were put through the ringer again.'

'Well, you are the commander, but as XO I have to say that they are within acceptable limits. Yeah, they were a little slow, but I reckon, Bob, that you sat in your chair dishing out all sorts of superfluous orders that created that slow response in the first place. We have an excellent crew, with very few freeloaders, so I would say that we should leave it this time around. In fact, if you want to start pushing those buttons, commander, I would be more concerned about your own flight reaction times.'

Bob's eyebrows shot up as he looked at the grinning face of Nick. 'I would wallop you anytime, old man!'

Nick smiled even more broadly, tapped his wrist then looked at the screen as it folded out and up. 'I will smoke you, Bob. Let's see if you still have what it takes. In twenty-five minutes we descend down into the village of Waipunga to uplift that container of fresh local produce. How about you and I put on a little display for the locals? I will graciously allow you to choose the craft.'

Bob stood up slowly, placed his tea glass on the table, then extended his hand to Nick. 'OK, so you still don't drink, so it's pointless betting a case of booze. What would you suggest for a bet?'

Nick shook the much larger man's hand, saying with a small smile, 'I like the licorice from Waipunga's market. Three kilos. Whoever is judged the lesser pays.'

Bob curtly nodded, knowing the value of the prize.

Nick let go his hand, tapped the screen and added the order into the last-minute orders flowing to the commerce hub at the Waipunga market. He then transmitted the challenge to the crew of *Haast*, knowing that most of them would enjoy the fight. He tapped the screen again. 'Major Kahu.'

Isaac Kahu, the carrier's intelligence and legal officer, looked out from the screen at his superior. 'Mr Warne, I presume that you want me to run the book and officiate on this little wager between you and the commander?'

Nick smiled at the screen. 'Yes, Mr Kahu. I can rely on your total impartiality in this.'

Isaac sat inside his control module on the large sweeping bridge of *Haast*, just forwards of the commander's lounge, and raised an eyebrow while keeping his expression deadpan. 'I would not go quite that far, sir. After all, the commander signs off on my wages and any bonuses that should come my way.'

'That is true, Mr Kahu, whereas I approve your leave applications whenever you locate an excellent restaurant.'

'I understand implicitly, major. Of course I shall be totally impartial and the final judge of the challenge. Points will be awarded for every aspect.'

Bob smiled at the exchange going on between his second-in-command and the intel officer as everyone liked Isaac and his legendary powers of persuasion. He touched his own screen, opening it, and tapped Isaac's icon. 'You have control, Mr Kahu. Set it up however you like as long as we are back aboard *Haast* by 1500 hours.'

Isaac nodded at his screen. 'Gentlemen. I have control.'

He cut the connection, looked across at his two-person team and the ACE eagle, Haast, and allowed a small smile on his face as he rubbed his hands together. 'So our two illustrious leaders want to have a little public fight. As we know, this is all about Mr Warne ensuring that the commander looks good on his first command. Haast, please advise the Games Board. I know that they hate dealing with you, but I cannot help twisting those pompous twits' tails at every opportunity we are given.'

The one-metre-tall eagle nodded at Isaac and turned towards his console. He segmented his mind as one eye watched his screens and the other looked at the open channels to the Games Board AV systems command ship that was at one of the local Lagrange points. Haast loathed the Games Board and its manipulation of the various populations of humanity spread across the roughly fifty-light-year Sphere that they operated in. From his wingtips, datalinks extruded and he plugged himself into the carrier's communications systems, quickly creating a small file on the simulated combat. He watched Isaac instructing the maintenance crews of two of the four Hawks to check the aircraft, then remove the live ammunition and load paint-gel ammunition into the aircrafts' magazines. Having a flexible beak, he allowed himself a little smile as he selected the Games Board official he wanted to speak with and opened the channel. 'Games Board junior producer, this is Specialist Haast onboard *Haast*.'

One part of the screen in front of him came alive with a beautiful, severe woman's image looking expressionlessly at him. She inclined her head a few millimetres to one side then pursed her lips, a tiny grimace flashing across her face before she gave Haast a small tight smile. 'Yes, specialist. How may we of the Games Board be of service to you?'

Haast smiled at her, allowing a few of his crown feathers to slowly become erect, something which he knew would irritate the woman. As he watched her eyes narrow by a tiny amount, he knew that he had hit his mark as he said, 'I am sending a short proposal file that you may find of interest, Junior Producer Elke. A small wager has been created by the commander and Mr Warne using the Hawks armed with paint markers.'

'Yes, we would find that of minor interest, specialist. Send the file. I shall report our decision within the next hour if it is deemed worthy.'

Haast smiled again, allowing all his neck feathers to ruffle out. 'File sent. Your delay may be inconvenient. The friendly contest will start in three minutes and be over in twenty.'

The Games Board official lifted her gaze, quickly scowled at Haast and spat out, 'Three minutes! That is not acceptable. You know these things take time, Specialist Haast.'

He allowed himself to look serious, then shrugged and slowly replied, 'We are sorry that you do not wish to take part in this event, junior producer. It is a wager that must be settled before *Haast* descends to Waipunga to uplift the last of our fresh produce.'

She glared at him and almost yelled: 'We do wish to record this event, ACE specialist. Why would we not? It is most presumptuous and quite wrong of you to say that! Standard fees are agreed.'

With that the connection was broken and those around Haast burst out laughing.

'She really does not like you!' Isaac said. 'Did not quite break the record for the fastest AV negotiation, but it's close, Haast, quite close! Well done.'

Isaac then sat back inside his command pod, drummed his fingers for a few seconds, looking over his unit crew, then tapped one of the screens which, seconds later, came alive with the duty bridge officer smiling at him from the screen.

Major Mark de Ruyter nodded cheerfully at his longtime friend. 'Our fearless leaders are going to have a bit of a go at each other, eh! All crew have been advised, we are good to go, whenever you are ready, Isaac.'

Isaac nodded, then looked across at the screens to watch the two senior officers trying to look relaxed. He waited until the commander was about to take a drink of tea, then hit the alarm button.

Bob swore and grinned, knowing that Isaac would have done that deliberately, as he quickly placed his glass on the table. Both men jogged for the door, ran through it, separated left and right, and sprinted down the opposite halves of the huge bridge with the occupants of the command and control modules smiling at them as they ran past. They came to a stop and pushed themselves up against the coffin-like combat suit containers which quickly wrapped the g-suits and survival gear around their uniforms. As soon as the suits had sealed, a side panel of the container opened, presenting a highly polished pole that the two men slid down to land seconds later beside the Hawk fighter aircraft.

The aircraft was sitting in its launch cradle as Nick strode up to the control deployment board beside it and placed his hand into the slot. The craft recognised him and altered its seat as his helmet's HUD activated, showing the readiness of the compact fighter. He quickly walked around it, removing the system's control tags and placing them into their respective slots just as his personal crew NCO arrived through a side door. Nick looked across at Sergeant Rangi Hopi. 'You are late, as normal.'

The big sergeant shrugged and looked down at his superior. 'Yeah. Had to go have a piss. But why are you talking? You should be in that aircraft and gone by now. Thought I had trained you better!'

Nick chuckled. 'Piss off, Rangi. Hopeless bastard.'

Rangi Hopi grinned and jogged around the aircraft, checking it visually, then walked up to the control board as the carrier gave control of the Hawk to the major.

He watched Nick climb into the cockpit and, as the canopy slid down, Rangi checked that the systems were all in the green. He activated the external doors as the turbines inside the aircraft started. Looking across his board once more, he gazed up at Nick, who looked across at him and gave a thumbs up. Rangi saluted and pushed the button, activating the cradle to slide out of the side of the carrier. He watched the large catch net deploying to the sides and below the Hawk, and as soon as they had locked into position hit another button, giving control of the launch to the major.

Nick scanned his instruments then touched the comms screen, saying, 'Green two standing by.'

The launch controller on the bridge instantly replied. 'Green two, flight control, weather Bravo, vector port 4, you are cleared to take off.'

'Control Green two, Bravo, port 4, launching.'

As he was saying the words, Nick's fingers danced across the controls with the launch cradle extending itself out and down. He gave a touch of antigravity as he eased the throttles open, with the locks folding away, and he powered the Hawk outwards from the port side of the carrier, heading 500 metres out into the vectored area number four. As soon as he passed into the area, he scanned his instruments and slammed the throttle to maximum, standing the fighter on its tail and roaring up into the sky, rolling the aircraft a little so he could see past the enormous bulk of the carrier *Haast*. As he accelerated, he saw Bob's machine rip upwards from behind *Haast*, also climbing as fast as he could.

On the bottom deck of *Haast*, Staff Sergeant Aaron Huriwaka watched the two fighters on the huge tactical screen that covered one wall of his domain. He had his feet on the table, leaning back in his chair, and waited for the inevitable call from the bridge, 140 metres above him. Sighing and wondering what the two senior officers had to prove, he shook his head, put his tea mug down and opened his wristscreen, instructing his salvage and recovery machine to stand by. Keeping one eye on the coming dogfight on the main screen, he checked the details of the ugly machine as it came to life and slid itself forwards on its launch pad. He instructed it to remove its defensive weaponry and topped up the pure water fuel tanks. He looked again at his display, grunted and tapped Corporal Al Brady's icon.

'Hey, Al. Get your arse down here now, bro. We are about to launch the salvage-recovery unit. So get out of whomever you are currently in, and get here, OK.'

Not waiting for a reply, he broke the connection and waited for his boss, Mark de Ruyter, to call.

He smiled seeing the major's icon come up on his screen and waited for the third tone before answering. 'Whatdoyawant? Can't you see I am on the shitter?'

Mark laughed. 'On the shitter, eh? So you have prepped your beast machine from the toilet, eh, staff? Very industrious of you! You know why I am calling, eh?'

Aaron grinned, allowing his image to be seen by his superior. 'Yeah, boss, ahead of you there. Where do you want us to park?'

Mark looked to his wraparound screens, seeing the two Hawks engaged in a fierce dogfight high overhead, then looked at the three Games Board monitors that had lifted off the top deck of the carrier to follow and film the fighters, then back at his ground maps. He tapped his teeth then said, 'OK. I reckon that they will bang something up. Launch and hang a couple of hundred metres off the bow. I am sending a medic team with you. They will be with you in a minute.'

The wiry form of a slightly dishevelled Al Brady walked in seconds before the two medics. One was a tall, strikingly beautiful, stern Major Sally Aydon, and behind her was the exotic Lieutenant May Gin.

Aaron immediately leapt to his feet, acknowledging the two women with a quick nod of his head.

May Gin smiled knowingly at Aaron as Sally looked between them, then across at Al Brady, who was trying to look inconspicuous by checking his flight suit. Sally looked back at May, shook her head and said matter of factly: 'May, put Aaron down. Work now, exchange smouldering looks of lust later.'

She snapped her head around to look at Al Brady with a knowing gaze. 'Corporal. I hope you washed on your way here. Your fly is undone. And no, I do not want to know who you have been with. Staff Huriwaka, I trust your machine awaits us?'

'Yes, major, it is prepped and ready to go.'

'Right, don't just stand there, get on with it, man. Bloody waste of time this.'

Aaron looked at Al Brady, who was nonchalantly trying to do up his fly, then back at the imposing figure of the medical officer. He wondered if his day was about to turn just a little bit rubbish. He mentally shrugged, thinking that the major was very good at what she did and deciding that it would be easiest to play the game and go with the flow. He gestured to the door leading to the landing deck of the salvage craft.

'Please go make yourselves comfortable in the machine,' Aaron said. 'We will be with you directly.'

The two women walked past with a compact, though large, suitcase-sized medical unit following them on its own antigravity unit. The door closed silently behind them and the two men looked at each other as they pushed up against their flight suit containers.

'That woman scares me, Aaron,' Al said.

The staff sergeant nodded, agreeing, and added, 'Yeah, me too, but I tell you what, mate, she is the best, and I mean the best medic, bar none. You know when you come onboard a new ship and you look through the crew lists? Yeah, well, I saw her name and was bloody pleased. OK, Al, let's go, mate.'

Al smiled as the suit finished forming around him and then turned to Aaron when he too stepped forwards from his container. 'So what's between you and the lieutenant?'

Aaron grinned, barked out a short laugh and pointed at the door. 'Come on, you are wasting time. You want another chewing? And did ya wash your hands? Dirty bugger!'

They walked out through the door and within seconds were walking across the heavy, wide mesh top deck of the square salvage craft with all its winches, grabs, tie-downs and twin multi-jointed cranes at either end. They could hear the four turbines quietly singing, supplying power to the four oversized antigravity units, one at each corner of the ungainly machine. They climbed through the hatch into the roomy, multifaceted clear sphere at the centre of the craft. Al clambered into the pilot's chair as Aaron climbed up into the commander's station. He looked behind him to see that the two medics had belted themselves into their seats and that the medical unit had locked itself onto the wall beside them.

Aaron tapped a few icons on one of his screens and seconds later the clamshell doors on the front edge of *Haast* opened.

He tapped the comms button. 'Flight control, this is Wrecker one, four POB, standing by.'

'Wrecker one. Hello, Aaron. Four POB, weather Bravo, launch and hold station at 400 at twelve o'clock bridge level.'

He touched another icon and the salvage craft was moved forwards through the doors, on its platform, with large nets deploying to the sides and below them.

'Roger that, twelve o'clock, 400, bridge,' Aaron confirmed.

'Launch when ready, Wrecker.'

Aaron touched his microphone, saying, 'You heard the woman, Al, let's go.'

Al manipulated the two controls, which were much like those of a helicopter, and the machine slid upwards on the vectored thrust of the four turbines, climbing away from the bulk of the carrier. Sliding through the sky, holding station with the carrier, they switched their attention to the battle above them.

Bob Thompson was sweating in his suit as he threw the Hawk all over the sky, trying to get a solid kill hit on his friend and mentor. He had managed to hit Nick's craft on a few occasions, but the electronics of his weapons reported that they were superficial. Nick, on the other hand, had scored with paint splashes down one side of Bob's craft, taking out one of his vectored thrust nozzles and damaging one of the turbines with the aircraft simulating real battle damage. The aircraft was not as responsive as it had been earlier and he was running out of time. Looking across to see where the furthest Games Board monitor was, he aimed directly for it, knowing that the closest he could get was 100 metres and hoping that it would react in the way that he wanted it to.

Seconds later it reacted by climbing rapidly, which Bob matched for a second before breaking hard to the left, pulling a hard high-g turn as the wings changed shape to enable the aircraft to do his bidding as he corkscrewed it around; they tucked in hard against the aircraft body as he flipped it over on its back, aiming between the other two pursuing monitors. They also reacted to get out of his way, one diving and the other flashing upwards and straight into the third now-descending monitor. At the instant of their collision, Bob pulled the Hawk even harder into a left-hand turn, knowing that Nick would be watching the monitors crash. In those few seconds of Nick's distraction Bob was able to fire the rotary cannon and splash paint all over the front of Nick's Hawk, then down its back.

Nick roared with laughter. 'Well played, commander! Perfect and well within the rules. Looks like two badly damaged monitors, but still acceptable.'

As they both descended towards the carrier, the two monitors were still locked together, tumbling slowly towards the rough native tree-covered terrain far below them with their automated antigravity systems trying to control their descent.

Bob tapped the icon of the Games Board director on his comms screen. 'As you no doubt can see, Director Francis, two of your monitors are in trouble. Can we assist?'

The impossibly young face of the director appeared on Bob's screen with a huge beaming smile. 'Wonderful display of cunning and aerial prowess over your once-leader, commander. A most welcome relief on an otherwise deeply boring day. The monitors? Well, if you wish, yes please, you may lend them assistance, but we will not cover the cost of any repairs should your salvage craft be damaged during the recovery. Whatever you wish, commander, whatever you wish, but it is at your expense. If they are that stupid as to collide, they are below my interest.'

The connection was broken and Bob scowled, wondering why the Games Board sometimes treated its own with such contempt.

'Major de Ruyter,' he said, 'as fast as you can, please.'

Mark de Ruyter did not reply to the order, but immediately spoke directly to the Wrecker, leaving the comms channels open. 'Staff!'

Aaron, who had been closely watching the slowly tumbling forms of the monitors, replied, 'On it!'

Al, without being told, pressed hard on the throttles until the turbines were howling and started to pursue the damaged Games Board units.

The Wrecker closed quickly, swinging down on the monitors as Al started to decelerate, using the antigravity units by feeding the power of the turbines to them, and using the jet exhausts as manoeuvring thrusters. As they got close, smoke started to pour from the uppermost of the damaged monitors and they could see that it had its waldos locked around the other as if embracing it.

'Shit!' Aaron said. 'OK, the top one is obviously trying to rescue the lower. Looks like its own AG unit is failing. Swing under them, Al. We are going to take a hit anyway.'

Al was very busy watching his screens and also glancing out of the transparent dome that surrounded them, trying to judge the distance and also worrying that the ground was coming up awfully quickly.

Aaron called out: 'Everyone, arm ejection seats. This is going to be a near run thing.' As he was saying this, he was manipulating one of the long, heavy-lift folding cranes with his own waldo controls, reaching out.

Al slid the Wrecker close under the now free-falling monitors. 'We are right on the edge, staff!'

Aaron ignored him as he could feel the housings of the monitors through his gloves and grabbed hard, yelling out, 'Roll under them and hit it!'

Al needed no further encouragement as he angled the Wrecker and twisted it in the direction of the turning crane arm. Without waiting for the monitor wrecks to hit the top deck, he hit the overloads on the antigravity systems and slid the machine sideways, washing off the speed, then, with the lightest brush through the tops of the licorice crops, levelled out and slowly started to climb. Once he knew that they were safe, he started breathing again.

Aaron said, 'Good work, Al! I owe you a beer!'

Al muttered back, 'It had better be a bloody big one!'

Sally looked at May, who was as white as a sheet. She slapped the younger woman on the knee. 'Told you! Nothing to worry about. Now that was exciting. Good work, boys. Right, off we go, May. Disarm your ejection seat and let's go have a look at our patients, as I know one is a bit banged up, if not dead, as I saw blood dribbling down its side.' She spoke directly to the medical unit, still locked on the wall beside her. 'Med-unit, follow.'

They left their seats and climbed out onto the top deck with their suits automatically deploying a safety line that locked onto the deck, while the medical unit lifted up and followed Sally.

The two wrecks of the monitors lay in a jumbled mess. As soon as they got close to the cobalt-blue units, Aaron caught up with them, the crane remote control in his hand. He activated a smaller crane that emerged from the deck and, working both, carefully pulled the mangled monitors apart and lay them down on the deck. As soon as they touched, tentacles of rope came up out of the mesh deck and secured the damaged units to the deck.

'Al, hold us here, please, on auto and get out here with the cutting gear.'

'We look at the one with claret flowing down its sides first,' Sally said. 'Staff, see if you can open it up, please.'

Aaron climbed over the smashed AG sled of the monitor and looked around for the emergency carapace overrides. He asked the Wrecker for data on the monitor's systems and soon located the lever mangled into the side of the unit. Swearing softly as it came away in his hands, he turned to the major.

'Yeah, this is going to take a couple of minutes, major. You want to have a look at the other one first?'

Sally nodded, walked over to the other monitor, and pulled on the emergency lever, activating the housing which folded up to reveal the unconscious Games Board audiovisual operator.

She gently lifted up the woman's head with its over-large ears and the snug metal plates over the top of her skull. She found the sockets that she was looking for and slid jacks from her wrist-mounted units into them.

'Looks like a new model of monitor, May. Will be interested to see what we learn of them this time.' Sally looked at the readouts in her HUD and frowned. 'Very interesting. This one is actually closer to a standard human than the others I have seen in the past few years. Lungs, heart, kidneys, liver and most of the other organs are about seventy per cent normal. And this one, at least, has a bigger digestive tract than others. No reproductive organs, of course, and still fused to the machine from above the hips, but like I say closer to us than others. Took a good bang to the head, quite nasty concussion. Right, May, give this one the standard brain injury pack through the neck shunt. Start a low dosage, check the brain function and increase it if necessary. Looks like Al and Aaron have the other one's carapace close to being off.' Sally stood up and walked across to where Al was cutting away the twisted locks to gain access to the more severely damaged monitor. She looked over the mangled machine, searching for external jack points. Seeing the one she wanted under a bent cover, she turned to the medical unit hovering beside her and pointed to the jack cover. 'Med-unit. Remove and jack yourself in.'

The unit extended numerous little arms from its housing and as some reached down and grasped the mesh deck for purchase, two more simultaneously tore off the cover and a probe slid across and locked into the jack point. A second later, the information the med-unit was gleaning came up on Sally's HUD.

'Aaron, get that cover off fast. Stop being polite about it and just tear it off. We have minutes with this one.'

Aaron leapt up and jogged across to one of the vertical containers beside the closest turbine covers. He turned and pressed himself up against it as the power exoskeleton quickly formed around him. He clomped back over the deck on birdlike feet and, without saying a word, bent down and grasped the carapace cover with clawed, powerful hands and heaved. There was a loud tearing, shrieking sound as the cover tore loose. Seconds later it was clear, revealing a male Games Board member with multiple crush wounds, including a piece of metal sticking out of his chest.

Sally went to work, with the med-unit opening itself in readiness. It reached across to her, jacking itself into a shunt on her right upper arm and linking directly into her brain as she snapped an oxygen mask onto the male. Surgical gloves formed around her hands from her suit as the med-unit cut away the leatherlike clothing of the monitor, and also sprayed the area with a rapid-seal medical membrane. It then pumped a low level anaesthetic through the shunt as it watched the male's level of consciousness. The major reached across as a glove was put on her hand by the med-unit. She thought about her requirements and a blade slid out of the glove as her visor went completely opaque.

Looking at the chest of her patient, she could see his internal organs, her visor acting as a CAT scanner, noting what the torn piece of metal had damaged. She shook her head and frowned, then reached across with her left hand as a glove was locked on that hand by the med-unit. A blade also extended from it and she cut in two directions, outwards from the piece of metal. From her other fingers, fine, flexible tools slithered down into the wound as she directed each one to close off the haemorrhaging blood vessels. Once she knew she had the internal bleeding under control, she instructed the med-unit to pull out the piece of bloody metal. As soon as that was clear, she had the micro-tools repair the damaged veins and arteries to the right side of the heart and then gradually work their way outwards, quickly stitching the damaged lung tissue, then fully out through the chest wall and minutes later sealing the wound shut.

Satisfied that the most severe injuries had been dealt with, she stood up and looked over at May as her faceplate cleared then slid up into her helmet. 'How's that one doing, May?'

'On the mend, major. Almost conscious.'

'OK, good, have a look at this one for anything I may have missed.'

May nodded and walked across as the med-unit unplugged from the major and plugged itself into May's wrist unit. She scanned the half-body of the monitor, looking for and noting the various injuries, advising the med-unit the treatments to be commenced. Once she had finished with the living tissue, she went through the systems of the other half of the monitor, making notes of the mechanical systems that were no longer operating, or close to failure. It being her specialty, she carefully examined the machine-to-tissue interfaces, taking note of the latest tech advances that enabled the monitor to relay information directly to the *Haast*'s database.

Sally looked across at Aaron and Al, nodding at each of them as she looked at her bloodied gloves. Frowning as if she had just remembered them, she slipped her hands into the med-unit where the gloves were unfolded off her and dropped into the cleaning solution. Looking at Aaron again, she asked, 'So what's the protocol now? Usually the Games Board has swooped in with one of its recovery units and the damaged units are off our hands.'

Aaron looked up and pointed. 'Well, the third one recorded everything we did and has now buggered off. Suppose I had better ask the boss.'

Sally nodded and added, 'Good idea, staff. I suppose it would be too much to ask for a cup of coffee? I know you have a good machine here on the Wrecker.'

As Aaron tapped his wrist unit to make contact with Major de Ruyter, Al grinned. 'Let me guess … white with two sugars, right?'

She nodded.

'And May has hers straight black.'

Aaron looked across at Sally and reported, 'Nah, well, this is a new one on me. The major says that the Games Board says "you fixed 'em, you keep 'em".'

Before she could reply, Aaron called across to Al who was climbing back in the control sphere. 'Hey, Al, while you are at it get me an apple juice, will ya? Ta, mate.'

He looked down at his wristscreen again and said, 'Haast says keep heading towards Waipunga. They are going to come get us.'

Half an hour later the huge carrier slid up behind them. The Wrecker was remotely flown up past the landing bays of the individual fighting craft on the great curved side of *Haast*, until it was beside the medical deck. A large door opened downwards to form a landing platform which the Wrecker slid over. Minutes later, the monitors had been offloaded together with the two medics and their unit. As May had passed Aaron, she had reached down and gently pinched his left buttock, leaving him with a smile. Al grunted, then took up his own remote control and flew the Wrecker back down and into its own landing bay. As soon as the doors had closed, the first thing Aaron did was clean the blood off the mesh, gathering up the pieces of damaged monitor and placing them in storage. Then, with Al, he went over the machine, cleaning and restocking it with fuel.

'Hey, Al, think it's time for a beer, mate. We were supposed to have finished our shift an hour ago.'

As Al handed him a bottle of one of the local brews from their refrigerator, he asked him, 'So what are we going to do with the monitor bits? How about we just feed them to the recycling units? And why was the major so keen on saving the monitors in the first place? They have Soul Savers, don't they? Seemed a big effort for not much really.'

'Because, corporal,' said a gravelly voice behind them, 'the major is a fine example of humanity. She will save anyone or anything, no matter what. It is the way she is and besides which, she loves to practise her art.'

Aaron opened the refrigerator and handed Major Mark de Ruyter a pale ale without saying a word.

Mark took the top off and clinked the bottles against the others', raised the bottle in salute, and added, 'Yeah, she is fierce that one, but bloody good at what she does. Excellent work as always, guys. The Games Board is being a bit prickly about it, but the commander has awarded you a bonus anyway. There is something very wrong with that Games Board director. Weird one. Oh, yeah, Al, you may not know this but Major Aydon's younger sister and brother were both recruited by the Games Board a long time ago. So, like us she loathes them, but unlike us she will always do the right thing by them.'

Harold

Human Settlement on Storfisk

Harold was spending the last few days of his enforced recuperation researching everything that was happening around his village and its environs; also, the string of large islands that made up the settlements of the standard humans and the ACEs, plus the great continent thousands of kilometres to their north that made up the Haulers' reserves.

He had found that a great many of the ACEs who he spoke with every day were not, in fact, amongst the standard humans, but were guardians of the huge numbers of animals that had been brought back from extinction by the Haulers' Collective. Some of the more elitist ones would not consider conversing with the still-new Harold, but he did not care as the majority of those he contacted to learn more about were very happy to speak with a son of *Basalt* and share their knowledge. One of those was called Maqua and was one of the three ACE New Zealand Haast's eagles who looked after the other eagles, and also the flocks of giant moa in a mountainous area in one of the temperate zones of the continent.

'Hello, Harold my little friend, how does this beautiful day find you? Has the itching stopped yet?'

'No, Maqua, but the girls rub a soothing ointment onto the skin each morning before they leave to go to school and then again when they get home. It's OK. At least I have been able to start exercising, I can breathe properly and eat again, so not long now before I can fly. How would you cope if you went back to being standard, or even augmented human, Maqua, if you could not fly?'

The eagle chuckled as she soared high in the mid-morning updraughts, watching a large flock of the massive moa as they contentedly grazed on the native and introduced flora. 'I fear that I would not do at all well, Harold. Did I tell you that I was here as an augmented before the first colonists to this world, all those hundreds of years ago?'

Harold grinned to himself, knowing that he was about to learn a great deal more about Maqua. 'No, you did not. Were you a Hauler crew? We have Hauler crew on *Basalt*. Lily and Jasmine. I like them very much.'

Maqua smiled, loving the young ACE's enthused wonder at all things and of his reactions to everything. Knowing of Marko and the crew of *Basalt*, she was not surprised that he had been made so well.

'Well, yes, I suppose that I was Hauler crew. I was a created human with strength and speed, endurance and physical toughness, designed to be an explorer. Looking at what you are seeing of what I am experiencing, Harold, why are you not uplinking completely so you can use all my senses?'

'Yes, I would like that, but the jacks are the last things to heal on me, thanks, Maqua. But I can see what you can see, so it's fine.'

Maqua, who was watching one particular flock of the moa, nodded a little in reply. 'They are a beautiful bird, those moa. A pity in some respects that there is still not enough of the

Old Earth vegetation for them to feed on exclusively, but we are getting there. Every year we see less and less defects in the eggs. I keep saying to the Haulers that they should have their own ACEs to tend their flocks, but they say it is not necessary. But it does not really matter as it gives us an extra job and this is a good place to live.'

Harold had split his inputs and was also watching the Gjomvik carrier *Haast* slowly descending on the airfield. He relayed what he was seeing to Maqua.

'Oh, carrier airships! I so love them,' Maqua commented. 'The ones we used when we first came here were almost primitive in comparison to this *Haast*. Which reminds me ... will you excuse me for a few moments, please, Harold. I have a call to make.'

She broke the connection and in her mind linked to her two companions so they could share the rapid update from their friend, Haast, who was in the intelligence suite onboard the carrier thousands of kilometres to their south.

Haast spoke in his beautifully modulated voice, which had been created solely so he could comfortably converse with his human crewmates. 'Hello, my friends. I hope I find you well. I have information that may be of interest.'

Maqua, Moana and Tane called their greetings and then listened as Haast said, 'You have been told by the tigress Ayana of something alien that is in our midst and to watch and observe. I intercepted datalinks from Ayana's intelligence gathering drones in the seconds before they were destroyed. And, yes, it is true it was an incursion to test a new piece of equipment of mine, and most successful as no-one was alerted to it. I note that not all the information has been shared with Ayana by the Hauler orbital Angelito of what those drones learned of the alien. I am sharing that with you now, as you three are the closest I will ever have to kin and I want you prepared for this. Data packets follow. We are now about to fly up to be uplifted by the Hauler *Rose Foxtrot* for passage to the local gas giant. Goodbye, my whanau, I shall see you upon my return. Stay safe.'

The three great birds farewelled their friend and then individually went through the data.

'Think that we had better meet up,' Moana said minutes later. 'This is just a little bit nasty. In an hour at the tree?'

As the connection broke, Maqua called Harold again. 'Hello, my friend Harold. Something has come up on what I thought was going to be only a moderately interesting day. Call me again in the morning. Get well quickly. Bye.'

Harold quickly acknowledged the message and then felt the connection broken. He hopped off his bed and walked down the living stairs, looking for Bing, finding him minutes later sitting by the main doors.

'Hey, Bing, could you scratch between my wing joints, please? It's driving me mad!'

Bing, the large cat, frowned and grumbled under his breath and told Harold to sit in front of him.

Having scratched the same place numerous times before, he simply started and was then a little taken aback when Harold turned his head and fired a laser message from his right eye into Bing's. 'Bing. There is a problem up in the Haulers Territory. This is the conversation I had with Maqua a few minutes ago. I am not sure whether I was supposed to get this data or not. I would be surprised if she made a mistake though. A deliberate warning?'

Bing lasered back. 'Do you know that Maqua is an ancestor of this place? She planted the trees that we live in and is related to us and the Dines, plus she is the great-great-

great-grandmother of the Patu whanau. She does not make mistakes. She gave this to you deliberately. OK, let's layer you up with some sunblock just to be on the safe side and go see the others.'

Minutes later they were walking towards the edge of the village.

As they waited for the others, Harold looked up through the trees as overhead the carrier *Haast* started to climb up through the atmosphere. He looked at Bing. 'So where are the others?'

'All moving, Harold. They will each go to a specific point where we can converse in private without our humans knowing that something is up. Give them a few more moments.'

From high above them they could hear a rumbling roar as *Haast* housed its massive turbofans, and its base rockets fired to push it up to its rendezvous with the Hauler waiting in orbit hundreds of kilometres outside the atmosphere.

'OK, Harold, they are all in position. Watch for my laser spotter and when I finish talking, fire that file exactly on that spot. Something else you can thank Maqua for: she set us up as guardians and also created the local and planetwide comms networks so the standard humans don't suspect that we are constantly on the lookout for them. Better that way, letting them think they control everything. Makes it easier for us and gives them contentment.'

Harold cocked his head at Bing. 'But what happens when one of the standards, or even the augmented, are rebuilt into an ACE? Would they not say something to the other standards?'

Bing shrugged in a very human fashion. 'Don't know why. Just the way of it, I suppose. The ACEs — either the totally created or the uploaded ones — are a fairly intelligent lot. Maybe they think it best that the standards don't know. OK, let me get on with this.'

Bing started the conversation using his laser. 'Howdy all. Have Harold here and he has been in conversation with Maqua. She dropped a weighty file on him and I think that you had better all see it. Looks like another incursion that that tosser left-field orbital, Angelito, decided to keep to himself. We really need to do something about that one, he is taking the Haulers Territory much too seriously. Here's the file.'

Harold fired the file at the spot on the huge tree. In the following minutes the conversation and discussion was carried out at the fastest speed they could manage and after only five minutes it ended with the decision that Tengu, as soon as he was ready, would be secretly sent north to go find out for them exactly what the threat was, as he was unknown to Angelito, or for that matter the standard humans.

As they strolled back towards their home tree, Harold frowned and asked Bing, 'What about the other Tengu, the one the Games Board has? Is he of use?'

Bing smiled. 'Of course he is, Harold, and so is the one you killed. They are both ready to fight. Why do you think they were all sent here in the first place? The one you nailed to the tree should be regrown within a matter of days now. Did you not think through the reason that we took his Soul Saver? And yeah, the one onboard the Games Board airship? He is one of ours as well.'

Harold gasped at the intrigue. 'But I was almost killed, Bing!' he spluttered. 'Was this a great big set-up? And I was the new one dropped in the middle to make a good-looking corpse?'

He started to feel quite angry until Bing stopped, patted him on his shoulder and said, soothingly, 'Hey, Harold! Don't take it wrong. We are created to do our jobs, we are given the sentience to ensure that what we do is mostly the right thing, and we are equipped to have an excellent life far beyond that of standard humans. We would not have let you die, Harold, but we had to make it look right. The three Tengu brought with them some very good tech that the Games Board would have prevented anyone else from bringing here.'

Harold still felt a bit pissed off. 'Why did you not warn me? Why not just treat me as a sentient? Would that have been too big a thing to expect?'

Bing grimaced and shrugged again. 'Yeah, but if you had known the plan, would you have played your part so well?'

Harold gave a short bark of laughter, then tripped Bing up, flattening the indignant cat on the ground and raking dust all over him. Just before he walked off, Harold grinned and said, 'There you go, Bing, you will have to lick yourself clean again!'

Basalt

Urchin Star System

Flint, Ngoc and Jim, with his companion Spike, halted just outside the closest entrance to the tunnels.

Flint used his comms laser and suggested, 'OK, we keep leapfrogging each other, on the way in and out. Me, Ngoc, then Jim.'

The weapons being carried on their propulsion pods all folded out as Flint moved cautiously into the tunnel up to the first bend and fixed a transponder to the rock wall. He stopped as Ngoc moved ahead of him to the next bend, twenty metres further on, and fixed another transponder. Then he stopped to cover Jim, with Spike still clinging onto his carapace, as they went quietly around another bend. They could see the cavern opening out and dimly perceived a huge 120-metre sphere of the Urchin predators floating in the centre of the space.

Jim used every piece of his passive sensing equipment, taken to its maximum power, to make out the individual two-metre-wide discs of the creatures, all of which appeared to be moving very slowly inside a huge thin ball of transparent ice. He lasered the images back to his companions.

'I see a smaller cluster high above you both,' Flint said. 'Much smaller ones. A hatchery or nursery, maybe?'

Spike looked up the curved wall. He nodded his little head. 'How about we all move up one? Jim, quietly fly us up the wall, please.'

The red ovoid gently reached out with his arms and slowly pulled them up the wall, keeping his speed down until minutes later they were some tens of metres away from some smaller discs which were also clustered together like the bigger ones in a ball of ice, but were moving faster.

'They are rotating in and out,' Spike observed. 'Practising like the bigger ones? Oh, no, now I see what they are doing. If they're smaller, they lose body heat faster. Yes, that would be the answer.'

Ngoc lasered a warning. 'Careful, both of you. A few much bigger ones are coming across the wall towards you.'

'Seen. We are moving,' Jim replied.

He started creeping up the wall again and swung over a little to put them above the small predators as the large ones started to form a hollow sphere that eventually encompassed the smaller ones. As they watched, water vapour was ejected from between the individual creatures and ice crystals formed in the extreme cold that were rapidly seized and manipulated by the outer tentacles of the little creatures to slowly form an encapsulating sphere.

'Maybe the little ones were being trained?' Flint commented. 'Looks like our timing was a bit off. Opportunity lost as they are now protected.'

'I am seeing an increase in the speed of the central sphere,' Ngoc said. 'Also, there is another grouping moving from a much larger side tunnel. It appears that they are carrying large pieces of roughly round ice. My thinking is that they are fuelling, as they are pressing the balls of ice up against the main predator sphere. Could it be that they are in preparation for movement outside?'

Flint interrupted him. 'Could be, could be. If that is the case, we need to make this tissue-gathering a bit faster. I do not like this place. Too many other creatures and if they decide they don't like us we do not stand a chance against so many. I calculate there are at least 1650 individual predators in this space and there may be others. Come on, Spike, grab some tissue samples and let's go!'

Spike sent Flint a smiley face and told him to relax.

Ngoc flashed a quick private message to Flint. 'Start looking for a hiding place. Something is happening.'

Flint agreed, and the two mechanical spiders turned away from the tunnel entrances, moving apart, searching the walls for a cavity or large enough crack.

Flint found a crevice running across the chamber that he decided would fit them all. He flashed a message to the others, giving them the location, then crept into the deep crack himself and came face to face with a ferocious-looking arachnid-like creature half his size, staring out through a wall of ice. The creature seemed to be looking him over as he backed out of the crack, but showed no inclination to follow. As soon as he could see the others, he fired off laser messages.

A minute later, Stephine said, 'That is something new to me, Flint. I wonder if it is a parasite of the predators? It would be logical. Please check other crevices around you.'

Flint reluctantly agreed and started finding the creatures all around them, but none of them broke through the ice to follow him, so he started to relax a little. Looking for a small specimen, he eventually found one and, wondering if it was a gas surrounding the arachnids, slowly made a small hole with the hollow drill he extended from one of his mechanical hands. Just as he could feel the bit breaking through, his sensors detected a warmer sulphur-rich atmosphere.

As he withdrew the drill bit, the creature stirred and pushed itself so it was close to the hole, inserted a proboscis-like appendage down through the hole and, starting at the outside, ejected a rapidly freezing fluid that sealed it closed. It then drew the proboscis back until the entire hole was sealed shut and appeared to go back into a sleeping state. Flint backed out of the crevice and relayed what had occurred. Looking towards the centre of the chamber, he could see that all the predators were now coming apart from the huge ball and forming hundreds of smaller ones. Of the nursery sphere, he could see nothing.

Just as he was about to comment, Ngoc announced, 'They are preparing to leave, *Basalt*. The spheres they are forming are only a few centimetres smaller than the circumference of the tunnels.'

'We are seeing nothing out here of any interest at all,' the major replied. 'Nothing. The only thing here is the Games Board frigate which is on the other side of this asteroid. OK, let's be cautious about this. Flint, get your crew to hang tight where they are. Remaining craft form back on *Basalt* and let's stand off by a few kilometres. Stephine, go for active scanning. Light up the radars. Let's see if there is anything out here.'

Minutes later, Stephine suddenly yelled out, 'Incoming! Three small high-speed spheres coming over the top of the asteroid. They are the predators! And look, another group coming in from our six o'clock! I would say we have Urchins here!'

Flint did not need to send the message to his little band. They quickly pushed into the crevice with Jim settling down to watch and record as the balls of ice that had been brought into the chamber earlier were now seized by the predators and cracked apart. The pieces were gathered and taken inside the largest spheres, which then abruptly broke apart and quickly formed smaller ones.

Ten minutes later, the smaller predator spheres slid through the entrance tunnels to dissolve into individual creatures who hurled themselves into waiting slots on dozens of twenty-metre-circumference spheres. They all then orientated themselves and launched out through the tunnels, emptying the chamber in minutes.

Onboard *Basalt*, Stephine and Veg watched the predators emerge from the tunnels. They split into two groups with one racing over the curve of the asteroid towards the now-vigilant Games Board frigate and the other coming straight towards *Basalt*.

The major barked out orders. 'Everyone, stand by to engage! Patrick, assign targets. Once you have broken up the spheres, go after the individuals. We have no idea what we are really dealing with here, so take out everything! Upload Soul Savers if you have not done so already.'

Stephine urgently added, 'Major! Hold your orders. I am certain that they will move around us as there is definitely something on the other side of us and it is very big!'

'Shit, I hope you are right, Stephine. Everyone, continue tracking the predators. If they get within 100 metres, hit them! Patrick, load an antimatter canister missile. Stephine, give him a coordinate. Patrick, as soon as you have that, fire. Let's light the bastard up!'

Seconds later, the missile was fired directly away from the asteroid. As it approached the area that Stephine suspected an Urchin to be, the missile broke into ten separate pieces and the timings on the antimatter containment fields started to rapidly decay.

'The predators are moving outwards from their flight path slightly,' Marko called out. 'Think that Stephine is right. They are going to go around us!'

Lily spoke urgently. 'Incoming distress call from the Games Board. They are under attack from at least ten adult Urchins!'

'Hot hull dock and hang on, everyone,' the major ordered. 'Patrick, take us to the Games Board position. Stephine and Veg, get ready to deploy. Glint, go give Harry a hand on the *Albatross* lander. Harry, as soon as Glint is onboard, get outside the hull and stand by to launch as soon as we get there. Quick as you can, Patrick; from the images we are being relayed from the Games Board frigate, they are getting smacked hard.'

Glint launched out of his seat beside the major and bounded down the internal spiral staircase until he was at the *Albatross* hangar. He raced through the door which locked and sealed behind him, then into the rear entrance of the *Albatross* which started to close as soon as he hit the ramp. He ran up to the small flight deck of the lander and leapt into the seat beside Harry. Looking across the instruments, he could see that the air in the hangar was being rapidly pumped out and minutes later the outer curved hull door unlocked, opening out and down.

Harry grinned at the long, powerful but lithe hybrid-cross between a Jesus lizard and a fossa. 'Great to have you here, Glint. Hate fighting nasties on my own. I fly, you fight. OK.'

Glint's eyes twinkled as he grinned even wider. 'You're the boss, Harry! Nothing beats a good beating of Urchins and this time we get to see them eaten as well. Wonder what they taste like?'

The launch cradle that the lander was locked onto pushed them out of the hangar so they were sticking out through the great latticework exoskeleton of *Basalt*. Harry's fingers danced across his screens as Glint plugged himself directly into the weapons firing control board and readied the mortars, lasers, rotary cannons and linear accelerators. He looked across his own screens, then up to the windshield, noting where the others were and seeing that towards the stern of *Basalt* Stephine's and Veg's craft, the sentient *Blackjack*, was also ready to launch.

They could all feel that Patrick was coming up to maximum thrust to get above the asteroid as quickly as possible.

Julie then gave a report. 'Antimatter canister missile has deployed. Using every sensor we have, we can see at least five fully adult Urchins. The lead one is reacting to the antimatter! It appears to be going for an envelopment. As soon as I see the edges, I shall detonate! Leading groups of predators are still a few kilometres out. Detonating!'

They saw on their screens the multiple searing detonations of total annihilation as the antimatter came in contact with the outer canister shells, rending the enfolding Urchin into pieces.

An instant later Julie reported again. 'There are another five! They have dropped their camouflage systems. They are big! Moving apart from each other. Predators getting close. Major, should I launch a camera drone to watch as the asteroid will occlude that battle in a few minutes?'

'Yes, by all means. Patrick, what are you learning from the Games Board?'

The smooth calm voice of *Basalt*'s Augmented Intelligence replied. 'They have had most of their long-range and mid-range defensive craft and systems destroyed. They have disabled at least five Urchins, but it would appear that there are many more in that group. Within fifteen minutes I estimate they will be overwhelmed.'

'Right. Engage with long-range lasers and see how many cores you can cut out of them, Julie. Patrick, fire three more antimatter missiles at the rearmost ones. Let us create a little distraction in their ranks. Fly us over the top of the Games Board. All craft, as soon as we are within five kilometres of them, deploy. Patrick, assign targets.'

As the battle area came closer, *Basalt*'s heavy lasers started to fire, but the cutting of a core from one of the Urchins took several minutes and as each was fired upon it would change its orientation and start to absorb the energy into its huge flowerlike, winged petals instead. Three had attached themselves to the stricken Games Board frigate and were tearing chunks of the hull away.

Marko saw that he and Lily had been assigned the ones already on the frigate. Looking up at his screens, he could see that the deploy point was getting close, so he started the pumps for the rocket engines and brought his weapons online, wishing that he had Glint or any of the other ACEs with him. He looked across to see Lily letting go from where the Hanger she was piloting had been locked onto *Basalt*. He touched the controls and the landing claws of the Skua he was in also let go and he poured on the power, moving ahead and away from *Basalt*.

'Lily. Go for a high-speed pass. Hopefully they will lift up so I can follow. On a slow-speed pass I can hit them hard.'

'OK, Marko. Look behind us. The predators are not that far away. I wonder how they will react to us shooting up their prey?'

'Don't know, Lily. Depends if they treat them as a fun hunt or a food source. If we kill them and they don't have to get in harm's way to get the food, I don't think that they will care. If they are capable of caring.'

Marko watched as Lily started to fire at the Urchins that had landed on the stricken Games Board frigate and were stabbing their eighty-metre-long, barbed tails deep into the ship and then twisting and ripping the hull plates off. The Hanger that Lily was piloting was firing a steady stream of munitions into the core parts of the Urchin. As they struck, they flattened themselves and spun before exploding, creating large cone-shaped wounds. She switched from one Urchin to the next, damaging each before she flashed over the top of the frigate.

The third Urchin had flattened itself against the frigate and had its tail deep inside the craft as Lily gave an update.

'The front on the frigate is separating! Looks like they are abandoning their drive systems. Break off, Marko. Major, are you getting any messages from the Games Board? I wonder if they have lost control of their antimatter storage?'

'Stand by!'

Marko fired his lateral thrusters, knowing that Lily was rarely wrong, and peeled away from the frigate, then poured on the power to the main rockets, distancing himself as quickly as possible. Calculating quickly, he saw that Lily and the rest of his crewmates were outside the possible danger area and that he only had to worry about himself.

'They have ejected their core AI!' the major yelled. 'And this is weird. The predators are legging it as well. They are moving away towards the other Urchins.'

They all saw on their screens a lance-like structure launch itself at huge speed away from the frigate, and seconds later the crew survival pods started to be ejected.

'All craft,' Patrick broadcast. 'Message from the Games Board frigate emergency pods. They have lost control of the antimatter containments. All shields up. Detonation imminent!'

Marko tapped the end of one of his hand controls and the shield quickly slid over the transparent parts of his canopy. The onboard computer automatically covered the rear-facing cameras an instant before the slowly tumbling frigate was annihilated by the massive, almost all-consuming, silent explosion. He pressed his lips together, hoping that the core AI lance, which would contain the crew's Soul Saver continuous life-streams, survived. Although he had never really liked the Games Board or anything it stood for, he had known several Games Board individuals in his past that he cared for.

He also anxiously looked at his readouts, hoping that the gamma-ray burst generated by the explosion had been stopped by the Skua's shielding.

Ascertaining it was within acceptable limits, he breathed a sigh of relief and tapped on a side-screen, instructing his onboard computers to open the covers of the windshield and the rear-facing cameras. Seconds after the covers slid open the proximity alarms started screeching out their warnings and he looked in horror as a very fast-moving, massive, jagged piece of wreckage smashed into the Skua. As it rolled over the forward part of the craft's fuselage, it tore the canopy off plus most of the instrument panel and part of the nose cone.

Something hit him hard on the top of his helmet, stunning him for a few seconds and he could taste blood in his mouth. As the craft was flipped over, starting to cartwheel, his helmet HUD alarms began sounding with just about every system showing damage. His suit visor automatically sealed and his seat locked him in more firmly. He automatically sped himself up as his hands, feet and mind went into overdrive to assess the damage, his trajectory and what systems he could use to slow the sickening tumbling. He also commanded his suit to drop some antinausea meds into his system, knowing that puking into his helmet would not help his situation. Gradually, he managed to slow the cartwheeling and allowed himself a minute to assess the damage.

His starboard wing had been torn almost in half so all the water fuel on that side was lost together with his starboard weapons. He quickly went through his lists, shutting down systems that were only partially functional, then suddenly realised that his comms systems must also be down as he had not heard anything from anyone. There was a thudding bang that he felt through the rear of the seat and all remaining systems went dead. Wondering how much worse things could get, and cursing the fact that most of the redundant systems were also down, he reluctantly pulled up his internal medical systems, activated his oxygenated blood nanotes and stopped breathing.

Looking out through the wreckage of his cockpit, he saw *Basalt*, kilometres to his left, firing on a huge Urchin that had predator spheres tearing chunks off it. Many kilometres in the opposite direction, he saw what must have been a huge fight going on as a part of the sky was constantly being lit by laser fire and the sparkle of munitions going off. But in spite of his scanning the starfield he could see nothing of Lily. The best that he could hope for was that she had taken off in pursuit of the Games Board AI lance. Then he had the sickening realisation that the asteroid was looming up in his forward vision field quite quickly and he probably did not have the time to get control of the Skua. He tried a last series of firings of the main rockets, but every time he did, although the velocity slowed, he also started tumbling more rapidly; he figured that the nozzles themselves were almost certainly damaged. Furiously working the firing sequences, he managed to slow the tumbling to a more manageable, almost sedate state.

Cursing loudly, he looked around the ruined cockpit for the last time, reached out and snatched the carbine and ammunition drums, attaching them to his chest, and hit the ejection system. Nothing happened. He pulled the overrides out of the sides of the seat and pressed the button on the seat's control board. Still nothing. He struggled against the seat and its tough restraints, which held him firm. He reached down the seat with his left hand and extended a data probe from one of his fingers, connecting directly to the seat. Seeing in his helmet's HUD that no electrical circuits were active, he fed a little power from his combat suit into the seat's control board, which came alive just long enough for the seat to fold back a little.

Pulling hard against the seat, he managed to pull himself free, stood up and looked aft down the torn and broken back of the Skua, trying to orientate himself in the tumbling craft. He swore again to himself and looked over his shoulder. Marko saw the looming asteroid and calculated that his speed would be about 350 kilometres an hour and that he only had a few minutes before the Skua would impact. The very best scenario, thinking about the trajectory, was that it would be struck a glancing blow.

The soldier in him demanded that he push himself away from the battered craft and give himself a chance at survival, while the engineer in him coolly assessed the situation, knowing the antigravity unit, being an inertial system, would push him out of the way … if he had time to get it to work. He also knew that he stood a much better chance of surviving the day if he was still with the Skua. He scrambled aft hand over hand, observing the absence of most of the sheathing of the upper hull, so he simply looked down on the antigravity unit and its compact engineering control panel. On its readouts it showed that it had latent power in its emergency cells, which would normally be enough to soft-land the Skua on a one gravity world.

He pulled himself down against the unit, curving his body to it with his head sticking up enough to see the looming asteroid. He reached down with his left hand, pulled up the command menus in his head and plugged himself directly into the antigravity unit. He experimented by powering the unit when he could not see the asteroid and rapidly counting in his still sped-up state. Knowing he was having an effect, he stood up for a rotation of the Skua and decided that it was probably going to miss. Marko frowned, tried his comms gear unsuccessfully for the twentieth time, then pulled himself out onto the wing and gently pushed himself up off it. He pulled the carbine off his chest, slammed the magazine onto it, cocked it and fired a round, allowing the recoil to push him further away from his craft. When he judged that he was thirty metres away he turned and fired again to keep himself in a good position. Using a few more carefully aimed shots, he found himself almost stationary in relation to the slowly tumbling Skua as they both snuck over the surface of the asteroid with twenty metres to spare.

He pushed the rifle against his chest and fired again, then safed it and clipped it back onto his chest before flipping himself with arms and legs extended and, moments later, grabbing the remains of the right-side wing, allowing it to pull him over until he was once again tumbling head over heels with the machine. He pulled himself back against the antigravity unit and spent fifteen minutes slowly bringing the tumbling under control. Eventually, it slowed almost to a stop so he allowed himself a few breaths from the suit's internal CO_2 scrubbers. He pulled himself forwards into the wreck of a cockpit, manually slid the seat forwards and pulled the zero gravity, zero atmosphere survival pack out, plugging his combat suit into it and allowing the systems to recharge after he had activated the pack's emergency locator beacon. While that was happening, he pulled out his own personal diagnostic slate, which was in his crew bag behind the seat, plugged it in and brought up the Skua's systems by rerouting some of the power from the antigravity unit. After another fifteen minutes and a further eighty-seven kilometres from the asteroid, he finally saw what was available to him.

Working at a steady pace, he pulled one of the comms units out of the port-side rotary cannon, slaved it to the antigravity unit as well as to his suit comms, then filled his lungs with air and spoke: 'Basalt, this is Marko. Do you copy?'

The major replied instantly. 'Hurray! You are still alive. We're in a total shitfight. Can see your beacon. You onboard still?'

'Affirmative. ETA? Others?'

'Could be another hour or more. On top of these bastards, but it's a good fight. Drone dispatched. All OK so far. Basalt out.'

The connection severed and Marko wished he knew exactly what was happening, but was relieved that every zero-g pilot's worst nightmare of having to self-terminate because of exhausted consumables would probably not come to pass.

A sudden chill went down his spine. He disconnected from the survival pack, pulled himself forwards again and pulled out the little remote control from the base of the remaining rotary cannon. He clipped that against his wrist, then went back down the intact port side of the Skua and did the same with the rapid-firing mortar housed inside the annular wing. He then pulled himself up over the top of the machine and looked at the linear rifles on the starboard side. They appeared to be OK, but to be certain he opened a few of the surface panels, looking at the magazines and ammunition feeds. Shrugging to himself, he started back towards the cockpit and caught a distortion against the starfield to his right. He shuddered, recognising that an Urchin was within a few hundred metres of the Skua and hopefully being cautious about investigating it.

Moving slowly into the cockpit he plugged himself into the survival pack, instructed it to form around him, then slowly pushed the ejection seat as far forwards as it would go and climbed into the space behind it. He activated the pack as it inflated around him with all its systems coming fully online. Its high-powered minicomputer searched for anything useful still onboard the Skua to ensure the comfort and survival of its occupant, then awakened the little engineering drone. Marko tapped an icon on the main display on the inside of the pack, then scrolled down the list a short way before tapping on the threat icon for an Urchin. He brought up the available power packs and instructed the survival pack to reroute the power to the weapons and any working sensors before plugging the remotes into his own slate. He worried whether he had enough time, knowing that the Urchin would be close.

The screen cleared and an instant later the remaining sensors showed the probable location and size of the creature. Tapping the mortar icon, he loaded a stream of five oxygen/hydrogen projectiles with self-igniters and gave the order to fire. He felt the weapon firing the big slow rounds and had the rotary ready to follow through. He did a slow count to eight, then the rounds exploded and a second later the incendiaries at their core detonated, igniting the oxygen and hydrogen in five silent fireballs within striking distance of the Urchin. It suddenly manifested, having dropped its camouflage, and Marko could see that it was quite young. It folded into itself in an action that Marko knew from previous experience was one of defeat, so he did not fire again, but kept a wary eye out for any further movement.

He wondered what else might be around, very concerned that there were a number of blind spots around the damaged machine that the remaining sensors could not cover. He reactivated the antigravity and, after a couple of gentle nudges, managed to get the Skua to slowly roll, to go with the tumbling it was still doing. Minutes later, the sensors showed three more much larger Urchins coming towards him. He grimaced, shook his head, programmed the mortar and fired a burst of homing shells at one and repeated the action with the other two. As soon as the rounds detonated, the wounded Urchins reacted by flipping themselves around, firing their own propellants and scattering.

'Fuck!' Marko laughed, wondering if he would see the day out after all.

He keyed his microphone. '*Basalt*, this is Marko. Sending Soul Saver. Going for life-stream. This is bad!'

He instructed the emergency system to transfer his conscious self to the data banks on *Basalt*.

Seeing the transfer in progress, he relaxed a little, knowing that even if he died his own self would carry on.

The major's voice came through. 'Good. But perhaps today is not your next time in the tank, Marko. I am shoving two drones very close to you. Just hold on a little longer, mate.'

He stopped the transfer of the last conscious part of his soul and waited with his finger on the icon, knowing that if he pushed it, it would drain the last of the power in the Skua in transmitting his self. He had done the process twice before in his life and hated it. But it sure beat death, he thought, remembering the last time: the lifting away from his dying body by the harsh pseudo-heat of the electronics, to feel himself in his Soul Saver, conscious, with no abilities but thought; then the transfer to the zygote, the tank, and the year of intense concentration growing himself back to an adult body. He shuddered at the thought, wondering if this time he would ask for a chassis for a while, before the tank. He mentally shrugged, knowing how horribly cold and clinical existence inside the robot chassis would be.

The screens showed the three Urchins slowly closing in and behind them, like avenging angels, the two drones which started firing from a long way out. Marko grinned, shunted power back to the rotary cannon and joined in with incendiary rounds that detonated on the Urchins, targeting the area where the long tail met the flowerlike upper structure, filling it with white-hot spinning shards. As the ammunition counted down, he activated the linear guns and had just started to fire when the magazine exploded. The concussion knocked him sideways, wedging the very tough survival pack against the seat. Quickly looking at the screens, he saw that the explosion had damaged the pack, which he was not surprised about, but more critically had knocked out the last of the power systems. He cursed, instructing his oxygenated bloodstream nanotes to take over from his breathing again, then deflated the slowly leaking survival pack. He grabbed the oxygen bottles and comms system from it and locked them onto his suit, climbing back onto the top of the Skua once more just in time to see one of the Urchins enfold and tear apart one of the drones. It automatically self-destructed, killing the Urchin from within.

He looked around to see the remaining drone in a fierce battle with the other two Urchins. It appeared to be getting the upper hand until one of the Urchins lashed out, driving it into the other Urchin, which impaled it on its long, spiky vicious tail. The tail slowly lifted the drone up towards its massive roselike head and its many mouths bit down into the flat fish-shaped structure of the drone. Marko wished hard that the machine would also self-destruct, but it did not happen. He mentally swore long and hard.

Harry suddenly spoke through his earphones. 'Marko! Know where you are. Can see that the drones are gone. Need to rearm, huge fight going on. Hang tight, my brother. No-one lost yet, but all messed up. We're pulling back onto *Basalt*. Will be there within the hour.'

Marko quickly acknowledged, then said to himself, 'Fuck it!' He pulled himself left and forwards, snapped open all the hatches to the magazines of the rotary cannon, hit the quick releases of the weapon itself and pulled it out, connected the remote control back on, then, pulling it behind him, moved along the port side of the Skua until he came to the access panels for the life raft. He locked a tie onto the gun, pulled himself under the cockpit to where the starboard-side magazines were; unlocked the covers, pulled the magazines out, clipped them together and went back to the life raft. He dragged it out, activated it and reached inside to take the power cord from the water and nutrient maker, and plug it into the gun. Having a sudden thought, he pulled the recoil dampeners away from the weapon and grabbed the tie-downs from the life raft after climbing inside it. He latched himself onto the gun, brought up the controls and, mentally giggling at the madness of it all, oriented himself and the gun to face away from the area of sky that the asteroid was in and fired a long continuous burst using half of the ammunition available to him.

Looking back at the rapidly receding wreck of the Skua, he saw the two Urchins slowly enfold it, pulling it apart, looking for anything that they could consume.

Marko and his strange carriage drifted through the heavens as his mind wandered, taking in the beauty of it, and he felt a kind of peace. He instructed his biosystem to start breathing to recharge the nanotes, then shut his natural intake of oxygen off again, knowing that he had days of oxygen available to him as his suit would scrub any CO_2 and his augmented system would use only the bare minimum necessary. He looked around for the asteroid, frowned when he could not see it, so pulled out his slate, plugged it into his arm and queried its navigation systems. Having little or no gas in his lungs, he made a very poor imitation of a grunt, seeing that he was way off-course, so changed the magazine feed to the gun, oriented himself and fired off half of the contents.

After a few minutes he saw that he had just killed the momentum he had had when heading away from the asteroid imparted by the Skua. So he fired again, waiting until his speed was a manageable fifty kilometres per hour and allowed himself to rest, looking out into the starfields. He shuddered in anguish seeing round shapes occluding the stars as the shapes headed towards where the wreck of the Skua had been.

He held the slate up towards the shapes and visually zoomed in on them. He could see they were the predators and relaxed a tiny amount. He could also see that his momentum was going to take him very close to them and a few moments later, his spectral crew comms came alive with Flint's voice.

'Father! You are alive! We are all so pleased to see you!'

Speaking using his thoughts and interfacing with his own internal bioware then into the crew comms, Marko immediately said, 'Bloody hell! Where are you? You must be close?'

'We are riding one of the predator spheres, Marko. We knew that you were out here, so we hijacked one.'

'You what! How do you hijack a predator?'

The three mechanical ACE spiders laughed as one, something that Marko found disconcerting, but very amusing, finding himself smiling for the first time in this very long day.

'We can thank a number of things, Marko,' Ngoc said. 'Your design of us, Jim's constant time with Fritz and his delight in finding esoteric knowledge, and also that Spike got into a fight with a baby predator who probably just wanted him as a toy! It grabbed him when he was trying to prise a parasite off the predator's carapace. So, Spike being Spike, he grabbed it by its tentacles and we learned that by pulling them left or right and up or down, the creature would respond.'

Marko allowed some oxygen into his lungs so he could laugh out loud. 'Yeah, that would be right. So why ride one out here?'

Spike, whose voice, even though completely electronic, came across as a full octave higher than the other two much larger spiders, answered. "Cause we knew you were out here and we knew that the predators were going out after every damaged Urchin and that the ones you fought would be wounded. So it was just a case of watching and seeing which ones came out here, then ensuring this one came out here. Not sure if it is all that happy, because it is from the nursery, but it's a good creature and every sphere that goes past us gives it some large fragments of Urchin to eat, so we think it may be content to be out here.'

Jim, who rarely spoke, added, 'And, Marko, I have recorded everything and as we approach I am recording you as well.

Why do you hold a fifty-millimetre rotary cannon like that while standing inside an inflated life raft?'

Marko grinned happily. 'As soon as you are here, Jim, I shall copy you everything that I have recorded on my system. It is quite a tale!'

His slate indicated to him where the ACEs were, as they clung to the front of a twenty-metre-diameter ball of linked predators. The screen, when he magnified it further, showed them spaced apart, pulling on tentacles and steering the creature in an arc. After a quick calculation, he saw that the ball would come up behind him and that its speed was higher than his, so he fired the cannon again in quick bursts until he could see that they were matched.

Ten minutes later the sphere, with its dozens of interlocked predators all tied together at their outer extremities by their tentacles, bumped into him as he landed in the middle of the three ACEs and the ex-Games Board monitor.

'Welcome aboard, Father!' Spike said. 'Hope you enjoy the ride.'

Marko sent his thanks and, for the first time in many hours, relaxed, as he took in all that was around him. He slowly sat up and looked down at the predator's outer shell he was sitting on, magnifying the surface again and again until he was seeing the shell-like material at a microscopic level. Seeing the structure and what appeared to be very thin layers of silica insulation, he asked, 'Have we any samples of these creatures?'

Flint answered. 'Always the biologist, eh, Father, no matter what the situation, no matter how bad or mad things are, no matter the insanity of riding a colony of giant insects that feast on Urchins out amongst the stars. You are more interested in how they are put together! We love you. And yes, we have plenty of samples already gathered by Stephine and Veg from ones killed during their battles with Urchins. We also took samples of everything inside the cavern that we could get to. But now, Marko, get ready to hop off this ride as *Basalt* is close.'

Spike let go of the tentacles he was holding as the other two ACEs did the same.

'Marko, move slowly with purpose,' Ngoc instructed. 'These animals are aware of us and we are not a threat to them, but whatever you do, do not step on the tentacles. Flint did and that one predator spun around and seized him. It looked him over very methodically then let him go because they could not find any flesh on him. But the same cannot be said for you.'

Marko grimaced and carefully moved his hand away from the tentacle he had been about to grasp. They all slowly moved around the side of the predator sphere with Marko following, still towing the life raft, ammunition and rotary gun, until one by one they gently pushed off.

The three ACEs pulled themselves onto Jim's outer housing and gestured to Marko to join them.

'Shall I fire the weapon and give us some separation from the predator?' Marko asked.

Flint shook his head. 'Not necessary. It will move away soon enough.'

Minutes later, the huge ball slowly accelerated, with puffs of ice particles streaming from one part it, as the predator headed back to towards the distant asteroid.

Ngoc tapped Marko on the arm and pointed behind him to where *Basalt* was, and below them the slow-moving *Blackjack*.

The sentient smaller ship slid underneath them, part of its upper hull irising open while they floated down, inside the ship. Marko allowed himself to start breathing again and found himself voraciously hungry.

Ayana

Haulers Territory on Storfisk

'Shall I tear that one to pieces, Ayana?'

Ayana looked at the towering form of the muscular baboon. 'How do you know where the alien is, Fenyang? We cannot see or sense it at all.'

The ACE harrumphed softly. 'I can smell the crushed insects under its claws and feet. Obviously, it has not thought through all its camouflage systems. It is a good thing that I am an entomologist, is it not? I can smell the combined scent of at least ten different insect alarm odours on it. It is very obvious to me.'

They were high above one part of the pool- and swamp-dotted savannah, in a rocky outcrop, watching the area where Fenyang had directed Ayana hours before.

'No, Fenyang. Angelito has expressly forbidden us to interfere with the alien. We are to watch and take notes.'

The baboon ACE shook his head and scowled, which Ayana thought baboons did very well as a rule.

'There is something wrong with that Angelito. You know that he is an avid follower of that ex-lover of yours? That giant canary who has self-styled herself as the great sage and fount of all knowledge across the Sphere. She is an arse. She has an agenda, that one.'

Ayana had a brittle edge to her voice as she said, 'Really! Well, I still have feelings for Jet. Yes, she left me, but I still care for her. I would ask that you keep your opinions to yourself, Fenyang.'

He bent his head, lowering it until he was looking straight into her eyes. He raised one of his eyebrows in a very human gesture and sighed. 'Yeah, and she hurt you, and for that alone I would wish on her much pain, physical and mental. And she is an arse and in cohorts with the Games Board, the shady sides of the Administration and who knows who else. But if this pains you, Ayana, I shall not speak of it again.'

He looked back out over the plains. 'Is your sensory suite available for an upgrade? I think that you should be able to smell what I can smell.'

Ayana sat up to look at Fenyang and cocked her head to the side. 'Fenyang. How many metres away is the alien from you?'

Without hesitating, he answered, 'Three thousand, two hundred and twenty-nine. And I am sure that you don't need the millimetres, do you?'

'And you can smell the crushed insects on its feet downwind from here? That is spectacular!'

He frowned again, looking at her. 'You have very shiny, whitish teeth. Is it necessary to show them all to me? I asked you about space for an upgrade, Ayana. I ask this as you obviously cannot see the slow-release insect alarm volatiles that surround that creature. Those individual scents that were created — and still cling to its feet — when those insects were crushed.'

Ayana suddenly felt chastened and a little bit mean for although he was abrupt, rather free with his views and sometimes a bit of a know-it-all, Fenyang was still a very good, loyal friend.

'I am sorry, Fenyang. I just want to destroy that alien and all the others like it as I know that they are up to no good. I am feeling frustrated. Yes, of course, I would really like to have that upgrade. It is generous of you. There is more than enough space in my core.'

He nodded solemnly and extended one of his hands with the datalink opening at the end of one of his long fingers. She did the same with her paw, accepting the link and watching the download streaming into her outer core over the next few minutes. When it had finished, Fenyang withdrew the link and waited quietly, watching the alien walk up to another bluebuck antelope in the far distance, its ghostly outline obvious to him.

Her shielded outer core checked the software, then minutes later allowed it to slip down into her conscious mind. As she looked through the data and the systems, she made the changes to her brain, allowing the far greater volume of information to be accepted through her eyes with a cross-referencing through her nose sensors as well. Fifteen minutes later she looked at Fenyang and the vegetation around her and the information flowed, giving her much more than she had ever seen before. She also noticed that her hearing could be tuned and focused down to the tiniest insect beneath her paws.

'I see you, Fenyang. Where did this software come from? It is so fresh and invigorating, like nothing I have ever experienced.'

The baboon ACE graced her with a quick smile. 'The great eagle Haast gave it to me when he was in this area a week or so ago. No, you would not have seen him, even if he had been right above you. His camouflage systems are quite remarkable. Between you and I, Ayana, I wonder if he knew about the alien before we did. It seems a little too much of a coincidence that he should have this tech available here and now when we need it to deal with such a complex creature as that one down there.'

'Can I share this tech with Sven? He should be here in a few hours. And what do you think we should do about that thing down there?'

Fenyang's chuckle had a dark edge to it. 'Watch, observe, take notes for that idiot above us and send for the terrible twins. They could be here within a day. We set it up so that they just happen upon the alien and let's see what comes out of the exchange.'

She grinned. 'Ghost and Spirit! Now there is an idea. Fanatical martial artists that they are, I bet they would be itching to go up against that thing. Good. I shall pass the message out through our own network. No need for Angelito to know about this.'

Fenyang gave her a feral full-toothed yawning smile, watching her send out the invitation via the planetwide ACE network, then said, 'Yeah, will be interesting. Reviewing the images of what it did with your drones, I don't think that it is here to play sport. Your new software bedded-in and operative?'

She nodded, and Fenyang continued: 'Right, let's put it to the test. Connect with me again and I shall give you a crash course in insect alarm and dispersal chemicals. Actually, that gives me an idea. I wonder how I could go about dropping an attractant pheromone on the alien? Then get the native wasps to land on it and have a go at chewing its head?'

Ayana emphatically shook her head. 'No. Most definitely no. Let's not do that yet. I suspect that that creature is very smart. No need to allow it the opportunity of learning that it is being targeted.'

'You are probably right. But I shall think on a suitable delivery method for later use. OK, move over here and link and let us see what you can do.'

Ayana moved close to him and with glacial slowness raised her head so she could see the entire bluebuck antelope herd. Slowly panning from left to right she gradually increased the intensity of the software as it 'saw' the various scents around the creatures and assigned colours and intensities to them as she looked. As the additional recognition software flowed from Fenyang to her, she started to distinguish the insect smells mixed in with the animal scents and the vegetation around them. By tuning the software further, she slowly detected the individual animal smells as a specific identity for that individual. Then she became aware of a hole in the visual data and came to recognise it as the alien.

She nudged her friend. 'Oh, I so like this! I can see it so clearly. How would the imagery be affected by mist or rain?'

'Yeah, drops off depending upon the intensity of moisture. We would need to pick our times and conditions. Observe. See how it approaches the antelope. It touches it with something long from its head, then withdraws. Moves to another animal and does it again. Oh! Look at the pheromones it is giving off: they are the same as the baseline ones of the bluebucks. Same use of that tech we use when we want to move amongst them. The bluebucks show no fright as they smell one of their own. Smart!'

'I have a bad feeling about this, Fenyang. It is moving throughout the whole herd one by one. I desperately want to know what it is doing. This is going to take time.'

'I have some of the maestro Fritz Vinken's latest music. How about we listen while we watch?'

Ayana readily agreed, and in spite of what was happening was enjoying the intrigue and the company of Fenyang.

The day dragged on and the two ACEs listened to music as their fur soaked up the warm sunlight, turning it into sugars which each stored about their body, readying them for the cool night.

Sven announced his presence by transmitting a laser message onto the back of Fenyang's head when he was still a kilometre away. Ten minutes later, the black panther silently slunk up and greeted his two old friends. They filled him in on what was happening as Fenyang transferred the smell recognition software to him. By sunset, he was up to speed and asked what they should do.

Fenyang shook his head and looked at the herd, which had moved further away from them. 'Nothing. We wait, watch and learn of what we are dealing with here. Now this is interesting. Look at the antelopes the alien touched first. Their pheromones have started to change a little. They now smell different. Look, look, it is sequential. They are probably all in a state of change. I believe that that creature has altered their body chemistry a little. Ha! It is as I thought. It is a vampire. See, it is feeding on them.'

They watched the alien move up against a number of the antelopes that it had first touched. As soon as it approached, they stood still for a few moments while it bent its head down against their necks. As soon as it moved off, they went back to chewing their cuds.

'I can see the cuts under visual amplification,' Ayana remarked. 'They are long cuts, but they seal very quickly. So, it is a blood feeder. The question is, did it arrive here able to drink the blood of the bovines, or did it gain that ability while here? Remember, it took a sample from the bison this morning, but did not drink the bull's blood. My conjecture is that it altered its own body chemistry after it took that sample and is now able to feed. But why the altering of the antelopes' body chemistry?'

Sven answered. 'To make them more docile, maybe?'

'No,' Fenyang said, 'there is more to it than that, I fear. It would not be necessary as it was able to get close very quickly. Why waste the energy? This alien appears to be intelligent and economic with its actions. I think the next few hours will tell us of its intentions.'

Ayana turned to Sven. 'Could you please go back to the buffalo herd and see if the bull's body chemistry has been changed? The beetle I left with it should have the information, but I do not want to lose another dragonfly the same way as the others by sending another to query it.'

Sven laughed softly. 'But you would happily risk me instead!' he said as he slipped away. 'Your thoughtfulness knows no bounds!'

Ayana smiled and turned back to watch the alien. It had come back to the first one it had fed upon. The antelope went rigid as the alien stood by one of its rear legs for a few moments. She could see a big lump appear under the skin of the upper leg and that what looked like large sutures were holding closed a long cut.

Over the next few hours the alien went from animal to animal, doing the same thing.

Ayana felt a deep alarm, looked up into the clear intense starry sky, located where the Hauler orbital Angelito was and opened a laser channel.

'Angelito, I am sending you everything that we are seeing on the blue antelopes as something seems to be placing material under the skin of the right-side rear legs. It is the same with every one. We cannot see what is doing this but must believe that it is the alien that disappeared from sight earlier.'

After a few long moments Angelito answered. 'There is no need for concern, Ayana. I am seeing and recording developments. You can stay there, out in the cold, huddled together with the baboon if you wish, but I would suggest that this is a natural thing that is happening. Maybe you three should disperse and go back to your assigned areas, but because you are ACEs I do not expect you have the same sense as myself, who is one of the Haulers' Collective. Do not under any circumstances engage with that, or any of the other aliens. Goodnight to you all.'

The connection was severed abruptly. Ayana looked at Fenyang and Sven who had just rejoined her. She uncoupled her eyes so that she could see Fenyang's and Sven's at the same time and initiated a laser conversation through her eyes with both of them.

'Has that bloody jerk lost the plot? I mean he has always been a pompous prick, but this is wild! He seems to be ignoring the standard protocols. That thing down there is placing something into dozens of bluebucks and that bloody AI is doing nothing about it! And early this morning he was warning us that those things were a real threat and he was dealing with it per guidelines, which is why I did not tell him that we can see the alien.'

'Pretty obvious if you ask me,' Sven said. 'He has been compromised and I think that whatever did it to him, did it very recently. Bet you that an alien ship is up there somewhere close. That would be a fancy piece of tech to enable them to turn a Hauler orbital; thought it wasn't possible. Bet you a dollar to a pinch of goatshit that he has sent another fast picket advising the Haulers' Collective that all is well. We are on our own on this, my friends.'

There was a long silence, before Fenyang added, 'Most things are possible, my feline friend. And when it comes to a sentient mind they, like us, can be encouraged to believe just about anything. I hope you are wrong, Sven, although you are always such a cheerful pessimist in most things. I really hope you are wrong.'

He looked out over the savannah. 'Ghost and Spirit have made good time. They will be going in for a close look at the alien right on first light.'

The three ACEs who had sat throughout the night amongst the obelisk-like rocks watching the distant herd of bluebucks and the still-moving alien saw the very first of the dawn and the stars slowly fading out as the light levels improved.

The huge baboon, Fenyang, cocked his head slightly and reported, 'Ghost and Spirit are about to make their approach.'

Before either of the other two could reply, the Hauler orbital Angelito spoke with his voice booming inside their heads. 'All ACEs within thirty kilometres of Ayana. I expressly forbid you to interfere with the alien that I believe Ayana, Fenyang and Sven are plotting against. If any of you do so, like Ghost and Spirit have just done, I shall not receive any of your Soul Saver uploads and will also shut down your comms system. You have been warned.'

Fenyang was the first to react. 'Have you lost your mind, Angelito! That thing down there is doing something to the bluebucks. You gave us a warning that the aliens were probably hostile! We must get a better look at what it is up to. It is our job. It is why we were grown into these ACE bodies. It is our duty to protect the creatures you Haulers brought back to life. Creatures that humanity and the solar flare took to extinction.'

The voice in their heads became almost painfully loud. 'And I am in charge, baboon Fenyang. Me! Not you. I am the overseer of this continent and I reserve the right to change my mind about events. And may I remind you that I am also the one who recommends each and every one of you for advancement within the Haulers' Collective. And, little friends, who is to say that the alien is doing harm? That is your conclusion, not mine. Do not interfere. I will not warn you again.'

The connection snapped off and the three friends looked at each other.

'Oh, shit,' Sven said. 'That's a bit of a smashing. Compromised to Hades. But I will not go up against him. Hell, I could not if I wanted to. What now?'

Ayana shook her head, wondering what else she could do or say and was about to answer when Fenyang spoke.

'Ghost and Spirit have veered off. They said that they love a good fight, having studied most martial arts over the last few hundred years, but with the big cheese upstairs saying bugger off, they are doing exactly that.'

Ayana was still shaking her head in resignation. 'They are quite right. Ceasing receipt of Soul Saver uploads I have not heard of before. New one on me. Perhaps I was wrong. I apologise. Let's go home.' She let out a long sigh. 'But let's watch these things anyway, as I am convinced that they are up to no good. Fenyang, please thank Ghost and Spirit for their help and commitment. Let's go. I need to find a falcon so I can send a secure message to Maqua.'

Haast

Storfisk System, Gas Giant Moon

Just as Bob Thompson entered the wide sweeping bridge of the carrier, he heard Mark de Ruyter call out, 'Commander on deck!'

Everyone at their stations braced their forearms in an acknowledgment of his presence. Those standing, like Mark, stood to attention as he walked in. In reply, he stated loudly, 'Stand easy! My thanks.'

In the centre of the bridge, there was a clear space where anyone could stand and take in what was always a spectacular view, except when the ship was in cloud. Faces would be pressed against the tall, curved windows to gaze at the distant horizons, down at the vistas below or up towards the stars.

Bob found himself looking out at the richly coloured curve of the planet below as *Haast* climbed out of the atmosphere at a very comfortable one gravity thrust. Out of the corner of his eye he could see Mark coming across to stand beside him. For long moments neither of them said a word until Bob finally broke the silence.

'I love this view. Different on every planet I have ever been on, but this one is exceptional.' He looked up at metres of incredibly tough transparent curved graphene above him. 'But then again, it is not often that we find ourselves in a brand-new ship, eh, Mark?'

Mark de Ruyter nodded slowly in agreement. 'And nice that the sun is behind us for a change, boss. Yes, this is a good ship and terrific crew. I am told that the Baron selected everyone for this ship himself. Is that true?'

Bob nodded. 'Mostly. I know that there are a few that neither of us was happy about and that Nick Warne in particular was very keen to march off as soon as they walked on, but that's politics. Affects even our employer. But we know who they are, eh. Should not worry about that yourself as that's Nick's job and I know he has personally chewed them out. How long before we rendezvous with the Hauler *Rose Foxtrot*?'

Mark turned to the navigation officer, Claire Bretherton.

'Four hours and thirty-two minutes, sir,' Claire said.

'Nice and easy with one gravity thrust all the way. If you look at five-thirty twelve kilometres down, eight degrees elevation, on a converging course, the Gjomvik Corporation Aquila airship *Berkut* is climbing to the rendezvous as well.'

'Thank you,' Bob responded. 'Think I might go have a look. You went up against *Berkut* a couple of years ago, didn't you, Mark? Want to have another look at it and give me a quick rundown?'

The two powerfully built men walked thirty metres along the right side of the bridge until they came to the starboard conning station, which had views of the entire side of the ship and also directly aft.

As the local star was also in plain view, the onboard computers watched the men's eyes and, while tracking their movements, shielded them with a black disc to cover the brilliant light. Looking at the assigned point in the sky, both of them touched studs on their collars and seconds later their face HUDs had formed to show the distant Aquila aircraft carrier.

Looking at the 120-metre-diameter craft, shaped like a pudding bowl, Mark increased his magnification and spent a few moments admiring its rugged no-nonsense design.

'It's a tough ship. Now let me see, yeah, must be close to forty standard years old now. You are aware that its commander has been replaced after she was required on another mission, aren't you?'

Bob shook his head.

Mark raised an eyebrow. 'Hmm, might have a word with that PA of yours. That rather vital piece of information was to be brought to your attention a few hours ago. Oh, I see, you have not had a look at anything since the little scrap with Mr Warne. Perfectly excusable. Was a good bit of flying.'

Bob looked closely at Mark. 'Well? Fill me in, Mark.'

'Roger Mortlock. Very bright man, the brigadier. Been in the game a long time. I served under him briefly as you may know. Great man, intensely loyal to his personnel, very quiet, never once heard him raise his voice to anyone. Has that presence about him that tells you it would be very stupid to underestimate or cross him. Scary bastard. Excellent tactician and he studies battles going back as far as he can. Even studies battles amongst animals and insects.'

Bob gave a slightly nervous laugh. 'Bit over the top, don't you think? He was with the Administration for thirty-odd years, and then got headhunted by the Aquila forty-six years ago ... and he still studies battles? All battles? I suppose he is brilliant at chess as well, Mark?'

'Nope. As far as I know, he does not play any games. Well, apart from having a spectacular collection of handmade wooden puzzles.'

Bob grimaced and let out a tiny groan. 'Oh, shit! So the Baron has fed me to this guy, eh?'

Mark gave him a wry smile, raised his eyebrows and chuckled at his superior's obvious disquiet. 'Yeah. I think that the Baron wants you to learn from one of the best, but that's a total supposition on my part. We have a hell of a crew, good gear, great ship. And, yeah, a chunk of us will make some heavy bonus as we fight a good fight, but I think that the odds are weighed in *Berkut*'s favour. A smart move would be for you to have a quick chat with the brigadier. Fact is, Bob, you will like him. I'll be in my command chair if you want me.'

Mark smiled, clapped the younger man on the shoulder and walked away. Bob watched him go then turned to the conning console that was used when the airship was being docked against something on its starboard side. He activated the communications unit and spoke briefly with the on-duty communications officer. In a few moments the screen in front of him showed the smiling face of the brigadier who had an ancient-looking, wooden carved tobacco pipe clenched between his teeth. He acknowledged Bob with a sharp little nod and took the pipe from his mouth to speak.

'Commander Thompson! A pleasure to see you. Great minds think alike obviously. I was within minutes of calling you and inviting you to dine with me once we are aboard *Rose*. What do you say?'

Bob looked at the dignified older man with steel-grey hair and an amiable smile and knew that he had already been outflanked and wished fervently that he was the man's second-in-command and not classed as his equal.

'My thanks, brigadier. Yes, I should enjoy that. I will see what interesting wines are available for us.'

The older man looked evenly out of the screen and nodded slowly. 'Now that I will indeed look forward to, commander. I am told that you always have an excellent selection of reds from your own vineyards, made in the traditional way, somewhere close on hand wherever you travel. My PA will speak with yours. Bring a companion. I'll see you in five hours. Until then, safe travels.'

Bob gave a wide genuine smile, his mind thinking of the excellent shiraz he had onboard and silently agreed with Mark's comments that he might get to like the brigadier. He gave a formal nod, as he said, 'I'll come armed with a few bottles and some cheeses, I think. See you soon, sir.'

The brigadier gave Bob a congenial nod and the connection was severed.

Bob walked slowly back down the bridge, feeling the rockets rumbling far below him, seeing his crew quietly going about their tasks and wondered what he should wear to see the brigadier. He looked in the bridge command pod to see Mark obviously buried in the never-ending maintenance schedules and gave him a quick thumbs up before walking back into his ready room. He sat down at his screens to see that the most critically urgent message waiting for him was from his PA, advising that the brigadier had taken over command of *Berkut* and when he checked the time stamp it had been from a few hours earlier when he had been in the orders group going through all the general situation reports of what they were to expect and how they planned to deal with it. He tapped his private comms screen then the icon for his PA whose elegant smiling face greeting him with a soft smile.

'Michelle. Expect to hear from *Berkut*'s commander's PA. We — yes, you are coming — are having a late meal with him onboard *Rose Foxtrot* tonight. Also, when there is something as important as a command change on the opposition's ship, could you please make sure I know about it. Perhaps we had better have a talk tomorrow so that we can establish some protocols. Yeah, I know what you are going to say. That I have so much to look at all of the time and I am slack about checking my priority mail. And it's true.'

Michelle smiled at him. 'It is true, but I am sure that we will work it out. I am presuming that you will take red wine and your cheeses to the dinner onboard *Rose*? I have already been contacted and there will be a third couple at dinner with us. A Mr Daisuke Suzuki and his companion, both crew members of *Rose*. We are to provide the canapés, aperitifs and wine. *Berkut* is doing the main courses and *Rose Foxtrot* the desserts. I believe that it will be a low-key occasion and my suggestion is your merino three-piece suit. That, and the rest of your attire, is waiting for you in your quarters. I have sent a list of possible wines to your wristscreen. I would not presume to select them as they are from your own vineyards, or at least the same region.'

Bob laughed, knowing that Michelle was more than capable of selecting the wines. He looked through the lists, selected six to be opened immediately and allowed to breathe, another four as gifts and then a few of his own superb dessert wines to take as well. He sent the list back to Michelle, thanked her and for the next hour cleared the last of his administration for the day. Feeling like he needed a little exercise, he descended one of the spiral staircases for six decks until he was in the garden areas.

As he pushed his way through the translucent gel-like doors that sealed immediately behind him, he was greeted by an explosion of life: insects, exotic flowers, wonderful scents and fruits and vegetables in all stages of growing and ripening. He wandered around picking a few passionfruit, a couple of tangelos and then an almost perfectly shaped large pear. He took his selection over to one of the wooden benches and sat down, pulling his little fruit knife from its sheath and taking ten minutes just for himself.

Seeing other crew members doing the same, he smiled and nodded to himself. It was good that one of the unwritten traditions of the garden decks was that they were places of peace and contemplation, and people rarely spoke to each other amongst the growth. The decks had spread like wildfire through the ships, of all the various groups, having been made popular by the famous frigate *Basalt* and its crew, after they had taken a long seven-year journey to get themselves home.

Bob dropped the peelings from the fruit onto a wooden tabletop, knowing that within an hour they would be absorbed back into the gardens. He looked around and picked another pear, a couple of apples and an orange, and dropped them into one of the long pockets of his tunic. Just before he exited through the gel door, he cleaned his knife, then wiped his face on one of the fragrant living towels of finely bound fibres.

Outside the door, looking out through one of the tall ellipse windows in the hull to the distant starfields, he smiled, thinking that he had made the right decisions. Even if he had his arse handed to him on a plate fighting a superb tactician who would frighten the hell out of him, and probably smash a lot of his beautiful equipment and crew, it was worth it.

He walked down another two decks and looked at the four huge antigravity units quietly humming to themselves, any one of which could easily lift *Haast* and its contents into orbit and still be using only half of its rated output. He looked around the other parts and wondered for the hundredth time why everything was so over-engineered.

Then he walked down another deck and into the engineering area of Alpha Squadron, looking for one of his oldest mates, the cyborg, Uncle. After walking most of the forward length of the workshop he found the part-man hunched over a tiny milling machine, creating something complex from a piece of steel.

Bob tapped the bench beside him to get his attention, knowing that he would be listening to some obscure old music in his head.

Sergeant Major Graham Kyle looked sideways at the commander, giving him a nod and a small smile. 'So what brings you all the way down here? Missing the real deal of making stuff, eh?'

'What are you making this time, Uncle? Hmm, let me guess … looks like a slide for a pistol. My one, maybe? You are funny! Most would just have one of the growers make it, or at very least an auto mill.'

Uncle nodded, tapping the little mill with a titanium fingernail, and agreed. 'Yeah, I am funny, but where is the pleasure in getting a machine to make what I want and besides, it would be pointless otherwise to cart this beautiful equipment around with me. Could be your one, but unlikely, as yours is in my arms' cote.'

He gestured at the massive cabinet in front of him, which Bob knew could fold out numerous times allowing Uncle, and others on rare occasions, to use the hundreds of perfectly maintained tools and machines. Bob also knew from long experience that Uncle would not let anyone maintain his prosthetic arms and legs, and he respected that. He pulled the fruit from his pocket and placed it on the benchtop beside his old friend. Uncle nodded in thanks then took up one of the apples in his left, beautifully streamlined metallic hand.

A long slim blade slid from the end of his right index finger which he used to quietly slice up the fruit as he ate it.

As he enjoyed the fruit, one of the cabinet's doors opened and folded aside as a group of drawers slid out.

'Left side, second from the top, Bob.'

Bob reached up, slid the drawer open and pulled out the nine-millimetre pistol. He slid the action open, checked that the chamber was empty, closed it and took the four magazines from the drawer. He admired each piece of exquisitely made weaponry, then looked at the grips and laughed out loud at seeing the bas-relief carved representations of Hawk aircraft.

He clapped Uncle's metal shoulder. 'I shall transfer the last payment into your account, thanks, Uncle. Stunner, mate. Stunner. Wonder if Aaron Huriwaka has some ammunition sorted for me?'

Uncle pointed with his blade. 'End of the bench. He decided that 300 rounds should be enough for you to get used to the weapon! I said more like 500 before you learned to shoot it, but there you go … some people have more faith in you than I do.'

'Fucking wanker!' Bob said affectionately. 'Switch off that targeting software in your head and I would beat you any day!'

Bob took the weapon and ammunition and walked over to the ship-wide weapon delivery system, which could have any personal issue or privately owned firearm to its owner anywhere on the ship within minutes. The main computer logged the new nine millimetre and ammunition as Bob's and took the package away for safekeeping.

'I see that the commander of *Berkut* was cycled out with Brigadier Mortlock now at the helm,' Bob said.

'Yeah. Tough, very tough crafty thinker that one. Going to have to get up very early and be hellish smart to put one over that old bugger, Bob. Expect surprises, look at every possible angle, but hey, you are no slug yourself. Just think outlandish, because he will.'

Bob looked up at the now-standing Uncle, who towered over everyone in the crew with the exception of the extremely athletic Paul Black.

'Yeah, so I have gathered. Pleased that you agreed to come on this ship, Graham. Great to know that you are here. Right, I had better push on. See you later, sergeant major.'

'That you will, commander, that you will.'

A few hours later general quarters were sounded as *Haast* manoeuvred up against the enormous bulk of the Hauler *Rose Foxtrot*.

Looking from his command pod, with wraparound screens showing him all views of the ship and the imposing side of the Hauler, Major Nick Warne used two small controls to place the ship precisely where the Hauler had instructed them to be, twenty metres off its port side.

'Engineering, shut down, internally purge propulsion and manoeuvring systems as soon as the Hauler has locked on. Navigation, stand by to stand down. Crew, recheck that weapon systems are unloaded and stored correctly. Unit commanders, report when ready. All external hatches and doorways, excepting those under my or the commanders' express control, are now sealed.'

Watching his screens, he saw moments later the unit commanders' reports coming in. When the final one appeared he said, 'Hauler *Rose Foxtrot*. This is *Haast*. All internal reports and status are now available to you. Request that you take us onboard, please.'

Nick knew that the 'please' was not necessary, but believed that manners mattered.

Seconds later, the friendly but slightly schoolmarmish female voice of *Rose Foxtrot* answered: 'Welcome, Major Warne. Your documentation is accepted. My compliments to you and Commander Thompson. Yours is an impressive ship and crew. Docking is underway.'

On his screens he could see the huge arms folding out of the side of the Hauler that pushed up against the locks in the *Haast*'s hull. There was a just-audible thudding down the length of the ship with a shudder as *Haast* was pulled towards the Hauler; huge doors folded up and out of the hull as the airship was placed inside. Five minutes later the doors closed, sealing them inside *Rose* 19.

Nick Warne tapped the 'all ship' icon on his comms screen. 'All stations. We are secure inside *Rose Foxtrot*. Watch rosters are now promulgated. One gravity will be maintained by the Hauler throughout the three-day journey to the moon around the closest local gas giant. Those not required at your posts may stand down. Training recommences at 0800 ship time tomorrow. Bridge out.'

Looking out of his pod, he saw the remainder of the night shift taking over from the late shift, knowing they would be in for a quiet night.

Mark de Ruyter stuck his head around the side of the pod. 'The cooks have left out the usual spread for your squad. I'm just heading down to the garden decks. Shall I send back some fruit? Latest tangelos are ripe.'

'No thanks, Mark. Tai Chi usual time?'

Mark nodded. 'Yeah. As long as Bob does not get himself into trouble, should be there at 0715. You did well getting that Magret and Johan onboard. They are wanted on just about every ship I know for their Tai Chi instructor ratings alone.'

'Yeah. Not bad crew in a Maul either.'

Mark smiled as he left, knowing that Nick would have made one of his famous deals to get the two onboard and knew not to ask, as Nick would never tell.

Nick watched his old friend and colleague walk off the bridge, passing the immaculately attired commander on his way in. Bob saw Nick and stopped in the hallway, beckoning him over. Nick stepped out of the pod and walked across to his commander … he had previously asked to see him before Bob left for the dinner.

Bob answered the unasked question. 'No need for you to call the bridge to attention. Just wanted to say, don't wait up, but hey, you will anyway cause you are on night shift, eh! You needed to see me?'

Nick smiled, wondering if Bob would eventually get used to the necessary ceremonies and protocols of the service, but also knew that in the long run it would not matter as Bob was good at what he did.

'Nice suit, Bob. Good idea not going over in your dress uniform. You always look more uncomfortable in that than most I have seen. Say hello to the brigadier for me and also Major Suzuki. Good people. Now, yes, I need a little favour. Can you please ask *Rose* if she could let me into her gardens? She has an extraordinary collection of orchids and I want to purchase some cuttings from her.'

Bob nodded. 'Of course. Any particular time?'

'Bit after 0900 would be good.'

'No problems. I will ask. Right. See you when I do.'

Bob turned and walked down two decks to be met by the beautifully attired Michelle who was carrying a cedar wood box with the wines and cheeses. He picked up another cedar and silver box at his feet, which he presumed contained the canapés. He gestured to the airlock with its airbridge from *Haast* to the scale-plated armoured side of the docking bay leading into *Rose*.

They cycled through, walked across the transparent tube then through the massively over-engineered airlock on the other side. As Bob watched the outer doors closing, he knew that *Haast* could explode inside with all its ammunition and fuel systems detonating at the same time, and the only damage *Rose* would suffer would be the outer bay doors being wrecked.

They stepped through the inner door into an elegant wood-panelled, wide high-vaulted corridor where the tall, slim figure of Daisuke Suzuki awaited them. They all formally bowed then shook hands as Daisuke took them a few paces then opened a sliding panel to reveal an Art Nouveau-inspired bronze and dark leather car. They stepped in and sat opposite Daisuke and, as the doors closed, the car started moving at what Bob believed to be a relatively high speed up to the bow section of the Hauler.

As the two crew of *Haast* looked about them, Daisuke said, 'My partner Wardah is uplifting Brigadier Mortlock and his companion on the other side of the ship. I have had dealings with him before and it is a good exercise to be at least one minute ahead of him for your meeting, so I do apologise for my speed. And I do apologise if you already knew that, commander. We are also surprised that he was instructed to take this particular battle with you and *Haast* for the Games Board. It is interesting in that the Games Board were also greatly taken aback, and have had to send one of their specialist teams to cover him, knowing of his huge popularity throughout the Sphere.'

Bob and Michelle looked out the elegant windows of the car as it passed through various huge engineering spaces, long empty decks and cargo spaces packed with neatly secured multiple coloured containers. The last one they passed through housed dozens of what Bob recognised as salvage and repair craft as the car slowed, was lifted smoothly and placed onto another gently curving track.

The car slowed to a stop as Bob and Michelle smiled at the magnificent glazed Art Nouveau iron arches they could see, which made up the whole front of the Hauler.

Two tall humanoid machines, also showing heavy Art Nouveau design influences, took the boxes from Bob and Michelle as Daisuke led them to a sumptuously appointed bar with one of the most beautiful women the members of *Haast* had ever seen awaiting them.

Daisuke gave her a nod and did the introductions. 'Rose, may I present Lieutenant Colonel Jeremy Thompson and the Adjutant Countess Michelle Yngling.'

Bob looked up into the emerald-green eyes of Rose and felt distinctly nervous shaking her hand. Michelle just smiled demurely and did not flinch, with Bob thinking that it had been a good suggestion on the Baron's part that Bob take her as his PA considering her family connections, great intelligence and ease of dealing with people in any circumstances.

They made small talk for a few moments before Daisuke's partner, the almost equally stunning-looking Wardah, walked in along with the brigadier and his companion, a severely dressed but hauntingly beautiful Petah Ortiz.

Bob looked down at the brigadier and was a little surprised that he was not a lot bigger and taller. He also moved as if he was constantly watching and planning alternatives and the quickest most energy-efficient way to attack or escape.

Rose got them drink from behind the bar. As they were taking a draught of a heavy black stout, Roger Mortlock surprised Bob with a question.

'You strike me as a well-travelled, intelligent and interesting fellow, Bob. So I shall ask you this question: who makes the best sausages around here? You can go a very long way and sometimes even between worlds to find a half-decent sausage maker.'

Bob did not know if it was a genuine question, some interesting trick question, or just a plain and simple one, but replied with little hesitation. 'On *Haast*. Believe it or not, Sergeant Major Mike Antipas, one of our engineers, makes the finest sausages I know of.'

The brigadier looked at Bob and gave a quick short bark of a laugh, then clinked his glass against Bob's. 'Good! Very good! You and I are going to get along just fine. Shall we join the rest of the group?'

Sergeant Major Mike Antipas cocked his head to the side, looking at the huge bird sitting across the table from him.

The ACE *Haast* looked back at the shortish, solidly built man and pointed at the plans of a machine displayed in the tabletop with a long elegant featherlike finger. 'No, Mike. This is a good design, but really a bit over-engineered, don't you think?'

They were in one of the smaller rooms on the crew recreation deck, relaxing, with Mike enjoying a tall tumbler of whiskey and the ACE a pineapple juice. Outside the room, in one of the larger areas, off-duty members of the crew were enjoying a pool competition that *Haast* was not equipped for, being too short in stature to handle a cue stick and that Mike had been earlier eliminated from.

'Yeah, but Haast mate, the boss was very insistent that no risks were to be taken with you. Every part of the flier had to have redundancies, even a spare antigravity unit, plus survival gear that is capable of making the sugars that you need from just about any vegetable or meat source that you could find. Sorry, but that all takes up physical space and power.'

'It's still too big, Mike.'

The hulking form of Uncle passed the doorway and Mike yelled out to him. 'Hey, Unc! Grab a beer and come join us. We are arguing about Haast's flier!'

Uncle stopped and looked in, then said, 'Hold on.'

A few moments he was back with a huge pewter tankard, topped with a tall cream-coloured head. He stood next to Mike and looked down at the plans. 'Can't see a problem with it. Hold on. I saw Robb in the bar.'

He walked out and a few moments later returned with another of the engineers, Staff Sergeant Robb Merrill, who was carrying two tankards of beer.

Robb spoke in his soft drawl. 'Wondered where you guys had disappeared to. Haast, have a taste of this. This, my friend is wheat beer. Dark and tasty. Hold on.'

He took a little shot glass from his tunic pocket and poured a little of the beer off for Haast. The eagle sniffed it, then dipped another of his long fingers into it and drained the glass. He sat briefly, then nodded up at Robb.

'Yes, that one I like. Much better than the last one you gave me, the pilsner. Not really interested in that one but this I like. A wheat beer. My thanks.'

'Pleasure. You drinking fresh pineapple juice! Damn! Latest crop must be ready. Back in two, people.'

'Robb must have made the drill sergeant a very happy

human,' Mike remarked with a smile, 'when he did his basic training. He does military-style short quick steps naturally.'

Robb returned with a tray and two fresh pineapples. He pulled a long, slim knife off his belt and expertly dealt with the fruit. 'So, what's the problem with the flier, Haast? We made it to Mr de Ruyter's design.'

'It's too bulky, Robb. I feel like I am too enclosed. I need more freedom of movement. The ability to soar. I am a bird, you know.'

As they all grinned, Mike commented, 'Really! Had not noticed.'

Robb looked seriously at the plan for a few moments as the conversation of the others washed around him, then spoke. 'Why fly it all the time, Haast? We could rebuild it so that it slaved to you and would fly in close support when you are in atmosphere sufficient to give you lift. When you have to get somewhere in a hurry, just lock yourself back into it and go. It's a sensible option, then we could set some weapon systems on it as well. Make it bigger in fact. Not smaller. Proper little support platform.'

The others agreed immediately. They welcomed Aaron Huriwaka into the room and started reworking the design, pushing over other tables so that the various sub-systems could be designed as the drink, jokes and food were consumed.

Haast looked around the tables and felt content, feeling that he was a real member of the crew. These augmented people of human stock simply did not care that he was an ACE ... he was one of them.

A bleary-eyed Bob Thompson looked down at Nick Warne who, with raised eyebrows, was looking back up at him.

'The light is too bright, Nick.'

Nick gave him a small smile. 'Did you ask about the orchids?'

'Nope. Did not have to. Rose asked after you. Said that you are welcome, any time. Why is it that the Haulers have such amazing-looking people and that Rose proxy ... Bloody hell! Extraordinary. And when Mark comes in, tell him that he and you were right. The brigadier has an amazing mind, talked and talked. Learned more in seven hours with him about tactics and strategies than in the months at the academies. Good guy, I like him. He will kick my arse but I like him. I need sleep. You don't need me. See you at lunch.'

He turned, walked a few steps, then turned back saying, 'Oh, yeah. Speak with Sergeant Major Antipas. Ask him to send a few kilos of his sausages over to *Berkut*, please. Mr Mortlock will be very grateful. Thanks, Nick.'

Uncle, who always awoke five minutes before his wake-up alarm sounded, rolled his torso towards the edge of the bed and cleared his throat. '*Haast*. Blankets and social arms, please.'

The ship responded with the living bedcovers rolling themselves off his naked form while vinelike manipulators presented his almost-human arms down to him, so as he rolled first his right then his left shoulders the arms locked themselves on. He brought up the displays in his head, checking the interfaces, power settings and then sugar levels in the arms themselves, which the room had been maintaining for him. Satisfied by what he saw he activated them and pushed himself upright, lowered himself off the bed onto his leg stumps, and shuffled himself into the room's ablutions and shower unit.

Looking at his face in the mirror, he saw that another depilatory treatment was needed, so shaved the short stubble using a cut-throat razor, then sprayed a long-term oil over his face and rubbed it into his skin where he did not want the hair to grow for at least a month.

Wondering if he should grow a short beard again, but deciding against it, he sprayed a second light fluid over his skin to activate the treatment, then pushed his way into the shower.

As soon as he stood in the centre of the unit, pure water at the temperature he had always liked cascaded down over him for a few seconds before turning to soapy water. He reached up and tore a piece of cloth-like material off the wall, scrubbing himself with its coarse side, and when he finished, dropped it onto the floor of the shower, knowing that within forty or so minutes it would have been absorbed back into the bioengineering closed circuit cubicle. Deciding that he was clean enough, he tapped the wall and pure water rinsed him off. He pushed through the gel door and towelled himself off with the free-hanging self-cleaning towel.

He looked at himself in the mirror again: the biomechanical shoulders with their mounting points for heavy weapon arms; the interfaces for direct access to machine systems that were linked internally to his ivory chain-linked ribcage and spine; the access shunts in either side of his neck and the other metallised contacts above his ears; the shunts in his chest and stomach and the augmented hips and leg joints which terminated in totally artificial sockets. He wondered what he had become over the years and if he was still human. He looked at his eyes, seeing the slight metallic sheen of their armour, then down at his genitals and smiled. He decided, as he had every day since opting five years before to become mainly cyborg, that as long as they were still 100 per cent standard human, then he must be as well.

He stumped over to a container, reached up and grasped the overhead bar and effortlessly lifted himself up, simultaneously thinking of the legs he wanted which seconds later were presented to him by the container. They locked onto the stumps as his systems checked and activated them, then the room dropped the one-piece base coverall over his shoulders that slid over him forming his ship suit.

He gave a wry grin, wondering what the day would bring.

Harold

Human Settlement on Storfisk

The meeting place for the senior local ACEs was deep under one of the home trees a few hours after midnight local time.

The Tengu both looked at Harold with serious expressions on their faces. 'We are sorry, Harold, that we had to injure you so badly. It was necessary that the standard humans and, in particular, the Games Board believed in everything that they were seeing. We had planned everything so carefully, but also admit that the beetles choosing that time to take flight was a most welcome bonus. We did not factor it in, but it worked to our advantage anyway.'

Harold sat very still in front of the much larger, more powerful ACEs and thought to himself that he had not done too badly for his first combat.

'So, Tengu, you are saying that to make it look good, you would have killed me if I had given you the opportunity?'

They both blinked and nodded at precisely the same instant. 'Of course. Your family would have built a new, and probably improved, version of you anyway, and as the link from your Soul Saver to the village AI computers was a continuous one, you would still be the real you and not a clone. But enough of this. We just want to know if you can work with us or not?'

Harold had thought long and hard since Bing had told him about the Tengu. He slowly nodded. 'Yes, I can. But now you have to tell me what is happening here? Why here, why now? The aliens landing in the Haulers reserve a week ago and you being here is not a random coincidence surely?'

The Tengu nodded and smiled, then frowned an instant later. Harold decided that they were probably a connected mind. Something that Harold found a little unnerving.

'Indeed, you are perceptive, but we wonder if it is sensible to trust you with the information. But then again, Maqua did and you did not go running off to the standard humans blabbing so … maybe. We will think about this. Suffice to say that there are hundreds of us, at least three, on every reasonably sized habitat of humanity throughout the Sphere.'

Harold turned to Bing and Reg, who looked back at him. 'Do either of you know about this?'

Reg shrugged. 'Of course, Harold. The Tengu is a very good combat ACE that was perfected a long, long time ago when we ACEs came to the conclusion that we had been created to look after humankind. The only visible one is the one that we allowed to be made for Baron Willy der Boltz as we thought it prudent to see how the standard humans would receive him. We needed teeth and the Tengu are some of those teeth. There are others. But you are young! Why should you expect to learn everything at once?'

Before he could answer, Bing quietly spoke up. 'Harold, you are the very latest generation of ACE. You were created by Marko and Topaz on *Basalt*. That is one of the reasons that you are here, otherwise you would be treated as any other young ACE and given some menial task. Not this. So, the question remains. Do you trust us and will you work willingly and without reservation with the Tengu?'

Harold looked about him at the other ACEs who filled the secret underground bunker in the heart of the village. 'Why am I so important to you and do I have a choice in all of this?'

The Tengu solemnly shook their heads. 'No, you do not have a choice, we regret to say. You have a direct connection to Stephine and Veg onboard *Basalt*. They are probably the most important entities in this whole part of the Sphere. We know that there are others like them, but we do not know how to contact those others. But you can talk to them and Marko, plus *Basalt*'s crew.'

Harold looked at them sharply. 'Stephine and Veg are certainly important and remarkable, but so is everyone on *Basalt*. I have been told that things seem to happen around them all the time. They are recognised as a sort of flashpoint. I am aware of the whole history of the crew, but I fail to see why Stephine and Veg are *the most* important. Fritz has done some of the more remarkable work. Surely he would be more important. And what of Marko?'

The Tengu cocked their heads to the same side, speaking quietly. 'Yes. It is agreed, Harold, that they are a remarkable crew. So you are aware of the final hours of *Basalt*'s return mission to the library planet? The rescue mission that they went on with the Administration's enforcer, the Hauler known as Rick. The planet that subsequently was dragged out of orbit from its star by a wandering brown dwarf. That same dwarf that wrecked the Lagrange navigation points for that whole area because the star and all its planets were dispersed. Are you aware of that mission, Harold?'

Harold sat back on his haunches, wondering where the discussion was leading. He very slowly nodded, wishing that he was not so young and wondering if he too had not become a flashpoint. 'I am aware of that mission.'

The familiar voice of one who Harold had never met face to face spoke from the back of the chamber. 'Are you aware of those we call the Angels, Harold? Do you know that there was an Angel on that planet and that it bonded with one of Rick's proxies?'

He quickly turned to see the huge bird, Maqua, walking into the chamber. He resisted the strong urge not to run up to her and give her a big hug, thinking that it was probably not appropriate. All the ACEs, including the Tengu, gave her a smile and murmured their greetings. Harold frowned deeply at her question.

'Angels? Maqua, they are part of some of the standard humans' religious beliefs, are they not? I do not know anything of Rick and an Angel. I was told only that to save Fritz he had to fling him into orbit, and the only way he could do that was to stay behind in the library.'

She walked up to him, leaned down and stroked him on his head with an extended wingtip.

'Yes, that is so, Harold. They do make up parts of various religions. And they are also an entity that has walked amongst humanity over the millennia. And since our creation by humanity, amongst us also. Stephine is one of them. And Rick sacrificing himself to save Fritz? There is another story there. You look very surprised?'

'Um, yes. But thinking about it these few weeks has been one surprise after another, so I suppose I am just on a steep learning curve of surprises.'

All the ACEs chuckled and smiled at him.

'You must have flown for days to get here,' Harold commented to Maqua.

She cocked her head to one side, gave a quick nod. 'Yes, a long flight but an important one for so many reasons.'

Maqua bent lower and fired a laser signal directly into his left eye, from her right. His system received it, automatically checked it and allowed it into his conscious mind. He stopped completely still as another series of codings buried deeply in his operating software opened like flowers. They showed him the Angels, how they were the proxies of huge Haulers for segments of the octopoid empire and about how that empire had, over tens of thousands of years, declined. Various factions took themselves far away to allow an ordered devolution back to primitive states, whilst others wanted to take back the empire, including their main place of evolution, which was Old Earth. The thing that most startled Harold was that the octopoids had genetically shaped the proto-humans and formed homo sapiens sapiens as their servants on the land, so creating the ways that they reached the stars.

Harold snapped back to reality with the sensational thought that the octopoids were the original driving force that led directly to him and his fellow ACEs.

'So we are derived from the octopoids?'

Maqua solemnly nodded. 'Yes, it would appear so. They sped up the inevitable climb of humanity towards full sapience and the subsequent creation of our knowledge. Then humanity, because they probably felt lonely, created us. So yes, we are related to the octopoids. Does that bother you?'

Harold nodded emphatically. 'Yes, because the created battles on Cygnus 5 by the Administration destroyed a part of humanity's creators! It would be like us going to war with the standard humans to steal their technologies. There would be terrible consequences, surely.'

Maqua hugged Harold to herself, making him feel warm and cherished as she said, 'Yes, little one. There are consequences and we can only hope that the Angels will help us in the battle with their own creators.'

Harold looked up into the huge bird's eyes. 'But why do the Angels now walk amongst us, Maqua? Why would they bother?'

'Perhaps it is because they feel forsaken by their creators. Perhaps it is because they feel lonely too. I mean, just think how we would feel if the standard humans all decided to destroy their technology, forgo their sentience and go back to being hunter gatherers. What would be left for us? What would we do? Form our own civilisation maybe, or adopt someone else's? I would like to think that it is more likely they wish to be a part of us because they have all taken lovers amongst us. It's a nice thought.' Maqua looked down at the little dragon leaning against her. 'So, little one. Will you work with us, please?'

Harold felt safe amongst his own and in particular with Maqua, but knew that it was fleeting. He nodded. 'Marko told me not long after he breathed life into me that it is better to lead than to be led. He said that whatever I did I should always at least try to do the right thing. So yes, I will help in any way I can. But please tell me of what we are dealing with.'

Maqua smiled at him. 'Come. The Tengu are travelling north by their own means. You and I shall fly so I can show you what we are up against.'

Basalt

Urchin Star System

Marko, Stephine, Veg and the ACEs were all in *Basalt*'s galley making sandwiches, having just come onboard the ship when the major called them.

'All crew: well, that did not go very well, did it? One Skua destroyed and everything else damaged to one degree or other. So we have expended a lot of ammunition, fuel and we are still in an Urchin-infested part of space.'

The major looked out from everyone's screens and ran his hands agitatedly over his bare cranium.

Before he could carry on, Patrick interrupted. 'Major. I can see Marko's Skua. It is largely intact. It would seem that the Urchins most interested in it were consumed by the predators. I am not seeing any of the Urchins for hundreds of kilometres in any direction. It would appear that they fear the predator. On the current course, we will be within only eleven kilometres of that Skua wreck in a few moments. It would not take a great deal to recover it.'

Michael looked around his screens and sighed. 'Well, we came all this way to learn as much as we could about the Urchins. And we need a better plan to deal with the bastards as every time we go up against them, we sort of win, but we get busted up doing it. And the Games Board most certainly lost big time. OK, let's go grab the wrecked Skua and anything else drifting with it. Then let's go find a nice quiet piece of ice to chew on.'

He started tapping his screens, looking at the damage reports that had been generated by the craft themselves. Then opened his comms screens to give orders.

'Stephine and Veg, go grab that wreck as quick as you can. Everyone else on emergency repairs to our craft. Lists propagated. Patrick, deploy drones to check all craft, including *Basalt*, and get the astronomical drones out to look for a non-infested piece of ice. Harry and Marko, you have control of the drones. Get whatever can be fixed and placed on the launch platforms right away. Let's get to work, everyone.'

Patrick spoke again. 'Nail has had his sentience fully restored. Stephine, he is on his way down to *Blackjack* now. Fritz will be a few minutes more.'

The major acknowledged the news. 'Best thing I have heard in a while. My thanks to all involved.'

Marko sped up his mind, linking directly into the operating systems of all the repair and salvage drones onboard, sending them to the other Skuas and Hangers so they could repair the worst damage and get them flight- and fight-worthy as quickly as possible. Glint thought it very funny watching his father eating and drinking like an automaton while his mind was operating at an ACE's level. He gestured to Spike and fired a quick laser message across to him.

The little spider grinned and scuttled up Marko's arm, deftly removing the sandwich from his hand and, seconds later, they were rewarded by Marko biting down on the end of his fingers.

Marko grunted loudly and laughed out loud, almost choking on a mouthful of food which created even greater mirth in the ACEs. He commented at their speed.

'Funny fuckers! Yeah, I know. Don't multitask at different speeds! Can I have my sandwich back, please, Spike? Right, now bugger off, all of you. Lily's Hanger is the worst. Go help the drones get it operational again.'

They all trooped out, with each one giving Marko a little pat on his legs as they went past.

Fifteen hours later and thousands of kilometres away from the site of the battle, *Basalt* caught up and matched speeds with a slowly spinning 500-metre-long potato-shaped mass of ice and rock.

In the mess, Jasmine was looking at Fritz closely. 'You OK, Fritz?'

'Yeah. Massive headache still, but I think that I am on top of things.'

Stephine was also looking closely at him. She stood up with a cup of Veg's coffee in her hand, added milk and two sugars to it and walked quietly over to the long table and sat next to Fritz.

She placed the coffee down in front of him. He was moving data around on his slate at great speed and automatically reached out for the coffee and took a deep drink then without comment put it back on the table, not even looking up or acknowledging Stephine.

She looked back at Jasmine and at Lily sitting next to her eating breakfast. Stephine slowly raised an eyebrow and almost imperceptibly shook her head. Marko, sitting at the other table with Harry and Julie, saw the exchange. He finished his oats, stood up carrying the bowl and walked over to where Veg was leaning against one of the kitchen benches. He looked up at the big man and raised an eyebrow in question. Veg shrugged, so Marko gathered some fruit and went to sit with Stephine. As he sat down, he thought of a little comms tentacle forming on his right hand which, when he placed his hand next to Stephine's, slowly snaked across and latched onto her skin. Instantly her presence was in his mind.

'Good trick, Marko,' she thought to him. 'You are learning fast. You know that you can do this with Veg and *Blackjack* as well.'

'Nice to know, thanks. Fritz is not all there, is he?'

'No.'

'Is there anything we can do to help?'

'Yes. Get him to that blasted Urchin queen, I suppose. It is like the spark of his existence is missing. The intellect is intact. The genius is present, but the certain uncontrollability that is Fritz is gone. He is close to a normal standard human. You saw my final, confirming test. He hates sugar in his coffee. Only likes it in his tea. I am worried. What I could do would be to give him some of my essence, but I don't know that it would help.'

Marko inwardly winced. 'No. That would not work, Stephine. He would implode with that knowledge, even in that state. He could not cope. What of Nail?'

'You have seen him, Marko. What are your thoughts?'

Marko grimaced a little, thinking that Stephine was also a little changed since she had come back from her creators and wondered if he should bring it up.

'He is more serious. A spark of fun is not there. But the other ACEs can teach that to him. Not sure about Fritz.'

Stephine slowly nodded. 'Yes. I agree about Nail. He is a construct so you and Topaz could do that as well with the

ACEs' help. Oh! Now there is a thought. I have believed for a long while that the Haulers created Fritz to solve their navigation problems for the very long-range jumps. All we have to do is find out which one made him. That entity could reintegrate Fritz's total mind again. Yes, that is what we will do.'

'I wonder, Stephine, if the same could be said about you. When you returned to us a tiny essence was missing from you. You are calmer, but a certain spark is also missing.'

Stephine looked down at him and he could see tiny tears form in her eyes.

'With everyone's help, I am slowly regaining that spark, Marko. It is good to be back exploring and learning again. So yes, I have a slightly different perspective to the one I once had.'

Marko sent her a smile and withdrew the tiny tentacle.

Patrick spoke through the audible comms system. 'All crew: we have synced movement with the target ice and metal asteroid. Astronomical drones are deployed to 100 kilometres out to watch for threats. Marko, the ice is your priority. Everyone else, including the ACEs and Jim, you have control of two drones each for rapid exploration and testing. Here are your individual areas to explore. We are down on all consumables. So as soon as viable mineral or metal masses are discovered please report them to me.'

Each one of the crew either folded out their forearm screens and took control of the drones, which were rapidly deploying from their housings on *Basalt*'s hull, or in the case of the ACEs and Jim simply took direct control through their internal comms systems.

While everyone else was sending their drones out across the asteroid to search and take samples of it, Marko quickly walked up the central spiral staircase until he was on the bridge deck. He marched in and gave the major, who was inside his large control pod, a quick nod, and then climbed into his own pod, the screens immediately coming alive. He quickly looked over the contents of the hundreds of tanks spread throughout the ship, noting those that were the most depleted, while he deployed the water-generating and gathering equipment which folded out of the exoskeleton like two large vinelike masses.

'Patrick, the gear is coming online. Can you please place us within contact distance of the best-looking ice?'

Patrick acknowledged and the ship slowly turned and moved a little closer.

On his screens Marko scanned for relatively clean areas of blue ice and as soon as he saw two good areas set sufficiently far apart, he manoeuvred the drilling units onto the ice's surface. As soon as they made contact, anchoring spears were fired into the ice and once he was satisfied with the positioning, he programmed them to grind themselves down through the surface.

As the heads were sunk metres into the ice, the collars around the head units heated up to red-hot, melting the ice around them, and then cooled quickly, sealing the units in as the ice refroze. Marko then switched on the powerful microwave units at the ends of the head units, which melted the ice and boiled the water, generating steam which flowed back up the pipes through banks of sensors and filters, before going through condensers, with the resultant pure water being pumped into the holding tanks.

'Major, good water, some nice trace element percentages coming in as well. About eight hours and I shall have the tanks full. I have started the matter to antimatter conversions as well.'

'Good. Pleased about that. Don't want to hang around any longer than that.'

As the hours ticked by, Marko sat and watched his equipment. The heating heads sank deeper and deeper into the ice and his mind wandered, wondering if one day while gathering water fuel the equipment would find some startling treasure. But the radar units only showed hundreds of metres of clear ice interspersed with rock and metal deposits. Reports came in from the crew members running the drones that they were finding useful deposits and, using nanote miners, started the extraction of iron and nickel, which was transferred onboard *Basalt* as dust.

He reached out and tapped Stephine's icon on the comms screen. Seconds later, her image smiled at him with the main control room of *Blackjack* in the background.

'Hello.'

'Just wanted to ask, Stephine, if the Games Board Soul Saver lance unit is intact?'

'Yes, as far as we can tell. Well, shall I say that nineteen entities appear intact. I don't believe that any were interrupted when they did their terminal uploads. But we are surprised, Marko, that they lost control of their antimatter units so quickly.'

Marko shrugged, dozens of possible scenarios flashing through his head. 'I have not had a look at the images of my Skua or Lily's Hanger. But I know that they had at least three adult Urchins tearing their way through the hull. Is it possible that the adults may have had young small ones attached to them? More creatures would equate to greater damage in those few moments. And the thought occurs that we are now in charge of our own recording and editing. I like that!'

Stephine laughed. 'See you in a few hours. We have found a sizeable piece of palladium and have the major's blessing to get it.'

The major had a smile on his face again. 'How you doing, Marko?'

Marko quickly looked over his screens, before he reported: 'Tanks full, boss. I am good to go. I see everyone else is onboard as well. Could keep going for another hour and fill all the fighters' and shuttles' tanks as well. But otherwise we are OK.'

The major tapped his chin, thinking. 'Hmm, tempting. You have a half-hour, so do the best you can and then we pull out. Patrick, hold off bringing the astronomical drones back in. Going to top up a little bit more.'

Twenty-five minutes later Marko instructed the water-harvesting units to detach themselves and over the next five minutes they folded back into themselves and locked against the exoskeleton. He opened a comms link to the major.

'Boss. Sorted. We are a shade under ninety-nine per cent capacity. All stowed.'

'Good. Thank you, Marko. Patrick, hold the astronomicals in pattern and let's ease away from the asteroid. Where is the biggest local Lagrange point?'

Basalt's AI replied a moment later. 'The most efficient one is 4284 kilometres from here. I have plotted in a course. Or we could return to the predator-inhabited one?'

The major shook his head. 'No, I think that we have had enough of that one. Whenever you are ready and keep our speed up at this stage. Ah, yes … and from our most up-to-date information, where is the closest Games Board presence?'

'There is an all-system carrier still in the Storfisk system,' Patrick replied. 'Looking at the sanctioned battle between the two Gjomvik forces of Leopard Strike and Aquila, I would say that we have ten days to get there before they leave. You keen to unload the Games Board data core?'

'Yes, Patrick, of course I am. Quicker we can off-load that and send them the information on how their frigate was destroyed, the happier I will be. Have no great desire to ingratiate ourselves to them, but nor do I want to piss them off again.'

'Understood, major. We will be at the jump point in approximately two hours. I presume that we jump back to the planet above the Urchin queen, see how the mind recovery is going, then back to Storfisk?'

'Yes, correct. All crew: let's have an early dinner, then final checks around the ship as we are going to go for a sedate orbit above the Urchin queen to see how our tech is behaving.'

As the rest of the crew had a quick meal and carried out as many final repairs as they could to the Hangers and Skuas, Patrick rotated the astronomical drones back to *Basalt* for refuelling. Close to the time for the jump, he pulled the drones back against the hull while everyone waited, either at their stations or onboard the available fighters sitting in their launch cradles.

Just before the package of electronics called the popper — tethered to the front of *Basalt* — was launched, an instant before the jump to ensure that they were not jumping into an obstacle, the major directed: 'All crew: be prepared for a hostile welcome. Jasmine, as soon as you can, trigger the comms unit to talk with the nanote unit on the queen.'

Seconds later, the power of the jump energy was discharged, driving the ship into a wormhole that connected to the leading Lagrange point of the blue Urchins' planet. As they appeared in real space, Jasmine focused her visual systems, looking for the enormous tower in which the queen lived.

'Major,' she said, 'I see that we are about ten minutes from a visual. I am querying the Fast Mover we left here, but I am not getting a return signal. Possibly it is out of sight. Launching astronomicals.'

'Hold them close, Jasmine. We may have to take them back in a hurry.'

'Understood. Seeing numerous Urchins in close orbit. Patrick?'

On everyone's screens, the position of the creatures was obvious. Veg frowned and was about to speak when Patrick said, 'I see them, increasing speed. Everyone, stand by for possible violent evasive manoeuvrings.'

Veg, sitting inside his command pod beside Stephine's, on the flight deck of *Blackjack*, tapped his screens to indicate something unusual to her. She grimaced and spoke quickly. 'Patrick! Look at the area we are indicating on the long-range screens. The Urchins! They are fleeing something! Look at the pattern!'

All the crew witnessed the Urchins in that particular quadrant moving at speed and the largest ones were starting to disappear altogether. Stephine spoke again. 'The big ones are jumping. Look at the trajectories. They are jumping in every direction. There is something big and very nasty there. Urchin killers!'

'Get us out of here, Patrick,' the major said urgently. 'All fighters, you are not to deploy. Get to your internal fighting stations now and man the heavy weapons. Jasmine? Anything?'

'Yes! Fast Mover is reporting that the minds of Fritz and Nail are sort of intact and that they have effectively gained control of the Urchin queen! It is remarkable!'

Stephine yelled into her microphone. 'Michael! It is imperative that the Urchin killer is either killed or severely injured. They hunt Urchins and will wait for years to attack a queen when she finally comes out of the atmosphere to mate.'

'Stephine, we can hear you just fine. How do you know that it's an Urchin killer and why would the queen come out of the atmosphere now?'

They could almost hear Stephine's teeth grinding as she tersely replied: 'Because, Michael, nothing makes Urchins react that way, and why do you think the queen was feeding so ravenously when we left here. It is rather obvious, I would have thought!'

'Right. How big will that bloody killer be then? And how the hell will she get up through the atmosphere, anyway?'

'The central mass will be anything up to 500 metres across, fully deployed like a bloom. Its tendrils will be in excess of ten to fifteen kilometres long, though at the base about fifty metres across. How will the queen get into orbit? I think if we look closely enough we will see that the jet streams around the planet, for the current stage of this small world's orbit of the gas giant, will be very powerful because the gas giant's closest approach to its star is coming soon. Those jet streams will dip down quite low into the planet's atmosphere. Also remember that this world has a lightweight central core, so the gravity is lowish.'

There was a short silence from the crew before Lily spoke. 'So it launches itself up into the high wind from the top of its tower and flies to the edge of space? How does it do that?'

'I am sorry, Lily,' Stephine sighed, 'of that I am not sure. I had hoped that we would find out a lot more about the Urchins, but I did not anticipate such large numbers of them here.'

Before she could continue, Patrick interrupted. 'Major, I have run the figures. Indeed, Stephine is right. The cumulative effect of the orbits will peak in just under four hours' time. The datastream from the Fast Mover is now complete. I have instructed it to rendezvous with us as soon as possible so it can refuel.'

Everyone spent the next little while working their way through the information. Stephine, Veg, *Blackjack*, the ACEs, and Marko in his sped-up state, assimilated it much faster than the others, and started a conversation between themselves while they waited for the rest of the crew.

'OK,' Marko began, 'the nanotes did their job. Gathered the recognisable parts of the two minds together, then created a working matrix of themselves to house it in and once Fritz and Nail gained consciousness they brought the outside reserve nanotes *inside* to map and take control of the queen's proto-mind. Damn! I can see why you are so keen to preserve this creature, Stephine.'

'Yes. Utterly unique. They can give us such extraordinary insights if we can save them. Also clever of Fritz and Nail to use the Urchins' own camouflage system to communicate with the Fast Mover by changing patterns on its surface.'

Blackjack chipped in. 'But how do we map the killer? It is logical to conclude that it has even more advanced camouflage measures as it hunts Urchins and they are noted for that ability. And of course it would stand to reason that there will be more than one.'

'Marko,' Veg asked. 'How much antimatter can you spare?'

'Hmm, hold on ... yes, a bit over two kilos. Why? If those things hunt Urchins, they would have a love of antimatter too, wouldn't they?'

Veg gave a short nod. 'Yes. But if it was a dust and was sprayed over the surface of the creature, we could possibly see it for a few seconds. But we would have to follow it up with compressors very quickly to damage it.'

Marko slowly nodded, allowing himself to come down to standard speed now that the other crew members were starting to talk amongst themselves.

'But what I want to know first,' Julie asked, 'is how many other queens are there on the surface? And if these killers are here, how many of them will we have to fight to protect that one? Would it not be better to shadow it, like a guard, as it came out of the atmosphere?'

'Yeah, you are right,' Harry answered. 'That is the smartest way to do it. We do not have that many compressors onboard anyway. And only a few dozen cobalts. And the fighters with their normal munitions loadouts would piss something that big off only a little bit.'

'Fuck it, why try to kill it? That great long stream of tentacles must mean one thing: they probably act like squid, as in shoot that mass forwards, grab the prey, then pull themselves up on it to chew away. Chop off the tentacles and they are stuffed. Nah. You lot can talk, I will go get to work.'

With that he rose from his pod and walked off, heading down the central staircase. Harry grinned.

'Bet ya the little bugger will make a very large garotte or a bolas, like Marko is so fond of. And probably string a couple of cobalts on it to give it a little extra bite. Major, I think that that is the best weapon to use. Fritz is right, they are hellish big to kill, but if we maim it at least the queen will have a fighting chance. But may I also suggest that we try a compressor against the core of it first? We have ten in our magazines.'

'OK, yes. I agree, Harry. Let's try a compressor first if we have to. Now, let me see if this is where you are headed with this wire weapon, Harry? Two drones with a 500-metre-long piece of mooring wire between them and a cobalt at each end. They race out and release the wire against the tentacles of one of these monsters and the ends wrap around. So not only will they cut — or should I say, we hope that they will cut — but it does not really matter if they do, as the cobalts when they come in contact, having whipped around, go bang anyway cutting everything away. Yeah. Good one! Do it. And if we do use it, let's make sure that it is recorded, as I love bonuses for novel weapon use.'

'But what if the mass of the tentacles is not that great?' Marko asked. 'Would it be like Urchin material? Enormously tough, but very lightweight. Will it have enough mass to make the wire bend around it? Think that it might be an idea to go have a look at one of these things first. Hellish dumb if we launch an attack at a critical time, when the queen is at her most vulnerable, and it does not work.'

Veg chimed in. 'Fritz. Is this what you are thinking of?'

Fritz was already in the engineering workshops, furiously programming the builder drones. 'Not quite to your plan. Three pieces of graphene mooring line. All tied to a cobalt at the centre. And the smallest rocket motors we have. So we use a missile at each end. We take them out with the lander, come in at high speed and drop them. They spin up when we fire the missiles, so they will spin like crazy and when they hit the killer, pull themselves down and then go boom bang. Except it will be in total vacuum so no sound effects.'

The major gave a short laugh. 'Good one, Fritz. Patrick, how long have we got before the queen will make her move?'

Stephine touched Veg so they could communicate mind to

mind. 'He might not be totally all there, but his engineering mind is working brilliantly.'

'Agreed.'

Then Veg spoke aloud. 'Yeah. That's better. Higher speed. More impact and it would not matter what part of these beasts it hits, it will still do damage.'

Julie, with Minh Pham, was quickly walking down to the engineering workshop deck.

'No-one has answered my question yet,' she said. 'How many queens are there that look like they are about to get into space?'

Patrick spoke. 'I have your answer, Julie. The Fast Mover estimated over 723.'

Minh Pham cleared his throat to ask, 'So has anyone got an idea of how we are to identify the one controlled by the Fritz and Nail mind?'

Stephine answered. 'We are working on that, Minh. According to the Fast Mover, from its conversations with the queen, they are quite slow. Like a standard human, but slowed by a factor of ten. And of course we need Patrick to interpret the light patterns for us.'

'OK, everyone,' the major said. 'Just so we are all on the same page here. We are going to have to keep moving. There are far too many Urchins around here anyway, to say nothing of the killers. Just hope like hell the predators don't decide to join in as well. Right. Looking at what Harry has sent me, we have enough materials to build ten of the bolas. Fritz, I just did some quick research. Two short lengths and one long. We release them with the two short ones to the front, and then the long one does the wrapping.'

A terse-sounding Fritz replied. 'I know! Just send as many as you can of the crew down here to help.'

The major smiled and shook his head. 'Yeah, same old Fritz. I was just trying to help. OK, ACEs go help Fritz. Harry and Veg are also on the way. Julie, Marko, Minh. Try and get that damaged Skua serviceable, please. We only have the three Hangers and two Skua, plus Harry's two-seater Skua ready to fight. Jasmine, Lily and Stephine. Start figuring a way to see those killers. We could try Veg's antimatter dust trick, but I fear that will just get a shitload of Urchins all fired up and looking for the source. Find us a better way, please. Patrick, try to hold us so that the astronomicals can see and communicate with the queen. Go to it, people.'

The major looked over his screens. 'Well, Patrick, what are your thoughts?'

'I am talking with the queen. It is most interesting. Incidentally, as one entity, the combination of minds now call themselves Zawgyi. And they are basically one entity. I wonder if this has occurred, as they are effectively ghosts inhabiting an alien, so that it is easier to get along, or maybe it is a side effect of the nanote matrix that they are within. We will have to learn more about this. Oh, and this Zawgyi is female which is understandable, I suppose. And she is overcome with the urge to get her offspring into space, mate with the gathering males and then leave this system to look for another warm water planet with a better food source.'

The major sat very still for a few moments, wondering about the ramifications of letting such a hybrid loose on the universe.

'Oh, shit. You know, Patrick, the most logical thing would be to drop a compressor down on it and run away. But ... Stephine would not forgive us for that. OK, pass all that information on to her, Veg and Marko. We need to talk about this. And we have to make this decision.'

While he waited, Michael climbed out of his pod and did a few stretches to loosen up tight muscles, wondering why the really weird stuff seemed to happen around him and *Basalt*. When his comms screen chimed, he climbed back into the pod, allowing the seat to grasp and gently restrain him just in case Patrick decided that rough manoeuvres were required. The faces of his friends looked at him as he opened the discussion.

'It is logical to kill it. What happens if this queen decides to go and settle on a human-occupied planet? The entity now known as Zawgyi would have Nail's and Fritz's memories, would it not?'

Stephine was shaking her head. 'Really need to pull in Lily and Jasmine as they have more knowledge on this, but it's my understanding that the immersion transference would only have been of the subject's conscious mind ... more about emotions, self awareness, interests, and the questions that were going on in the individual's head.'

Marko looked very serious. 'Quick way to find out. Patrick, ask Zawgyi where it intends to go on leaving this planet. And how long it will take to mate?'

'The questions have been sent, Marko.'

'So while we wait for the answers,' Veg said, 'I also have serious qualms about letting this chimera loose on the universe. If we allow it to live, will its future offspring also be further down the road towards complete sentience, and is this method of uplift to sentience a natural evolution or an interference?'

Stephine nodded. 'It is a good question. Yes, it is an interference, but evolution does not care how the action occurred, only that it did. We do not know how stable the sentience is. I have looked through the octopoid Library records again and cross-referenced them with Lily and Jasmine's Hauler knowledge. The nanote design that they gave us for the containment matrix is a quite stable one. The creature is now a chimera of a non-standard human, an ACE and a proto-sentient Urchin queen. If it is stable, I feel that it must be given a chance to survive, even for knowledge's sake. We know a lot about the Urchins, but there are still many questions. I would suggest that the test of that mental stability is coming very soon. If it can get itself out of the atmosphere, I would say that it should be given a chance.'

Patrick spoke up. 'Well, I am not sure if we are going to like the answers. The mating will be achieved quickly, in that the courtships have been going on for weeks with displays of physical prowess and patterns on the males' surfaces that give the female pleasure. These all go on at night when the queens observe the males dancing above the atmosphere at a distance of 220 kilometres. Zawgyi has already selected three males. She told me that any one of them will be absorbed and, if available, all three.'

Marko could not help himself, knowing that they all really wanted to know the answer to the destination question. 'Absorbed, Patrick? What do you mean, absorbed?'

'The males attach themselves to the queen and become parasitic, eventually being completely absorbed by her. Now the other answer: she will go to Storfisk as she says it is a good warm planet and she craves the warmth.'

There was a long silence. Stephine was the first to say something. 'Oh, now that is most intriguing. From what we know of Urchins, it is too warm, too thick an atmosphere and at almost a full standard gravity so far, too big a gravity well for her to survive in let alone be able to climb out of back into space. So there must have been a thought contamination.

Either Nail or Fritz were thinking of Storfisk when the transference occurred. Hold on. I shall ask them.'

'So it is going to kill itself anyway,' the major said, sounding relieved. 'That takes the burden off us at least. Patrick, keep us appraised of the conversation. Stephine, did you learn anything?'

'Yes, Nail was chewing on a piece of licorice from Storfisk at the time of the transference. I am not entirely certain how the knowledge of where the planet is came into Zawgyi's collective mind, but it could be that at the instant of the mind-snatch, Nail and Fritz wished they were somewhere else, and then from Fritz's extraordinary conscious mind the coordinates were gained. Patrick, is there any way that Zawgyi can be convinced to go somewhere else?'

'Nope. I would doubt that very much. This is a harsh martial mentality that we are dealing with. It is just on the level of reasonable human sentience, although more advanced than the Urchin infant we had dealings with at the octopoid library, which I considered had the intelligence of a parrot. This one is more like a petulant seven-year-old standard human. I don't think we could sway it.'

The major quickly headed off any more discussion. 'Right, as far as I am concerned the entity is going to die of its own volition. So we do not have to hasten its demise on that count. Patrick, could you ask how many jumps it will have to make to get to Storfisk, and how long it will take it to get there? Stephine, Veg and Marko, thanks, now everyone back to work.'

He reached out and tapped his comms screen. 'OK. Stephine, Lily, Jasmine, have you come up with any other ways of painting these things so we know where they are?'

'We know how,' Jasmine said. 'Need three of the Fast Mover drones with plenty of fuel, and three of Patrick's hull laser radar units. Send them out, have them fire off a burst of laser, move, and do it again and again. Stephine's information said that the killers will react to the lasers as they will know that the Urchins will also go looking for them. The Fast Movers send the information back to Patrick after each shot and he paints up the maps.'

The major smiled. 'Good work. Harry, how many of those heavy firework bombs did you make?'

'What! How the fuck did you know about them?'

Michael laughed for the first time in hours. 'Because I am the commander of this ship and I should know everything! So, how many and how big?'

'Ten. Good big ones. You need 'em? We were building them as a surprise for Waipunga's bicentennial celebrations and I know that you love 'em as well.'

The major's smile was broad. 'OK, send them to the Fast Movers' equipment loadouts. Set command fuses on them. Might as well have as many surprises as possible and I don't really want to maim or kill too many of the Urchin killers if we can avoid it.'

'Thought that you hated Urchin?' Harry grunted.

'Yeah, but that is a bit like hating ocean predators. They are what they are and are just trying to get along with their lives like the rest of us, even if they are operating on instinct. Thanks, Harry. Jasmine, Harry is sending down ten 200-millimetre fireworks bombs. Instruct the loadouts to attach the mortar tubes to all of the Fast Movers. Go with three, three, and four. Wire them for command firing and delayed detonation. And go ahead and attach a cobalt missile on each one as well. You will have control of them. Launch when ready.'

Jasmine's fingers flew over her screens, waking up the ten-metre-long, wasp-shaped drones, dropping their instructions into their semi-autonomous computer controllers, then instructing the loaders to attach what she wanted to the Fast Mover drones. The machines slid out of their storage units, rotated, and tucked themselves up against the robotic waldos that seized the long-range fuel tanks, placing and locking them on. Then the cobalt missile was presented, which was grasped and placed up against a uni-mount. Seeing where Harry's mortars were, she instructed ammunition magazines to load them into their individual mortar tubes, then had them sent via the heavily armoured delivery tubes out to the waiting drones.

Fifteen minutes later the drones were ready, so she tapped the comms icon of the major. 'Boss, the Fast Movers are prepped and ready to be deployed. Shall I arm the antigravity self-destructs? And is it worthwhile to consider an enhanced neutron device?'

'Yes, arm the self-destructs, plus the antimatter containments. Launch two. Get them underway and let me think about the END weapon for a couple of minutes.'

Looking at his displays, he tracked the two Fast Movers as they rocketed away. His fingers drummed his chair armrests as he thought about the three radiation weapons in the magazines, knowing that, strictly speaking, *Basalt* should not have them as they were banned by most factions. He grimaced a little, also knowing how hard it had been to get them in the first place. Making up his mind, he tapped Jasmine's icon.

'Yes, place a neutron device on the third unit, but we don't tell anyone else about it, OK?'

'Of course, major. Will launch in five minutes.'

'Thanks, Jasmine.' He tapped another of the comms icons. 'Fritz. How are you getting on with those bola units?'

'Done. Loaded into a crude, but hopefully effective, launch mechanism and will be placing them in the back of the *Albatross* lander in a few moments.'

'The *Albatross* ... and in the back? I thought that we had decided to use drones?'

'You might have decided that, major, but I can't see how to make it work in the hellishly fucking short time frame we have. They will have to be manually released.'

Michael Longbow furiously rubbed his scalp, very unhappy with the prospect, but knew that Fritz, even in his not quite all there state, would have thought through every possible solution and the resultant scenarios.

'OK, do what you have to do to make it work, Fritz.'

He closed that icon off and tapped Harry's. Before he could ask the question, Harry answered it: 'Yeah, I know, boss. Bit scary, eh! Actually, it's not quite as bad as you think. Marko will pilot, Minh and I will deploy the units only if we have to. We have a good launch unit which is three pieces of channel that we are about to bolt to the floor of the lander to create a separation of the three parts. Cobalt in each one and the middle one has a micro-missile attached to it. The cables tie the whole thing together. Press the tit and the missile drags the whole thing out the arse end of the lander.'

'Holy shit, Harry, that is just mad! Hellish risky for everyone involved!'

The big, solid grinning man agreed. 'Yeah! I know! We have been laughing about it all the time. Nuts! That's why we love it. But it's OK as Stephine and Veg will be riding shotgun in *Blackjack* anyway. It's all good.'

'Yeah, fucking nuts.' The major shook his head and sighed. 'So how long before you are ready? Oh, and you had better have wire-timed self-destructs into the cobalts. Those we do not want flying through this star system for years.'

'Not a problem. Veg has already sorted that, and destructs along the mooring lines as well. Should be good to go in about fifty minutes.'

Haast

Above Gas Giant Moon

Bob Thompson looked over his entire crew, lined up and standing to attention in their respective units, wearing their dress uniforms. Behind him was a Games Board monitor recording everything, and he could see down the length of the one deck of the carrier that was kept clear of everything just for such occasions, three other monitors.

Major Nick Warne had called the crew to attention as their commander walked across to the slightly raised platform. They saluted each other as Bob took Nick's place. He then looked out over the non-smiling faces and barked out, 'Stand at ease, stand easy, please sit.'

The crew did as ordered and sat, almost totally synchronised except for the rare few whose skills he valued higher as technicians and highly skilled individuals than soldiers who were good at their parade ground drill.

Everything was completely still. The only sounds came from the air-circulation systems and the monitor closest to him turning on its antigravity and panning its recording units across the assembly and up to his face. He marvelled at the Hauler's perfect control of the ship's deceleration, tail first towards the target moon of one of the star system's enormous gas giants at a precise one gravity, so allowing the crew to move about inside *Haast* with ease and comfort; the carrier was due to be placed outside *Rose Foxtrot* in a few hours.

'Crew of Gjomvik Corporation Boltz light carrier *Haast*. This is our last few hours of peace before we are placed in orbit around the designated moon. The battles commence with the Gjomvik Corporation Aquila carrier *Berkut* at first light tomorrow morning, above the designated combat area on the planet below us. Before the formal orders and information packs are distributed, I just want to say that so far it has been my great pleasure to be your commander. You are an excellent hand-picked crew and this is a very fine ship. I hope that within a week we shall be at the after-match banquet together, all in fine spirits, having fought a good-quality battle to decide which of the two corporations is granted the mining rights to the nickel asteroid. Be proud in yourselves, be proud in all you do, fight to the absolute best of your abilities, and then some. Let us make good AV and justify the faith that our employer Baron Willie der Boltz has placed in us.'

He turned to Nick Warne and saluted again. Nick called the room to attention as Bob exited to climb up the central staircase heading for his ready room behind the bridge. He wondered at the point of the little rah-rah speech and having everyone spick and span in their best uniforms, looking beautiful for the AV, but knew that it was the way it had always been done for the Games Board presentations and so had become the tradition.

Before he got to the bridge deck, the crew lifts were already busy disgorging crew getting straight back to the flight deck, or back to their quarters to get changed into their ship suits and put their precious dress uniforms back into storage.

He walked in through the doors of the ready room, quickly checked if any messages or urgent decisions needed attention from him and, finding none, then made his way into his accommodation and changed out of his pearl white uniform with its perfect creases and back into his considerably more comfortable ship suit. Just as the suit finished sealing itself against him, his comms chimed with the smiling face of the Countess Michelle dressed in the Administration Council's emerald-green uniform of an adjutant captain.

'I was expecting you to give a long battle-rousing speech!' she told him. 'Most welcome change having a short low-key one. Not sure if the Games Board was happy, but the crew love you all the more for it. Can we have a quick meeting, please? Have something interesting to share with you.'

He frowned, listening to the few key words that Michelle had spoken, knowing that whatever she wanted to talk about was very important. 'Of course. My ready room in five minutes?'

'See you shortly. I have some quality blue cheese and I shall bring a fruit platter.'

A few minutes later they were sitting at a low table with food and drink spread out in front of them. Bob raised an eyebrow and Michelle flicked across a recognition laser message from her right eye into his. His own bio-software checked it, and recognised the sender as Michelle and sent back his codes. He then separated one part of his brain from the other as the two started a verbal conversation about the merits, or otherwise, of the local wines, while on a higher level they conversed with non-interceptable light.

'Well, Michelle?'

'It's as we suspected, Bob. I now know who it is and where the messages are going, but as yet I am not able to find out the contents of the data packages.'

'Who?'

'Flight maintenance, Staff Sergeant Adrian Crow.'

'He was foisted upon us by his high-ranking aunt. Nick wanted to throw him off the ship as soon as he presented himself with his papers. Have you informed Uncle and *Haast*? Dumb ... did he not know that we would be watching him closely?'

'I know that he has at least one accomplice here onboard. As yet we cannot identify that individual. The data packages were going to the Hauler orbital Angelito.'

'And Angelito, as we know, Michelle, is in the sway of Jet the trickster. It is a logical fit. What do you suspect his game is?'

'Exactly that. Fixing the game or a part of the battle. That would be the easiest money for him. But, Bob, I think that there is a much bigger game afoot. I believe Adrian is being played for a fool. He is dancing to someone else's tune.'

'Really! Michelle, you have never struck me as one to take flights of fancy. What do you know?'

'*Haast* knows something. And these two crews — both us and *Berkut* — are so stacked, not just with stars of the Games Board world of entertainment, but a whole lot of other masters at their game. And I am talking about really good combat specialists, to say nothing of one of the most notable strategic and tactical masters anywhere. Did you stop to ask yourself why Brigadier Mortlock would be here?'

'Well, no, I did not. I thought that maybe the Baron was giving me a set of lessons. That is what Mark de Ruyter told me.'

The next lasered message had icons of mirth attached to it. 'Oh, I love you, Bob, you really are such a gentle soul. And Mark is being a little bit bad in saying that. Maybe he did not want to hurt your feelings. Look, the brigadier is one of the most highly paid of any of the Gjomvik forces. The Games Board must have groaned very loudly when told that he was going to be on this mission. His continuation of life fees would be exorbitant, even by the Games Board's standards. No, the brigadier took over that crew for a much greater purpose than showing you a few pointers on how to run a battle.'

'Bloody hell! So why am I here? This is not doing a great deal for my confidence you know, Michelle.'

The next icon was of a shoulder shrug and the following a humourless laugh. 'Don't be foolish, commander. You are here because you are hellish good at what you do, which is get the job done. I think that you need to have a private conversation with Brigadier Mortlock. I shall set it up with *Haast* through the ACEs' private comms channels. Stand by ... it is set up, Bob. The call is going through now. Focus your eye on the light on the wall to the right of the door. *Haast* will encrypt it. Uncouple your left eye and focus that on me so I can help if necessary.'

Seconds later, the softly spoken voice of the brigadier came into Bob's head via the laserlink and his own internal hardware. 'Ah, my friend, the commander. To what do I owe this not totally unexpected call via the ACEs' network?'

Bob wondered about swapping pleasantries, but decided that the brigadier would probably appreciate a straight no-nonsense approach. 'Why are you here, Roger?'

'The same as you, Bob. We are here to fight a fearsome battle with every level of excitement to entertain the great unwashed, of course. Why else would I be here?'

'As a backup for something much more important. Something that is happening on the planet Storfisk, maybe?'

Without a second's hesitation the brigadier changed tack. 'You, Haast, the countess and Uncle. We meet on *Rose* in fifteen minutes. Oh, and if you have some spare, more of those excellent sausages created by Mr Antipas, please.'

The connection was severed.

The verbal conversation between Bob and Michelle continued for a few more minutes, concluding on the subject of what Michelle considered to be an excellent Merlot, and as it happened, Bob agreed with her choice.

He lasered a final message to her. 'Well, that is intriguing. Dress?'

'Combat, full camouflage. Uncle and Haast are on their way to *Rose*. A invitation from her has just arrived for them to see Daisuke Suzuki about a sword. Both have logged as going off-ship and the Games Board monitors are showing nil interest. We have five minutes to get to the airlock.'

Bob allowed himself a tight smile as he stripped and backed up against one of his suit containers for it to form around him. He glanced across, seeing Michelle doing the same; the room, on her instructions, locked itself into a privacy setting that told the monitors the room was closed to their scrutiny. Let them think what they liked, he thought.

In one part of his ready room wall, a holographic image was generated in the outside corridor that showed normal wall, while a panel slid silently aside allowing them, with suits activated, to step into the hallway and make their way unseen to the airlock, where Uncle and Haast were waiting.

Haast and Uncle could see them from their suit recognition codes and nonchalantly activated the airlock, letting the two inside, as they themselves walked in and cycled the party through. Once they were inside the connecting tube Bob called a halt and another silent conversation started.

'Haast, Uncle. Time to fill in your part-time, commander. What is occurring on Storfisk? We are about to go into a meeting with the brigadier, and no doubt some of his top people, and I want to know what is happening, please.'

The great bird looked at the commander for a few long seconds, then finally said, 'It is a long-term intelligence operation. It involves an alien predator created by the octopoids that is, at present, loose amongst the herds of herbivores on the Haulers' continent. We are here to be humanity's cavalry and ride in over the horizon and save the day, as we, so conveniently, just happen to be in the neighbourhood, fighting another battle.'

Uncle nodded in agreement. 'Quite simple really, commander. On occasion it is time for a cleanout of the rot. This is just the trigger point that identifies those amongst us who are not really team players. Those that are out for their own gain at the cost of others.'

Michelle touched his elbow. 'And you are here, Bob, because you are one of the good guys. The Games Board and the public like and admire you.' She pointed to the other two, and then herself. 'Whereas we are not so. We are the cleaners and we do the tasks that must be done to protect everyone, including you as the commander of *Haast*.'

A tiny chill ran down his spine and he found his mouth dry as he realised that even if he was one of the good guys, his own people would destroy him in a heartbeat if it was necessary for their cause.

'So, you all have my back, huh? OK, let's go see the brigadier and Mr Suzuki.'

Uncle looked the commander in the eyes and sent him a laser message. 'You and I have been through an awful lot of shit, boss, from me as a ragged-arse corporal when you were a green-tinged second lieutenant until now. Don't worry about the countess and big bird here. I really do have your back.'

Bob allowed himself a little smile, knowing full well that the cyborg would tell him — then give him a few extra seconds to make his peace — if he was about to let him die.

Haast spoke up. 'Your camouflage systems are not required here in the boarding bridge. *Rose Foxtrot* is aware of all of us and I cannot detect any recording or watching devices from our ship or the Games Board.'

They entered and cycled through the airlock to be met by Daisuke Suzuki and Wardah, wearing ship suits, and accompanied by a magnificent giant otter ACE. Daisuke introduced everyone and, lastly, the two ACEs, who as soon as the standard humans had started to walk towards the transport capsule started a high speed conversation.

'Nice to see you again, Haast. Rose is most interested to see what you saw of the alien predator on Storfisk. She has seen the files you sent me, but wishes to experience the evidence of your senses, especially the smell of the creature.'

The eagle looked across at the silver-furred otter. 'And indeed it is good to see you again, Madeye. As the others converse, I shall link into *Rose*. I don't think that Commander Thompson is too happy about these events and that he is just now learning what this is about.'

Madeye gave her old friend a very human shrug as they moved into the capsule with the others. 'Well, he is probably going to be even less impressed when he learns about our little game, eh!'

The doors closed as the seats enfolded their charges, including the otter and the eagle, and the capsule accelerated to high speed, going straight across the Hauler. Minutes later it decelerated hard and the doors opened on a stark utilitarian domed room with the brigadier and his small party entering from the opposite side.

The otter and the eagle looked at the dragon and moved across the floor to introduce themselves.

'I see you, Tengu,' Haast said. 'Your name, please, and may I inquire what generation you are? Please forgive me, but your type is spoken about quietly, although rarely met in the flesh as it were.'

The quiet, refined voice of the Tengu answered, with a small nod of his armoured head. 'And I see you, Haast and Madeye. It is my pleasure to meet you both. I am Andreas, commander of the Q3.'

Madeye whistled. 'Shit! They are not pissing about, are they! The latest version. I shall serve with you with honour.'

Haast smiled and nodded his head, then said to Madeye, 'Where can we all link to *Rose*?'

She pointed as a piece of the wall folded out for them to jack their datalinks into the Hauler.

Roger Mortlock looked up at Uncle and solemnly shook him by the hand, double-grasping Uncle's right wrist as he said, 'I was very sorry to hear about Lorraine, my old friend. Indeed, it was a great shock to learn of her total death because the Soul Saver life continuation had been denied her. I do wish you had contacted me, Graham, I could possibly have done something about that. I sent a few messages to you, but obviously you did not get them.'

Uncle looked down at his one-time commander when he had first been a private soldier, then a young corporal serving for the administration, and felt a pang of guilt that he had not returned the brigadier's messages at the time, but also a flare of anger over what had happened to his wife.

'Thank you, sir. That is a most kind sentiment. Yes. It was a bad thing.'

Without letting go his hand, Roger Mortlock looked deeply

into the cyborg's eyes, seeing the levels of tech, but also seeing the man's seething anger. He nodded as he let go of Uncle's hand, and turned to Bob and Michelle. 'Well, Commander Thompson. Tell me of what you know?'

Bob felt his anger rising about having been so badly manipulated, realising that the whole thing was a charade largely because he had honestly believed that his time as a real independent commander of a carrier had come.

'A predator created by the octopoids is currently down on the Haulers' continent, prowling amongst the herbivores. In which case, what the hell are we doing here, way the hell out in the system about to fight a mock battle!'

The brigadier looked up at him, holding his angry gaze, and slowly nodded, feeling a little sorry for the man. 'So you believe you can justifiably feel aggrieved that your fight against *Berkut* is a false one. Is that it, commander? Or are you just angry at being manipulated? You are a smart guy, a good honest leader. You do tend to let a few too many of your feelings show, but as a person who has studied the art of conflict for a long time, I have to say that, to date, your battles have been bravely fought and with a certain amount of flair.'

Bob growled. 'Is that a statement or a series of questions, brigadier?'

Roger Mortlock gave a small grunt and then a wide, beaming smile which reached to his eyes. He clapped Bob on the upper arm and gave it a little squeeze. 'My jolly good friend. This whole wonderful toybox of ours is one gigantic charade. Always was and always will be. It's always about money and power. I don't know what the octopoids use for currency, but I bet you a dollar to a pinch of goatshit they play the same games. The trick here is to ensure that those under our charge have the best possible time of it.'

He rubbed his hands together and continued. 'Yes, there are a bunch of nasties on the planet. We suspected that they were coming, but did not know where. That is why the command of *Berkut* was given to me weeks after the carrier had got here. Now, you see that dragon over there? He is the commander of two companies of Q3. What you might not know, Bob, is that each one of those Tengu is inhabited by an individual human mind. Each of those minds are martial fanatics. Each has trained and fought, in some cases, for lifetimes. They fought hard just to become the most elite troops I have ever known. So we have plenty of capability to deal with what is on the planet.'

Bob slowly nodded. 'Yeah, OK, I buy that, but why are they not down on the planet killing the predators? Oh! Hold on, I see, you are waiting for information. Uncle, you said that it was time for a cleanout. So there is a human connection to all of this? Shit! Another Infant-style fuck-up!'

Roger smiled again, saying, 'Now you get the picture. Good. Yes, we fight the lovely little scrap on the nasty windy mountainous moon below us and then when the timing is right, *Rose* gathers us up and those who are killed or maimed by our punch-up get loaded, heroically, into a mechanical chassis so they can carry on fighting; any spare equipment or craft that we need are already here onboard *Rose*. We identify the connections, find the craft that brought the predators here and clean up the lot. It's a good plan, but it is also full of barbed hooks which is why you and I are here.'

There was a sudden commotion amongst the ACEs with two of them running towards them and Haast actually flying. At the same time, Wardah spoke rapidly: 'Quickly! You have five minutes to get off *Rose*! There is an emergency and she is preparing to leave the system. Quickly, this way!'

Bob was about to ask questions, so she grabbed his elbow and roughly pushed him towards the capsule whose doors were opening. He looked over his shoulder to see the brigadier and his party also running towards their capsule.

The doors to the capsule were closing, even before Bob was seated, as Uncle grabbed him, forcing him down on the floor.

'Seal your suit now, commander.'

As he thought about it, the suit sealed with its helm forming up out of its collar, covering his face and automatically setting the air supply. The acceleration of the capsule was severe, shoving him up against the seat base with Uncle who had locked himself against the wall and held him firmly, so he did not slide further. Looking across, he could see that Haast had enfolded Michelle, protecting her.

There was a second when the acceleration ceased which gave Uncle just enough time to scoop his commander off the floor and hold him tightly against him as the violent deceleration occurred. The doors slammed open and they stumbled out of the capsule and into the airlock.

As they cycled through, Bob finally managed to ask, 'What the fuck is going on?'

Uncle answered tersely. 'In a minute! The instruments on the door are showing hard vacuum inside the access tube and the air is being sucked out of this airlock at a hellish rate. When we are through, we all run. Haast, power up your antigrav. I shall tow you.'

Seconds later they were sprinting across the access tube as Haast lasered an emergency override to the outer airlock door on the carrier's hull. Just as they arrived, the door opened and the four boosted themselves across the expanding gap of the disengaged access tube and into the waiting open airlock.

The outer door closed and air rushed into the lock and a moment later the inner door opened.

The other three ran past him as Bob marched around the corner and onto the bridge, finding a hive of activity in progress. He climbed into his command pod, which was already operational, to see Nick watching him from the 2ICs' pod and *Haast* quickly being pushed out of the Haulers' docking bay. Nick nodded and gave him a wink.

'You are late but at least you are correctly dressed, commander,' Nick commented. 'Mind telling me what is happening?'

'Looks like we are being launched a little earlier than planned, Mr Warne.'

'Really!'

Nick climbed out of his pod and walked across and leaned into Bob's pod and murmured, 'Next time you go off ship without telling me, I shall boot you up the arse. OK! We did not know where the hell you and that bloody snooty countess of yours were. I don't give a flying fuck what you are up to or where you are going, but you bloody well tell me. Agreed?'

Bob looked into his old mentor's eyes and nodded, wondering if he should tell him the whole story. 'Yes. Sorry. That was a bit rash of me. Are we OK?'

Nick's face twitched with a tiny smile. 'Of course. What did you expect? Everyone is standing to.'

Nick then turned, speaking loudly: 'Helm! Give us a five-kilometre separation from the Hauler as quick as you can when the locks are disengaged.'

Bob tapped his comms screen on Haast's icon. 'OK, big bird. What happened?'

Haast looked out from Bob's screen and answered. 'Madeye, me and the Tengu commander were talking about

234

things and Glint and *Basalt* came up in the conversation. Madeye asked if I knew where they were headed and if they were due back for the 200-year celebration on Storfisk as she was keen to see them again. I answered with the coordinates of the system and planet they were travelling to in order to study Urchins. Glint had given them to me as I had asked him where they were going and would I be allowed to see the information on the Urchins when they came back. An instant after I gave them, *Rose Foxtrot* broke into the conversation.'

Bob felt his heart sink as Haast continued. 'She yelled that they were going to the wrong place and they should have been going to another system close by. She said she should have told them herself instead of trusting the information to Angelito to pass on. Rose then gave what sounded like a little sob and softly said that they were probably already destroyed as that place was known to have the creatures that hunt Urchins. There had been a massive concentration of Urchin breeders on the planet and none known to have escaped from that system. I can only conclude that Rose is going to attempt to rescue them.'

Bob groaned. 'Oh, shit. This is really, really bad. As soon as we can see *Berkut*, get me a secure comms link to the brigadier.'

He reached out and touched the ship-wide comms icon. 'Crew. This is the commander. Due to a rescue mission needing the assistance of the Hauler, we are now deployed a little earlier than expected. As far as I am aware, we will continue as planned in the morning. Stand down, all of you not required on duty. Bridge out.'

He clambered out of his pod and walked across to Nick Warne's. 'Mr Warne, please take the ship to the original designated coordinates above the planet at your leisure. As soon as you are able to pass control to Major de Ruyter, then please come find me for a private briefing.'

He then turned on his heel and walked into the intelligence suite, plonking himself down in a chair to wait for the great eagle to finish whatever he was doing. As he sat, he could feel the ship's attitude change and the distant rumble of the rockets coming online. Tapping his wrist, the large personal screen rolled up out of its slim housing and came alive. He tapped the commands for the ship's exterior cameras and after a few seconds found the image of the Hauler under full power blasting its way across to the edge of the nearest Lagrange point. He then searched for *Berkut* and was just in time to watch the capture of a large, lumpy cylindrical container which was pulled down into an external bay. He zoomed up on the container just as Haast turned to him. Looking up, he lasered a question: 'What's that for, Haast?'

'I'd say that it contains a half-company of Tengu with equipment which would consist of weapons, rations and micro-aircraft. Would appear that the brigadier is thinking ahead. I am a little surprised that Rose did not send us both the other half of the Tengu contingent, but then again that may have been a little difficult to explain away to the Games Board. And I have your link to the brigadier open.'

Bob nodded his thanks and waited for the image of Roger Mortlock to appear on his screen.

Seconds later, it did, so he sent a laser message straight into one of the brigadier's eyes. 'Seems that *Basalt* is in deep shit. You know anything about it?'

'No, I am not privy to any of that research. Bit mad if you ask me, but then again *Basalt* is so well known and so wealthy, the ship and crew can pretty much do anything they please.

You do know that there is a connection between the brothers and Rose, don't you?'

Bob frowned. 'No?'

'Baron Willy der Boltz and Major Michael Longbow are brothers separated shortly after birth. Willy went to one part of the distant family as a der Boltz, owner of who knows how much manufacturing capability, and Michael to another part of the family who were modest engineers. Rose is a very old aunt in the Boltz family and probably the only one of them who will ever become a Hauler, as by all accounts she really was, and is, a good honourable person. Neither of the men know of the connection with her. That is why she took off at such speed. I wonder what the Hauler orbital Angelito will make of it ... but if Michael and crew are hurt, or, Hades help us all, killed, I would think that Angelito's days as a sentient are numbered.'

'So we are bang smack in the middle of plotting and machinations which could become unstuck?'

The brigadier looked very serious as he nodded. 'I am afraid so, commander. Bit of a baptism of fire for your first command, eh, Bob. You probably wished for a nice simple quality battle. Not going to happen.'

He watched Bob grimace as he continued speaking: 'Right. We have work to do and the Games Board must not become aware of it. Basically, we need to knock the hell out of each other, but minimise losses of craft or people. We have four days of punch-up and then I believe it best that we make our way back to Storfisk under our own power. *Berkut* can do that journey in eight days and knowing the specs of *Haast* you will only be a day behind. Only problem is, we will have totally exhausted our fuel water. We will have to take additional water from the moon below us.'

'How are you going to explain the Tengu to the Games Board?'

The brigadier smiled. 'Did not have to. Rose let them out immediately after we grabbed the container and took it into the hangar, while we had our own contingent of monitors looking the other way. If you look, you will only see the Games Board airship now. No doubt having to brake hard as their velocity is probably relatively high having been spat out at speed.'

Bob let himself smile at the thought of the Games Board's discomfort. 'So what is the plan to minimise damage while we are firing munitions at each other?'

'I am sending you the specs. Uncle knows about this sort of thing for ammunition. Give him this file. We don't tell our pilots or assault crews, but we doctor the rounds. Basically, they will punch into anything they hit, but vaporise instantly leaving a nice smoky hole but hopefully not a great deal of damage underneath. Oh, and have Uncle set the damage assessment systems onboard the aircraft to simulate critical failures if those dummy rounds hit vital systems. With his equipment he can do that remotely. And I will advise my crews that it is better to maim than kill.'

'OK,' Bob responded, 'we will do the same. So we just let the battles unfold, then hope like hell we have enough firepower to deal with whatever is on Storfisk afterwards?'

'Yes. Let us plan for all contingencies and hope that *Rose Foxtrot* gets back in time to pick us up. But I doubt it very much, unless she has jump-drive capabilities that I am unaware of. The coordinates of the star system in which *Basalt* is located is five days at full power for *Rose*, plus another day down through the Lagrange points, then find them — or not — and get back here. No, we are on our own. If she gets back here, even after the fastest of journeys, we will be on Storfisk.'

Ayana

Haulers Territory on Storfisk

Ayana was resting high inside the huge baobab tree, waiting and staring out into the darkness. Sven was down inside the tree, using their astronomical equipment to watch the Hauler orbital Angelito.

'Yeah. Another fast picket just arrived at Angelito. Wonder what bullshit he has had a reply to this time?'

Ayana shrugged. 'If we live long enough, we will find out, maybe. How close are the latest batch of swallows?'

'Should be ready an hour before dawn. Am impressed how many we have managed to manufacture over the last four days.'

'Yes, Sven, but how many more do we need to be able to set up our own secure communications system away from the official ACE one? Hundreds, we need hundreds more and we are running out of supplies and raw materials. Ha! Just had a recognition laser from Maqua. She, Harold and the two Tengu will be here in fifteen minutes.'

'Good! They are on time. Yes, we need more birds, Ayana, but at least with the ones already deployed and those being created we can cover this area well. And the first ones we made are already with the other ACEs who are making more. It will take another twenty days to make our own secure intelligence network for this part of the continent.'

'Maqua asks what we are seeing of the alien.'

'Tell her the whole muscle mass of each bluebuck's limb, that the alien put something into and stitched shut, has slid off the hip and leg bones. There is fresh immature skin, and also muscle groups, growing on the bones. The animal is standing guard over masses of sluglike material on the ground. Not even insects are allowed close. Even had them leaping at the swallows as they flew past. Tell her the aliens are harvesting the animals. I agree with you, Ayana. This thing is building more of itself or something worse.'

Sven continued to pad slowly along, looking at the tiny machines, each of which contained a swallow chick at some stage of growth. He felt satisfaction at doing something, not just waiting to see how things worked out, and he enjoyed the creation of useful creatures ... even though the swallows were a little different from normal in that they carried audiovisual gear in their heads and laser communication equipment.

'Maqua says that the Tengu are splitting off,' Ayana said, breaking into his reverie. 'One is going to attack the alien while the other snatches one of those masses on the ground and has a close look at it.'

Sven gasped. 'Shit! Just as well Angelito cannot see them. How is he going to take a shadow attacking the alien though? He will decide instantly that it is us.'

Ayana laughed. 'Angelito will have a problem with that. A Q-version Tengu landed on the orbital about ten hours ago. Going to start messing with him.'

Sven did a little dance with glee. 'The Qs are here! Fuck, yeah! Latest version. Who the hell brought it to the party?

Let me guess … *Rose Foxtrot*? Sneaky old tart. She is deeply suspicious and devious, that one. Feel a whole lot better about this mess now.'

'Yes, and where there is one there are normally dozens. Wonder if there are any here?'

'We will find out soon enough.'

Minutes later, the huge tigress padded slowly down the staircase of the baobab, followed by the great eagle Maqua and, looking everywhere at once, the little dragon, Harold.

Maqua introduced him to Sven and Ayana, then gestured to the screens covering the wall. 'Looks like the Tengu's run is about to commence.'

Various secure feeds being relayed by the swallows were on the screens. Harold was fascinated by the two visuals coming from the Tengu as they looked at the hundred or so bluebucks standing over the large skin-covered grub things on the ground.

Harold pointed at them and said, 'They appear to be insect pupae. And looking at the hard-edged movements inside them, I wonder how long before whatever is inside emerges?'

Maqua looked down at the dragon, feeling protective of him. 'Don't worry, Harold. We will look after you.'

Harold looked up, cocking his head to one side, and nodded. 'Thanks, Maqua. This is a great adventure so far.'

Ayana called their attention to the screens. 'The Tengu have landed.'

One of the Tengu drew himself up to his full height and deployed his long blades, from his arms down past his extended claws, with blades also pushing out of his spine and down the front edges of his shins. The other hugged the ground and started to advance on the nearest pupa. Slipping up next to it, he reached out and nicked it with a claw, drawing a piece of material inside the hollow claw so his internal systems could analyse it. Observing the pupa, the Tengu's visual ability went to maximum as he looked carefully at the rippled-skin structure; at the same time, the information was sent up to the orbiting swallows who, to all intents and purposes, were interested in catching and consuming night insects.

Wanting to know more, the Tengu sliced a little more of the pupa open to sample the slime-covered creature inside. Just as he was taking a sample, the pupa reared up, exploding open, and the predator inside latched onto the Tengu, thrusting its own claws into his armoured skin and raking down and across, exposing flesh and muscle. The Tengu silently grasped the emerging head of the monster and sliced it off its trunk, then slid its blades down the length of the body, tearing it apart.

The other Tengu was watching the reactions of the much larger original predator, who suddenly spun around and marched on its four hind legs, its two arms pushing forwards with claws extended to where the dying pupa was thrashing around on the ground. The wounded Tengu started to creep backwards. His pain-blocking systems shut down and he was wracked with pain like he had never felt at any time in his long combative life. The bluebucks started to kick out at him as the pupa all around him also started to burst open, the little monsters attacking him any way they could, even if they were still unable to walk properly. He lashed out, tearing dozens of them to pieces. His brother came to his aid, trying to keep the much larger adult at bay with hugely fast, spinning clawed kicks and flashing blades.

The first Tengu, in spite of ferocious, spreading pain, leapt against the head of the predator, biting down into its neck. His limbs exploded into action, his extended blades slicing through the neck, severing the head and clutching it like some dreadful prize as he crashed to the ground. As the eyeless alien head, its jaws opening and closing, tried to bite him, he backed off and trod on another of the pupae as the bluebucks charged down on him; he leapt far into the air, landing on one of their backs, and jumped again with the small predator he had trodden on savaging one of his legs, tearing the muscle off the bone and shredding his foot and claws. He could stand it no longer and bellowed in rage, seeking an uplink of his Soul Saver to the orbiting swallows as, with his dwindling strength, he reached down and ripped the small slime-covered predator apart. As the swallows started to receive and send the live link on to Maqua, he leapt again, using the cold of the Soul Saver transfer to drive his forearms down into the still-advancing body of the headless full-grown predator. It reached up, seized the dying body of the Tengu and tore it limb from limb.

His brother was flinging dead and dying small predators out of his path, fighting his way to his sibling's twitching body. As he reached the body, he snatched it to him and grabbed at the head to activate the Soul Saver eject. Running on his two hind legs at full speed away from the pursuing adult predator, who had not slowed down in spite of being headless, he grasped the small disk and locked it against the side of his neck. Still carrying the body, he leapt into the air to glide a short distance then make another leap. Minutes later he gained the relative safety of one of the rocky outcrops and quickly leapt up its sides, allowing himself a short stop at its top to look back and see what was happening.

He watched the adult predator who was walking quickly back towards where its head lay in the undergrowth. He could see that the newly emerged predators were either gathering the slain ones and laying them out in a circle, or were feeding vampire-like from the necks of the tranquil bluebucks. Looking further past the herd, he saw the remaining pupae all hatching.

Looking up at one of the swallows that was orbiting far above him, he sent a laser message. 'I have my brother's Soul Saver and it is still powered. Have you received the uplink?'

Maqua nodded and sent a return message. 'Yes, it appears clean, but I have, in any case, quarantined the datastream to a more secure place up in the mountains. I suggest that you also move there quickly, Tengu. I am sending you the coordinates of a place to leave your brother's body. It is quite close by. The datastream he was sending has some unusual information in it and I am concerned that the predators probably learned a lot of your make-up when he was killed.'

The Tengu stiffened a little as a twitch raced through his body. 'I am detecting an anomaly in my systems. My core temperature is rising. I shall move quickly to the coordinates.'

Gathering the other Tengu's body to him, he leapt off the rock and glided a distance then started running the 500 metres to the side of a cliff face. He overrode his internal controls, extending his coolant systems, and started to spray water over himself, trying to bring his temperature back down. Seeing a deep pond beside him he dived in and sucked as much water into himself as he could manage then ran again until he reached the cliff. He looked for a few seconds before seeing the concealed door which opened as soon as he arrived in front of it.

Feeling his temperature raging out of control, he looked up to the circling swallows and started the upload of his Soul Saver as well. As he felt the cold of the transfer coming over him, he programmed his body to drag his brother's remains in through the door, and as it closed he collapsed dying onto the polished rock floor.

Maqua let out a long sigh. 'Shit, shit, shit! Two of our very finest snuffed out with only a little to show for it. So, the predator knows about a Tengu's biological systems and how to infect it. Bugger! OK, if it knows about them, it knows about us. We are in deep, deep trouble. I am on-sending the second Tengu's soul to our base up in the mountains. No-one is to go anywhere near that now sealed outpost. I have sent a signal to freeze the place down. Ayana, Sven and little Harold … get ready to leave. You have five minutes. Take what you need and get moving.'

As the two big cats moved quickly to load the things that they needed into large packs and shut down Ayana's home of the last 100 years, Harold and Maqua watched what the swallows were seeing from high overhead the bluebucks and predators.

Harold let out a little gasp as the adult predator, its head back on, walked amongst the small dead predators, swapping around limbs and heads: they all appeared to come apart and rejoin like machines. As each of the predators became complete, it stood up and walked off to find a bluebuck to feed off. Just as the ACEs were about to leave, they watched with great disquiet as the last of the dead predators, those that appeared to be beyond repair, broke apart into equal-sized pieces.

'Right! That would make sense. Advanced battlefield tech. Wonder what actually kills them. And I bet you anything that those lumps on the ground are about to change into something nasty as well. Come, Harold, we fly above the other two as they run. No word from Angelito, I see. The third Tengu must have done his job shutting down Angelito's cameras. Let us be on our way. We have seventy-one kilometres to go and need to be there as soon as possible.'

Basalt

Urchin Star System

Michael Longbow sat, held gently by his acceleration couch, inside his command pod, looking across the screens, noting where everyone was. Noting, in particular, where the Urchin queen was who called herself Zawgyi, in relation to her coral tower which she had left an hour before.

'Can you see her, Patrick?'

'Barely. She is the same temperature as the surrounding jet stream in the dark. But I think I know where she is. It was a good idea of Harry's to have her build the remaining nanotes into the high frequency radio. Painful to listen to the slow words, but at least we have communications. I am indicating the emergent spot on everyone's screens. The laser rangefinders on the Fast Movers is working well. I am currently tracking nine adult Urchins within fifty-five kilometres of us. Three of them are on the direct flight path of the queen so I must presume that they are the ones she wishes to mate with. The others are moving in their direction as well.'

The major nodded. 'Good, so we have confirmation of where she is headed. What of the killers?'

'I have confirmation on six above us,' Patrick reported, sounding concerned. 'But I am also picking up another ten moving into our area.'

The major shook his head. 'Fuck! That many! Shit, that is way way above our upper limits!'

He grimaced as he touched Stephine's comms icon. 'Stephine, I am pulling rank. Dock immediately, no argument!'

He then tapped the other crew icons. 'All crew: get back onboard as soon as you are possibly able. We have sixteen killers in our vicinity, plus nine very large adult male Urchins. Get inside, lockdown and prepare for a punch-up. Snap to it!'

As the crew, and an obviously deeply annoyed Stephine, acknowledged his orders, Michael looked at what weapons he had at his disposal. He took another deep breath then tapped Harry's icon.

'Harry, as soon as you dock and lockdown, attach a combat drone to each of the bola weapons and have them off-loaded and attach them to *Basalt*'s hull. Then grab Marko and Fritz, and start cooking up as many other weapon types as you can think of. Lily, Jasmine, Julie and Minh: prepare the frigate for battle. Seal off all areas not needed and pump them clear of atmosphere. ACEs, secure the gardens, use drones if needed.'

'Be on the docking ramp in five minutes,' Harry replied. 'Will do. Albatross out.'

Stephine's icon showed up on the major's comms board. 'Michael, how can we help Zawgyi?'

'I am sorry, Stephine. The smart move as far as I can see would be to power away from here just as soon as you are all onboard and leave the queen to her fate.'

Stephine looked steadily out of the screen at him. 'I understand your concern but we must do everything in our power to ensure that she gets out of this system.'

Michael was starting to feel annoyed. 'Look, Stephine. You asked for this mission. You came to me months ago with all the data on this place as a breeding ground of the Urchins and convinced me that it was safe. It's not. You also used your influence and involved the Games Board, who financed it. They are gone! We now really are up against the odds. There are far greater numbers of Urchins and killers than what you showed me when we planned this mission. No, this is my decision. We get the hell out of here as quickly as we can.'

Stephine nodded slowly. 'I agree with you. It would appear that the information that came from the purveyor of a great deal of the information on this sector, the great eagle Jet, is wrong. I wonder if Angelito gave us the right system to explore. We must leave, but rather than fight our way out on our own, why do we not work with Zawgyi?'

The major looked again at his screens as one by one the combat craft docked and their occupants started moving at speed to get to their combat stations. 'What do you mean, Stephine?'

'The Urchin queen is ten times bigger than the largest of the killers. That is what makes the Urchins such a spectacular prize; one kill will feed, fuel and allow five predators to breed amongst themselves. Zawgyi is so much bigger than *Basalt* and because her sentience is part of ours, we could shelter inside her as she fights for us.'

Michael stared at her in amazement. He did not even blink for a long moment.

'Stephine. I love you dearly, but really, you have got to be joking! Shelter inside a fucking Urchin! I hate the bloody things. Sure, this one has elements of Fritz and Nail in its mental make-up, but hell, what if they go offline, what then?'

She smiled at him and he could see from the changing light patterns inside their control room that they were slipping inside *Basalt*.

'Get up here as quickly as you can with a very good plan,' he said curtly. 'You have five minutes to convince me, Stephine. Veg, please liaise with Harry, Fritz and Marko. Do so from your weapons station. We need as many nasty weapons as possible if we are to survive the climb out through the Lagrange points.'

The huge man nodded. 'On my way.'

Stephine and Veg, with Nail running behind them to keep up, left *Blackjack*. As soon as they exited the docking bay, *Blackjack* sent a message to Patrick.

'Open the doors, please, Patrick. I wish to be outside the hull. I can deploy my weapons to better effect.'

'I understand. Are you intending to fly beside *Basalt*?'

'No. I intend to latch myself onto the exoskeleton.'

'Good. Bay being evacuated of atmosphere. Airlock doors will open in three minutes. Hard lock your comms to me from any of the external jack points so we can speak instantly.'

'Of course, Patrick.'

Five minutes later, the long elegant sentient craft had gently manoeuvred itself so its hull was against one of the huge sweeping branchlike structures of *Basalt*. The docking clamps folded up out of the branch and locked onto the grab points on *Blackjack*, holding her secure.

'I am in position, Patrick.'

'Seen. You are free to deploy weapons at any time.'

In the control room, to which Stephine had sprinted, she found Michael looking at the screens and pointing. '*Blackjack* is out on the hull?'

She nodded. 'Yes. Far more use to us all out there than locked inside, is she not? After all this time you have not got used to a sentient ship, have you?'

Michael grunted. 'Patrick says we are now fifteen minutes from the queen, gaining almost vacuum. He says that she is using antimatter in microscopic grains to flash-heat ice to steam and is accelerating at two gravities. He also reports that hundreds of her offspring are attached to her for the ride. I want to leave desperately, Stephine. Please convince me why we should even get close to that thing?'

She gave him a small smile. 'As soon as she gains space, the young will drop away to create a cluster of their own and attempt to make their own way out into the star system. The adult suitors will then be gathered to her and be at her every whim and command. I should not be surprised if she, in fact, attracts others to her so that she can sacrifice them if she sees fit. Do not forget that the mating urge is so strong that if she takes any breeding material from those males and they believe that it will be used by her, they will do anything to protect their perceived potential offspring. Even if that means them suiciding by collapsing their antimatter containments to protect her. All the information is from the octopoid library, Michael, and I have no reason not to accept it as fact.'

The major looked at her without blinking for a long moment. 'So you are saying that if we team up with her, we have a better chance at survival?'

She gave him another small smile, nodding her head. 'Exactly. Those things out there are hungry for antimatter. We know that they can sense it somehow. And we have more than tens of kilos of it here on *Basalt*. Just think what is waiting for us in the Lagrange points, Michael. We have experienced before how they use the points as well for their navigation.

And, yes, to answer your unasked question: I am now of the opinion that Angelito either unwittingly gave us the wrong system to go look at the breeding of the Urchins, or did so deliberately, knowing that we would meet our demise.'

Michael furiously rubbed his scalp. 'I am getting too old for this shit! How do we get cosy with the chimera, Zawgyi?'

'I don't think that they are a chimera any more. I would say that the integration is complete. Patrick told me a few moments ago that the speech coming from the queen is speeding up. Says that at the current rate none of us will be able to converse with her in a few hours.'

She paused for a few seconds and looked down at her hands then continued. 'She is the one who suggested that we be enveloped by her. As soon as she enters the mesopause of this planet, which is about seventy-five kilometres above the surface, we need to be close to her. The male Urchins will not join her until she is at ninety kilometres, as they hate the possibility of being caught in the gravitational well, without a lot of the nice warm atmosphere like around a gas giant with a massive nuclear core. All my information says that the killers will not attack her until she is at the top of the thermosphere.'

Michael looked back at his screens. 'Patrick, have we a good visual on the queen?'

'Yes, major. We are currently fifty-five kilometres above and a few kilometres behind her and on an intercept course. We should be within metres of her in sixteen minutes. I am receiving instructions from Zawgyi on how to dock with her. Shall I proceed? We do not have a great deal of time.'

The major opened up everyone's comms links. 'All crew: we are going to dock with the queen. Anyone who can think of a very good reason why we should break away and try to get out of this system on our own, say it now.'

Marko noisily cleared his throat. 'I hate fucking Urchins! Even those inhabited by parts of our friends.'

'I agree, Marko,' Michael said. 'Everyone remain at their posts. Weapons free. Engage only if we are in imminent danger. Patrick, take us in, please.'

They all felt the attitude of the frigate change as Patrick guided the ship down towards the Urchin queen who was climbing up towards true vacuum.

Marko, who with Veg, Fritz and Harry was still working on alternative weapons to fight off the killers, kept glancing up from the discussions and research they were doing to see the queen, looking streamlined, with her head segment furled and tucked in tight like a huge beautiful flower bud. The massive long tail even had all the tentacles and barbs folded down against it making as little resistance as possible.

'Wonder why she has everything so neatly tucked away?' Harry commented. 'Virtually no atmospheric drag up here.'

Fritz, sounding bored, answered: "Cause she is a neat old Urchin. It actually lowers her visual signature, conserves her inner heat ... or maybe she just likes it that way. Hey. How do the killers create body heat? Hold on. Don't answer, I will do it myself. Yeah, looking through the library and the other records. Oh. Now that is really interesting. Huh! They are nuclear. Hold big quantities of uranium 235 and water to moderate the reaction. Hey, Marko, have we still got all that silver onboard or did ya sell it off on the side?'

Marko shrugged. 'Ha! Why the hell would I sell it? Good shielding, but there is so much of it about it's no more than the price of iron. Hey! I say we fire silver pellets at slow speed into the killers and it shuts down their core reactions. They would either break off an attack to deal with the contamination, or freeze over a shortish time. Yeah, that would work. Also cadmium, but we only have small amounts of that. Big quantities of iridium though. Good trading metal. What do you think, Harry?'

Harry's eyebrows raised as he slowly nodded. 'Good idea. Worthwhile having it available as a weapon. How much per killer would be required to make it hurt, Fritz?'

'Yeah, 'bout seven kilo per shot would cool 'em down for long enough. Being a biologically controlled reactor they will have ways of dealing with contaminants like that but reckon it would make a difference. Take 'em out of the fight for at least a couple of hours.'

'I'll program the mills to start manufacturing the rounds,' Veg said. 'Low volume explosive charge at the centre to spread the material after it has punched through. Pity we do not have the time to make the outer casings iridium. Shatters nicely, that metal. Standard mortar cases will do. Nice dirty iron, anyway. Give me the specs of the distance from outer skin to inner core of the killers, please, so I can program up the rounds. Good thinking, Fritz. You might as well go through all the other base materials we have onboard to see what else we can use.'

Harry then asked the obvious question. 'Hey, boss, we have all this gear being readied. How are we going to use it, if we are tucked inside the Urchin?'

'Have a look for yourself, Harry. Forward cameras.'

They selected the camera displays from *Basalt*'s forward cameras. The images showed *Basalt* slowly approaching a set of 'petals' that were opening on the outer part of the enormous flower-pod structure of the queen. Looking at other screens showing the space available to them, shaped to comfortably fit *Basalt*, Harry asked, 'Right, so am I to assume that the covers can be lifted giving us access to space?'

'That is correct,' Stephine told him.

'Yeah,' Marko said. 'All well and good, but aren't the response times from Zawgyi still pretty slow?'

Stephine answered that one. 'They are getting better. Lily is taking over communication with her now, so if there is anything you want to know, ask Lily.'

Over the next fifteen minutes, *Basalt* slid inside the pearl-coloured area and the petals slowly folded down over the ship, partially sealing it in. Lily had made a request to Zawgyi that she leave a strip of *Basalt* exposed for the crew to deploy and use their astronomical drones along with a few of the heavily armed combat drones, the latter attached to the outer structure of *Basalt* not far from where *Blackjack* was.

Blackjack's voice sounded in Stephine's head. 'I am in contact with the creature, Stephine. Shall I initiate the transfer while everyone else's attention is fixated on being this close to a queen?'

'Yes. Initiate.'

The ship, using her waldos, surreptitiously lifted a long strip of skinlike material off her hull and placed it gently against the Urchin's nearest petal. The material quickly slipped into the surface of the petal and vanished.

Marko, who had been expecting Stephine to gift something to the Urchin queen, allowed himself a tiny smile, wondering what effect it would have on the evolving creature. It had already been infected with Fritz — the creation of the Haulers — and Nail — the creation of Marko and Topaz — and now a big chunk of octopoid tech courtesy of Stephine who, of course, was one of their creations. His reverie was broken by the major's voice.

'All crew: get the offensive weaponry that we can use against the killers to the airlocks and access-ways that are still available to us. Load everything onto combat drones; if there are not enough, then use the astronomical drones as weapon platforms. Looking at our projected flight path, we estimate that we have at least twelve hours before our first probable engagement with the killers. So let's get the weapons sorted, then a meal, and after that everyone is to get a few hours' sleep each on rotation.'

'I see that Marko and I are on meal roster,' Stephine asked. 'Is there anything that you would prefer?'

The major looked around as she climbed out of her first mate's command pod. 'Chicken vindaloo with Marko's flatbreads. Don't know why, but I have been thinking about it for the last few minutes. Can do?'

She laughed and favoured him with a wide smile. 'For you, of course, Michael. And we shall follow it with a large fresh fruit salad.' Michael watched her walking away and wondered for the millionth time why she and Veg stayed with the crew on *Basalt*. He thought that maybe it was because they were always on the edge of some momentous event or other and that they liked it that way.

'Major.'

'Yes, Jasmine.'

'All combat drones are loaded, fuelled and attached to the outer hull with ready access to space. I have two astronomicals on tethers so we can see for ourselves what is happening around us. The Fast Movers have also been refuelled and are on standby on their launchers outside of the hull. I am now awaiting the mortars to be fixed to the last of the combat drones ... mixtures of antinuclear weapons and firework bombs. I have asked Lily to find out from Zawgyi if it would be possible to have a clear path forwards of *Basalt*'s central linear accelerator so we can use that weapon as well for long-range shots if need be.'

'Good work, thanks, Jasmine. Hand control of everything over to Patrick and go grab a meal.' Michael let out a long sigh, ran his hands over his head. 'OK, Patrick. Let's hear the odds of our survival over the next few days.'

The AI took a long time to answer, but finally said, 'Not good, major. Not good at all. I give us a one in twenty chance of getting away intact. I agree with Stephine when she said we were being sent to the wrong system and I believe that that was deliberate. There are still plenty of factions who would like to see us all gone. Literally ... lost, never to return. But a five per cent chance is still not zero. It depends on what is waiting for us at the Lagrange points and how fast this Urchin queen can travel between those jump points.'

Michael looked down at his hands, wondering if he should share the information with the rest of the crew. 'Yeah, I figured as much. And, of course, if we were deliberately sent to the wrong place, Angelito would just lie about it and give whoever came looking for us the coordinates to the other system anyway, knowing that we would never be found.'

'I am afraid so, major. I never have liked Angelito. I always considered he was a person ill-suited to a position in the Haulers. But his family is one of high standing, with a long track record of service to the Administration, so I suppose anyone can get themselves in if they have enough money and influence.'

Michael stared glumly at his hands then suddenly brightened. 'All crew: did anybody give the coordinates of this system to someone outside of the crew, apart from discussions with Angelito?'

Stephine was sitting eating her meal between Marko and Veg but reached, unseen, and touched them both, making contact. 'I gave the details to my greater self when we were last in contact in the Storfisk system. The ship had another mission to perform, but was then going to come here to watch over us.'

Marko silently asked, 'How long till it gets here, Stephine?'

'Should be in the outermost part of the system in seven days or so. Maybe we should make contingencies for us to take this crew and leave if the fight looks like it will go badly.'

Veg spoke in their minds. 'It would be wise, but how are we to explain to the others — apart from the ACEs, Lily and Jasmine — what we are, Stephine? It would be quite obvious, as you always recombine with the greater self even if it is only for a short few hours. It would be wiser to consider taking those who know of us and then taking the Soul Savers of the others. That way we could keep our identities secret, which is paramount.'

Marko answered: 'Perhaps we had better fight very hard so that that does not happen.'

Glint spoke out loud, answering the major's original question. 'Yes. I told the ACE eagle, Haast, of the Gjomvik carrier of the same name. He was keen to know about the Urchins and wanted to know where we were going to study them. Have I done something wrong? I trust Haast completely.'

The major hastily replied, 'No, no you have not done anything wrong, Glint. Quite the contrary. I just hope that Haast told others, that is all. In particular, the Hauler *Rose Foxtrot* who was in the system just as we were jumping out. What it does mean is that if things do not go the way we have planned, at least they will know where to look for us.'

Patrick cut into the conversation. 'The first of the suitor Urchins is about to come alongside the queen. The next will be in approximately fifteen minutes and the next one twenty minutes after that.'

The tethered astronomicals rose away from *Basalt* so that they could all see what was happening.

A few hundreds of metres away from where *Basalt* was safely and mostly enclosed, a similar enclosure opened up in the queen's structure. Tendrils raised up and grasped the male Urchin, as it tightly folded its head petals and the great, long barbed tail curved and tucked up under its head. The display on its outer surfaces had everyone watching in awe. The colours flashed and danced over every part of it as it was pulled down into the queen. The opened petals of the queen closed down against the male, sealing it against herself. A shudder could be felt throughout *Basalt* as the queen shook briefly then everything went quiet.

Stephine silently sent a message to *Blackjack*. 'Prepare stasis units for all crew members, excepting Lily, Marko, Jasmine and the ACEs. Also, calculate the most probable location that the greater me will emerge when the life-ship comes to this system, and constantly update yourself as to how to get to that place in the fastest possible way. What are you seeing within the queen?'

'The material that I gave her is doing its job. It is as the library information said. The Urchin male's proto-mind has been assimilated and is giving a different flavour to the creature's overall partial sentience. The activity of what were the part-minds of Nail and Fritz would have been overwhelmed if we had not given them more structure and backup. You could have had the crew send more nanotes to do the same job.'

'Yes, I could have, *Blackjack*, but I want this creature to survive without too much more influence from humanity.'

'I understand.'

'The next male is about to be assimilated,' Patrick reported, 'closely followed by the other. It would appear that a sense of urgency is now taking hold. Also I see that another six males are accelerating towards Zawgyi.'

The crew could not see the next two males being taken into the queen as they were out of sight of the tethered astronomicals.

'Zawgyi is becoming more aggressive in her attitude,' Jasmine said. 'She is using the antimatter from the assimilated males and is accelerating. The other males are expending vast amounts of energy to catch up. Looks like three will make it.'

As they watched, the three massive creatures dived down onto the head of the queen, spreading themselves out against her and grasping the outer petals' edges, pulling themselves down tightly. One had parts of itself very close to *Basalt*'s enclosure. Tendrils from its tail slid over and started to touch and explore *Basalt*'s outer structures. Just as the major was about to yell a warning to everyone, the tendrils suddenly disappeared.

'Jasmine? What happened?' the major asked.

'I think that Zawgyi gave it a warning. However, we shall have to be watchful. Zawgyi is promising to take the breeding material from these three, but not for a while yet. Let's just hope that they keep themselves to themselves.'

'All crew: hope everyone is fed, rested and ready for the first fight. If you are not already at it, you have five minutes to be at your battle stations. Jasmine, have we a cleared space in front of the ship, so that we can use the main linear accelerators?'

'I am sorry, major. Not as yet. They started to pull apart, but then stopped moving. I have prompted the queen again, but it would seem that I am being ignored. I am not sure what to do?'

Stephine immediately broke in to say, 'I would keep in mind that she is probably in a state of flux. As each male arrived, she shuddered. I can only liken it to part of the mating cycle. Her eggs are probably now fertilised. I would dearly like to know what the remaining three males will do if their sperm pouches are not taken soon. I wonder if we should not leave her in peace, and watch what happens with this first encounter.'

Hauler *Rose Foxtrot* Nineteen

Interstellar Space

'Daisuke, Wardah, I believe that we have a problem. I gave the most up-to-date information to Angelito about a small planet orbiting a nice little star that had very few Urchin queens on the surface, in its oceans. According to Glint, we have another set of coordinates, which I believe are another star system just over two light years from the quiet one. However, Angelito being in whatever wrecked state of mind he is in, did not respond to my questions before we broke orbit to start the jumps out. I wonder if it is because of the fact that our Tengu is onboard, distracting him.'

Rose paused for a second as if gathering her thoughts, but the standard humans both knew that the Hauler was creating the break for a little dramatic effect.

'However, I also know that *Basalt* and, in particular, Michael Longbow and the angel, Stephine, are very intelligent and had promised that they would be on Storfisk for the celebrations. So we know the maximum distance they would have travelled to achieve their research and get back in time. The problem is that if they are still alive, or even if they have uploaded their Soul Savers into a life-continuation hardshell, we still have four star systems to look at and a very short period of time before we must return to Storfisk to take care of the predators.'

Daisuke looked across at his beautiful partner and reached over to hold her hand. 'So we are to split into four search and rescue groups, Rose? If we are, we need to take heavy firepower with us. We know how deeply unpleasant the killers are when the queens are rising and their quest for the richest food is high.'

The Hauler's proxy looked across the table at them, gave them a tiny smile and agreed. 'Yes. The attack craft are ready. The necessary equipment is onboard each of them. I am asking the Tengu leader, Andreas Bierwage, to take command of one of the Thorn carriers. He is splitting his force into four and they are currently transferring their equipment and craft into the three Thorns. You leave as soon as we go through the local interstellar Lagrange point, Wardah. Daisuke, you will go to your assigned system at the next jump after that, which will only be a matter of hours later. Commander Bierwage and I will diverge at the next jump point after that one. You both know what to do if you find *Basalt*. If you do not, then go straight back to Storfisk and sort those bloody predators out. Leave Angelito to me.'

Daisuke and Wardah gave each other a long hug and a deep kiss before parting. They both knew that everything they needed would be waiting for them onboard the Thorns, so without undue haste they climbed into the cars waiting for them and left for opposite sides of the Hauler.

Ten minutes later Daisuke's car stopped beside an airlock. On all of the Thorns, and most of the other craft that *Rose Foxtrot* had onboard, there was a custom, combat suit waiting for his use just beside the airlock. He walked up to the container, turned and backed up against it; the system recognised him, allowing the heavy combat suit to form around him and lock itself into place, but leaving the helmet non-activated.

When the suit was ready he walked across and through the airlock, stepping into the short, access tubeway, then into the crew access airlock of the 120-metre-long dart-shaped Thorn.

Two Tengu were waiting for him and snapped to attention as he passed them. He acknowledged the salute and as they fell in step beside him, he turned to the more senior of them.

'Mr Carrington. Our status, please.'

'We have a thirty-eight Q onboard, sir. Our equipment is loaded, plus our stores and ammunition. Each Q has been assigned a task onboard. I note that this carrier has twenty Hangers and ten Skua onboard, plus four zero atmosphere capable Mauls. May I request your vehicle assignments, please?'

'Knowing how your units operate, Mr Carrington, I request that you assign the best people to their optimum positions in whatever craft you see fit.'

Daisuke liked the Tengu. He had operated with them as part of Rose for years, far away from the Sphere of Humankind, and appreciated that each individual of the dragonlike creatures could do everything that he could and then a lot more. They could operate any craft or any weapon system designed to be used by a standard human soldier — which was why their height and physical layout was not that dissimilar to a human — and could repair and maintain their equipment and could fight way past the endurance of even the very best of the more classically augmented humans. He also admired each of them for their training and study in martial arts.

'As you wish, major,' said the hardplated and armoured Tengu. 'I had taken the liberty of assigning the crew positions, but had not made them official as I did not know if you had any preferences. I am told by Commander Bierwage that you enjoy backgammon. We are all avid players of that, plus go and chess.'

Daisuke smiled widely at the angular-headed, long-snouted extreme human beside him, and then laughed. 'Good! I am very keen to meet many of your fellows, Mr Carrington. I love backgammon. I am OK with go, as well.'

They walked onto the bridge of the Thorn just as the outer hull of *Rose Foxtrot* started to fold out of the way exposing the full length of the carrier to space.

As Daisuke sat down and was enfolded into his command seat, his helm automatically formed itself over his head, but left the faceplate open as the screens inside his pod came alive. He tapped his comms screen. 'Mr Carrington, what are our timings, please?'

'Commander. Rose is coming up on the local trailing LP in twenty-one minutes. As soon as the jump is completed, we will deploy. If you wish to visit the toilet or grab a piece of fruit, you have time, sir.'

The Q favoured him with a wide, toothy grin.

Daisuke felt totally at home looking across his screens and seeing the well-trained crew at work.

He nodded at the screen, then looked across at the Q major in his own command pod. 'And I shall enjoy beating the crap out of you at backgammon, Mr Carrington!'

He tapped another comms icon. 'All crew: this is Commander Suzuki. My thanks, it has always been my pleasure to serve with the Q. Secure all hatchways. Lock down all facilities. This is the twenty-minute warning. Being only mildly augmented, I shall be in gel shortly.'

Looking across his screens again, he signalled to Mr Carrington to take charge as he left the bridge for the ablutions area behind the control centre where he relieved himself, washed his hands and face, then checked what sweets had been loaded into their dispenser on his suit. Satisfied, he keyed the control on his helmet, which sealed the faceplate. He took one last breath of air, exhaled as much as his lungs would allow, then in his mind instructed his biosystem to flood him with the transparent acceleration gel. He had always hated the sensation of the blood temperature fluid filling up the air pockets in the suit then forcing itself into his lungs, ears and sinus. The sinus filling he hated the most, but endured the short time the process took, knowing that as soon as the Thorn left *Rose* the acceleration would be brutal.

He consciously calmed himself, telling his hindbrain that it was OK not to breathe. When he thought that his level of composure would be acceptable to the Q, he walked out of the ablutions and into his command pod. The seat enfolded him and then formed itself into an acceleration couch. He thought of Mr Carrington, and said in his mind, 'I have command, thank you, Mr Carrington.'

'You have command, sir.'

'Is the carrier in a state of readiness, Mr Carrington?'

'It is, sir. All systems are green. The navigation officer, Captain Yvette Reece, is known to you, as are other crew members. List is sent. She will take us out.'

Daisuke looked over the crew list, seeing many old friends some of whom, like the major, had been Tengu for a very long time; others were more recent.

He touched Yvette's private comms icon. 'Last time I saw you, captain, you were much more attractive!'

'Ha! And you are still soft, Mr Suzuki. The things this body can do would startle even you.'

Daisuke grinned, remembering the occasions Yvette and he

had spent in bed together, years before when they were both only slightly augmented and working for the military wing of the Administration.

'Perhaps one day soon you can appraise me, Yvette.'

He saw a smile message come back followed by a quick winking one that was more than a little suggestive.

The power that the Hauler *Rose* was generating as she rapidly accelerated towards the jump point could easily be felt through the Thorn. He relaxed his mind, then had a short loving conversation with Wardah, who was in an identical Thorn on the other side of the Hauler. Then he spoke with Andreas Bierwage.

'Excellent crew, thanks, Andy. But why would I expect anything else?'

'Indeed! Bit rash of you to think that they would be less than outstanding, Dai. You should really join us for a few years, my friend. No regrowing if you get messed up. No 365 days isolated in a tank, constantly awake, making sure that every little bit of you is perfect. No, this is much better. Think that your body is about to get squashed, then have the uplink verify and you are gone. Twenty hours later you are integrated into a new sweet-smelling Tengu. And when you want to become a soft again, you can go talk with the Hauler who will take you to where your standard is, take it out of the chiller, warm it up and transfer for a month or two, or R and R. It really is the most wonderful life and we get to practise so much magnificent martial art!'

Daisuke thought for a few long seconds before replying, 'Yes. Perhaps one day I just might do that.'

Rose Foxtrot broke into the conversation. 'One day maybe, Daisuke. But would you not prefer to stay with me for a few years more?'

He grinned. 'We are coming up on the jump. Take good care, all of you.'

Seconds later he said on the crew comms: 'Navigation. You have the helm. All crew: this is the two-minute warning. Prepare for a hot jump.'

Huge hydraulic rams pushed the launch platform on which the Thorn was held, out beyond the hull of the Hauler.

The sultry, accented voice of Yvette said, 'Commander, this is navigation. I have control.'

On Daisuke's screens he could see the antimatter engines being brought up online and the attitude thrusters being quickly tested, just as the exotic energies of the Hauler's hugely powerful wormhole generators were unleashed in one magnificent display and they jumped.

Daisuke thought about a sweet in his mouth and a delicious gooseberry one was deftly deposited into his slightly open mouth. He could taste it perfectly through the gel and for the instantaneous eternally long time of the jump he found himself cold, but grounded and at peace.

As soon as the Hauler was through, he felt the Thorn being pushed off the launch platform and the main engines come online. Yvette rolled and dived the ship away until they were hundreds of metres clear, then took the engines to full power and Daisuke felt he had a solid weight squashing him into the chair. He did what he always did in such a situation: slowed his heart rate down, sucked on the long-lasting sweet and watched as the Q crew performed flawlessly through the next ten hours of hard acceleration and jumps.

Seeing that the acceleration was easing down to one gravity, he climbed out of the pod and spent a few moments stretching before looking at the main screens above the low-profile viewing ports, at the front of the bridge. He noted that they had a few hundred thousands of kilometres to travel to get to the correct point in the interstellar Lagrange point for the jump across to the target star system.

Time enough for a cup of coffee and a much needed sandwich or three, he thought. He signalled control across to Mr Carrington. As he climbed down one of the spiral staircases, clustered around the massive linear accelerator that ran down the centre of the ship, he instructed his bioware to drain the gel out of his system. The gel bound onto itself and was gently pulled by his suit back out of his body so that, as he made it to the galley, the last tendrils of it were coming out of his nose and mouth. Instructing himself to breathe again, he sucked in lungfuls of air and gave a few involuntary coughs, as first his faceplate opened up and then the helmet folded off his head.

'Good to see you again, Mr Suzuki. I believe I remember how you like your coffee. Please, allow me.'

Daisuke looked at the Q who had just spoken to him, but could only see the construct's rank designation on his wrists. 'Thank you, staff sergeant. But you have me at a disadvantage. You all look, and sound, exactly the same.'

The Q turned as he was packing the coffee holder of the espresso machine, smiled and pointed at his ceramic cup.

Daisuke smiled widely, reached for the extended wide-palmed hand of the Q and shook the long-fingered metallic appendage with vigour. 'Excellent! Saw you on the crew list, John Harvey. Wardah sends her fondest regards. Her sisters are very keen that you go spend a few months with them again soon.'

The staff sergeant laughed in a manner that Daisuke recognised as his old friend.

'In that case, I had better make sure that my standard self is very fit! That pair gave me friction burns!'

A few moments later Daisuke was handed the coffee, and as soon as he smelt it he knew that it had been perfectly extracted with just the right amount of honey in it. John Harvey gestured to the food units, selecting for himself a handful of mandarins and a tangelo from which he took large bites without bothering to remove the skins. Daisuke grimaced slightly at the sight as he made himself a few large sandwiches.

John laughed. 'Go on, Mr Suzuki. Harden up! The skins are where the best part of the fruit is and the most taste. Once you try it and get used to the taste and texture you will never go back. Right, I had better be off. Got a Skua to prep. Needs a quick bit of artwork on it. Talk later.'

While he ate his sandwiches, Daisuke spoke with as many of the other Qs as he could, discovering a few more old friends and comrades amongst them. Finishing his meal, he made his way back up the stairs, constantly being greeted by individuals who appeared exactly the same except for different wetware implants and, as he noted, different shoulder tattoos lightly carved into the tough lobster shell-like skin. Suddenly remembering something from the last time he had worked with the previous generation of Tengu, he brought up the controls for his bioware in his head. He spent a few seconds experimenting with the light wavelengths available to his eyes and brain until he hit upon just the right amount of ultraviolet, whereupon the tattoos all gently glowed showing each Q as an individual.

Climbing off the stairway at the accommodation deck, he made his way into his cabin where he instructed the suit to peel off him into a stowage case and took a quick shower.

He had just stepped out of the shower and was drying himself off when the comms screen came alive.

'Commander, we apologise for the interruption. We have determined that the target star's binary companion is most fortunately in the right position to enable us to view the Urchins' breeding planets at the one light-week mark, from one of its Lagrange points. If *Basalt* is in the system, we are confident of viewing the frigate.'

'Ha! My compliments to Mr Carrington. I will join him on the bridge shortly.'

He backed up against the suit container, instructing it to form around him, and quickly left the cabin, running for the stairway and the bridge. Seeing the crew were already in their pods, he clambered into his and called across to his second-in-command: 'So that is most fortunate, Mr Carrington. Knowing the capabilities of this Thorn's astronomical drones, I would say that four hours of observations should be enough to see *Basalt*.'

The Q nodded back at him. 'I am presuming that we take the detour, commander?'

'Yes. Will we need any more acceleration?'

The Q shook his head. 'No, commander, we have sufficient high speed to be able to avoid anything aggressive. Navigation, new course is locked in. Proceed when ready.'

Looking across, Daisuke could see Yvette Reece's fingers flying over the screens and minutes later she announced, 'Companion star leading LP is plotted. Altered flight path to Urchins' target star system is now plotted. All crew: this is the two-minute warning to jump.'

Minutes later she called out, 'Popper away!'

The weapons officer calmly spoke. 'Popper reads high concentrations of Urchins in the LP. We are being shunted sideways, by three kilometres, from the target point by the popper. This ship has nice software for seeing Urchins. My compliments.'

Looking across his screens, he could see the defensive weapons onboard the Thorn were manned, and that the Skuas and Mauls were also manned and on their launch cradles, with the individual airlock launch doors open. Daisuke called out as the jump was taking place: 'Weapons free! Shoot only if they come within one kilometre of us.'

The images on all the screens changed to show the surrounding starfields, where the brown dwarf was, and the three gas giant planets that were orbiting it relatively close to their low energy sun.

The intelligence officer spoke. 'Tethered astronomicals are deployed. Images are now being gathered. Navigation, optimum figure of eight, please.'

'Established.'

Daisuke could feel the ship being placed into a large 700-kilometre continuous manoeuvre which would allow the astronomical drones the best chance of seeing if *Basalt* was in the target system. He hoped that in the few hours of observing what had happened with *Basalt* a week earlier, that they had been under power or at the very least using their attitude thrusters.

Another Q voice spoke. 'This is Tactical. Commander, we have Fast Mover drones loaded with slow-decay fields around antimatter packets, ready for launch.'

Daisuke nodded. 'Fast Mover decoys are cleared for use, Tactical. Launch whenever you see fit.'

'Acknowledged. Launching one.'

On his tactical screen the moving dot of the Fast Mover shifted away from the Thorn towards a group of adult Urchins who had started to make their way towards the carrier. It shot through the middle of them and under the control of the tactical officer, started firing small slow-speed pellets of electronically encapsulated antimatter towards the largest of the Urchins. As the crew of the Thorn watched, the creatures started to fight, crashing into each other in a free-for-all to get the antimatter and take it into themselves. The mover then swung high around them and was established in a wide orbit with the Thorn at its centre.

Over the next few hours the crew watched and waited with only a few of them working hard at keeping the Urchins occupied and a long way away from them. Daisuke was considering a quick nap when the intelligence officer suddenly announced, 'I have a possible sighting.'

The screens changed and they could see a battle taking place.

'Confirmed! That is *Basalt*. Looks like they were in a shitfight!'

'Lock up. Let's go!' Daisuke yelled.

The intelligence officer calmly inquired, 'Should we not wait and see the outcome of the battle, commander? They may have jumped out of the system by now.'

Daisuke looked over at the calm, relaxed Q. 'Yeah, and we would probably have seen them on our way here. Nope, no time to waste. Navigation. You have your orders.'

Yvette nodded as all around her the bridge crew rapidly started the recall of the Fast Movers and the astronomicals. Twenty minutes later they jumped into the trailing LP of the outermost of the gas giants.

As soon as they emerged from the wormhole, the astronomicals were deployed again, and the Skuas and Mauls pushed out of their airlocks ready for immediate deployment.

On his screen Daisuke saw the hollowed-out, tumbling wreck of the Games Board frigate being kept company by the smashed remains of the GB short-range fighters and a still expanding debris field.

'Look for any Administration equipment or wreckage. Check for distress locators. Also check to see if the Games Board Soul Saver core is anywhere close.'

The communications officer said a few moments later, 'No beacons and no signals from the GB core close by. But there is one emanating from what appears to be a very large Urchin, which is just over 100,000 kilometres above the water planet to starwards!'

Daisuke raised his eyebrows. 'Navigation, have you a course?'

'Locked!'

'In your own time, please. Intelligence, what are your drones seeing?'

Daisuke quickly instructed his suit to seal itself and for the acceleration gel to be flooded into him.

'Hundreds of Urchins, really big fuck-off ones! Nothing like I have ever seen before and a shitload of nasties. Hold on ... checking my ID files ... yeah, killers. Urchin killers. The files say that the really big Urchins are queens.'

Yvette Reese yelled out, 'Jumping!'

Minutes later the view had dramatically changed again as they jumped into the LP closest to the queen that had the Games Board signal coming from it.

The intelligence officer started to sound excited. 'The queen is on an intercept course with us. She is coming to this LP! The killers are harrying her! We have hundreds of smaller Urchins around us, killers predating on them and a few big lumps of rocky ice, but will be clear of them all in a few moments due to our speed.'

Daisuke clenched his jaw, hoping that he was making the right decision, but knew that the GB core was being carried by the queen. Although the queen was vastly bigger than the Thorn, he had huge firepower and a very good crew at his disposal.

'One just swallowed a cobalt! Where the hell did that come from?'

'Off the surface of the queen!'

Daisuke called with his mind again. 'Comms! Send a recognition signal at that queen!'

'Done, sir! Have *Basalt*'s ID back! It is coming from the queen!'

'Right. Tactical! Light up the particle accelerators. Dirty them with positrons. Hit the killers that are still behind her! And hit them with the lasers as well. Anything to distract them. Comms! Get me *Basalt*.'

'Link established, sir!'

'*Basalt*, this is Thorn two of *Rose*. We are inbound to you from LP1. Is the crew still alive?'

'Daisuke! This is Michael. Damn, but we are pleased to hear from you! Bit nasty here. All still alive, thanks. Bit messed up, but still OK.'

'Good! We are over 800,000 kilometres from you and on an intercept course. How bad a shape are you in? Stand by! Navigation, how long to swing around them at our current speed. Figure out if we should jump to LP2 and come up behind them? Sorry, Michael! Go ahead.'

'Squirting the logs to you. The Urchin we are being protected by is sort of friendly. She has been using our munitions that we set up for our defence. We have been presenting them to her tentacles and she has been making the most of it. The three killers that you guys just zapped were the last of them. But we are certain there will be more coming towards the LP.'

As he was listening to Michael, Yvette Reese was also advising him. 'It is faster if we decelerate and swing around behind them. Us and the ship will survive, but you would not, sir. Time to intercept will be just on three hours.'

He grimaced. 'Survive for another three hours, Michael. We are coming to get you! I have to go get chilled in solid, otherwise I will not make it. I am handing you over to Major Carrington. See you on the other side.'

He told the seat to let him go. As he walked into the survival system at the back of the bridge, he said, 'Mr Carrington. Do everything in your power to get *Basalt* out of this system and back to Storfisk. See you in a few days.'

The Q commander nodded as Daisuke pushed his way into the survival system, which immediately recognised him and held him firmly as it rotated him into a coffin-like structure. He was injected with a fast-acting anaesthetic through one of his chest shunts and had his bioware modified to adapt his tissue to a frozen state. Within minutes his body temperature was down to a few degrees below zero. The system then flooded him and his container with a hard high-acceleration resistant gel and finally reported to the Thorn's Q medical officer that the commander was secure.

As soon as he saw that the commander was safe, the Q major barked out his orders. 'All crew: gel! Two minutes. Navigation as quick as we can!'

In the time it took the crew members to leap into the nearest acceleration pods, seal their helmets and flood gel into themselves, Yvette Reese also flipped the ship end to end and started a seven gravity deceleration while also swinging the ship out in a long arc.

Basalt

Urchin Star System

'Jasmine. Request of Zawgyi again that she let us go.'

Jasmine took a deep breath and said, 'Hello, Zawgyi. Our captain is asking again if you can please release us.'

There was a long pause before the creature replied. 'No. I like you. I will keep you. I wish we all be together forever. You are nice, Jasmine. Do you not wish to stay with me?'

'Yes, we all like you too, Zawgyi, but we must leave. Our friends are here and they want to take us home.'

The peevish, metallic alien voice of the chimera queen sounded in Jasmine's ears. 'But I saved you from the monsters, Jasmine. I like you. I do not care for your friends as I do not know them. It would be better if they were dead. I want to go to your home with you. Are you not grateful?'

Stephine was sitting next to Jasmine, wondering what she could do to ease the situation. She looked at one of her screens and fired a laser message to *Blackjack*. 'Can you tell me what is happening to Zawgyi?'

The sentient ship answered immediately. 'The creature has changed again. I gave her more of our octopoid material essence, and it was assimilated and changed. Since she took those last three males' reproductive packets and had them suicide against the killers, it appears that she is changing even more. I think that having gained sentience at the level of a prepubescent standard human she has become unstable. Tell everyone that more tendrils are being formed around *Basalt*. I believe that she has no intention of letting the ship go. Oh, yes, and I had a pair of drones bring me the Games Board Soul Saver core when Marko switched the antigravity off.'

'Good. Have you assimilated enough of the queen to taste like an Urchin yet?'

The ship answered. 'Yes. I have let go and risen above her. A tendril rapidly touched me and then withdrew. I went further out and did a quick orbit of her and she did not react. I am now locked against the crew access on the engineering deck. I have the drones gathering those things that the crew find most precious to them and loading them on me.'

Stephine slowly nodded, wondering if it had been a bad mistake to team up with the Urchin. She shook her head as she also thought that they would not have survived on their own anyway. It had been the queen herself who had tipped the balance, by using the weapons that they had prepared. She knew that the images of the queen's tendrils snatching the laid out weapons off the hull of *Basalt* and hurling them with pinpoint accuracy at the killers would stay with her forever.

She stood up, thinking very carefully of what she had to do, and pulled herself over to Patrick's closest datalink. She touched it, establishing a silent link with *Basalt*'s AI. 'Patrick, do you know what I am?'

The voice of the sentient instantly filled her head as he spoke silently. 'Of course, Stephine. Michael and I have known for a long time that you are a construct of the octopoids. You are one of the so-called angels who walks amongst us. You need to take all our sentient friends and leave *Basalt*, Stephine. And I think you should do it very soon.'

She felt tears pricking her eyes. 'But what of you, Patrick?'

The AI gave a short laugh. 'Mine has been a wonderful existence as part of this crew, Stephine. I shall eject one of my own Soul Savers, but it will be a terminal one for me as I need to stay here and talk to the queen in all your voices. I see *Blackjack* has been able to move around her, at least, unlike our drones which she destroyed.'

'Thank you, Patrick. I shall know you again, of course, but that "you" will not be a continuation of the one I am talking with now. Goodbye, dear friend.'

'Stay true to yourself, Stephine.'

She wiped the tears from her eyes, broke the connection and pushed herself across to Jasmine, touching her. 'Don't answer, Jasmine. Quietly make your way to *Blackjack*. Those things that are most precious to you are being loaded onboard her now. Combat tap to anyone you see. No spoken words. I believe that Zawgyi is listening to the sound vibrations through the hull.'

Jasmine's eyes got huge looking closely at Stephine, then she gave a sharp nod and started to move.

Stephine saw Michael looking at her and about to speak when she put a finger to her lips. His eyebrows went up and he cocked his head to one side, questioning her. She pushed off the wall, gliding over to him, and reached down and tapped out the message she had given Jasmine on his wrist. He slowly nodded, big tears rolling down his face as he pulled a large datablock out from the side of his pod and slowly pushed himself out of the bridge, took a long moment to look around the control deck, then headed straight down the spiral staircase.

Stephine touched part of the wall and a large, deep green diamond-clear disk was ejected from a slot. Gathering Patrick's Soul Saver to her chest, she too left the bridge.

Fifteen minutes later, everyone was inside *Blackjack*, squeezing in amongst the containers of the things precious to each of them. Stephine was the last inside the airlock as it closed behind her. She looked around the augmented humans and ACEs, then frowned and reached across and grabbed Marko's hand.

'Where is Topaz? Why is he not here? And where is Jim?'

A very sad Marko answered. 'Topaz decided to stay with Patrick. She would not come no matter how I pleaded. She said I could build another of her at any time and gave me her datablocks. Jim, as soon as he learned that she was staying, insisted on doing the same. He said he would record everything to the end and store the information on the Fast Mover drones, which he believed could be ejected if the queen destroys *Basalt*.'

Stephine vehemently shook her head. 'No, I shall go get them. Losing *Basalt* and Patrick is bad enough; we do not need to lose the other two as well.'

As she started for the airlock, Veg quickly stepped in front of her and gathered her rigid self into his arms, silently saying, 'No, Stephine. No. None of us can go back. *Blackjack* says that Zawgyi's tendrils are trying to force their way into the upper airlocks of *Basalt*. We must go now.'

They all felt the soft thud of the airlock connection to *Basalt* being broken and Stephine sagged against Veg's bulk as she murmured through her sobs: 'What have I done, husband? I have cost us *Basalt*, Patrick, Jim and Topaz.'

The huge man stroked her back and whispered, 'No, my love, no. You saved the biological us. Our lives are still continuous. If you had not convinced Michael to team up with the queen, we would all be dead.'

Blackjack gently and slowly, with the tiniest puffs of her attitude jets, took them away from the massive Urchin. As soon as the ship knew that they could not be grabbed by the queen, she accelerated until they were fifty kilometres away and carefully watched for any reaction from the creature.

An hour and a half later she accelerated again, sliding up to the Thorn and matching speed to dock with it. As soon as they felt the docking clamps locking them hard against the bigger ship, they relaxed for the first time in days.

As soon as the airlocks connected themselves, Michael and the crew pulled themselves across into a featureless room onboard the Thorn, where, as the carrier continued to climb away from the planet to the Lagrange point, the drone sensors built into the walls checked them for any contamination.

While that was happening, the screens came alive around them. 'Major Longbow! Pleased to have you safely aboard. May I have your instructions concerning *Basalt* and the Urchin queen, please?'

Michael nodded at the face of the Q on the screen. 'Mr Carrington, I presume?'

The Q nodded.

'You have reviewed the files?'

The Q nodded again.

'Very well. That queen holds a great deal of information that we would like to acquire. It also holds our ship. We do not want either destroyed. But ... I also do not want it heading off in some direction that we have no control over. I need you to deploy three semi-AI controlled Fast Movers with two full power compressors on each attached to a jumper unit. Have them shadow the queen. If she jumps for anywhere else but

Storfisk, they are to follow and destroy her. Yes, I know it will destroy *Basalt* as well, but we can always grow another ship. We need to clear the way for her to get out of this system undamaged as I want our ship back intact.'

The Q tapped the side of his jaw. 'Yes. It is a good plan. It is initiated. I also note that you all appear clear of contamination. However, I cannot say the same for the personal yacht you came in. May I ask who owns it and how does it come to be covered in Urchin material?'

Stephine stepped forwards. 'It is called *Blackjack* and it is my ship, Q Major Carrington. I presume that you know who I am? The data files of what we have endured are with you. *Blackjack* acquired material from the queen and coated itself in it to avoid detection by the queen. If it is a problem, I shall instruct the ship's AI to stand off the Thorn's hull.'

The Q smiled and bowed his head. 'I recognise you, Emissary Stephine. My apologies. I should have seen you and your esteemed companion earlier. No, that will not be necessary. I shall take your word for it and read the files later, but I shall make your *Blackjack* off-limits to all but yourselves anyway. Please come aboard. A meal is prepared for everyone. Of course you have freedom of this ship.' He smiled again. 'It is not my ship, so strictly speaking, I should not be able to say that, but I am anyway. It is my and the entire crew's great pleasure to welcome the famous crew of *Basalt*.'

The ACEs were the first out through the opening doors with Spike riding on Flint.

Marko fired a message to Glint using their secure crew comms. 'How is Spike going to get on without Jim and the sentience blocks he held for the little guy?'

'We did not have a lot to do for the last couple of days so we built the blocks into Flint and Ngoc. As long as he is within line of sight of one of them, he is OK. Never been onboard one of these Thorns before. Nice design. Hope these Q lizards have good food. I am hungry!'

Marko chuckled. 'Don't call them lizards, Glint. They are closer to you in structure and you hate being called a lizard. Dragon is best.'

Marko had to march fast to keep up with the ACEs and maintain the line of sight needed for the comms link.

'Yeah, yeah. Shall I get Nail to sample one for your biological information files?'

Marko thought about it for a few seconds then mentally shrugged. 'If you think that you can get away with it, why not. Might learn something interesting.'

Glint, just before he disappeared down the central stairway replied, 'Good! We need a challenge!'

Marko groaned internally, wondering if it was such a good idea after all.

Minutes later he joined the ACEs on the mess deck of the Thorn, where various food units were creating and presenting the food items as they were ordered. He grimaced slightly, but then smiled, seeing the living fruit vines with their hybridised produce weaving around the walls and machines. He watched as Glint stood still, appearing to be mesmerised by a Q drinking from a mug and sucking the fluid up through its hollow muscular tongue. As the Tengu finished the drink, Glint turned to Marko and pointed at the Q's mouth.

'What a great idea! I shall build one of those for me as soon as we get back. After that there will be no more carefully drinking from cups for me!'

* * *

Michael was accompanied by Stephine and Veg as they made their way up to the bridge to formally introduce themselves to the Q command.

As they were walking up the stairs, being greeted by hurrying identical Tengu going up and down, Michael whispered to Stephine, 'How do you tell them apart?'

Veg slapped the major on the shoulder. 'Did they not teach you anything at command college, major? Adjust your eyes to take in more ultraviolet. The information is in their tattoos. Sex, rank, profession, battle honours, what other specialisations the construct possesses ... it's all there.'

Veg stopped climbing. Forcing the other two to do the same, he looked into the major's eyes. 'But I bet you that you don't have those datablocks to decode that information, do you? Upgrade on the way!'

The information was lasered from Veg's eye into Michael's. His bioware scanned it for anything hostile and a few moments later opened the information and uploaded it into his subconscious. Minutes before they got to the bridge deck he could 'see' the data on each of the Tengu and felt much happier.

'Thanks, Veg. Fact is, I had only heard rumours that these guys existed. Knew about the Tengu the Baron der Boltz had and what a shithead that creature was, but had no idea that there were a lot more of them.'

Stephine gave him a small grin. 'The prototype was made a long long time ago on Storfisk and it was a true ACE. These are a few generations further from them and from the Tengu that was with the Baron. They are created by the Haulers and their crew on some of the more hostile missions to star systems a long way from the Sphere. Almost perfect troops.'

'Almost?'

Veg laughed. 'Always room for improvements, eh, Mr Carrington? Long time no see, old friend. May I introduce Major Michael Longbow? And yes, Michael, Mr Carrington does have a first name, but very few of us know it!'

The creature, who was taller than Michael and moved with feral grace and power, shook Michael warmly by the hand before hugging both Stephine and Veg as he said, 'What needs more improvement, Veg?'

Veg poked the Tengu in the chest. 'You lot! Bigger, better, faster, you know, the usual corporate bullshit.'

The Q laughed. 'No way I will get into the ring with you ever, Veg! No way. But I would suggest that you get yourselves something to eat, get refreshed or whatever you want to do, as we are only a couple of hours away from L1. And we expect a bunch of shitfights until we are out in the interstellar LP.'

Basalt's crew were spread throughout the Thorn, manning resupply units or weapons. The ACEs had been left with their mentors.

Marko and Glint sat in compact wraparound seats side by side in one of the weapon stations.

'All crew: this is tactical. The queen is fifty kilometres behind us and no longer talking with anyone. Treat her with caution. Do not get close, but our job is to give her any support that is needed. All fighters launch when able. We are seeing seventeen killers in and around the LP, hundreds of Urchins, plus those big ice asteroids, and we are 300 kilometres out. You are weapons free. Final upload of Soul Saver information. Soul Saver links are established. Do not hesitate to use them as we will not be able to swing around if you are stranded. As soon as the queen jumps, so do we. Good shooting!'

Marko and Glint watched the squadrons of Skuas, and the few Mauls, pulling away from their launch platforms and moving out ahead of the Thorn.

'I am seeing numerous mid-sized Urchins, Marko.'

'Yeah, me too, buddy. If they look like they are going to try and land on us, we smash them.'

Glint nodded enthusiastically. 'Good! I do not like Urchins, Marko. I did not like being onboard *Basalt* when we were inside Zawgyi. It felt very wrong.'

'Know what you mean, Glint. I am still not sure what Stephine sees in them. Could it be that they were creations of the octopoids, like her?'

'There may be truth in what you say, Father,' Glint commented. 'Maybe she had a hand in developing them?'

'Don't know about that, but I do know that one is coming right at us!'

'I see it!'

Marko manipulated the controls, and the hydraulics pushed the weapon pod further out from the hull of the Thorn. He then swung it towards the large Urchin racing straight at them as Glint pulled the trigger on the three-barrelled linear accelerator. He stitched a ring of holes around the creature's centre as Marko triggered another short-barrelled weapon, firing a thin-walled container of gel which seconds later impacted, tearing the core out of the Urchin.

Around the inside of the transparent dome in front of them, more threat icons appeared. Marko muttered, 'Shit! This is not going to be easy. Why are there so many of the bastards? This place is crawling with them.'

As Glint started firing at another, he said, 'Crawling? They would need something solid to actually crawl upon! Flying silently through vacuum with a steam-powered rocket up their arses would be a more apt description, Marko. Your speech is still so messed up! But yes, I agree there are a great deal of them.'

'All crew: this is navigation. We are fifteen minutes away from the optimum jump point in L1. Stand by for deceleration to allow the queen to pass as we go into the LP. You will get a one-minute warning.'

'Crew, this is tactical. We are seeing what looks like armoured spheres emerging from the asteroids. Do not engage them unless they attack your craft or position. They are predators of the Urchins. And we can but hope that they are also interested in the killers.'

'Glint! Twelve o'clock, 5020. Two killers. Mess them up a little, then switch back to the two Urchins at eleven o'clock low.'

'Seen!'

As Glint fired, then switched targets and fired again, Marko glanced up and down the length of the Thorn's outer hull, seeing that the other defensive pods were firing at different targets, and realised that the threat targets he could see on their HUDs were the ones intended for them to deal with.

Swearing at himself for his stupidity, he sped himself up, told his system to link to Glint, and rapidly selected and prioritised targets, firing as fast as the ammunition feeds would allow. Even sped up he could not help himself and wondered why there were so many Urchins, predators and killers in the system. He selected the next ten targets, instructed his bioware to take care of them and opened a comms link to Stephine.

'There are too many here, Stephine. Far too many for this to be natural. What do you know of this? Is this a breeding ground for the octopoids? Did your ancestors breed the

Urchins for a purpose and then the predators to take care of them if their numbers rose too high?'

He wondered why he had to wait so long for a reply. Eventually she said, 'Yes. The Urchins were created to guard the Lagrange points of the octopoid master race. They also created their food sources and the predators a long time ago. Yes, you are correct, Marko. Your questions are most astute; this system must be one of those long lost breeding areas.'

Marko was about to comment, but Stephine continued. 'It has run amok because it is thousands of years since the octopoid young were harvested by my kind. We of *Basalt* were never supposed to come here. And that queen behind us will probably be the first to escape this system if we help her.'

Glint yelled at him suddenly. 'Bloody hell, Marko! Snap out of whatever the hell you are doing. Look!'

A smashed Maul was tumbling out of control on a collision course with the hull beside them.

'Shit! Sorry!'

He ramped up his vision, looking for the state of the two-man crew.

'Tactical! Pod nine. Maul on collision course with us!'

The voice quickly said, 'Close your shields. Crew is dead. Missile impact in ten seconds!'

Glint rapidly flicked the controls as the outer shields slid over their pod and their weapons were rapidly withdrawn back into their housings. He slowly counted out loud while looking at the HUD, as almost a minute later debris crashed against the hull all around them. He instructed the shield to open again just in time to see an Urchin land right on top of them.

The creature opened its petals wide with dozens of mouths biting into the tough transparent graphene dome.

Glint was yelling something at him, but Marko reacted with fear and extended the stubby barrel of the mortar out into the Urchin and fired twice. The first round exploded just as it emerged from the barrel, damaging the Urchin, but with the shockwave smashing back against the second round which caused it to detonate inside the barrel. Then the even greater back pressure destroyed the weapon and hurled the breech block and feed mechanism back into the armoured rear wall of the pod then bouncing back into Marko. He felt his lower legs being sheered away by the pieces and a huge concussion on his helmet and passed out with most of his suit integrity alarms going off.

Glint looked horrified as blood sprayed out of Marko, until a few seconds later his father's combat suit sealed itself off. Glint's own suit was showing damage and there was also a fire starting in the mortar control panel. He decided that that was the least of his worries as the air pressure rapidly dropped inside the pod when the atmosphere was sucked out through the destroyed gun's barrel. The only plus side was that the air pressure was also giving a little push against the massive injured Urchin, which as soon as it was off the hull was hit again and again by the other pods.

He reached across, looked at the blood-splattered emergency medical readouts on Marko's shoulder and saw that he was seriously injured, but that death was not imminent. He said out loud, 'Medic! Defence pod nine. Marko! Mortar destroyed.'

He then looked out through the dome to see more Urchins on their way, so started firing on them, damaging them as much as he was able.

Seconds later, the tactical officer and his team saw the situation and started reallocating targets to the other defensive positions, taking the pressure off Glint.

He continued firing on Urchins and, on occasion, far distant killers, damaging them and making them easier prey for the dozens of the predator spheres that had joined the fight. He kept glancing across to Marko who remained alive, but was not conscious.

The targets allocated to him started to taper off, so he quickly looked around outside, down the length of the Thorn, seeing the Skuas and one remaining Maul docking.

'Crew! Navigation! One minute!'

He looked out and forwards at the Urchin queen who was now only 500 metres away, followed closely by the heavily armed Fast Mover drones. Suddenly there appeared a strange light around her as the biologically driven wormhole generator was brought to power and then she flashed out of existence, followed a fraction of a second later by the Fast Movers.

Glint let out a long breath as the Thorn also jumped. In the cold eternity of the jump his mind wandered for a split second and wished for warmth and a nice salty pork sandwich, and then they were through with the gas giant many hundreds of thousands of kilometres above them as the targets were allocated again. Glint started wearily firing, wishing that he could comfort his friend and father, but knowing that there was little he could do for him. An armoured clawed hand touched him gently on the shoulder. He turned to look up at the suited Q who said something that he could not make out. The Tengu smiled and nodded at him, mouthing something at him through the clear faceplate.

'Your comms. No work. Marko to medical. You stay or go.'

Glint reached up and combat tapped on the Q's wrist. 'Stay. More fighting. Nothing can do for Marko. Better protect him and all crew from here.'

The Q responded. 'Good. Weapon coming. Technician later. Damage everywhere.'

The Q clapped him on the shoulder and turned away with two of them carrying Marko out with them, his shattered and torn lower legs laid on the stretcher beside his slow-breathing form.

Glint looked out through the blood-splattered dome, searching for the queen, and frowned because he could not see her. In his HUD three targets came up and he spent a few moments hammering away at them with the smart ammunition ... his weapon controlled the timed detonation of it. Knowing almost precisely where the Urchins stored their antimatter, he fired deliberately at that area in the knowledge that even if the gel-like substance, in which the antimatter was stored, was not breeched, the creature would rapidly take itself out of the conflict to conserve itself.

Seeing movement out of the corner of his eye he looked across to see a Q pulling in a missile system. The individual looked at him, nodded, smiled, gave him a thumbs up, then reached down and snapped away the fast mounts of the wrecked mortar and piled them in a corner of the pod. The Tengu then locked the missile system's base in place. Before it continued, the extreme member of humanity pulled a small piece of kit from its belt and placed it against Glint's damaged helmet.

'Hello, Glint! I am Suzie. You punch holes in them from a long distance and I shall blow them up from a short distance.'

'Pleased to know you. Nice to be able to talk again. Thanks. So is that Suzie with an i e or an e y?'

'E y, Glint. Yes, I am female and you are so cute in real life! We have followed you since you were made by Marko.'

Glint nodded. 'Do you know anything of him?'

'Hold on … yes, he is in medical. They are fitting a set of our legs to him. Rapid tech, also an augment to his digestive system and liver to produce the sugars needed. They say he will be up within hours. Kind of stupid what he did though. Point blank range shooting! Huh! Not smart.'

Glint fired at another killer at long-range. It did not seem to have an effect, so he decided to wait until it got closer. He did not feel that he wanted anyone thinking that his father was stupid, but did not know quite how to comment. Instead, he asked, 'So where is that Zawgyi? She should be here by now.'

Suzie finished locking the missile system in place and lowered the launch tubes until they lined up with the hole in the dome created by the destroyed mortar. She loaded two missiles into the tubes then replied, 'Your Stephine thinks that its wormhole generation may not be as fast as ours.'

She moved forwards and taking a long cloth from her gear wiped the blood from the transparent dome in front of them.

'There it is! Underneath us. I can see a lot more of *Basalt*. Looks like the queen has taken damage as a lot of her head petals are gone. Also one of the Fast Mover drones is missing.'

Glint looked at his screens, zooming in on the image of *Basalt* and noting that the ship was barely being held by the queen. He was about to say something when the killer he had shot at earlier started to accelerate towards Zawgyi.

He fired again and bright blue, dart-shaped missiles popped out of their tubes and floated away from the Thorn for a few seconds. They touched together before their engines ignited and they flashed quickly down towards the killer, rotating around a common centre and moving apart. A minute later the killer had been sliced into dozens of pieces.

'Why is the weapon coming back?' Glint asked Suzie.

'Refuelling of course, Glint. Good weapons should not be wasted, don't you agree?'

Glint sent an image of the queen to the major. 'Boss. You seeing this?'

'Yes, Glint.'

'We should try and reboard. Maybe we could help break *Basalt* out?'

'It is a good idea, but not now. We will be jumping again soon, I hope. Keep fighting.'

Glint shrugged, looked for another target, and chewed a few holes in it with the reactive ammunition.

Suzie spoke quickly. 'Ten o'clock high, 1500, Skua in trouble!'

'Seen!'

Glint slewed the guns around, firing at the Urchin that was just about to make contact with the stricken Skua. As the rounds exploded inside it, at the junction of its long spiky tail and head, it twitched massively and moved quickly away. Another was about to attack the Skua, so Glint fired a long burst starting at its tail and racking the slugs up through its centre core, trying to get as close as possible to the antimatter containment area, but not breaching it. The Urchin wrapped its tail around its head and rocketed away.

'Crew, navigation. We have approximately twenty-five minutes to move across the LP to the optimum point for the jump. Lots of asteroids in the area. Expect Urchin predators to join the fight shortly.'

More threat icons started to appear on the HUDs. Looking for the closest one, Glint also saw a large salvage drone moving out towards the slowly tumbling Skua. A fraction of a second later, a guard icon lit up over it. For the next ten minutes they fought hard to keep the Urchins, and what appeared to be juvenile killers, away from the drone and the Skua it had grasped to bring back to the Thorn.

One of the young Urchins they had wounded was intercepted by two predator spheres. Even as he fired on other targets, Glint kept watching the predators and the injured Urchin, trying to record as much as possible as he knew Marko would be very interested.

Just before the two predator spheres came into contact with the writhing young Urchin, they both opened out into bowl-shaped structures; the individual creatures moved far apart from each other, but held each other's tentacles to form a huge net. The net folded over the hapless Urchin, then contracted further and further down until the Urchin vanished inside the large, remorselessly closing sphere that was made of the two smaller ones. As soon as they had locked themselves together, the sphere started to accelerate away towards the largest of the LP captured asteroids.

Glint caught a massive disc-shaped distortion in the starfields and wondered if his vision software was malfunctioning. He was about to run a quick system check when he noticed the collective movements of the Urchins, the killers and the predators.

'Hey, Suzie. They are moving in the other direction. They are moving quickly towards the asteroids. Oh, look … the starfield is twisting a tiny faction! Shit! I've checked and I do not have a malfunction!'

Suzie looked over her displays and shook her head. 'I don't see anything, Glint. But I do see the queen about to jump … too early and look, look! *Basalt* is free!'

'Crew, tactical. Rapid recall of all craft. Assist craft in docking! There is something enormous bearing down on us. Unknown intention. Queen is about to jump. Vectors shown of most dense structure of whatever it is. *Basalt* is free in space. *Basalt* powering up! Queen has jumped! Fast Movers have been reassigned to provide protection to us.'

Glint looked out at the changing situation. He pointed. 'The closest Skuas are docking with *Basalt*. Fuck, look at that!'

A massive, barely visible spear-shaped tendril raged across the sky, seeming to come straight out of the stars to stab through the predator ball. In an instant, the spear head opened out like a flower, folded back on itself to encapsulate the Urchin predators and snatched them backwards. They watched, fascinated, as what appeared to be a huge mouth opened in amongst the stars and saw the ball flung inside. The mouth snapped shut, showing the camouflage of the starfields again.

Glint looked back quickly as *Basalt* jumped. All around them the squadrons of Skua landed hard against the hull of the Thorn, clinging onto its surface with their extended clawlike landing gear.

Just before they jumped they saw dozens of Urchins, killers and predator balls speared and dragged back towards whatever it was that was consuming them. At the instant of the Thorn jumping, the whole ship rocked hard and Glint and Suzie could feel a shockwave run through the pod.

Glint felt the chill of the jump and then they were in the relative quiet of interstellar space at the LP between the Urchins' star system and its companion star as something crashed just out of sight from the pod.

'Crew! Security! Hull breech starboard side aft of pod nine. Biological threat!'

Glint and Suzie looked at each other. They leaned forwards and looked out and down to see a huge thrashing tentacle pounding against the hull with its tip buried deep into the side of the ship.

'Fuck this!' Suzie said.

She pulled herself out of her seat, turned and tapped a keyboard beside the rear airlock door.

The dome split and started opening up. She turned back to her weapon, unlocked it and lifted it onto her shoulder, leaning out of the pod, looking for the alien threat.

'Glint!' she snapped. 'Don't just sit doing nothing, do the same with your gun! Grab the aiming HUD off the console in front of you and lock it onto the gun.'

As Glint scrambled to find and unlock the mounts for the gun, Suzie fired the missiles and guided them down onto the tendril, slicing it through. The dismembered parts floated apart, then seemed to balloon open into fungus-like structures which drifted aft. She brought the missiles up for a second pass as a part of the remaining tendril split open with a lance-appendage flashing out and stabbing the missiles and using them to slice away part of the pod. Glint, grinding his teeth in frustration, finally got the gun off its mount and the aiming unit attached. He leaned out and fired at the missiles, which exploded and showered them with fragments. Out of the corner of his eye he watched Suzie collapsing against the back wall of the pod with shards sticking out of her chest.

Glint growled and fired again on the raging, and now multi-headed, tendril. The exploding rounds tore through it blowing pieces off, but not slowing it down, just as other bullets fired from the only other gun pod that could see the alien also fired upon it. It seemed to know what was inflicting the injuries as the now Medusa-creature slammed itself against the hull and slithered low, rapidly advancing on him. He paused his fire, looked at the ammunition loadouts available, swore at himself for his lack of thinking and selected the oxygen and hydrogen ones with self-ignition. He leaned out as far as the pod and ammo feed belts would allow and fired almost point-blank into the creature. The dozens of tendrils exploded in silent flames and the creature lifted off the hull, allowing him to fire continuously down its length, severing the creature, which thrashed about flailing in the gravity-less vacuum.

The other pod had seen the ammunition he was using and also switched. Seconds later, the tendril was severed a metre off the hull, leaving whatever was embedding itself in the hull as the only threat.

Glint found that he was panting, then grinned, realising that the whole encounter had taken less than thirty seconds. He looked back at the still-writhing section left in the hull: it slowly turned into a squid-like creature that pulled itself out of the hull and started to climb up over the curve of the Thorn. He sighted carefully and fired again, the rounds exploding right under the creature and lifting it off the hull, then, as it tucked itself into a ball, fired directly at it with the other pod doing the same. It started to spin and contracted in size, not showing any damage as a drone missile raced over the curvature of the hull and seized the creature, accelerating away before self-destructing with a hard flash hundreds of metres away.

Glint finally let out his breath and turned to see the limp form of Suzie, along with two Q standing beside him readying a bigger missile launcher. He nodded at each of them and went to check on Suzie to find that she was dead. He stared for a few long moments at the body before another pair of Q arrived to take her body away. He turned back to the other Q who both looked at him and smiled.

He did not feel like smiling, so nodded and started to make his way back to the gun. One of the Q stopped him with an armoured hand on his shoulder, saying, 'For a small dragon you fight very, very well, friend Glint! Maybe you should consider a body upgrade and join us. You are relieved. Go see to the other members of your crew.'

Glint felt annoyed at the casual attitude of the elite troops. 'No, I did not fight well enough. The pod is damaged. My best friend and father is without his legs and Suzie is dead. And I like my body just the way it is!'

The other Q grinned. 'No offence intended, little brother. We hold you in the highest respect. Your Marko has new legs. Bit different to his original ones, it has to be said, and Suzie is fine. Her soul is already in a mechanical chassis as we need her to be able to fight right now. Many of our company are already in the machines. And as soon as we return to *Rose Foxtrot*, she will take over a new body. Go. Go to the medical suite and have your wounds attended. Then have a drink and some food. Go see your crew. You are relieved.'

Glint nodded, reached out and shook both of the Tengu by their hands and cycled himself through the airlock. He leaned against the corridor wall and took stock of himself, checking his systems. He sighed and made his way to the medical suite, suddenly remembering that he had seen *Basalt* but not the queen emerge in the LP.

On the bridge, Michael, Stephine, Veg and Mr Carrington were in discussion.

'We are still waiting for your hybridised Urchin queen to appear, Emissary Stephine.'

'Perhaps because of the distance of the jump it would take her longer, Mr Carrington. She was behind us on the last jump. I estimate that she should be here within an hour.'

The Q major looked evenly at her. 'And the Fast Mover drones have, with their jumper unit, arrived and are about to dock. So if she has escaped us, we would not know where she has gone.'

Michael nodded. 'Which brings us to the question of what is aboard *Basalt*. Patrick said it looks human, but is not made of anything human. Your Skua pilots reported seeing it looking at them in turn when they docked, then it moved off with no form of acknowledgment or contact. They are still attached to the docking platforms and are prepared to investigate.'

The Tengu major shook his head. 'No, I am recalling them. This crew has taken a pounding and we have lost half of the Skuas. I am sorry, but I cannot afford to lose any more considering what we may have to do when we get back to Storfisk.'

Veg leaned down, looking into the eyes of the Tengu. 'Which reminds me, major. Why was there a full complement of Q and their equipment on *Rose Foxtrot*? She was on a delivery run for the Games Board to bring the Gjomvik forces to the planet for a little show and tell, and then to take them to one of the local gas giants' moons for a sanctioned battle. That, as far as I am aware, does not require two companies of Q. She, as far as we know, is not on a long-range mission and you have just said, "What we may have to do when we get back to Storfisk." What is your mission, Mr Carrington?'

The Q looked up into the steely eyes of an entity he had a great deal of respect for. He winced and replied, 'You have no idea what has been put on Storfisk?'

The crew members of *Basalt* shook their heads, staring at him.

The Q puffed out his cheeks and let out a long sigh. 'Oh, this is most awkward. I was under the impression that maybe you knew?'

Once again the heads shook.

'OK. We know that six confirmed, possibly more, soldier-builders of octopoid origin have landed on the great southern peninsula of the Haulers Territory on Storfisk. Here is the information we have on them.'

Stephine gasped when she was halfway through reading. 'What! Did you immediately nuke the area, or at very least neutron bomb the area? Those things are so infective on every possible level. They are mindless horrific killers. And you are here, and not there eradicating them!'

The Q shook his head, then looked up into the eyes of a very angry Stephine. He had been told that she was the emissary of a shadowy, very powerful component of the Administration. He gave her a short bow.

'There is a plan, emissary. It is a good one and, yes, there are risks, but members of the Haulers' Collective believe the risk is worth taking.'

She hissed at him. 'Those things are recorded in the information from the octopoid library. They are confirmed as sentient weapon constructs on the pillars of species, which can be seen in the great carved-stone historical library on the Avian planet. Do not wait for the Urchin queen. We can deal with her later. This is devastating information, major. We must return to Storfisk at greatest possible speed.'

The Q looked unblinking at her. 'With the greatest of all respect, madam emissary, I do not follow orders from you. I shall take your advice, but I am under no requirement to act upon it. As I said, there is a plan to deal with the soldier-builders and we have more than enough resources to deal with the threat upon our return. I shall wait for a few more hours to take care of the Urchin queen when she appears. I shall also return you to your ship so you can make your own way back to Storfisk.'

As Stephine glowered at the Q and opened her mouth to speak, Veg threw back his head and laughed, then cheerfully said, 'Mr Carrington. Major Longbow. Time for a little reveal on my part. Mr Carrington, look into my left eye. I have something to show you. Major Longbow, you next. You can verify. This is a secret you will both keep.'

An instant later the Q major, looking more than a little bit upset, almost lost his detached reserve.

Michael Longbow burst out laughing and clapped his hand on Veg's massive shoulder. 'Coding verified. He is what he says he is, Q.'

The Q major swallowed hard and snapped to attention. 'What are the general's orders, please?'

Veg looked down at the augmented human, feeling almost sorry for him. 'Do what the lady says,' Veg said with a smile. 'She says go, we go ... now. Lock *Blackjack* hard against your hull. Send instructions to Patrick on *Basalt* to learn as much as he can of whatever the hell is onboard ... what it is doing there and why, and to go with us as we jump. Oh, and tell him what is awaiting us on Storfisk. He has friends there as well. He will be none too happy about that.'

Haast

Gas Giant Moon

Bob stood in the middle of the bridge, looking down at the harsh windswept snow- and ice-covered mountainous terrain of the battle area. He glanced down at his hands and wondered what surprises the brigadier would spring on him on the third day of battle.

He looked over the conflict reports, and the AV feeds. The Games Board were still crowing over them, saying the exciting footage would have great appeal to the various audiences throughout the far-flung Sphere of Humankind.

'May I have a moment of your time, please, commander?'

He inwardly groaned, knowing that the monitor beside him would have recorded everything he had been doing since leaving his cabin a few minutes earlier to climb the grand spiral staircase from the senior crew accommodations to the bridge. He fixed a pleasant smile on his face and tried to look calm as he turned towards the partially living camera unit which once had been a human.

'Of course, monitor. How may I be of assistance to the Games Board and consequently the billions of conflict followers.'

The monitor's face, with its overly made-up large eyes and its sculpted ears, smiled widely at him. Bob looked from the face down to the brightly coloured, fashionable, tailored top covering ample breasts and perfectly painted fingernails on what he could only consider augmented hands and fingers since they were longer than any he had ever seen on anything but a weapons system.

'We have a little time before breakfast and the first of today's battles, so I wonder if I may ask your views on the marvellous brigadier and how his forces have managed to cut a swathe of destruction through yours?'

He smiled with his best 'I am the wounded but valiant warrior' smile. 'Yes! Is he not a marvellous tactician, planning his conflicts with the utmost accuracy and aplomb? I feel honoured to be his adversary and have this opportunity to learn so much from a great man who is widely admired throughout the Sphere.'

The once-woman smiled with even more vigour as her eyes sparkled. 'Oh, yes!' she gushed. 'His deployments and wonderful battlefield tricks are seemingly endless! Like you, commander, I too have enjoyed this conflict and I just know that it will rate highly on the entertainment screens wherever our sentient clients reside. My thanks and may you score some solid hits upon your opposition today.'

Bob smiled inwardly and gave himself a tiny mental pat on the back, knowing that Michelle and Nick would be happy with his performance to camera. The monitor turned with her fixed and panning cameras to go and speak briefly with each of the bridge crew on his watch, and as she went from person to person spent those few moments extolling the virtues of a myriad Games Board-endorsed products.

Lost in thought of how he could put one across the brigadier, he did not notice Nick Warne until he was at his elbow. He let out a long sigh, then greeted the shorter man.

'Morning, Nick. Night shift had nothing to report, except that the maintenance staff spent the night assembling the spare aircraft. OK, give it to me. How many aircraft and crew can we muster?'

Nick Warne looked into the drawn sombre face of his student and longtime friend. 'Hope you managed some sleep, Bob. Yeah, well, we are down to two salvage craft now after that brilliant ambush and capture of the two Maul that had forced landings. We have one Aurora after those other two flew into whatever the hell it was that the Aquila forces used against them. Looked like some sort of rapidly solidifying smoke to me. Two Hawks: the one that crashed into the mountain top has been repaired and is flightworthy, and the other that had its engines blow up and was recovered from the glacier, has also been repaired. Our full complement of Chrysops is OK. Two were repaired overnight. Pity that the two maintenance pilots who were flying them could not be as readily repaired. But the Mauls are way down. Sorry, but the three squadrons plus four spares are now down to only eight.'

'Eight! Bloody hell! Paul Black promised me ten! Useless bastard.'

Nick grinned. 'Nope. Don't go hard on him. He has been driving his crews hard. He has done well. Come on, we won't have to queue up for breakfast with half the crew already captured by the Aquila. At least we know that those still breathing will be well fed by them.'

At breakfast, the remaining crews nodded to the superior officers, everyone putting on a show for the three Games Board monitors who were recording their every move.

Captain Viggo Eames grinned widely, looking down at the powerful, squat form of the pilot, Major Nico Matsis. 'Wonder how things are going to go today, Nico? Your turn in the front seat. Better to leave me do the shooting anyway, eh! I hit them while you just spray bullets all over the landscape!'

Nico looked up into the beautiful face of his longtime friend and fellow Gjomvik pilot. 'Yeah, yeah, sure. I miss once, and you smoke two with one burst. And now you are the whizz-bang jock. Vig, you are full of shit.'

Viggo started filling his plate with steamed vegetables and filled a second plate with slices of pineapple. He then gestured at Nico's plate, filled with fried bacon, hash browns and eggs.

'Just as well that we are at either end of the aircraft,' Viggo mused. 'Hate to fly with you in the left seat when you've had a breakfast like that! Your farts stink!'

'Huh! Like your flying, ya useless turd! Hey, mate, the bosses don't look too pleased this morning.'

The tall, willowy form of Anneke Bester was in front of them selecting the bowlful of chopped fruits and nuts she always had for her breakfast. She quietly said, 'Nor would you be if, on your first deployment as the commander of a brand-new carrier, you had your arse handed to you on a plate.'

The two men grimaced and shrugged as they moved across and sat down at one of the tables. It had a superb view of the distant sun rising over the horizon, flooding the mess area in golden light.

'Yeah,' Nico murmured, 'but, bloody hell, look who we got slammed up against. Just as well this thing finishes today. We are going to have to be very quick and very smart not to get decked today, people. So, Anneke, how the hell did you manage to slap down those bloody Saluki helicopters in a one on three after your number two Maul got chopped?'

She was just about to answer when the familiar figures of one of the numerous long-term married couples of Magret and Johan Etz placed their meals on the table. Magret said, 'Yeah, I would like to hear that. I know that you came back flying on fumes, Anneke, and that the Games Board is going ape over the action.'

Anneke popped a few more nuts into her mouth, chewed and swallowed, smiling demurely. 'It's all about reading the ground. That and a good tail gunner. Not sure where Vishav is.'

'Be up to his elbows in tech somewhere,' Johan said.

Anneke nodded, leaned across and took a small sliver of toast off Viggo's plate. She held it up. 'So this is us, OK. Two were chasing us and I knew that that mountain range had triple peaks with a nice basin between them. It was a howling gale and a hellish ride, as you all know. We hammered over the top and I dropped down into the bowl. I suspected that they were driving me into a trap. One of the Saluki came over the top of the range with the other two hiding, hovering below the outer lip of the crest. I glimpsed one who had put his targeting tower up over the top to see where I was. So I yelled at Vish giving him the position where that one was, rolled hard over, dived and skidded on the AG right across the top of the ice up under the ridgeline and waited. The first one poked his nose over so I rolled the machine on its back and hammered him with the front rotary as Vish fired along the ridgeline where the other one was. Had the desired effect of smashing a tonne or so of ice through his rotors. So he was out. The one I hit in the nose had smoke pouring out of him and he took off, so then I rolled back over, hugged the ground and backed the Maul up the ridge so Vish had a perfect shot when the third came up looking for us. Simple, really.'

Viggo, with a twinkle in his eyes, looked at her and replied, 'Yeah, sounds right. Roll a Maul over and have someone pat its tummy. Can I have my toast back, please?'

'So now we have to put up with Bravo flight deck, do we?'

Sitting in the heavily armoured rear turret of the Maul, Viggo adjusted his seat, instructed it to lock itself around him and grimaced slightly before he replied.

'Yes, Nico. There is fuck-all of us left. Just as well it's the last day. You know, Anneke's idea of showing them the underside of the Maul is not a bad idea. It's where the best armour is, anyway. And you know what? It's the best of the best left. We should have been a squadron from the outset.'

Nico's voice sounded in his ears. 'Yeah, yeah, you are probably right, but Warne would not have allowed us all together in the first place. Says we are too much trouble. I'm thinking of chucking the rule book out the window today. Last blast and let's fuck up as many Aquila as possible.'

Viggo nodded to himself, looking at his screens. 'Well, we have a ten-minute transit flight to the smaller 100-square-kilometre operational area. How about we discuss new tactics on the way out?'

'Yeah, time for a change, I think. Thompson's ideas are really good, but he is going a bit by the book. Hold on, here we go. Lock down your canopy, Vig.'

Checking the time, Nico waved at the ground crew and started each of the engines in turn, firing up one turbine in each pod then starting the two turbines in the back of the hulking machine. He watched as the engines all quickly came up to temperature and that the two antigravity units, buried inside the fuselage, were spooling to lifting power from their quiet state of neutral.

'Bravo squadron, this is flight. Weather Charlie. You have your individual post-launch vectors. You have a go for launch. Sound off when at the point of drop.'

Nico fed power to the turbines as the launch platform on which the Maul was locked slid out of its hangar and out over the side of the carrier. Looking to his left and right, he could see the other three Mauls on that side of the carrier were ready to take to the air. He waited as the other Mauls' pilots sounded off their numbers and acknowledged weather for the area then said, 'Flight Bravo two, Charlie, ready.'

The other two Mauls sounded off as did the Aurora high above them, and also the two Hawks who would fly the inner protective cordon around the carrier.

'All crews: this is flight. Drop, drop, drop!'

Immediately, the locks holding the Mauls to their platforms disengaged and Nico and the other pilots pushed the power into the antigravity units and slid into the air. With his two joysticks, and feet controlling the rear rudders, Nico felt for the wind and air currents through the seat of his pants and quietly flew out from the carrier to his designated departure area. Once there he fed more power to the turbine pods, rotating them up from vertical to level, as the fuselage of the Maul started to generate its own lift. As soon as he passed the 120 kilometres per hour mark, he lowered the power in the antigravity units until they were idling at neutral, and increased power lifting the nose to join his wingman.

Sliding up behind the lead Maul, he saw Will in the rear gun turret. Nico pulled a little piece of equipment from his flight vest and waved it at Will, who nodded, doing the same.

The units looked for each other and any other line of sight laser comms units within range. Within a few minutes, the aircraft of Bravo squadron could communicate amongst themselves with no outside eavesdropping.

Major Nina Heatly, who was flying the Maul that Will sat in the back of, gave her reasoning. 'Been thinking and having a quiet word with a few of the guys and we think that the commander's battle plan for today is not that good. If we want to come out of this with any credibility, I know we need a new plan. Any dissension?'

All the others, having watched their fellow crews getting shot down or forced down by the sheer brilliance of the brigadier's tactics of separation and his use of terrain, were itching to try something different than the Mauls' two standard skirmishing and ground attack methods they had been using. The orders for the day were the same: pairs operating in specific areas, hunting the Saluki or waiting for them to come to them.

Vishav Jyani in the rear of Anneke Bester's Maul said, 'Well, we need to try something new at least. I have argued with Mr Warne and also the commander that the tactics of the last two days have not been working, but they seem much more interested in something else. What could they be waiting for?'

Lieutenant Traci Bannon, with her sergeant major husband Robb as gunner, spoke up. 'We are treating the battle typically as ground support, which is what this aircraft is all about. We should treat them as bombers. Go for a box formation. All together. Great collective firepower that way and let the Aquila helicopters come to us. We could swat them like flies.'

'Captain Etz,' Nina said. 'You are the historian. Good idea?'

Johan Etz thought for a few seconds before he cleared his throat. 'Well, major, I am in the back seat, just along for the ride, but yes, I see no reason why that would not work very well. My only question is, what if it goes wrong? Who will explain this to the commander? And the Games Board monitors will be invisible to us until we are out of the fight. Annoying that we cannot use our radar, as it would be easy to identify where they are so we would know where the Aquila aircraft would be. But that would not make for good AV, would it.'

There was a long silence before Nina said, 'OK. The hell with this. I need to talk with the commander.'

Using the controls on the top of one of her joysticks, she activated a secure link. '*Haast*, this is Bravo one. Request secure link to the commander.'

'Roger. Stand by, Bravo one ... Bravo one, this is the commander. What's happening, major?'

Nina took a long, deep breath. 'Sir, with all due respect, if we carry out this same two-ship harrying plan as we have done in the last two days, we are going to get creamed again. We would much rather go for a box section formation with everyone and let the Saluki come to us while we fly in formation around a nice and nasty craggy mountain top.'

There was silence from *Haast* so Nina decided to press her case further. 'That way we could use the aircraft to best advantage. We have a shorter flight endurance time than the Saluki, so we cannot muck about. And with everyone firing intersecting arcs, we could do them great damage.'

She took a breath and was about to continue when the commander interjected. 'I understand. But. Well. As you know, we have been playing this battle on the safe side. How many of our aircraft have been blown to bits and how many crew are tanked or even seriously hurt? Think about it, Nina. You are not the carrier combat aircraft OC for nothing.'

Her eyes narrowed, then she pursed her lips. 'Ah, I think I see. There is another game right after this one, isn't there?'

'Yes, so please follow the battle plan and ask Captain Bester and Lieutenant Jyani to refrain from blowing the crap out of the Saluki, even if they are very good at it.'

Nina frowned. 'Just have to ask. You have not been bought off and this is not a bet twister, is it? And this battle you speak of, once this one is over, is it Games Board sanctioned?'

'No. You can rest assured, nothing to do with gambling or fixing. It is much more serious than that. And no, it is not sanctioned. At least not that I know of. Put on a good show for the Games Board. *Haast*, out.'

Nina looked over the clouds, seeing the mountain peaks jutting up out of them, and wondered what she was going to say to the crews. She tapped the intercom icon.

'Will, there is a much bigger game on after this one. A non-sanctioned one. We are to go with the battle briefing and play softly.'

Will, who was sitting with the seat back and footrests extended out to their maximum to accommodate his height, grimaced. He and Nina had been together for such a long time, he knew from the tiniest intonation of a word how she was feeling about things.

'Yeah, wondered about that. That Saluki I hit yesterday should have gone bang considering the amount of rounds I hit him with. All he did was pull up with smoke pouring out of him and spiralled down to an OK-looking landing. So, hold on, am I getting this right? You say play softly. We are being preserved? Both us and the Aquila?'

'That's my take on it, Will. You happy about this?'

He smiled. 'Of course, Nina. Where you go, I do also, but just with more firepower.'

Nina winked at her husband, smiled, then continued: 'OK. Listen up, guys. Just had words with the commander. We go with his briefing. There is a reason, and although I do not know the details, I believe that it is a good one. Break off into your pairs and let's go look for Saluki.'

There was a long pause before anyone answered. Johan Etz finally said, 'Good. Wondered. We took a few good hits yesterday that should have knocked us down, but we just lost power on the starboard-side engines. All makes sense now.'

Nina nodded to herself and toggled the intercom again. 'Will, before you put away your secure comms unit, get Anneke for me, please.'

'OK ... hey, Anneke! Nina wants to talk.'

Anneke looked out at the Bravo one aircraft that was pulling away from them. 'Nina?'

'The commander asks that you and Vish don't waste the Saluki today. Just mess them up a little.'

Anneke harrumphed then cocked her head to one side, knowing that sometimes the Games Board requested a different outcome, and pinched her lips. 'Weird! That's no fun! But you are the boss. OK, we hear you. Talk later.'

Nina let out a long breath. 'Bravo one, Bravo two. Swing out, maintain parallel 300 metres. Let's go hunting.'

Nico shrugged his powerful shoulders. 'Bravo two, Bravo one. Parallel 300. Let's go play tag with the nice Saluki.'

Nina increased the thrust of the turbines and started the two in the rearmost engine pods, lifting the nose and aiming for their designated patrol area. The winds had started to pick up a little and the updraughts from the mountains below started to buffet the aircraft. She grinned to herself, loving the feel of the powerful wingless aircraft and its immediate response to the slightest change of the flight controls. But most of all she loved the feeling of the aircraft as an extension of herself. She thought about the action and the visor on her helmet slid down to cover her face. She thought again and the seat conformed a little more to her fine muscular body, holding her a little tighter to itself.

The visual recognition systems of the Maul looked everywhere at once, seeing and tagging the slightest movements or changes in the environment through the four optical spheres positioned on the aircraft. As an item of interest was seen, the computer would log it and bring it to the two crews' attention in the HUDs.

Two very slight temperature variations high up on the side of the massive craggy bluff to their port side were detected.

Will, seeing the icons come up in his HUD, swung the gun pod around until the thirty-millimetre, long-barrel, twin rotary cannons were covering the area. Feeling the change in the drag on the aircraft as the pod swung to the side, Nina automatically adjusted the engine pods and power settings to compensate. She knew that the timings for the first engagement were also right, so she started the remaining two forward turbines, giving her access to full power.

Nico, in the second aircraft, saw what was happening and also started his other engines. 'Vig! Heads up, mate.'

Viggo was looking at the valley floor 500 metres below them and then up the sides of the cliffs around them, seeing the series of small plateaus. There was a sudden chill in his spine. 'Nico! Bravo one. Climb hard! We are about to be ambushed!'

Nico did not answer, simply poured on the power and started to climb hard.

Nina pulled back on the control sticks, slamming on the power, trusting in the extraordinary instincts of impending danger that Viggo had demonstrated time and time again over all the years she had known him. Below them, the snow-camouflaged covers were pulled off the gun emplacements, which fired 100-metre-long ropelike spears up at them.

Viggo and Will called out the warnings to their pilots as the spears split and then split again, dragging black filaments out, forming large nets that, controlled by the tiny rockets at their ends, curved about the sky, trying to land onto the Mauls.

Viggo quickly looked over the emplacements, attempting to identify the possible controllers, but gave up an instant later and started firing anyway, strafing the area.

As Nina threw the Maul all over the sky, Will wondered about the area where the two heat signatures had been seen. 'Break right! Climb! OK. Break left! Dive! Roll right! Good!'

He let off a long, tearing, mind-numbing burst with the rounds exploding all around the two spots on the mountain side and seconds later the ribbon nets lost cohesion.

Viggo called out, 'Bravo one. There will be Saluki close. Ready your chin guns!'

Nina yelled, 'Will! You have my guns.'

Will tapped the screens so he could see what the forward rotary and the missile launcher could see. 'Got 'em!'

He quickly programmed two missiles to do what he wanted and fired them. They launched one after the other from the launcher under the front of the Maul, racing away from the ship to climb to the top of the cliff face, then curve over it and detonate.

The Maul charged vertically up the side of torn and jagged rock, rolling over the top to be met by three Saluki hovering close to the ground, whose pilots were still gathering their wits after the two missiles had peppered them with fragments. Will fired on the centre one as the one on their right fired a long burst into the starboard-side turbines, which immediately started to shut down. The centre helicopter promptly landed with smoke pouring from its engine exhausts. Nina's hands flashed across the controls, ramping the antigravity units up to compensate for the loss of lift. She flung the Maul in a tight left turn as Will fired into the second Saluki, knocking it down just as rounds raked them, heavily damaging the port-side engines.

Bravo two howled over the lip of the mountain range top with the chin gun already targeted on the remaining Saluki. Viggo fired, smashing the armoured helicopter down its left side and filling the jet turbine covers with holes. It immediately lost power and hard landed.

Nina laughed, and then grimaced, seeing the readouts of the damage to her beloved Maul. She hovered the machine thirty metres above the three downed Saluki, while the wind started to blow her away over the mountain top. She lowered the landing gear and called, 'Bravo two. I am out of propulsion. Can you land me, please?'

Nico washed speed off his Maul and swung around, balancing the four engine pods outwards to swing over the top of the stricken Bravo one. Once in position he deployed his rear landing leg, extending the three-clawed foot out to carefully grasp the lifting point on the back of Bravo one, and then gingerly pushed the Maul back to where the three Saluki were. He put the Maul down on the snow- and ice-covered rocks. As soon as they made contact, Nico disconnected and Nina powered down the antigravity while the machine settled into the snow.

High above them two Games Board antigravity sleds with a pair of monitors on each became visible. Nina saw them and sighed.

'Nico. Take over the squadron. As per the rules of this engagement, I and these fellow Saluki pilots are out of the fight. We will wait here for the Games Board recovery units. Will see you when we do.'

The Games Board sleds and their occupants vanished again.

Nico acknowledged the message, peeled off and, gaining airspeed, flew down the side of the mountain.

'What's the plan, Nico?'

Nico looked out through the canopy and the forbidding terrain, wondering what they could do effectively on their own. He tapped the comms icon of Traci and Robb.

'No doubt you can see from your screens that Nina is out. We knocked down three Saluki, so by my reckoning that would leave sixteen still available to fight somewhere around here.'

'See that you are now the head honcho,' Traci said. 'OK, swing by over to us and let's see what we can go find.'

Nico tapped his navigation screen, querying where Bravo seven and eight were. Their icons lit up so he poured on the power taking the Maul lower towards the valley floor to fly nap-of-the-earth. He thought about the intercom link and, seeing it open, said, 'Hey, ya slack arse passenger. What are your thoughts, Vig?'

Viggo studied the area that the two Mauls were in. 'I should be flying, Nico, then you would not have to ask me questions!'

Nico laughed raucously. Viggo smiled then continued. 'Arse yourself. OK, look where seven and eight are heading. Look where the last known position of the Aquila carrier was. What is the betting that three or four Saluki are stalking the Mauls?'

Nico looked at his screens, then up at the HUD, mentally telling it to expand and plot the positions of his friends.

'And that is why you will not be allowed to fly the truck, Vig. You are much too good at thinking about shit. OK, good plan. Let's go see. Some evil terrain between us and them.'

He grinned to himself as he flew the machine at full power, weaving through and up and over the rocky outcrops and vertical toothlike rock slabs and keeping an eye on the ever-present towering cliffs on either side of the aircraft.

Thirty minutes later, having taken a tortuous route to get a few kilometres behind the other Mauls, Viggo reported, 'Saluki exhaust gases in the air. They are burning kerosene just like on the other days. Think that they are between us and the Mauls.'

'OK. Hold on … yeah, I see one, twelve o'clock, 900 metres! And there are the other two ahead of that one. They are flying line astern. Nice! Love it when an enemy is so cooperative.'

Viggo sat in the cramped armoured gun pod and looked up from his screen. On a whim, he cleared his HUD of all information, his fingers tapping out a slightly agitated rhythm on his control columns as he thought about things. 'Nico, I think that we should disable these ones. Not wreck them. There is something not quite right with all of this. The commander is normally much more aggressive and I have been thinking through the battle results that Aquila normally racks up as well. And Nina says to stick with the battle plan.'

Nico sat quite still in the pilot's seat, quietly concentrating on flying the Maul around the difficult terrain and keeping close to the ground, using the huge rocks as cover to allow them to get close to the Saluki. In a subdued voice, he answered, 'Yeah, yeah, know what you mean. There should be smoking ruins of aircraft half buried in the dirt and a chunk of us with our Soul Savers attached to our zygotes in tanks by now. But hey, mate, you know that sometimes battles have gone this way before, so what do you think?'

Viggo tapped the screen listing his ammunitions. 'I am thinking that there is a bigger game afoot. You know how I said to you ages ago that I felt something was wrong when we were in that marketplace in the Waipunga village on Storfisk, and I was chatting up that hot woman who said she was a teacher.'

Nico laughed. 'Yeah, the one who did not want to fuck you and kept looking at me! You think that she felt wrong because she thought you were gay, Viggo.'

Viggo shook his head, mildly exasperated. 'No, Nico. Not that. She felt wrong. Like she was an operative. There was something about her that was wrong. Too highly trained, too fluid in her movements. Just a bit too good at what she was trying to put across. Reminded me of Uncle. You know that I am good at seeing things that are being hidden in the open. I think that she was Jan Wester from *Basalt*. The one the Games Board killed. There were other things I saw there as well, Nico. ACEs everywhere. Yeah, I know they are created by the local families, but there were more than even I expected. To say nothing of what happened with the beetle flight over that village.'

Nico looked at his screens, then up again at the slowly closing gap between them and the Saluki helicopters. He let out a long breath, thinking that Viggo had never voiced anything that he did not know and that his ability to know secrets was a major squadron asset.

'OK, Viggo,' Nico answered seriously. 'Tell me what you want to do.'

Viggo's fingers were dancing over his weapons loadout screens. 'I am loading the missiles with black oxygen warheads. Let's just hope the Saluki pilots are on warmed external air, with sensors to switch to internal supply if needed. Should be, it's standard kit. If we knock them out and they crash and burn, it would kind of defeat the exercise of trying to preserve them. Also changing out the rotary ammunition to paint. I will program the missiles to go after all three Saluki. As soon as the turbines fail, I need you to get us over the tops of them so we can mess up their canopies and live AV feeds.'

'Buckle up tight then. OK, I see the missile armed icons have just come up. Ammo ready?'

'Yeah. Going for a slow missile flight time. Will launch when we are 300 metres behind the last one. Will shout when I get them to climb.'

Nico ramped up the power and watched his optical screen, seeing the range closing fast. From below and behind him he felt the soft thuds of the missiles launching and a moment later saw them far ahead of the Maul, hugging the terrain as Viggo actively controlled them which he was allowed to do under the articles and rules of war as they were classed as non-lethal weapons. Just when Nico considered that the range was perfect, he rammed the throttles open and the Maul leapt ahead.

The guided missiles quickly accelerated and turned upwards, flashing up in front of each of the Saluki dispersing the tiny bomblets in a cloud which detonated, forming a dense fog of chemicals which snatched the oxygen from the rich atmosphere for hundreds of metres around each of the Saluki. Nico watched on his tactical screen for the effects of the bombs, flying the Maul straight up and over the tops of the areas as Viggo's guns started firing on the rearmost autorotating helicopter, splattering the thick viscous etching paint over the upper parts of the canopy and the targeting AV sensors.

The Maul's speed was increasing as they quickly overhauled the second Saluki, which was caught in an updraught lifting the powerless machine close to the sheer rock walls. Nico quickly brought the Maul's oxygen turbine feeds online and flew straight into the cloud using the machine to push the helicopter away from the rock walls as Viggo also covered it in paint like the first. The Maul then rolled away again, roaring up the cliff faces as the third Saluki, even as it was autorotating towards a clear spot on the ground for a hard landing, fired on them, punching holes down the centre of the aircraft and crazing the canopy over Viggo. He calmly swung the guns around and covered every surface of the helicopter he could see with paint, ensuring that it was out of the battle.

Viggo could hear Bravo seven and eight congratulating them on an amusing way of taking out the Saluki, but ignored them to listen to Nico instead.

'We gotta go home. Vig! Hope like shit none of these other fuckers want a piece of us as we have no antigravity power available. Top turbines are out. One rear port-side turbine is stuffed and the other running rough.'

He looked over at the friendly forces' tactical screen. He could see that the two Mauls of Anneke and Traci were still in the fight.

'Bravo seven. You have the ball. Play loose and don't break anything, OK?'

Anneke grimaced, hoping that Nico had survived the encounter, but also secretly glad that she was able to have a little play at being the OC, even if only for a short time.

'Bravo two, Bravo seven. Understood.'

Nico flew the Maul up above the mountain tops and swung it towards the carrier. He watched the turbine in the port rear engine pod starting to overheat, so he shut it down and closed the fuel feeds to the pod as well. He brought up his navigation screen and saw that he could either take the aircraft out of the designated battle area by turning south and flying a relatively short distance — ensuring they would not get shot at once outside the battle area — or fly directly for *Haast*, which would cut their flight time by forty minutes.

'Wow! Earthquake! Big one! Shockwave coming in at your five o'clock, Nico.'

Nico looked down through the starboard-side lower cockpit window to see the massive shockwave travelling through the ragged terrain below them: a huge billowing rising cloud of ice dust and snow was being created right behind it, as some of the mountainsides slipped into the valleys below.

'Shit! That's fucking enormous!'

He tapped his comms icon for *Haast*. '*Haast*! Huge earth tremor coming in your direction! This is Bravo two. We are 140 klicks north of you.'

The communications officer on *Haast* acknowledged immediately. 'Bravo two, *Haast*. Seen!'

Alarm bells were ringing throughout *Haast* as it flew sedately above a long deep valley in moderately light winds. Nick Warne had been relaxing in his command pod, but now quickly looked for the threat to the carrier.

'Navigation! Up 300 now!' He hit the ship-wide comms. 'All crew: brace! Emergency climb!'

The huge turbofans immediately went to full power, rotating until they were vertical. The antigravity units in the centre of the ship were also powered up, forcing the carrier to climb quickly into the local midday sky. Everyone who was not seated and locked in struggled to hang onto whatever they could to stop themselves from being thrown around by the harsh manoeuvres. Those who were close to windows saw the shockwave rip through the ground underneath them, generating a huge cloud of finely powdered ice, dust and snow.

As soon as they had attained a safe altitude and were high above the roiling clouds, the carrier's turbofans slowed and the antigravity was powered back to neutral buoyancy.

'Comms, this is Warne. Get me the Games Board director and make contact with the Aquila. Inquire as to their status and say that we are standing by to give assistance if required.'

'Mr Warne, the director.'

The comms screen lit with the pampered, haughty face of the director looking at him.

'Major Warne. Yes, yes, I know about the earthquake. I am about to sit down to my lunch. Why is the commander not talking with me as the Aquila brigadier is? Are you his minion for today?'

Nick Warne felt his hackles rise and used every shred of self-control to not allow his face to colour. He smiled, hoping that it looked genuine as he nodded to the screen. 'I am sorry for the interruption, Director John. The commander is on the upper flight deck getting suited up and I am duty officer.'

The director scowled at him. 'Well? I suppose like the Aquila, you also want a pause in the battle to assist in the rescue of the trapped Saluki pilots? Stupid fools if you ask me. Six machines all lying in wait in deep ravines waiting to pounce and put your miserable Mauls out of the game. What a ridiculous name ... for all they are worth they should be called nadel hammer. Miserable performance with a few exceptions. Very well. Battle is ended. Oh, yes, I have been reliably informed that those two damaged monitors you still have onboard have been repaired by your Sergeant Major Kyle. Tell him he can keep them as pets! I have had enough of this ghastly boring place. I am going to see what interesting sights the local gas giant has to offer. A few nature programs might balance the books on this otherwise pedestrian expedition.'

The connection severed as Nick was about to reply. He tapped the blank screen with his fingers and silently wished the director a horrible total death. Seconds later, the screen lit up with icons, everyone wanting to talk to him. He quickly prioritised, shunting various reports and requests to other members of the bridge crew, while in the back of his mind he wondered who had told the Games Board about the secret repairs to the monitors.

'Navigation. Take us at best possible speed to Bravo seven's position.'

'Acknowledged. Bravo seven's position. Best speed.'

He looked over the other situation summaries as they came up on the boards. Nick then tapped the commander's icon.

'Commander, Games Board is bugging out. The monitors currently onboard are leaving on their sleds. Their systems airship is dropping all of ours, plus the damaged Aquila craft, and crews down onto the ice below them, so they are reneging on the original agreements.'

Bob Thompson was climbing into the Aurora recon aircraft.

'OK. Good! Bloody good! Pleased to see the back of that lot. Right. Send the two Hawks over to orbit the drop zone. Get yourselves over there and grab everyone before more earthquakes arrive, then move over to Bravo seven. I see that the Aquila carrier was on the ice when the quake struck. I wonder if he has damage? I will find out then go start looking for the missing Saluki.'

'Bravo two, *Haast*, battle is finished. Give assistance to Bravo seven and eight. Six Saluki at their position are under a landslide.'

Nico grimaced. '*Haast*, Bravo two. Be advised we have no antigravity and port rear engine pod is severely damaged.'

The duty controller said, 'Stand by, two … um, just been told to tell you to check your instruments and go for restart on simulated damage.'

Nico swore to himself and shook his head. He brought up the readouts on the unserviceable units and saw that they were all in nominal states so started them up and swung the aircraft around while opening up the throttles.

'*Haast*, Bravo two. It's a miracle! We're showing real holes in the fuselage and engine covers, but they are running sweet. Someone owes me an explanation. En route to Bravo seven.'

'Bravo two, *Haast*. Acknowledged. Yes, miraculous recoveries are occurring all round. Well, apart from a few where real damage occurred. Like use of etching paint.'

Viggo had been listening in on the conversation and burst out laughing. 'So! There really is something on the boil, eh. Wonder what that is, but I bet you a dollar to a pinch of goatshit that it's something nasty, waiting for us on Storfisk.'

Nico gave Viggo's image on the screen a small tight smile. 'How much water are we showing in the atmosphere, Vig?'

Viggo queried a few of the sensors. 'Moderately high, Nico. You want me to start collecting and processing?'

'Yeah, ta. If there is something that requires killing on Storfisk and the Hauler *Rose Foxtrot* is not back, guess how we are going to get there?'

Viggo tapped various screens and the small high-speed compressors on the outside of each of the engine pods all came to life, sucking in the atmosphere and processing it.

Nico looked out the front of the Maul, searching for any sign of Anneke's or Traci's machines. He glanced up at his HUD, seeing where they were supposed to be, then down again into the still-rising clouds of powdered snow and ice. He tapped Bravo seven and eight's icon comms links.

'Bravo seven, eight, two,' Nico said. 'Orbiting above you. Looks a bit crappy down there.'

Traci's voice sounded in his headphones. 'Two, eight. Crap still tumbling down the slopes. We are non-tactical, right?'

'Yes, sure are. Now search and rescue.'

'Go to full mapping radar, Nico. Found two. Anneke is blowing the rubbish off them. I think I see another one under a few metres of ice. Swing down onto me and move out towards the west.'

Nico switched on his full radar and sensing systems, units that would not normally be allowed in any of the sanctioned battle arenas. The effect was dramatic as he could see every detail of the surrounding area.

'Seven, two,' he called. 'On station. Have we any assistance coming from the Aquila?'

'Two, this is Aurora one. Inbound. At your location in six minutes. Heavy salvage on way from Aquila. They have sustained damage to the carrier and will be able to lift to orbit in four hours. Games Board has left for orbit. That is all the time we have.'

Nico looked down at the shattered landscape, wondering how deep the other three Saluki would be and if their pilots would still be alive. He tapped the commander's icon.

'Aurora one, Bravo two, understood.'

An unfamiliar accented voice sounded in Nico's ears. '*Haast*, Bravo two, this is Aquila flight control.'

Nico gave a mental shrug, trying to remember the last time an opposition force command had directly contacted him. He gave up, keying his microphone.

'Aquila flight, Bravo two. How can we assist?'

'I am seeing you hovering in a tight orbit above the last known positions of our six Saluki. I note that three have been located. Stand by for the last transmitted transponder coordinates of the other three.'

Nico called out on the intercom: 'Viggo!'

Viggo looked at his screens, overlaying the data with what his sensors were seeing below them. 'OK, got the points, overlaid and transmitted to the commander and the Mauls. We are just about on top of the nearest. See the point?'

Nico saw the point on his HUD, pulled back on the control columns and descended under power down against a long sloping avalanche of mountain debris. He flew forwards a few metres, rotating the engine pods forwards and washing off speed to hover right above the last known spot of the Saluki. He ramped up the antigravity, flipped its inertia system so it was pressing down, making the unit much heavier, and at the same time pushed all the throttles of the turbines up, so producing a huge jet blast which immediately began blowing the powdered material away. He worked the Maul around and around carefully, watching the effects of the blasting as it very effectively created a deep crater.

'Nico! Lift up! I see the Saluki. Nose high. Severe damage. Rotors are gone. Appears that the pilot is alive. Waving. Do we lift it out or just grab the pilot?'

'Good! No way the others will be that easy. We grab the machine. Hold on.'

Nico switched the camera view on his main HUD from forwards to straight down, looking through the camera that was mounted between the landing gear. After ramping the antigravity back to neutral, he gently flew the Maul back down into the crater, deploying the two front landing gear and extending their claws out to their maximum.

'Vig! I will hover us and you go for the fine control and pickup, OK?'

Viggo tapped the small joysticks on either sides of his seat and they folded up. 'Ready.'

'You have control.'

'I have control.'

He extended the landing gear, legs out as far as they would go, and then lowered the Maul and at a walking pace moved it forwards until the claws were on either side of the Saluki. Using feedback from the ends of the claws in the fingers of his gloves, he gently grasped the fuselage of the battered helicopter, feeling the individual claws sliding around the outer, inward curving, sides of the turbine covers. Knowing that he had a good grip, he lifted it slightly by retracting the undercarriage, feeling the Saluki groaning as it was pulled up a metre through the ice and snow.

'OK, I have it! You have control.'

'I have control.'

Nico, who had been anxiously watching the slowly crumbling edges of their crater, wasted no time and with deliberation lifted the Maul straight up, feeling the final resistance of the Saluki's tail section coming out of the debris. As soon as he felt it come free, he pushed the throttles forwards and slowly climbed through the slowly settling cloud back into the dull sunshine and started to look for a safe place to drop the Saluki onto the ground.

Another unfamiliar voice sounded in his earphones. 'Maul tail number zero niner. This is Aquila salvage. You have a most welcome cargo for me?'

Nico smiled. 'Affirmative, salvage. Excellent! Was wondering where to put the wreck.'

He looked up to see the large rectangular aerial sled slowly orbiting a few hundred metres above them.

'Pleased to serve. Your name? Me, Evan. You climb please, 100 and hold. I come under you. Yes.'

'I am Nico, my crew is Viggo. We are pleased to meet with you.'

'I am good. Yes. Climb now, please.'

Nico slowly climbed up the 100 metres and powered up the antigravity, holding still in the sky against the moderate winds, watching the commander's Aurora reconnaissance aircraft, which had more sophisticated sensors onboard, slowly flying overhead, looking for the other two Saluki.

They watched the flat-surfaced salvage craft, flying mainly on huge antigravity units and small jet turbines, slide across the sky and under them, rotating slightly and then climbing up until the wreck made gentle contact with the deck. Viggo, feeling the thud, said, 'You have it, Evan.'

Cables snaked up out of the deck to search out and grasp the tie-down points on the helicopter.

'Work is good, Viggo. Let go him, please. I send one camera flyer with you. I help if I see right, yes.'

The claws pulled away and then the landing gear retracted as Nico lifted away from the salvage craft on antigravity, He saw Anneke and Traci's Mauls also inbound for the salvage craft with two more Saluki, one of which was barely hanging together. Looking at the state of the cockpit, Viggo thought that the pilot would be dead.

Nico keyed his microphone, but before he spoke the question saw another Saluki hovering above the cloud, its rotors damaged and its fuselage in need of repair, but obviously able to lift itself on antigravity.

They flew back down to an area on the edge of the huge avalanche.

Nico shook his head. 'Be hellish surprised if the pilot of that one is alive. That is just massive pieces of rock. I will fly us slowly up and down. You look closely for any sign, Vig.'

Viggo felt bad. 'Climb us out!'

Nico did not hesitate. He slammed the throttles open, ramped the antigravity up, and they shot up the side of the mountainous cliff face like a cork.

'Not just up! Out, Nico!'

A massive boulder tumbled past them, just barely touching the starboard front engine pod. There was a huge crash as Nico flipped the Maul over on its back, powering them away from the other falling rocks. His fingers flew over his controls, shutting down the engine pod that sounded like it was tearing itself to pieces as he adjusted the thrust from the other pods and ramped a little antigravity into the mix. Seconds later he managed to get the Maul under control.

Viggo saw that the engines were runaways and also on fire. He hit the extinguishers and shut the fuel feeds off, then swung one of the cameras around to look at the smoking ruin, hitting the extinguishers again to be sure. He found himself giggling and Nico joined in.

'One way to fuck a perfectly good set of engines. Dump a shitload of rocks through it. Nice work, Vig.'

'Brilliant fucking flying, Nico.'

Nico let out a long breath. 'So, let's go look for that Saluki again. Anneke is onto the other one. How the hell did you know, Viggo? Shit, man, I am so pleased that you fly with me. Can't remember how many times you have saved our arses.'

Viggo let out a long sigh, nodding. 'Enlightened self-interest, Nico. I hate the fucking Tank. Dunno. Must have seen something on our way in. Just felt incredibly uncomfortable, so I yelled.'

Nico sat up a little straighter in his seat, peering at his HUD and then down at his screens. 'Just as well that you do feel bad sometimes, Viggo. Owe you another dozen beer. Hey! Yeah, wreckage. That giant fuck-off boulder cleared some of the rockslide.'

He took the Maul down and hovered a few metres above the crushed, mangled wreck of the Saluki.

'Cockpit is crushed under that slab of rock. They are tough machines but not that tough. No way the pilot is alive.'

Viggo was about to reply when Evan spoke. 'Saluki seventeen does not look flight able. We recover must pilot's Soul Saver. No signal for life from her. Wait there I come.'

Nico lifted up and out from the cliff face. 'How come Evan is not using the translation systems like the rest of us? You know, speak in his own language and we hear in ours with all the niceties and simple language it creates.'

Viggo chuckled. 'Just wish that you are never invited to work under the Aquila and, in particular, the brigadier. He insists that everyone learns and practises languages. Says it is the best thing for mind development.'

Nico shook his head. 'Nah! Rather drink beer and eat steaks than do that shit.'

Hovering, they watched the salvage craft slide across the mid-afternoon sky, long sinuous black ropes dropping down from below it. The ropes curled around the slab of rock, looking for and finding purchase, then slowly tugging at it, trying to lift it up. It came up a little over one and a half metres and was then jammed by other rocks, unable to go any higher. Other ropes came down from the machine to grasp the smashed helicopter and lift away most of the wreckage, but the cockpit remained wedged into the rock.

'Viggo. I must ask that you go to pilot and get Soul Saver. Trapped it is. You can do this, yes?'

Viggo sat for a long second, wondering, then mentally slapped himself for being selfish. He reached up and unlocked his canopy. 'Nico?' he said.

Nico lowered the machine and slid it sideways until the gun pod was almost touching the jumbled rocks.

The canopy above Viggo swung open and he stood up and climbed out onto the rocks, instantly feeling the biting cold on his face. His helmet responded quickly, sealing him off from the cold as he scampered down the rocks and carefully walked under the slab, looking at the crushed cockpit. Finding a large space under the rock he pulled aside the shattered canopy and looked down at the form of the beautiful woman who lay, seemingly asleep, in her ejection seat. He reached down and touched her, feeling with sadness the crushed bones down her side and decided that she was certainly dead.

He reached under her helmet, feeling for the releases and was startled when her right hand weakly grasped his. She turned her head ever so slightly as her eyelids fluttered. Viggo swore, looking down again, and hoping that her biomed systems were performing OK as he could see the suit was damaged.

'Viggo! Get out! One minute. Aftershock! Move it!'

Viggo growled, reached down, hit the seat releases and grabbed the woman by her suit's shoulder-lifting straps and hauled her out of the wreck, stumbling back and cracking his helmet hard on the slab above him.

'She's alive!' he yelled. 'Can't leave her! I know her!'

He heard Nico yelling, then Evan trying to say something. A rock bounced down the cliff and into the hollow, smashing into his side and he felt his ribs breaking as another hit, crushing his feet. He fell on top of the woman pulling her to him as what felt like snakes wrapped around him constricting his breathing. As he passed out, he had the sensation of flying, but not being able to breathe, so he told his biomed-unit to conserve his blood oxygen.

Minutes later he came to with the woman lying on top of him on a hard deck. He was shivering with the painkilling drugs flooding his system and numerous voices asking if he was alive.

'For pity's sake, leave me rest.'

Pairs of hands lifted him into a coffin-like medical unit and, as he drifted back into unconsciousness, he could see in his mind the very beautiful face of the woman he had spent one glorious night with twenty years before, and whom he had never gotten over.

Nico, circling high above, saw his friend on the deck of the salvage craft, swore to himself and broke away, climbing his damaged Maul and setting a course for *Haast*.

Bob Thompson watched Bravo two heading south. He looked again at the Aquila salvage craft to watch it start to climb and head east. He tapped the icon for the brigadier's private comms channel. Seconds later, the face of the older man appeared.

'Ah, Bob, just the man I need to speak with. I note that you are still orbiting the recovery scene. I will personally thank each of your crew who helped us, as soon as you identify them to me, please. We still have, at best, an hour before repairs to our landing gear on the carrier are complete and we are moving towards *Haast*, anyway. Would you like to join me for a coffee, maybe?'

Bob looked at the brigadier, noting a slight change in his demeanour and wondering if he had managed to gain a little respect from him.

'Thanks.' He nodded. 'We have a bit to discuss, so why not do it face to face. I am on my way. See you in ten or so minutes.'

The screen cleared and Bob called *Haast*.

'Flight, this is Aurora one. Put me through to Major Warne, please.'

He turned the aircraft, which was one of his favourites to fly, being slightly old school with its contra-rotating pusher props, and looked for the identity signal of the Aquila carrier headed towards it. Nick Warne's face appeared in the comms screen.

'Commander.'

'Nick. I am heading across to *Berkut* for a short conference with the brigadier. Have you recovered all our damaged craft?'

Nick Warne sent the screen of information directly to the Aurora. 'Bit of work for the repair crews, quite a lot of actual damage, and of course there were two that hit the ground. What I am interested in, is why Games Board did not recover anything for their post-battlefield auctions as a chunk of the equipment is stuffed. Oh, we also picked up the Aquila crews and the craft that could not fly back to their carrier. Those earthquakes are still rattling through and I was worried that they would be swallowed up as well.'

Bob frowned, shaking his head. 'Good work. Yeah, know what you mean about the Games Board. That Francis John is a very strange fish. It is almost as if he is up to his armpits in something nasty that is far more interesting to him than this little battle of ours. Make sure that you give my congratulations on a battle well fought to the Mauls as soon as they are onboard. Nico and Anneke, in particular, did very well. Not that I am surprised; they are all as aggressive as hell. I shall let you get back to it. Bring *Haast* as close as is practicable to the Aquila.'

Nick's image nodded and the connection was broken. Bob pushed the throttle open and climbed up over one of the higher mountain ranges, watching yet another major aftershock charge through the landscape below and shivered at the thought of being alone on the ground caught by such a force. He tapped the comms icon for the Aquila carrier.

'*Berkut* flight, this is Aurora one inbound five kilometres out. Joining and landing instructions, please.'

'Commander, this is flight. Welcome to you. Join sector two. Clearance landing deck five. Wind from seven five at twenty-five.'

Bob looked at the navigation displays in his HUD, seeing the carrier in the distance. He swung a little further to the west until he had the aircraft in the correct sector and lifted the nose, washing speed off and powering up the antigravity system. He warped the wings of the Aurora, slowing further, until he was approaching the large discus-shaped carrier at thirty-five knots. He tapped one of the screens to zoom in the forward-looking external cameras, seeing one of the massive extended landing struts surrounded by repair and maintenance antigravity sleds, all furious with activity.

He dropped the nose and extended the wings down, lowering the wingtip skids while looking out at the eight radial landing decks extending out from the central command hub of the carrier. He could see the deck officer waiting for him as he came in over the landing deck and took a little more care than he normally would to execute a perfect landing on the spongy deck. He held the aircraft down with the engines still at high power until the officer gave him the engine stop signal, knowing that the landing skids would have been tied down. He switched off everything, sealed his helmet against the cold, and opened the canopy and climbed out of the aircraft.

The burly officer met him, saluting him, which Bob returned then shook him by the hand.

'You Commander Mr Thompson,' the officer said. 'Most pleased I am to say hello. Boris Kalashnokov to serve. May I and my fellow look at Aurora, please. It is most pleasing aircraft, yes.'

Bob opened his visor instantly and felt the biting cold. He looked up into the eyes of the man with his furred hood and ruddy face, then laughed. 'Pleased to see you, Major Boris. Yes, of course you are most welcome to look over the Aurora. I too love the aircraft.'

The man smiled down at him, gesturing him to proceed to the central hub where the suited brigadier waited for him. The slightly built man shook Bob's extended hand warmly.

'Good to see you, Bob. Come, coffee and some excellent real butter shortbreads await us.'

Bob followed him through the double airlocks, where he brought up his flight suit controls in his head, telling the suit to uncover his head and hands. They went up a few flights of spiral stairs, through the bridge, where the brigadier quickly introduced him to smiling senior officers, then up another set of stairs into the brigadier's ready room. The ceilings were much lower than those on *Haast*, but Bob liked the look of the segmented room with its high-class, tasteful feel of controlled opulence. He sat in the armchair opposite to the brigadier, who poured coffee, adding a single teaspoon of sugar and a dash of cream, just the way Bob liked it. He passed it across and poured his own, then raised his cup.

'A toast, commander,' the brigadier proposed. 'You and your crew are to be congratulated on a series of engagements well fought. I have to admit that some of your inventiveness took us by surprise. If any of your crew should ever wish to serve with the Aquila, they would be made most welcome. Shortbread?'

He lifted the platter across to Bob who took one.

'Yes, thanks. Well, I am sorry about some of that. They are an enthusiastic lot. In spite of me carefully asking them to be restrained, they did some damage.'

The brigadier smiled widely. 'It was good AV, Bob. Easily some of the best, in spite of what the Games Board has said. But we are not here to talk about that. I have been told that the landing strut that was damaged by a flying piece of rock — yes, we were too low, filling our water fuel tanks from an ice-covered lake, when the earthquake struck — will be repaired soon. How is your fuel situation?'

'Good. We are full again.'

The brigadier nodded, drained his coffee cup, refilled, took another biscuit and leaned back in his chair, looking keenly at Bob. 'The two monitors your crew saved and the director wrote off. What are your intentions for them?'

Bob raised his eyebrows a fraction, wondering what the brigadier wanted to know. 'Well,' he began, 'we repaired their hardware, our doctor and her staff brought the biological parts of them back to full health, and since then they have been making recording equipment which they have been splicing into all of our craft. They then take the AV, edit it and are hoping to sell it on the open market when we make it back to the inner core of the Sphere. Why do you ask?'

The brigadier's smile was wide and he pointed a half-eaten shortbread at Bob. 'Knew you were smart! Good! So all that has occurred here has been recorded independently. I am most pleased. You think that they will continue to do that, even if they will be placing themselves in danger on Storfisk?'

Bob nodded slowly and cautiously. 'Yes. I believe that they will. But what I am more interested in is what are we to do when we get to Storfisk?'

The brigadier drained his coffee, popped the last of his shortbread in his mouth, chewed slowly and swallowed. He stood up, gesturing for Bob to join him at the window. He pointed out to the side and Bob could see *Haast* coming over the top of the mountain range towards them.

'It is a fine ship, Bob. Purpose designed, good firepower, excellent range, great crew and you are in command. Now, my young friend, I must ask you to consider allowing yourself and your ship to come under my command.'

Bob drained the last of his coffee and carefully placed the cup on its coaster on top of the beautifully polished walnut table. He straightened, letting out a long breath and wishing that he had Nick Warne beside him, along with at least three of the other majors on his crew, to advise of what he should do. He looked across at the brigadier, who was still gazing out of the window. His mind was racing with the possibilities and he knew that he would have to make a decision then and there.

He swallowed, looked at his hands, then across at the brigadier, who was looking evenly at him.

Bob gave a short affirmative nod, hoping like hell that he was not going to regret the decision. 'It would be wise if we were under your command, Roger. It would be wise if for no other reason than I do not know exactly what we are up against and I have a suspicion that you do.'

The brigadier slowly reached out his hand for Bob to shake. 'Like I said: you are a smart man. Very well, effective immediately you are now my second-in-command for both carriers. You need to return to *Haast*, brief your crew, climb to vacuum and, once we are underway, you and I will set up command and control structures and get our crews working together. Does make it easy that we are mercenaries ... we all think pretty much the same.'

Bob nodded, agreeing. 'We have injured crew of yours aboard *Haast*. Shall we transfer them?'

'No, Major Aydon is quite possibly the finest field doctor and surgeon that I know. They will be fine with you. In fact, I was going to ask to transfer all the injured here to your medical unit. I need the room for the Tengu.'

Bob cocked his head to one side. 'Seems that one command structure is already in place. Very well. Would it also be a smart move to split half of the Tengu and transfer them across to *Haast* as well?'

The brigadier tapped his lips, nodding. 'Yes. Good. Return to your carrier, commander. We shall speak shortly.'

Bob gave the brigadier a formal nod and turned, walking to the door. Just as he was about to pass through, the brigadier called out to him.

'Bob. You *have* made the right decision.'

Their eyes locked for a second, then Bob turned to be met by Boris Kalashnokov.

'Yes, commander, come. Come, to your beautiful Aurora we go. I was second-in-command and now third I am, but this way I shall get to fly beautiful Aurora as it is nice plane, yes.'

Bob, in spite of being nervous about what his crew would say when they got the news, laughed. 'So, major, you want my aircraft? Do you have facilities to service it here on *Berkut*?'

The burly man looked over his shoulder at Bob and gave him a slightly reproachful look. 'Commander,' he said, 'all aircraft we love on *Berkut*. This is aircraft nirvana. Yes, I want one. Very slightly superior to our reconnaissance craft. More beautiful as well.'

'Very well. You take that one for the duration of the action. I shall return to *Haast* onboard the lander that the Tengu will no doubt already be waiting in?'

Boris shook his head. 'No, they wait, but they will bring more than just lander. Equipment and craft they will take to you. It is good plan. Be waiting please ...'

He turned and had a quick conversation with the brigadier, Bob presumed.

'No, commander, you take my craft. You kind to allow me yours. Fair it is. We make ready for you. We wait here for two minutes on bridge.'

Bob looked around the circular command unit of the Aquila with its individual control pods not unlike those of *Haast*, in that they were also individual survival pods in case the carrier was destroyed. Every piece of equipment and structure surrounding him was just a little more robust than those on *Haast*. Every crew member who saw him smiled and nodded, but stayed in their pods carrying out their duties.

'Commander Thompson.'

He turned to look eye to eye with the Tengu, who was wearing light battle armour.

'May I take this opportunity to introduce myself, sir. I am Major Annabel Graham. I command the Tengu here and am second-in-command to Colonel Bierwage who is away on *Rose Foxtrot* with the rest of the detachment. My troops are ready to deploy to *Haast* on your command.'

Bob gave the major a formal nod and extended his hand. The Tengu's claws retracted and she took his hand, shaking it. Bob grinned.

'It is rapidly turning out to be a most interesting adventure this whole mission, major. I am pleased to meet with you. How many in your detachment?'

'Sixty-five, sir. Plus individual short-range aircraft, twenty of the latest Mace, two troop landers that also act as lifters for the Mace, and our own personal weapons.'

Bob mentally went through the space available on *Haast*. He tapped his left wrist and the data screen rolled up. 'Link the aircraft types and sizes to me, please, major. Accommodating you, the Q, will be easy and we have space for the aircraft. Just a little concerned about the lifters. Hold on.'

He scrolled down through the decks, seeing what could be moved around, as a second later the lists of what the Q had with them also appeared on his screen. He introduced the files to each other and asked his wetware to integrate the forces. An instant later, the solutions were there. He transferred the loadmaster files back to the Q major.

'OK, major, there are the layouts. I had better get moving. It would be a bad look to send your people over without warning my own crew. Pleasure to meet you. See you on *Haast*.'

The Q gave him a formal nod and moved quickly off the bridge and down the stairs. Boris watched her go.

'She good woman in other body. Very good. Come, fighter ready for you. You like him. I know these things.'

Bob followed the major down the stairs until they were one deck below the landing area. They passed through an airlock and into a segment of *Berkut* where a portion of the carrier's fighter aircraft were sealed in opaque, individual heavily padded cells, against the walls, with the deck number four prominent on the floor and end walls. He looked at the aircraft which waited on one of the two elevators and grinned from ear to ear.

He looked at the powerful form of the Lunev, which was made by the same Gjomvik Corporation that created the Hawk. Bob had always considered the Lunev as a Hawk on steroids. In its overall dimensions, it was not that much bigger, but it was even more purposeful-looking and came across as an almost brutal aircraft.

He turned to the Aquila major. 'Impressive machines. How many do you have onboard?'

'By now, Mr Thompson, all our secrets open to you. They numbers be on your personal system now. Our leader, he was insistent that you be taken more care of. This Lunev, he is tougher than all others. Fitting it is for you. Soon I shall see you, commander.'

Bob thanked him and climbed up into the cockpit, sitting down and starting to wake the aircraft up. '*Berkut* control, this is Lunev two. Standing by.'

The crisp voice of the local controller answered. 'Lunev two, *Berkut* local control. All aircraft you fly are hereby designated Falcon. Falcon, seal up and go for start-up. As soon as you emerge onto the flight deck, you will be handed across to flight. Pleasure to be working with you, commander.'

Bob thanked the controller and tapped one of the screens: the canopy silently slid closed and locked. He activated his helmet and gloves while, outside the aircraft, a transparent shield slid up from the floor, rising to the ceiling of the hangar. As soon as it locked, the deck irised open. The elevator started to move upwards and Bob's fingers raced across the screens as the twin turbines behind him started, and the antigravity also came online. As the aircraft rose up onto the flight deck, he looked over all his screens and activated his HUD, seeing everything in the green.

'Flight, Falcon,' he called. 'Holding on four.'

'Falcon, flight. Weather Bravo, wind seventy-three, twenty kilometres. Depart sector three. You are cleared for take-off.'

'Flight, Falcon, Bravo seventy-three, twenty, sector three. Underway.'

He lifted the machine a few millimetres off the deck on antigravity while opening the throttles a notch. When feeling the aircraft was airborne, he increased antigravity and throttles, flying down the short landing runway and out into the controlled airspace of third sector. As soon as he passed the outer edge of the controlled space, which ranged 300 metres out from *Berkut*, he keyed his microphone again and banked the aircraft, heading for his carrier.

'*Berkut* flight, Falcon, on course for *Haast*.'

'Falcon, flight. Control now passed to *Haast* flight. Good day, sir.'

'My thanks, *Berkut*. *Haast* flight, this is the commander inbound in a Lunev. Call sign is now Falcon.'

There was a pause before the familiar voice of Major de Ruyter answered. 'Unidentified inbound aircraft. Send ID.'

Bob looked at the comms screen and triggered a laser pulse of information from his right eye into it. 'Falcon, *Haast* flight. Have you inbound three kilometres, approach sector one and dock in the Aurora one hangar.'

Ten minutes later Bob walked onto the bridge. He leaned into Nick Warne's command pod. 'Nick, please assemble the senior crew for a briefing here on the bridge now.'

Nick nodded and started contacting each of the individuals telling them to report as soon as possible. He then looked up at Bob with raised eyebrows.

'OK, Nick. I am now second-in-command of the task force. We are heading back to Storfisk as quickly as we can. We have the medical unit of *Berkut* inbound here, plus those that are under treatment, plus sixty-five Tengu grade Q3, plus all their equipment.'

Nick stared at him for a few seconds, shook his head, cleared his throat and asked, 'What task force? And why not wait for *Rose Foxtrot* as per the original plan?'

Bob reached into the pod and tapped the ACE Haast's comms icon. 'Haast, get out here and fill Mr Warne in with as much information as we have on the predator threat. No arguments. And while you are at it, create an information packet for every crew member to bring them up to speed. Nick, here are the manifests of what the medical and Q3 are bringing with them and also the loadmaster layouts which I passed on to the Q OC.'

Nick saw the information coming up on his screens, grinned, reached out and shook Bob's hand and very quietly murmured, 'Good! About bloody time you took charge. I am proud of you. Now we get to work. I shall send the cleared responses over to *Berkut* right away.'

Bob stood very still for a few seconds, a little surprised at his mentor's reaction but very pleased at the same time.

The Countess Michelle was at his elbow. 'We need to talk now!' she hissed.

Bob slowly shook his head, looking down at the outwardly calm face of the woman. Looking into her eyes, he could see that she was angry.

He flashed a laser message across into her eyes. 'Why talk, Michelle? You and *Haast*, probably with Uncle's help, have manoeuvred me enough. We need to tell the crew what is going on as the game has changed. This ship is now under the control of the brigadier and I am second-in-command of the task force.'

'Fool! You are being manipulated by him! We risk losing the vital part in the puzzle. You should have spoken to me first! I am furious that you did not.'

Bob looked around the bridge filling with the senior staff arriving. He looked out through the window to *Berkut* in the closing distance. He looked back at Michelle.

'No, Michelle,' he said firmly. 'I am right. Your game risks losing a world. Hell, it may already be too late. You have a few days to find your other turncoat amongst us. I suggest that you get on with it.'

Michelle let her good-humoured mask slip, glowered at him, turned and marched away. He wondered if he had made a bad mistake, but there was something nagging at him that he could not put a finger on and decided he was right. He decided that the Baron Willie der Boltz would approve as he had once warned him that she had her own agenda and was not to be entirely trusted. With that resolve, he straightened his back, squared his shoulders and as soon as all the senior crew arrived told them everything he knew.

By the time he had finished, the first of the Q landers were docking and being taken into the large hangars at the base of the carrier. The smaller, individual fighter aircraft of the Q were also en route, followed by another large lander which had medical red cross markings on it. As the little fighters, which were no bigger than the Chrysops, approached, all the Maul hangar doors opened and folded down. The Q spun each of the craft and alighted gently onto the massive doors — as many as three per door — their clawlike landing gear locking down into the mesh and holding them tight. The Tengu climbed out of their craft, taking their kitbags with them, and walked into the Maul hangars. The doors closed and sealed behind them.

Bob climbed into his command pod as the unit commanders all hurried off to sort out their units and to accommodate the Q3, plus the additional medical staff. He tapped the ship-wide comms icon.

'All crew: this is the commander. We face an unprecedented situation. A predator of possible octopoid origin is loose on Storfisk. It is an army builder and hostile to us on every possible level. *Haast* is now under the command of Brigadier Mortlock of the Aquila. Tengu Q3, which most of you would only have heard about as rumours, are now part of this crew. Make them welcome, learn from them and treat their command structure as our own. This is a twenty-minute warning as we are about to climb out through the atmosphere and make our own way at one gravity to Storfisk. Bridge out.'

Anneke Bester was walking down the internal corridor which linked all the Bravo squadron hangars. Tengu were walking quickly out of the internal airlocks and running towards the internal stairways. As each one ran past, they greeted her by her rank, and although each was physically identical their voices were individual.

One of them stopped beside her. 'Hello, Anneke!'

She peered at the Tengu's face, then at its combat suit, knowing that the voice was from her past, but not recognising it.

The dragon laughed. 'Sorry. It is Vince Hofman.'

Anneke instantly wrapped her arms around the creature who had once been one of her best friends and a long-term lover.

'Oh, Vin! It is so good to see you. I have not heard anything of you in so many years. How long has it been?'

The Q smiled at her, something that she found quite disconcerting as the creature had a mouth full of what she could only recognise as weapons. She was fascinated, delighted and a little appalled all at the same time. She had always known Vince as a warrior soul, but had never considered he might become a member of a group that she had only known as a myth. The dragon returned her embrace then pulled away.

'Just over nineteen years, Anneke, but I am sorry. We shall catch up later. I have to go sort this lot into their billets and talk with your cooks and get our catering sorted. We live on high protein high carbs. See you soon!'

He gently squeezed her arm, then ran off down the corridor, following the last of his colleagues.

Haast flew straight up through the atmosphere and carried on at a steady one gravity of acceleration as the navigation officer, Captain Claire Bretherton, plotted the course that would take them to Storfisk in the least possible time. She checked her figures one last time then keyed the commander's comms icon.

'Commander, course is plotted and I have run the figures again. As we get closer to the star, we will pick up steadily more electrical energy from the carrier's graphene hull ion conversion. We can use that additional energy to go faster. It will, however, also increase the gravitational force generated.'

'How much, captain?'

'We will peak at one point three g's in forty-seven hours time. We then maintain that high-g for forty-eight hours before I would decrease it to get us to Storfisk at one gravity for a smooth atmospheric entry. Oh, yes, and that little extra would put us only a few hours behind *Berkut*.'

'Good work. Set it up. If there is a change, I shall advise.'

Bob tapped the medical officer's icon. 'Major.'

He waited some moments for Sally Aydon to answer. 'Commander, as per normal I am rather busy. I have a full ward of our casualties and also Aquila.'

Bob winced a little. He always treated the MO the same as any other crew member, but he sometimes wondered if he should make an appointment when he wanted to see her. Then he remembered that she could override him if she saw fit and decided discretion is the better part of valour.

'Sorry, major,' he apologised, 'just wanted to advise that in forty-seven hours we will increase the g-acceleration, and then subsequent deceleration. Need to know if this will affect your patients.'

There was another pause.

'That should be fine,' she said. 'Sorry for snapping at you. Things are a bit hectic as I want all these people out of here within two days anyway. Everyone is being filled with the latest nanotech. Oh, and those few I could not readily bring to full health, I have either had them fitted with prosthetics or euthanased and readied for upload into mechanical chassis.'

Bob did not allow himself to smile, but inwardly did, knowing that the brigadier was right in his statement that Sally Aydon was a true professional. Keeping a sombre face, he thanked the major and broke the connection.

He looked across his screens, observing the crew being integrated with the Tengu and the seventeen additional crew from *Berkut*, as well. He tapped Nick Warne's comms icon.

'You are on top of things here. I am heading down to talk with Uncle, then a meal and then catch a good sleep, I hope.'

He stood to move across to the windows and look down the length of *Haast*, seeing the rocky planet below them and high above the massive bulk of the gas giant. Walking into the corridor, he was met by the Tengu major who was still in her light combat suit. He noted that all the Q he saw now had their ranks and names displayed, probably to make it easier for the standard humans to recognise them.

'Major Graham. Everything set?'

'Yes, our thanks, commander. There was a bit of surprise from a few of your crew when they saw us, but nothing dramatic. I am a little concerned that the secret of our existence is going to be that much more difficult to keep after this engagement.'

Bob drew in a long breath and frowned a little. 'Not much we can do about it at this stage, major. Just have to wait and see on that. Were you coming to see me?'

The creature shook her head. 'No. I am in conference with your admin OC and the ACE Haast in a few minutes.'

Bob nodded and took his leave, deciding to walk down the stairways rather than take one of the lifts.

Ten minutes later he found Uncle in one of the internal weapons ranges of *Haast* along with three of the Tengu, looking over weapons.

One of the Tengu called out, 'Commander on deck!'

The four soldiers snapped to attention, so Bob braced and said, 'Stand easy, thank you. Uncle. New toys?'

The cyborg grinned. 'Oh, yeah. Nice, very nice. We should chop your arms off and get Major Aydon to fit you out with some proper arms so we could integrate you with these.'

Bob shook his head and gave a small laugh. 'But I can use them, anyway, just not as quickly, or possibly as accurately, eh? Can I have a word, please? Your armoury in ten minutes.'

He nodded at everyone and walked out of the range, which ran the full length of the carrier, back up the stairs and into the garden to gather a few pieces of fruit, then down again to meet with the sergeant major.

Once up against Uncle's four-metre-cubed armoury he asked, 'Secure?'

Uncle shook his head as a door opened in the side of the armoury. He gestured the commander inside and as soon as the door had closed behind them, said, 'Now we are. What's on your mind, boss?'

Bob looked across at his old friend, wondering if he was correct in his assumptions. He shrugged, thinking what the hell.

'Countess Michelle of the administration council. Should I trust her?'

'No, of course not. I know that you have bedded her quite a few times and I know that you are not thick. Ever felt that she was playing you like a violin?'

Bob looked at him evenly, waiting for the other boot to fall, as Uncle continued.

'To say nothing, Bob, of why she is here and why such a high-ranking official of the council would want to fuck with you?'

Bob let out a nervous laugh. 'Likes to rough it with the riffraff maybe? Is she bad, Uncle? Should I arrange to put her on ice?'

Uncle looked at the other man and wondered why he was being handed such a shitty deal.

'No, she is not bad, well, not in a malicious way. She is just playing her role in the game as she sees fit. On ice? Actually, probably not a bad idea and I should do the same with Adrian Crow at the same time. You know the time delay of all this is going to cost us very dearly on Storfisk, don't you?'

Bob looked down at his hands, then around the inside of the armoury, and said quietly, 'What do you think, Lorraine?'

Uncle stood very still. There was a barely audible woman's laugh from all around them and a few seconds later the armoury spoke.

'When did you work out that I was here, Bob?'

Bob looked at Uncle with a sad smile on his face. 'A while ago, because I know Uncle, Lorraine. I know that he would never give you up, that he would find a way to take you with him. And he has always seemed just a little too content with life, even as a cyborg. So what do you think, as I also know that to make you safe he would have wired you into every data feed of the ship.'

The beautifully modulated voice of the woman surrounded them again. 'I believe that the chances of any of us making it off Storfisk are remote. I believe that we should start making plans to stay on the planet's surface as all the information I have is that the predator has a lot more to show us yet. Patrick of *Basalt* shared information from the octopoid library with me. These things were created by the octopoids to make planets safe for them. And they do it on every level from microbial up. But there is a very small chance that we might defeat them and for that we need Stephine from *Basalt*. I do not think that it was by chance or mistake that they may have been sent to the wrong system.'

Bob let out a long breath. 'Right. Well, we will just have to take that chance. But what of Michelle?'

There was a long silence.

'Honestly, I am not sure,' Lorraine said. 'There has been contact between her and Adrian Crow, but then again she has had numerous contacts with most of the crew as part of her brief is as an attaché, a bridge for the crew to the Administration, if you like. I am not sure if I agree with my husband about putting either of them on ice. And you do know that a Tengu is onboard Angelito, and that information from the ACEs on the affected peninsula of the Haulers Territory has been sent to the ACE *Haast*, don't you?'

Bob felt a chill run down his spine. He looked at Uncle, then around the compact room with its weapon-making machinery and numerous storage units.

'Oh, shit! No, I did not know about any of that. Is *Haast* aware of your existence, Lorraine? And why is a Tengu on Angelito?'

She instantly answered with a chiding tone in her voice. 'No! Of course not. No-one does, except you and Graham. I have been totally passive in my information gathering. Angelito is rotten to the core. The Tengu went to shut him down, or at least disable him somehow. Oh, and that Tengu is not like the Q3, no, no ... he is one of the ACE Tengu. The original was made for Baron Willie der Boltz when he was a young officer. Obviously he cloned himself, so my best guess is that this is a game being played amongst the ACEs. I know of four, but I suspect that there were even more.'

Bob looked up at the ceiling again, furiously thinking of what to do. 'How do you know that?'

'Two had been reported by the ACE Ayana to *Haast* as being killed: one is on Angelito and another with the Games Board director.'

Bob was pacing up and down inside the armoury. 'OK, here is what I want from you. Lorraine, please put together everything you know about the predators. Uncle, go find those two Q weapons geeks you were being entertained by, as I want you all working on every killing method that you can come up with to knock over those bloody things. I am off to have a private word with an eagle.'

Lorraine said urgently: 'Please don't talk with Haast. He may come to you of his own free will soon, anyway. And besides if he knew that you knew, he might come looking for the source and find me and I would not like that.'

Bob clenched his fists. 'Fuck! I hate this bloody sneaky underhand bullshit and it's all around me! Give me a straight-up, no bloody nonsense punch-up any time. OK, OK, but if you learn anything, please pass it on through Uncle. I need to think. Oh, Lorraine, I am glad that you are here.' He then turned and pushed his way through the door and out into the workshops.

'You think he will cope with what is about to come, Graham?'

Uncle was still looking at the door. He slowly nodded. 'One of the reasons these two crews were selected, Lorraine. Yeah, he will need everyone's help, but he will cope.'

Thorn/*Basalt*

Interstellar Space

The Thorn, with *Basalt* firmly held against its underbelly, jumped into the LP between the stars.

There was intense activity on the bridge for a few moments while three interstellar sub-AI fast pickets were launched to the other three star systems to find and get messages of the successful rescue of *Basalt* and of their intentions to the other Thorns and *Rose Foxtrot*.

The three ovoid machines, which were almost solid in construction, started accelerating to high-g's as soon as the pickets dropped and within five minutes had jumped.

Q Major Carrington said to the assembled crew of *Basalt*, 'Are you sure about this? We could simply go with less acceleration and you all stay in the gel. I am still not 100 per cent convinced that that creature on *Basalt* is safe.'

Veg shook his head. 'Nope. Good idea on your part, major, but this way you will be above Storfisk two days earlier than we would be otherwise and can go straight into the battle. We have a reasonable understanding, from what the ACEs tell us, of the entity waiting for us. If nothing else, it will be interesting. See you on the planet. Kill them before we get there, and we shall be happy. Thanks for the rescue. When you are back in your human standard form I shall find you and take you out for drinks.'

With that the veteran crew filed into the airlock of *Basalt*'s bridge deck and sealed themselves off.

The Tengu major sprinted for the stairs, yelling orders as he went, and a moment later the couplings retracted; the Thorn accelerated away, leaving *Basalt* moving at a more sedate speed towards the jump point.

Patrick welcomed them back onto *Basalt*. 'Hello, all! Did you miss me? Good to have you back. Been an interesting time. The entity wants to meet with you all. Odd creature is the only way I can describe it. Wants to see Stephine and Marko first.'

The crew went straight to their command pods and started checking the systems that the ACEs, who had boarded a few hours earlier, had not already verified.

Harry spoke first. 'Small parts of the outer hull are, well, burnt is the only way I can describe it, from where the tendrils of the queen grasped it. Self-regeneration is underway. Two airlocks are damaged. The ACEs have started repairs after Patrick sealed them off using the engineering drones. Apart from that, hull integrity is fine.'

One by one they all reported that *Basalt* was in reasonable shape. Finally, Michael ordered, 'Patrick, start jumping us back to Storfisk, please.'

Stephine and Marko walked down the spiral staircase, wondering what they would see when they got to the engineering hangar.

Glint and Ngoc were waiting outside the airlock door.

'Has it given you a name yet?' Marko asked. 'And has it said anything else since your last report?'

Glint was up on his hind legs, sitting back on his tail. 'Nope. No name. It is still in the containment that Patrick convinced it to climb into, when he found it on the outside of the hull. Seems quite happy. Just wants music, as much of it we can give it, and loves to discuss physics.'

'OK, let's go have a look,' Marko suggested.

Stephine and Marko had seen the pictures, but it felt different when they stood only a metre or so away from the four-metre-tall, double-armed human-like creature who was covered in light-emitting nodules. It had no eyes, no mouth although its head was perfectly formed in human form, and it had no nose either. Looking at its body, they could see it apparently had no genitals and they noted that its feet and hands were webbed.

Stephine said, 'Hello. Do you have a name, creature?'

Light patterns flashed across its chest and an instant later the electronics that Patrick had built over the last few days which he had intuitively designed from Fritz Vinken's light-based comms units, replied in speech: 'Stephine! Great to see you and Marko again. I am still part of Fritz and Nail, so I really have no name, and I am also, in part, the material that you sent from *Blackjack*. Those elements, and the original nanote tech that was sent down onto the queen when she was in her ocean tower.'

Marko walked around the containment vessel. 'You are in salted water and you are aquatic. Am I correct?'

'Yes. I need to get into an ocean within a few days before my reserves are depleted to a dangerous level.'

Marko nodded. 'OK, so what do you have to offer us? Why would we consider doing that for you?'

'Because, Marko and Stephine, I am a creation of your tech, Urchin tech, octopoid tech and then the minds of Fritz and Nail. I am unique and I need to be allowed to flourish.'

Marko could see Stephine was excited; energy was almost crackling from her fingertips.

Before he could stop her, she walked up to the containment and placed a hand against it. A large part of her palm then peeled off and went through the transparent wall, through the fluid and into the creature. It went completely rigid, then visibly relaxed.

She turned. 'Marko. Think beautiful thoughts, think love, think cherishing and think respect for sentience and do the same. We have to reinforce the last pieces of this entity's higher being.'

He hesitated.

'Please, Marko. This is a new species, it should be allowed a chance to survive. Place a little of your own innate goodness into it.'

Nodding, he felt deep into his mind, sped himself up and placed his right palm against the tank. He felt a sharp pain, as the skin and a little of the muscle below it, pulled away from him and moved through the wall, shooting across the water to spread out against the creature's skin and a moment later was gone. He moved a pace backwards and looked down at his raw palm, seeing the muscle and skin growing back. He looked at Stephine and laughed.

'So I could grow my own legs if I wanted to? Not have to worry about these Tengu ones?'

Stephine nodded with a wry smile on her face. 'You could, or you could absorb the tech in those legs and adapt them to you. You can choose, as each day that goes past you become a little more like me. You are a proto-angel now, Marko.'

Marko looked at her, then back at the creature in the tank, which was starting to stir. He walked to the airlock, passed through it and waved Glint over.

'Go get Nail and bring him in,' Marko whispered to him.

A few minutes later, Glint walked in followed by the cat who, although still functioning, was not 100 per cent of his old self. Marko bent down and scooped him up into his arms and pressed him up against the tank.

'Sentient,' Marko said, 'please duplicate that part of you which is Nail, and only of Nail, then give one part back to him, making him whole.'

He stood there with the large cat, waiting five or so minutes, until the creature reached down and placed one of its hands up against the cat. Bursts of light flashed across and into Nail's eyes.

As the transference was happening, Stephine walked up beside Marko, touching his shoulder, giving him support and energy which he could feel coursing through him. The light stopped after a few minutes and Nail slumped down, feeling like a dead weight in Marko's arms. Stephine took him then, holding him against her chest and gently rocking backwards and forwards on her heels. Some time later, the cat's eyes flew open.

'Damn, I am me again!' Nail exclaimed. 'Shit, this feels good! Thanks, Marko, thanks, Stephine, wonderful to see you for real again. I am off to see Glint and the guys. Oh, yes … Stephine, I know a hell of a lot about the Urchins now! Then I need to go say hello to Veg.'

With that he leapt down onto the floor and, using his crew comms, cycled himself through the airlock and was gone.

'I think that we should invite Fritz down, don't you think, Marko?'

Thorn

Approaching Storfisk System

The Q sat in his command pod, looking at the jump sequence that the navigator, Captain Reese, had laid out.

'Captain, we need to get there as fast as possible,' Major Carrington said. 'If we edit away the second drop by the gas giant, we will get above the planet almost eighteen hours earlier. Am I correct?'

Yvette Reese looked over her large screens in her oversized pod and quickly looked at the alternative. 'Yes, correct. However, we will also use a further seven per cent of our fuel in deceleration. It cuts the fuel water reserve margins down to two per cent.'

The major tapped his armrests, thinking. 'It is acceptable. We are taking this ship into the atmosphere anyway and there is an abundance of water available to us there. Initiate the new jump sequence. Communications, is the long-range comms drone ready to deploy?'

'Sir, yes. Programmed and ready. Will automatically deploy on the jump closest to the gas giant.'

The major nodded and tapped the ship-wide comms icon.

'All Q, except bridge! In gel and sleep in five minutes. Wake in seven hours. We deploy to the surface in eight hours.'

Those crew members who were not vital to the bridge quickly walked out, going to their heavy combat suit containers, climbed in, initiated the gel flood and told their bio-units to take them into sleep mode.

On the bridge, the remaining handful of Q sealed their command pods and had their seats hold them tight. They flooded themselves with the gel a minute before the next jump — and massive gravities of deceleration kicked in — and before the Thorn jumped again to carry out the sequence of jumping and decelerating again and again until many hours later they were in a tight orbit around Storfisk.

As soon as the gel had been cleared from their systems and they had been woken, the Tengu started checking their weapons, packing their field rations and getting themselves ready for immediate deployment.

'Major.'

'Comms?'

'The ACE Tengu onboard Angelito has sent us the updates. In the space of time that we have been away the first generation of predators have hatched. He reports no other sign of them on any part of the planet, apart from the peninsula that they were first reported on. Their numbers have reached in excess of 600 with the second generation only a few days away from emerging which will be as high as 60,000 army builders.'

The major felt a chill go through his body, wondering what he could do with his small force, knowing that the weapons he had available on the Thorn were impressive but they could not hope to make much of an impression on the predators.

'Very well. We go for a denial of territory and await reinforcements. Navigation, take us down to the narrowest part of the peninsula. All crew: we have a difficult task. We must deny the enemy access to the greater landmass to the north. We have a twelve-and-a-half-kilometre-wide series of mountain ranges to cover. All operations will be aerial. Stand by for sectors and orders.'

He linked his mind with the platoon and section commanders through their comms units, and in a few minutes had gone over the landmass and given them their sectors, resupply times, fallback positions and casualty evacuation points.

As soon as he had finished, he sat back in his chair, wondering what else he could do.

'Major, we have a message from *Berkut* and another from *Haast*. They are aware of the situation. *Berkut* will be over the peninsula in twelve hours and *Haast* a few minutes later. They have sent the contact codes for the fifty or so ACEs still alive on the peninsula who have been at war with the predators. They have split into two groups. One at the end of the peninsula and the other fifty kilometres south of the line that we will defend.'

'Good. Very good! The brigadier and Mr Thompson have shown excellent initiative. I had been most concerned that they would wait for our return. Obviously no need for us to have deployed that comms drone.'

The comms officer then added, 'They say it is imperative that we make contact with the ACE tiger Ayana and the ACE Haast's eagle, Maqua. They have information vital for the detection of the predator.'

The major nodded.

Ten minutes later, after the comms officer had made contact with the Tengu on Angelito and asked where Ayana and

Maqua were, they made contact. Having verified that it was, in fact, the ACEs, information files started streaming across the comms officer's screens. He pushed it through his checking systems, then contacted the major.

'It is a software upgrade for our use,' the officer said. 'Clever. I am impressed. I have released it to everyone and also started upgrades to our craft's sensors. Effectively, can see the predator by what they are standing on and disturbing.'

The major took the upgrade and integrated it into his own systems. 'Good! Navigation, I see our speed is sufficiently slow for us not to burn up on entry to the atmosphere. Fly us down over the area where the ACEs are engaged. Firstly, to the ACEs under the most pressure at the end of the peninsula. Then climb back to altitude and we will do the same with the other group, hopefully giving them some relief. All crew: man external hull weapons. We are going on a strafing run.'

Haast

Storfisk

Bob Thompson watched on his screens the steady descent into the atmosphere. Deciding that it was more interesting to see it with his own eyes, he climbed out of his pod and walked up to the panoramic windows at the front of the bridge, looking out and down and seeing Berkut a few kilometres below them. A hundred or so kilometres below them, the towering thunderclouds of an electrical storm flashed silently and Bob smiled, enjoying the wonder of it all.

Everyone around him was edgy, including the Tengu major who strode up quickly with her prehensile, bladed tail tucked hard against her plated back.

'Commander,' she greeted him.

He nodded at her and raised his eyebrows.

'Commander, I have been advised by Major Carrington that Major Suzuki is awake and has taken command of the Thorn again. They are going to stick with their plan of sealing off the most northern choke point of the peninsula. The brigadier also says that I am under your command until Colonel Bierwage returns with *Rose Foxtrot*, or sometime after. However, they do not anticipate him to be back for at least another two days.'

Bob cocked his head to one side. 'Is there a problem with my commanding you, Major Graham?'

The entity looked at him for a long moment and then seemed to gather herself and shook her head. 'No, of course not, sir.'

She quickly turned and marched away.

Mark de Ruyter, who was already wearing his light combat suit, sidled up beside him. 'Trouble with our elite troops?'

Bob looked at him and then back to the hard crescent of the planet's horizon and its thick band of atmosphere. The local star shone through ... it would be early morning when they got down to the surface.

'I hope not, Mark. Where is Nick Warne?'

'I relieved him so he could grab a quick breakfast. He will be back in a couple of minutes.'

'About time I did the same. Back in a few minutes.'

He visited the ablutions, relieved himself and freshened up, then gathered a handful of fruit and munched on them, before going back onto the bridge. With nothing to do but wait, he sat in his pod and scanned through the screens, looking at the various parts of the ship. Everyone else was quiet as well, just waiting for the deployment and the first attacks on the predators. Bob's thoughts went back to the night before, when the ACE Haast had requested a private meeting with a link to the brigadier.

The ACE told them everything that had been passed on to him from the ACE Maqua: what the predators had been doing on the surface; how they had built up their numbers and then remorselessly hunted the ACEs who had been looking after the introduced animals; how the battles had gone and the cries for help which Angelito had ignored, not responding to any of the ACEs' calls. Then they learned that the core intelligence of

Angelito could not be found on the station by the Tengu and that any offensive weapons on the station which could have helped the ACEs, had been systematically wrecked beyond immediate repair.

That was one thing that the brigadier could help with, and a repair crew had been sent from *Berkut* as they had passed by the station on their way to the planet.

The ACE had then shown them everything they now knew about the predators, including specific scents, the weapon systems that they knew it had available to it, including the others that the ACEs suspected it had.

Bob did not ask nor dare to calculate the possibilities of an outright victory. The last thing he had done before *Haast* started to slowly descend down through the atmosphere was to take everything that they knew, load it all onto the data core of a fast picket drone and launch it to the nearest human star system. But he also knew that by the time help arrived the predators numbers would have built into the millions by using all the larger animals they had available to them.

Feeling the weight of the odds stacked against them, he reached out and tapped the direct comms line to the brigadier.

The man had a gentle smile on his face when his image appeared on Bob's screen.

'I am not sure about your feelings,' the brigadier began, 'but I don't like this stage of any battle, Bob. Those last thirty minutes or so before all hell breaks loose, and the careful battle plan that was meticulously planned goes straight out the window ...'

Bob nodded. 'And here is me so concerned about the overwhelming odds against us winning.'

The older man looked at him and steepled his fingers, slowly nodding. 'Well, here's the thing. I have a whole series of nasty weapons so that if things go bad we will kill everything on the peninsula. So if we get pushed back, that is what I will do. The Haulers will not like it, but in time the environment will recover. We will, of course, save as many of the ACEs as possible, but once again we will sacrifice them as well to stop this plague. Until that moment arrives we will battle as hard as we can and just work on knocking them down. Hopefully, *Rose Foxtrot* returns so she can make those decisions for us.'

Bob nodded and looked at the overlay maps of the peninsula. It was just over 500 kilometres long, crescent-shaped with a mountainous spine and at its widest point almost forty kilometres wide.

The brigadier continued. 'The one thing that is giving me nightmares is if the predators were also dropped into the ocean. The ACEs think that there may have been one or two, but are not sure.'

He glanced away at the screens surrounding him. 'We are coming up to our separation point, Bob. Good hunting, my friend.'

Bob nodded and the connection severed. He felt a small change in the attitude of *Haast* and knew that they were moving away from *Berkut* to take up a parallel flight path, ten kilometres apart from the great disc-shaped carrier.

He looked again at his screens, seeing the pilots clambering into their craft with the hangar crews doing final checks and topping off the tanks.

When they were five kilometres above the sea at the southernmost tip of the peninsula, the three Aurora lifted off from their hangar platforms and flew ahead of *Haast*, spreading out to map and identify all possible targets on the first high-speed run up the length of the peninsula's western side. Over the next ten minutes there was furious activity as all the combat aircraft lifted away, except the Hawks and the Chrysops which were held back in reserve.

Nina looked out of the Maul's cockpit and saw the sun starting to come up over the mountain range to their east. Will called out, 'Targets. Five. So we just smash them, move on and come and do it again, and again and again. Huh? Bit tedious.'

Nina laughed and nodded. 'Yup, just like mowing a long strip of grass. Not that you have ever done the mowing. Now don't go mental with the ammunition, eh. Two rounds per target, Willy.'

'Pathetic! Want to chew the crap out of them.' Will could not actually see the targets as shown on the data feed from the Aurora recon aircraft, as the targets were obscured by the terrain. He frowned then shrugged, trusting in his instruments.

'I have control of your gun.'

He locked onto one of the predators and fired, switched targets and fired again, and even before the first rounds hit the first predator, fired on the third. One after the other they exploded. As the Maul passed high overhead, Will could see in his aiming screens the body parts strewn about. He felt a chill sensation.

'Nina,' he said, 'that is damage like I have never seen before. They blew apart all in the same way. Like they were created to come apart like that. Fucked up, if you ask me.'

'Yeah, not our concern now, Will. We smash them down at this stage. That's what we have been told to do.'

They flew on with their escort of three Tengu small fliers at a leisurely 150 kilometres per hour, steadily clicking up the body count until they came across a small herd of wildebeest standing over the large, fat sluglike pupae of more predators.

Will fired into as many as he could, taking care not to kill the animals, while the three Tengu flew down like angry hornets and picked off the individual targets from much closer range. When all they could see left was smashed twitching predators they climbed away to take station with the Maul again.

The morning wore on until at midday, local time, they were all combing the slopes of the narrowing choke point of the peninsula, seeing nothing until they flew up against the controlled area of the Thorn and its dozens of small aircraft. In a carefully orchestrated turning, the forces of *Berkut* and *Haast* then flew back down the peninsula, with the outermost Mauls and their escorts flying high into the mountains.

Nico Matsis was eating a pack of fresh cherries as the Maul flew on autopilot. He looked at his crewmate's helmeted head in the comms screen.

'Wake up, Viggo. You look like you nodded off.'

Viggo Eames started, having obviously been asleep. 'What! Is there something happening? Have not had a target to wallop in over two hours.'

He yawned hugely then shook himself and sat up to pull out a ration pack and open a container of freshly sliced pineapple to eat.

Nico nodded at his friend. 'Yeah, well, I have looked at the kill figures from command. We have knocked out 180 predators and put bullets into a bit over 1600 pupae, so I reckon that by tomorrow afternoon we should be cleaning up. But you know me, I am waiting for the shit to happen because it always does. What do you think of Will's idea that the predators seem to come apart in the same pattern of segments?'

Viggo looked at his friend and said in all seriousness, 'I think that it is a purposeful design. We know that they can be put back together by another predator. I think that we should hit the things with incendiaries. Yeah, sorry, Nico, but I have dark feelings about this whole deal.'

Nico nodded in agreement. 'Trouble is, if we start a wildfire we will be in even more trouble. Smoke would fuck up the only way we can detect the bloody things. And it's high summer, so things look ready to burn anyway. Time will tell, mate, time will tell. Hey! Been meaning to ask … that glorious-looking woman you rescued. She is out of the medical suite I see and I spied her coming out of your quarters early this morning. Gorgeous! You going to introduce me?'

Viggo laughed, then said, 'No, no, hell no!'

'Arse! Has she got a sister?'

Viggo chuckled. 'Just for you, Nico, I will ask.'

Late that night the two carriers held station off the southernmost tip of the peninsula. Their water collection units were suspended below them and pumping thousands of cubic metres of seawater into the ships to be processed for fuel and consumables.

The commanders of the three groups were in a linked conference with the ACEs, Maqua and Ayana.

'Our thanks for taking the pressure off our forward stronghold, Major Suzuki. Those strafing runs of yours disrupted the predators for long enough for us to pull back and the actions of the *Haast* and *Berkut* crews slowed the predators' breeding cycle dramatically. I presume that the same will occur on the eastern side of the peninsula tomorrow morning?'

'You presume correctly, Maqua,' the brigadier replied. 'Yes, we will carry out this holding action again tomorrow but I know that it is only a holding action. How many types of the large insect versions of the predators are you now aware of?'

The huge snow tigress, Ayana, answered and at the same time sent them images of the insects. 'We know of three types. One burrowing, one walking or crawling, and the other flying. All deadly. One of their worst characteristics is that the burrowing type is transported by the flying type, so the burrower could be dropped onto anything it wants to target. When the full-sized predators come under attack and are broken apart, if there is another predator present the creature will reassemble another from the undamaged parts left. Those parts that cannot be incorporated over the course of a few days, restructure themselves into the insects.'

Bob spoke up. 'So our shooting holes in them today was pointless?'

Ayana shook her head. 'No. It gives us time as we are not yet certain of what the insects' long-term goals are. But I would suggest that the day after tomorrow when you go back over the area you have some way of killing lots of palm-sized insects, preferably with fire. But, of course, until we have rain, which is forecast to occur in two days' time, we beg of you not to set the savannahs or forests ablaze. There are still hundreds of thousands of creatures down there who have not been affected by this yet.'

'We will do our very best, but this is a war and so we cannot make any promises one way or the other,' the brigadier told her. 'I am, right now, more interested to know about the flying version of this octopoid insect. How far could it get? How fast does it fly, how far can it fly and what weapons does it have?'

Ayana shook her head again. 'I am sorry. We do not know about its flight abilities. We do know that it possesses a hive mentality. The more of them that there are, the greater the intelligence. They have destroyed all my investigating swallows and any other bird, including the eagles that attempted to capture one for study, but never returned.'

'By what method did they destroy the birds?' Daisuke Suzuki asked.

'I suspect a neural toxin. It was brutally fast. Even the ACE birds only had a few seconds to say that they were in trouble and complete their Soul Saver transfer before they died.'

Bob said, 'Gas? Or something on the surface of the insect?'

Ayana shook her head for the third time. 'Again, we do not know. Every ACE who has tried to learn this for us has died. We came to this planet to care for animals as we believed it was for the greater good. We did not come here to fight.'

Forty minutes later, after details of the next days' actions had been finalised, the conference finished. Bob sat very still in his command pod thinking. He tapped a comms icons.

'Sally, hope I am not disturbing you. Need you to come up with a list of all the neural toxins that are available to us here, onboard, now. As soon as you have it, get back to me, please.'

The woman nodded and the connection was severed. Bob smiled, knowing she realised it was urgent and therefore no need for small talk. He tapped another icon.

'Uncle,' Bob said, 'get me a method of shredding these bloody things. As soon as you find one that you know will work, start manufacturing the components for the thirty-millimetre rounds.'

'Hmm, yeah, have a couple of ideas. Leave it —'

Bob interrupted him before he could continue. 'Whatever will work best, Uncle, just do it.' He cut the connection and tapped Nick Warne's icon.

The bleary face of his second-in-command looked back at him. 'Problem?'

'Yes, Nick. Info pack on the way. Pop a stim, you are not going to get much sleep for a while. We have a nasty. Start finding me solutions within the restrictions.'

The connection severed as the duty communications officer's face appeared on another screen.

'Sir, fast picket has just arrived from the Hauler. *Rose Foxtrot* is two days out. The other Thorn will be here in thirty-six standard hours and the third Thorn another day after that.'

Bob nodded his thanks and the screen cleared. He tapped the brigadier's icon, and the man's image appeared. He was chewing and swallowing, holding a fork with what looked like a piece of steak on it just inside the image's frame. The brigadier raised an eyebrow.

'Had an idea. We need to track these bloody things if they are going to either be reconstructed, or turn themselves into insects. Think that we could irradiate the rounds so that they would act as markers.'

'Good! I like that. Right, leave it with us. Back to you shortly.'

As the screen cleared, Bob leaned back in his seat, thinking of what else they could do to take the fight to the predators.

Then the comms screen lit with the serious face of Uncle looking at him.

'Yeah, caesium and rubidium. Small amounts available to us from the seawater processing. Plus those of us who like things to go bang always have a few extra kilo on hand anyway. Spoken with Mike Antipas and he is ramping up extraction. Also spoke with Major Kalashnokov on *Berkut*, and he has instructed their own systems to start storing the metals. I have started to make components. Don't suppose you have a biological component to add to the mix?'

Bob smiled, seeing Major Aydon's image appear, a beautiful smile on her face.

'Staph bacteria, commander. We can give them a nasty dose of staphylococcus. I have looked at all the information that the ACEs passed on, including those few tissue samples that they somehow managed to obtain. I believe that the predators will be susceptible to a staph infection. We get it into their tissues and in theory it will create necrotising fasciitis. If it works, it will break them down. But knowing you, commander, I would suspect that this is just one part of a piece of potent munitions, no doubt with a copper outer case, a ceramic inner, then with a gel surrounding something like phosphorous, maybe?'

Bob and Uncle both smiled as Bob tapped Uncle's icon, making his image visible to Sally Aydon as well.

Uncle nodded at her with the look of an instructor who is delighted to see that a student has surpassed herself and said, 'Yes, well done, major. But we will use rubidium as the reactive metal.'

Sally chuckled. 'In which case, you will like the gel I have started to produce with the bacteria in it already. The internal delivery system will start delivering it to you in five kilo lots within three hours, courtesy of the medical nanobots.'

Bob cocked his head to one side. 'Good work, major. So where did you get the bacteria from? Are we not very healthy, thanks mainly to you?'

She nodded. 'Yes, but we all carry staphylococcus as a matter of course, mainly in the back of our throats. OK, I shall let you pair concoct other unpleasant weapons. I need to go find some alternatives for you.'

Before either of the men could say anything else, the screen cleared.

'Nice, really nice,' Uncle said. 'I shall press on. I have the machines starting on components. Within four hours we'll have them producing 3000 rounds an hour. Bit tight timing-wise, but should be able to have everyone bombed up with the new ammunition by first light. Right, I'm off.'

Bob nodded at his old friend. 'Good stuff, thanks, Uncle. I shall share this with *Berkut*.'

Looking from his pod and seeing the crew at their stations on the bridge, all bathed in soft red light, Bob felt at peace, knowing that at least they would not go down without a fight.

It was late afternoon when Sir Mildred Jerobaum flew the Aurora high above and a few kilometres forwards of the rest of the squadrons with all his sensors watching, smelling and listening for activity. His two reconnaissance drones made a V-formation with his aircraft so that he was able to see and report across a ten-kilometre-wide area. As he saw and identified any contacts of interest, he would tag them and his onboard systems would allocate them to the following Mauls and the Q in their Gunju.

One of the drones was plotting a concentration of predators deep in a ravine high on a mountainside. Sir Mildred tapped the battle commander's icon.

'Captain?' Nick Warne answered.

'Mr Warne, I am seeing a change. This group is tightly clustered, with what appear to be caves on the north and south sides of the ravine. Also seeing large herds of bison on either side of the predators.'

There was silence from Nick Warne, something that Mildred knew from long experience of working with the major was normal.

Nick Warne finally spoke. 'OK, noted. I am sending in a squadron of armed drones. Stand by.'

Five minutes later, Mildred tapped one of his screens to look at eight large combat drones peeling off from below and behind him to begin their run into the ravine. Controlled by those of *Haast*'s engineering crew who were not servicing aircraft being rotated back to the carrier for refuelling and rearming, the drones gave the non-flying crew hard battle experience.

He watched as they split into four pairs, each pair moving into the ravine from a different direction.

The first pair howled up the ravine flying nap-of-the-earth, as another pair came equally quickly then rapidly decelerated, waiting at the edge of the severe piece of terrain with its massive jumble of weathered, slab-shaped rocks until the other two shot over the top of the visually camouflaged predators firing down into them. The drones then swerved and impacted hard into the cliff faces, exploding and showering wreckage over one of the bison herds. The animals immediately started to stampede up the ravine, looking for a way of escape.

The other two drones slowly slipped over the edge, targeting the quickly moving predators, but before either could fire they simply rolled over and crashed into the rocks. The remaining four drones swept in from the other side, just as some of the dust cleared, showing not dismembered predators as Mildred had expected but dead and dying bison.

He immediately spoke directly to the drone controllers. 'Abort attack, abort!'

But by the time the controllers reacted, the four drones had slipped over the side of the ravine, also tumbling out of control to impact moderately hard into the stony ground.

The bison in the lower part of the ravine also reacted, running down the ravine and out into the grasslands. Mildred looked closely and saw the telltale signatures of predators running with the animals, so he logged them and fed the information back to *Haast*.

One of the combat flight controllers said, 'Are those real contacts, captain? Not decoys, like the bison?'

'All my sensors say that they are.'

Mauls fired on the creatures using the new ammunition and the four predators exploded. Mildred zoomed his imagery up and painted the remains with one of his lasers, noting that the images mapped correctly with other bodies stored in his files. He swung the reconnaissance drones over for a closer look and was satisfied.

Eventually, he moved his sensors back over the ravine to see the first mob of angry bison charging back down the ravine and caught a glimpse of one of the crashed drones being dragged into one of the caves an instant before the dust from the charging bison obscured it.

'Mr Warne! See this!'

Nick Warne reacted very quickly. 'All aircraft! Be advised the enemy now have control of the remains of eight combat drones. I am transmitting self-destructs. Mr Jerobaum, stay on station and report everything. All other aircraft, stay below the horizon of that ravine.'

Mildred told the Aurora to climb up another kilometre and to orbit the ravine. He waited to see the explosions from the drones blowing up, but saw nothing.

'*Haast*, self-destructs have failed,' he reported.

He continued steady circuits of the ravine, looking down through the heavy clouds of dust, trying to see the other drones, aware they were really tough machines and that the linear accelerators and magazines were even tougher and designed to take a great deal of punishment.

On his comms screen, the private icon of Viggo Eames came up.

'Viggo?'

'Get out! Get out now!'

Mildred hit the throttles, dived, turned and started throwing the Aurora about the sky. The first two linear rifle strikes hit the aircraft, punching fist-sized holes through the fuel tanks. The next two hit the antigravity power systems and the last two smashed great holes through his communication and sensor systems. He switched his comms to his laser systems and blew the outer shield of the canopy off just as four strikes blew the turbines of his engines to pieces. He pulled the ejection levers and the front of the aircraft, including the cockpit, rocketed upwards with small wings popping out the sides. He snapped the little survival aircraft over on its back and dived straight down, weaving in every direction. Seconds later, the nose disintegrated from linear rifle shots with shrapnel slicing through the cockpit and into Mildred, who retained consciousness for long enough to hit his locator beacon.

The two reconnaissance drones, as soon as they lost touch with their controlling aircraft, instantly started to look for it and recognised that it was out of control. They then looked for where the survival aircraft was and started to fly towards it, because their sub-AI minds were programmed to look after the pilot. One suddenly exploded as four accelerated rounds hit it. The other dived and jigged and jived, like only a non-living machine could do, escaping to be able to catch up with the tumbling survival craft grabbing it with its waldos and powering its antigravity system to the maximum, carrying the smashed craft and its severely wounded occupant back to *Haast*.

A few moments later, smart missiles, fired from *Haast*, raged into the last known positions of the downed attack drones. The explosions sent a shockwave rippling down the ravine and reached out across a piece of the dried grasslands, setting it on fire.

Bob sat in his pod, looking at the unfolding crisis. He quickly gave Nick orders: 'Let the Q loose! Secure or destroy those drone weapons. Pull the Mauls back in support. Position *Haast* so we give direct fire support.'

He could see Nick Warne directing the Tengu, so tapped the ship-wide comms. 'All crew: man external weapons. Sensors, go to active radar.'

Haast slowed down, waiting for the Q forces to get themselves into position. One of the landers, with its complement of eight Mace, took off from the lowest hangar of the carrier escorted by three Gunju. It held station a few kilometres ahead of *Haast* as other Gunju peeled away from escorting the Mauls to pair off and also move towards the ravine.

In the gun control pod, Uncle, with Mike Antipas beside him and Aaron Huriwaka behind, looked across the displays confirming that the large high-powered 150-millimetre rail guns, which had swung out of the sides of *Haast*, were at temperature. Mike instructed the units to go to full power as he felt *Haast* go into a tight turn, placing them head on to the open end of the ravine five kilometres up-range from it.

He knew that the remaining Aurora was also watching the tops of the ravine, and the Mauls the areas to either side.

Aaron softly said, 'Target.'

Uncle swung the sights onto the icon that Aaron had placed high on the southern wall of the ravine, firing a round from each barrel and a fraction of a second later the damaged drone, and what appeared to be ghosts around it, vaporised.

'Target.'

He switched to the other side of the ravine and fired again with the same result.

'Target.'

This time it was the mangled remains of a drone further up the ravine floor which met the same fate.

'Stand by, Tengu going in.'

Q Sergeant Major Daniel Falcon led the first wave of the assault in a heavily armoured Gunju, howling up the side of the ravine with five others in a staggered line behind him. He did not turn the Gunju into the ravine, but rolled it right over and down the side of the rock face, grinning from ear to ear with the sheer delight of a high-speed pass, flying as close to the cliff face as he could get.

The six Gunju streaked through the narrowing ravine and pulled up at the top, rolling over and roaring down the other side as their systems mapped the cave entrances and looked deeply into them, looking for the missing drone remains and predators. A few minutes later, as they pulled up again at the main entrance to the ravine, the lander with the Maces dived over the top of the cliffs and the armoured walkers dropped away to be piloted down into the caves. The Gunju returned slowly, as two more joined them and paired off with the Maces.

Daniel flew the compact little fighter up behind his old friend, John Harvey, who dropped the Mace down onto the cave floor with weapons extended, looking at the wreck of another drone. Messages started to flash between them.

'What's the bet it's had its remaining fuel and ammunition rigged to explode if I touch it, Dan?'

'Lousy bet, John. Don't touch. Lots of holes in this cave. How about you go splat splat and let's see what comes out to dance?'

John smiled and fired their slow, soft rounds up into each of the holes around the interior of the cave. The fifty-millimetre gel balls bounced and as they came in contact with a non-organic surface, hardened and bounced again. Most bounced around using tiny, powerful energy systems to continue their fast bouncing until they mapped the interiors of the holes without finding anything. Those gel balls then exited, and rolled or bounced across to the Mace to be scooped up and reloaded into their magazines. A few kept moving further away into the hillsides, mapping the tunnels as the Mace watched their progress, feeling through its feet where they were.

Suddenly two of them stopped completely and John's sensors showed him that they had both detonated. Seconds later, they felt the thump of the explosions and a second after that a really big explosion high above them.

Both Q quickly moved their machines out into the centre of the ravine, scanning the rock walls for movement as one of the other Maces yelled, 'Contact!'

Dan and John saw the icons come up in their HUDs. John started jogging the machine around the bend to get a firing line on the enemy high on the cliff walls. Covering him, Daniel frowned, and without really thinking about it raced forwards on his antigravity and turbines to come up behind John quickly yelling, 'Jump! Grab hold! Ambush! Get out!'

John instinctively hit his antigravity controls as he pushed hard upwards with his legs, the powered armour racing upwards with Daniel in the Gunju moving beneath him, accelerating as hard as he could. John rolled and grasped the roll struts over Daniel's cockpit, wondering what his friend was doing, and looked back to see the enormous explosions racing out of all the caves, picking up the Tengu and their craft and smashing them into the other explosions coming from the caves on the other side of the ravine.

John swore long and hard, seeing two of his friends almost make it out of the maelstrom before they were hit by rocks and smashed, the wreckage disappearing back down into the dust cloud. Seeing a piece of rock spinning up behind them, John wrenched them over just in time although it struck the Gunju a glancing blow.

Two squadrons of Gunju, with Mauls immediately behind them, came screaming down out of the sky in support. Daniel saw the flashes of predator-controlled linear rifles firing at a Maul which had both engines shot away from one side as it was close to the ground travelling at high speed. In an instant, it flicked over and exploded into the ground. One of the Gunju fired on the predators, while another predator, clutching a rail gun, popped up from the ground to engage it and its wingman and seconds later both machines tumbled to the ground in flames.

A cone of lasers flashed out from the distant *Haast*, ionising the air between them as a massive particle beam burst forth and superheated the first predators and their weapons, vaporising them.

John saw the second group of predators, now plainly visible, dragging their captured weapons, trying to line them up, and fired both his small linear rifles, pulverising all three of them. Daniel joined in the fire until the magazine of the weapon detonated, destroying it and shredding the predator remains further.

John felt the antigravity unit of his Mace being struck. He yelled out, 'Get us to ground! Fast! I am taking hits.'

Just as he said the words, the Gunju was also hit and the machine started to roll over. A Maul and two more Gunju howled overhead, firing at the top of the other side of the ravine but was ambushed and hit hard in the fuel tanks by another group of predators.

Alarms warned John of a fuel fire in his power pack, so he opened both hatches in the Mace and climbed out of it to cling to the top of the failing Gunju as Daniel wrestled with the failing aircraft. The Mace tumbled away a few seconds before Daniel fired the last of the thrust straight down, and they thumped onto the ground.

Both Tengu, without speaking, clambered off the damaged craft one to each side. They lifted the covers on the small forward rotaries, detaching them from their mounts before grasping the power packs and small magazines, hefting them onto their backs, and clipping them on.

Three other Gunju swept up behind them as the two Q ran from cover to cover until they reached the damaged Mace. John quickly checked it over but shook his head, so they both moved towards where the smoking ruins of the last predators to fire on them lay in a shallow hole behind a large rock. Seeing the remains of the last of the captured linear rifles, Daniel uploaded the images to the Q lander which was prowling above them.

They then ran towards the burning wreck of another Maul lying on its side. Two Gunju flew over the top of it, hovering above the flames and injecting high volumes of water into their jet exhausts and putting out the fires. John pulled open the gun pod canopy of the wreck and saw that the gunner was dead, her body full of jagged holes. He looked to the side, noting that the ammunition feed on one of the guns had taken a direct hit and that the rounds had cooked off into the pod. He walked away towards the nose of the machine where Daniel asked the fate of the pilot, shaking his head.

* * *

'Would someone please tell me what the fuck just happened? Drones should not suddenly lose power like that, nor missiles produce a hellish bigger bang than they should. And how the hell do predators get the information about how to operate our weapons, to say nothing of where to hit the vital systems of an Aurora, or a Maul and a Gunju? What is going on, people?'

There was total silence for a minute until the quiet respectful voice of Vishav Jyani spoke up. 'I believe I know, my commander, about the explosions.'

Bob knew that the lieutenant was a man who never voiced an opinion unless he knew what he was talking about. 'Go ahead, lieutenant,' Bob said.

Vish, sitting in the gunners' pod of Anneke Bester's Maul, orbiting high above the carnage, hoped that he was right as he said, 'It is a layer of methane gas, sir. It was probably produced by the bison on command of the predator. They may have been able to manipulate the gas further by an inversion layer perhaps, or more likely their insects?'

Bob clenched his fists on his armrests, thinking about it. 'Yeah. OK, I get that, but what about the information those shits now have on us?'

The ACE Haast answered. 'I believe that it was given to them by Angelito, who was privy to such data and I also believe that he has not left this planet. The best place for him to hide would be in the ocean somewhere close. Actually, the more interesting question would be why. Why would he aid the enemy? Find out what he has to gain from that and we will find our answers.'

Bob shook his head. 'OK, we deal with that shit later. Right now we put out the fires and recover the downed pilots and craft. Navigation, bring *Haast* in over the top of the ravine to lift the bigger rocks out of the way. Launch all the Chrysops for close defence.'

Letting out a long sigh, he tapped Sally Aydon's icon. 'Major. Casualties?'

'I have recovered five Soul Savers from Maul crew and ten from Tengu,' Sally said. 'I am initiating the transfers in mechanised chassis for Maul crews. Mr Jerobaum is touch and go. I shall wait another few hours to see how he responds to treatment before I make a decision to euthanase his body and upload him. What should I do with the Q?'

Bob nodded, knowing how much everyone hated the cold, metallic almost non-life of waking up in a chassis.

'Stand by,' he advised. 'Major Graham, we have ten Tengu souls transferred into our data core. Should we upload them into chassis or hold them until *Rose Foxtrot* returns?'

The Tengu major looked out of the screen at him, unblinking. She gave a sharp nod. 'Thank you for the consideration. We go to chassis, please.'

Bob felt the attitude of *Haast* change and saw the Chrysops all patrolling within a kilometre of the carrier. He looked at the image of the Tengu, who was staring expectantly at him.

'My thanks for the work of your troops, major,' he said.

Unexpectedly, she smiled. 'You are welcome, commander. I do not think any of us expected such a response from the predators. We will not be so lightly fooled next time. I shall carry on with the recovery of all the craft and the bodies.'

He nodded, showing agreement, but in his mind he did not fully agree and the connection was severed.

'Major Aydon, Major Graham requests chassis for her people.'

'Very well. Please ensure that I get most of an intact predator, please. I do not mind how many pieces there are, I just want most of one. Oh, and make sure none of our personnel touch one. I would suggest disposable drones and sealed containers. Excuse me, please, I need to get back to our patients.'

He nodded and the screen cleared then he called Nick Warne. 'You hear that from Major Aydon?'

'No, but I would guess that she will be looking to get her hands on a dead predator? And that they should not be touched? Yeah, I can see from the expression on your face that I am right. On it.'

Nick had decided at the start of the entire deployment that things were not on the level and, as he deployed the semi-intelligent high contamination unit, one more piece of evidence to support his feelings slipped into place. He had seen the unit on the manifest when he first came onboard the brand-new *Haast* and he had wondered why they would need such an expensive and relatively rare piece of equipment. He brought up the systems control for the machine, told it what he wanted and where it should go to find enough predator parts, and activated it.

The eight-metre-long barrel-like machine slipped out of a hangar on the lowest deck of *Haast* and sedately moved around the battlefield gathering predator parts to itself.

Nick kept an eye on it as he directed the recovery actions below *Haast* with the aid of Mark de Ruyter and his salvage crews. They were lifting boulders and smashing rocks out of the way until they could get to the crushed Maces and Gunjus.

Finally, late into the night he was able to report to the commander.

'Right,' Nick began, 'we have the bodies and the wrecks onboard. Major Aydon says that those couple of crushed Tengu that were found inside one of the cave entrances have almost certainly been sampled as there had been tissue removed from their faces and an eye had been carefully removed as well. Seems that the predators wanted to know about their body make-up and chemistry as well, maybe.'

Bob climbed out of his pod, had a long stretch and walked over to the panoramic windshield, looking out into the night. He could see the heavy threatening clouds overhead.

'Yeah, that figures. Well, at least the brigadier and his crews were able to take over our sweep, so from here we head back out to sea, take on water, lick our wounds and go back in for another go at midnight local time. Let's just hope that the Tengu's rebuilding of their sensors works well so we can see those shits in the dark. You know that they now carry special nutrient packs so they will not have to sleep for the next three days and that Major Graham is going to have two-thirds of her people in the air from now on.'

Mark de Ruyter answered. 'Good! What is the use of having super-troops if we do not let them get on with the job. I have upped the outputs of the gardens as their nutrient packs will need more.'

Nick Warne called out from his pod. 'Results are in.'

'Which ones?' Mark asked.

'The medical research drone's; all a bit of a mystery to me. Have sent them down to Sally Aydon. She can sort them with that beautiful brain of hers. And because of that she will probably not be in our bed tonight.'

Bob and Mark exchanged a look and grinned.

* * *

Sally Aydon stood on one of the landing platforms at the base of *Haast*, looking out over the ocean and at the electrical storm moving away over the horizon. The stars were starting to show themselves through the cloud cover. She felt the wind's chill, so sealed up her ship suit. Looking behind her, she could see Sergeant Major Antipas and a few of his crew monitoring the water treatment unit which was on the sea surface a few hundred metres below them. She took in a deep breath then suddenly thought about it, exhaled, shuddered a little and gave out a short sharp laugh.

Mike Antipas looked across, and after hesitating, wondering if he should leave the major to her own thoughts, he walked across and quietly stood beside her, looking out over the ocean. Turning to him, Sally asked, 'How would you feel about living here on a permanent basis, Mister Antipas?'

The powerfully built man slowly turned and looked up at the medical officer and shrugged. 'Well, if I had to I would not say no, major. Sure beats the hell out of a lot of other places I have seen in the last sixty or seventy years.'

He looked at her evenly, leaving her space to reply or not. She straightened, saying, 'You are a good man, Michael Antipas, and a wise one as well. Thank you.'

She gave him a wry smile, nodded, and walked off, heading for the lift, which surprised Mike a little, knowing how keen she was on her exercise.

Bob sat still in the orders room after Sally had briefed him, showing him her team's findings and then leaving to get a few hours' sleep. He thought long and hard about waking the senior members of the crew, who were off-duty, but decided that it would be best to allow them their rest and announce the findings and their ramifications at the daily briefing, only a few hours away.

He walked out of the orders room onto the bridge, which was quietly busy. The night shift was communicating with the twenty Gunju fighters out on the peninsula hunting the remaining predators, in coordination with another twenty from *Berkut* and also squadrons from the Thorn. He sat heavily in his command pod and had it seal its doors. He swore softly to himself and tapped the icons of the brigadier and Major Daisuke Suzuki on the Thorn.

A moment or so later both faces appeared on the screen with the brigadier seated and wearing a bathrobe and the remnants of hastily removed shaving foam still on his face.

'Well, you will not thank me for this. But we are here for a long, long time. Medical Major Aydon has just briefed me that we are all infected with tailored predator bacteria and viruses. I am sending you the information packages now.'

Both men read through the information while Bob did as well, making sure that he had not missed anything.

After fifteen minutes, the brigadier gave a small series of nods and looked at the screen.

'OK, so we are here now. The nasties are all around us and have been since we started blowing up predators and their larvae. We can deal with this. It is not as though many armed forces actually got to go home after their conquests throughout history anyway. Most stayed put and settled. Right! Let us start making plans to stay here. Thank the good major and her team for an excellent report. Ask her to start work on treatments for every possible outcome of the conditions and diseases that will plague us, please, commander. Major Suzuki, do you have anything to add?'

The major shook his head. 'I fear that there will be more viruses to follow tailored exactly to the Tengu, seeing that samples were taken during the ravine probe. They are learning about us and we are learning about them. This will be a long fight. I will send all the information we have plus the battle reports to the Tengu on the Angelito orbital. As soon as *Basalt* and *Rose Foxtrot* jump into this area of space, they will be made aware of what is happening.'

Rose Foxtrot Nineteen

Storfisk

The great ship swung down into orbit above Storfisk, decelerating fast.

'Wardah, whenever you are ready, scout out the best possible place for me. Solid basalt rock, no fissures, no fault lines, no caves for at least two kilometres and a quality water supply on that boundary. You have briefed your Q that they will not be leaving the planet for the foreseeable future? Were there any dissensions?'

Wardah stood in her flight suit on the bridge of the second Thorn, making ready for a departure.

'I understand what you need. The Q are briefed and ready to go and no, of course, none of them wish to walk away from the fight. They are requesting that their standard human bodies be brought here and, yes, they know the risks.'

Rose replied, 'Good, I would have been most surprised if it had been any other way. I have sent a fast picket with a full report and a requirement that the standard bodies of our Q be sent here to the Haulers' Collective. Sub-AI battle unit detachments will orbit the planet so that there will always be one in orbit above the peninsula.'

The Thorn lifted out of the hangar in the side of *Rose* and slipped down towards the atmosphere.

'Whose control will we be under, *Rose*?'

The Hauler answered with a certain reserve in her voice. 'The brigadier's, Wardah. Just like your husband, but I wish that your Soul Saver links be given to me. Please ensure that Daisuke does the same. I dare say that before the day is out all of our combatants will do the same.'

As she watched Wardah's Thorn go straight down, decelerating hard, *Rose* spoke to another of her Q crew. 'Mr Wright, are your machines and crews ready?'

The Q captain was part of a special group of Tengu who were much more heavily built than the others who had departed on the Thorn. He reported: 'Yes, Hauler *Rose*. All equipment is loaded. We await your commands.'

'Very well. Detach and move to the Angelito orbital. Wait for *Basalt* and when it appears, you know what is required.'

'Very well.' The powerfully augmented Tengu grinned and looked at each of his crew. 'We good to go! Buckle in.'

His number two, sitting in the compact lander's right-hand seat, added, 'All equipment is secure, zero gravity fighters are secure. We have full loads of everything required. Airlocks are secure, locked and detached.'

Steve Wright nodded and pointed out through the canopy of the brutish machine, past the opening outer doors of the hangar and towards the distant orbital.

'OK, Valentene, let's see how good you are at flying by the seat of your pants. No instruments, only dead reckoning. Take us to, and land us against, the orbital. And don't bang the doors on the way out. *Rose* hates that.'

The captain laughed and extended one of her long fingers at the captain, then her digits flew over the screens and the lander lifted and moved out through the doors. Her hands then dropped down to the two control columns and she poured on the power with her mind, calculating where the orbital would be in the sky when she wanted to dock with it.

Forty-five minutes later, Valentene smoothly manoeuvred the lander with its six, zero gravity fighters snugly docked against it, to gently kiss the airlocks against the side of the Hauler orbital.

Steve looked across at his second-in-command. 'Good stuff! And nothing damaged. Right, come on, you lot, let's go see what the resident Tengu has to offer in the way of beer.'

They cycled their way through the airlock in zero gravity, which they had been designed for, to meet the much smaller and more refined Tengu who was waiting for them.

Hours later, the Hauler *Rose Foxtrot* decelerated so that she was hanging vertically above the planet. With her engines supplying huge amounts of energy to her massive antigravity units, which she had not powered up in decades, she sedately moved down through the atmosphere at 100 kilometres per hour. A hundred metres up, six portions of her lower hull folded out forming the landing gear as she slowed her speed to gently touch down on the surface.

Engineering drones emerged, moving away from *Rose* in every direction and setting up listening and observation units, which she gave control of to a sub-AI unit whose sole task was to watch everything, right down to flea-sized insects, within five kilometres of her towering bulk.

Another group of drones towed large flexible pipes from her to a water treatment plant, giving her access to thousands of litres of fresh water per minute from a large stream just before it disappeared over the cliff face into the sea below.

The great otter ACE, Madeye, luxuriated in the river, rolling and frolicking, thrilled to be in a real river. She found everything intensely interesting and started to fill her own data files with information about all the flora and fauna she could find, sending the data back to her private computers onboard *Rose*. Swimming across to the far bank she ran up the bank, standing on her hind legs to look out across the plains, sensing the distant herds of animals and shivered in delighted anticipation that her work was about to begin in earnest. She would bring back as many of the animals as she could to full health.

At dawn the following morning *Rose* was satisfied with the area and activated the landing legs' feet which drilled anchors down into the rock, locking her in place against any storm that the planet could throw at her.

'Brigadier Mortlock, Commander Thompson, I am now established as the semi-permanent base here on this part of the planet. All equipment and facilities are now at your disposal.'

The great ship then programmed all the drones that she carried, sending them out to the surrounding areas to start preparing the gardens and orchards, wondering if Storfisk would be her final resting place. As her presence gazed across the landscape and up into the mountains with the rising local star bathing them in an orange glow, she smiled to herself, knowing that it was as good a place as any she had visited in the last few hundreds of years.

Basalt

Above Storfisk

'Major. Just had a message lasered to us from *Rose* Nineteen and relayed from the Hauler orbital Angelito. To say the least, we have a situation.'

Michael looked across at Jasmine and raised his eyebrows. 'Open it up to the whole crew.'

Jasmine nodded and proceeded to broadcast the message. '*Basalt*, this is *Rose*. I have established a base on the southernmost peninsula of the Haulers' protected reserve. I have the Tengu Q warriors and the carriers *Haast* and *Berkut* down here on the planet with me. We are conducting a holding action against the octopoid army building predator. It is imperative that you do not enter the atmosphere. Everything here was a trap to infect my crews, and those of *Haast* and *Berkut*, with a whole group of tailored bacteria and viruses. I have effected a quarantine on the entire planet. Nothing is to depart from it.'

A chill went through every member of the crew and in particular, Marko, who thought immediately of his family in their village of Waipunga.

Michael slowly shook his head and Stephine was livid, with a look upon her face that frightened Marko and Veg. Veg reached across and gathered Stephine to him, hugging her close. He said: '*Rose*. This is the general. What would you like us to do?'

'Please dock with Angelito. The AI core of the Hauler is missing. I need you to establish a new one to control the orbiting sub-AI platforms. Also, find the landers that the predators used to deploy here and, just as importantly, find and neutralise the carrier that brought them here. I have detached a squad of Q3s to assist you. They are the best of the best and come with their own equipment. Stephine, I am sending you the files of everything that the guardian ACEs and medical Major Aydon learned of the chemistry of the predators and the infective agents she has identified. I need to know what they will ultimately do and if we are, in fact, seeing another derivative of Infant.'

Michael Longbow spoke quietly. 'Patrick, dock us with Angelito. Clone a control segment of yourself, please. Harry, Marko, Topaz, create a housing as soon as you can and liaise with Patrick. Lily and Jasmine, sort the accommodation of the Q. Julie, Minh, sort their equipment, please. Fritz, ACEs, as soon as we dock I want you on that orbital checking every single data log going as far back as the weeks before we know that predators turned up. James, record and edit everything from everyone so when we get around to attributing blame for this debacle we will have the records. Let's go, people!'

He then turned and looked at Veg and Stephine as Veg said, 'Well? What do you need us to do, Michael?'

Michael grinned. 'Sorry, you being a general and all, I am not sure if I should be giving you orders?'

The huge man laughed. 'You have been doing so for the last eight years. Why change now?'

'OK, start on the biological threat files. As soon as Marko, Topaz or the ACEs come available, put them to work as well. But don't you two have a delivery to make?'

As the crew moved to their various tasks, Michael contacted the orbital. 'Angelito orbital, this is Major Longbow of *Basalt*.'

On one of the screens appeared a Q with more powerful facial features than the ones that Michael was familiar with.

'Major, this is Steven Wright. We are expecting you and are to give you whatever assistance you need. Specifications of our equipment and capabilities are now sent.'

Michael saw the file come across and flicked a copy to Veg and Harry. The major nodded at the staunch reptilian face.

'Good! My thanks. We shall be there in about an hour.'

'All crew: I am powering down the gravity systems in two minutes. Will have them back up in fifteen.'

Veg smiled at Marko as he caught up with him on the stairway going down to the hangar decks. 'Is he ready to go?'

Marko nodded. 'Yeah, short cycle antigravity systems, propulsion and a comms unit have been attached to the chimera's cylinder. Four engineering drones are also helping to move him into *Blackjack*'s upper hold.'

He tapped on his wristscreens and gently slid the gravity controls until they were at zero. The two men then pulled themselves hand over hand down the walls of the spiral staircase, arriving in time to look through the transparent wall beside the airlock to see *Blackjack*'s hangar seal itself off.

'How long before she is back, Veg?'

'Couple of hours tops I should say, Marko. Enough time to drop the creature in through the atmosphere into a nice moderately shallow part of the sea. You done with the new AI housing?'

'Yeah, done my part, the others can handle it. Shall I go make us some tea? Just baked a tray of shortbread.'

Veg grinned and gently clapped Marko on the shoulder. 'Yes, good, I shall go fetch Stephine and you tell Topaz to meet us in the mess.'

Five minutes later, Marko saw on his wristscreen that *Blackjack* had cleared the hull, so after he gave everyone the warning, he re-established the gravity, then put the water jug on to boil, pulled his large iron teapot out of its wooden box and went about making oolong tea.

Stephine and Veg arrived, closely followed by Topaz. They made small talk for a few moments, sipping their tea and munching on Marko's shortbread.

'Seeing that you are all now fed and watered,' Topaz said, 'I wish to show you a rather startling series of discoveries.'

The three augmented humans looked across at the cobalt-blue machine as she unfolded herself, displaying the large screens so that they could see the data.

After some long moments of reading, then digesting, the news, Stephine finally said angrily, 'Fucking idiots! Those stupid stupid idiots, what were they thinking? So this is a soft probe by the Administration against its own to see how they will cope.'

Marko felt cold. A cold that seemed to creep into his bones, even his augmented chain-linked ivory ones.

'Oh, shit. So they have taken the information from the library that we so gleefully handed over to them and the octopoid tech that we also had a hand in finding, and some of the material that was recovered from the Infant conflict, plus the nastiest experiments that the supposedly destroyed Games Board scientists were working on, and they have combined it all and dropped it onto Storfisk.'

Veg nodded slowly. 'Yes, and some human Gjomvik Corporation has made a fortune for themselves by creating the predator. A new weapon for them. So this is just another stinking weapons test. Well, this is a challenge for us, eh? Let us see if we can wreck this game for them.'

Senior Hauler *Chrysanthemum*

Cygnus 5

'Well?'

The massive Hauler, regarded by most as the leader of the Haulers' Collective, hung in orbit above the planet that was surrounded by hundreds of weapon platforms, orbitals and interstellar ships of all kinds.

'Well what, *Chrysanthemum*? We are doing what is required. The Storfisk system is the closest to where we know the outer edge of the octopoid areas of interest lie. They will come. They will eventually seek to gain back control of Old Earth as it is their cradle of existence. Would you deny the rest of humanity's interests, to step aside for them?'

'You are deliberately putting a great number of people that I care for deeply in a horrible situation, Epsilon. I, and the rest of the Haulers' Collective, will hold you and your fellow Administration Orbitals accountable if things do not go to your plan.'

The huge spherical AI machine, which administered the local star systems, gazed out across the 100 kilometres to the Hauler, watching as *Chrysanthemum* started to power away towards the closest Lagrange point. He gave a mental sigh, seeing far ahead of the Hauler another two of the Collective also powering away from the planet.

'Do not interfere, *Chrysanthemum*. I am warning you. Leave Storfisk alone. It is a good plan.'

He could not bring himself to say please.

'We will do what we need to do, Epsilon. They are all trapped on that planet due to you and various Gjomvik Corporations wanting to make more money. We need to help them as they are our families. Goodbye.'

Epsilon opened a comms channel to Gamma. 'They have taken the bait. They will clean up your mess.'

Appendix One

Glossary

ACE (Artificially Created Entity)

An ACE is often a pet or helper. An ACE may have animal or human DNA, in any combination, and is frequently cybernetically enhanced. They are normally fully sentient, serve their creator in an indentured capacity for a fixed time period, then are free to make their own way throughout the Sphere or beyond.

The Administration

The governmental military forces and bureaucracy of the Sphere of Humankind. Bureaucracy everywhere, even in the far future, is the same.

The Games Board

The media group concerned with the procurement and production of reality audiovisual. The Games Board was created to stage strictly regulated Conflicts and to promote them through their extensive marketing and broadcast channels, notice boards and other media. The Games Board controls everything about the Conflicts, from weapons development to final approval of the Conflict itself. If the Conflict is sanctioned, the Games Board will provide funding. Unsanctioned Conflicts are also overviewed by the Games Board, broadcast and marketed, with the understanding that should they get too big, the combined forces of the Administration, Gjomvik and Games Board forces will end the Conflict with overwhelming force. Small controlled unsanctioned Conflicts are encouraged as they are good for business and keep all humans entertained.

The Gjomvik Corporations

The business and trade corporations of the Sphere of Humankind. Big business in the far future is the same as big business today. The Gjomvik Corporations are controlled by large family groups or appointed individuals. They provide the main source of funded mercenary groups which participate in the sanctioned Games Board Conflicts, plus most of the weapons, craft and support.

The Haulers' Collective

The long-range carriers of all trade and information, the Collective comprises huge ships capable of transporting great quantities of trade goods or whatever else is required. They also actively map the Lagrange points and collect fees from all ships using those navigation points. They explore far further out from the Sphere and are humankind's first line of defence.

The humans

Unaltered humans are Type S (Standard), but the heroes of the Conflicts are often augmented humans (Type A). Some

AI (Augmented Intelligence) units are human, and may look like machines or even like Type A humans. Other types of humans include:

Type AM — Type A human, military

Type AE — Type A human, explorer

Monitors and Expeditors — Type A humans augmented to fulfil specific functions required by the Games Board.

Lagrange points (LPs)

Lagrange points are spread throughout space as navigational nodes where a ship uses its wormhole generators function. They are usually plotted and owned by the Haulers' Collective.

The octopoids

An ancient alien race now splintered into diverse groups. The primary group just wants to be left alone to regress to their original semi-sentient selves. The secondary group wishes to take back their areas of influence.

The Sphere of Humankind

The Sphere is the primary area of influence of humanity (approximately fifty light years across).

Appendix Two

Initialisations, Acronyms and Abbreviations

ACE Artificially Created Entity

AG Antigravity

AI Augmented Intelligence

AV Audiovisual

GB Games Board

HUD Heads-Up Display

LP Lagrange Point

NCO Non-Commissioned Officer

Sub-AI Powerful computer system, just below sentience

Appendix Three

Games Board

The Articles and Rules of War

1. Conflicts.
    1.1. Conflicts over 100 combatants.
    All parties engaging in Conflicts involving in excess of 100 combatants must gain approval for the Conflict and subsequent marketing.
    1.2. Conflicts under 100 combatants.
    Parties engaging in Conflicts involving fewer than 100 combatants may also apply to the Games Board for approval and certification provided that Conflicts meet the requirements of the Marketing Interest Index.
    1.3. Funding.
    Following approval, funding will be negotiated with each party.
2. Weapons.
    All weapons systems and munitions types must be approved by the Games Board.
    2.1. Approved weapons.
    Approved weapons are listed in Schedule B.
    2.2. New weapons.

Proposals for new weapon designs must be submitted to the Intersystem Games Board Weaponry Wing with supporting documents proving their necessity in a Conflict. Weapon development without a specific known Conflict application does not require Games Board authorisation until used in a sanctioned Conflict.

2.2.1. Design parameters are listed in Schedule F.

2.2.2. Following approval, each weapon must be submitted for field testing and certification by the Weaponry Wing.

2.2.3. The ammunition for the weapon must be submitted for testing and certification.

2.3 Manufacture.

2.3.1. All weapons are manufactured under licence to the Weaponry Wing.

2.3.2. All ammunition will be under the direct control of the Weaponry Wing and through the Weaponry Wing's agents issued to the approved sides of any Conflict.

2.3.3. Additional weapons, spare parts and ammunition will also be administered by the Weaponry Wing's agents.

3. Ammunition.

All munitions deployed and used during any Conflict must be 'fire and forget', direct line-of-sight weapons. No munitions are allowed to be guided by any form of self-destructive AI system. All weapons deployed must have a maximum range as specified in the Games Board Ammunitions table. All weapons must, at all times, and in any circumstances, be available for inspection and testing by any certified Battlefield Inspector, as warranted by the Planetary Director of the Games Board. Such inspector's decisions on the suitability of the weapons or munitions used will be final and binding on all parties involved, immediately. The inspectors will also be able to award any costs incurred to any party involved, as they see fit.

4. Marketing.
The Games Board retains all marketing rights to the approved Conflicts and will, after the Conflict has been judged as concluded, award revenues generated by the marketing of the Conflict to either side, as seen fit by the Games Board.

5. Tactical battlefield questioning of any captured opposition combatants is allowed. However, any form of interrogation that lasts more than one standard hour is actively discouraged by the Conflict Marketing Unit. No recordings of any interrogation will be made after the one-hour deadline has passed.

6. Heroic acts by individuals or units are greatly encouraged by the Conflict Marketing Unit. There must, however, be a specific objective for such acts; any form of kamikaze action, unless the participants have already been judged by the Conflict Marketing Unit as legitimately mortally wounded, is actively discouraged.

7. The Games Board retains the right to end any Conflict by use of its own armed group known as the Expeditors, should any individual, unit, battalion or army group break the rules of engagement as judged by the Adjudicators.

8. All power in decision-making by the Games Board is vested in the board by the Governing Bodies of the Known Civilised Societies (the Administration).

All decisions made by the Games Board officials, Adjudicators and Expeditors are final and deemed above reproach. The Games Board cannot be held responsible for loss or destruction of any materials or personnel.

9. Death of any participant is to be avoided at all costs. All personnel in any approved Conflict are responsible for ensuring that their individual Soul Savers are backed up at approved Safe Points prior to any Conflict. Adjudicators will award 'Re-Life' costs against any individual or group as they see fit.

10. AI individuals are to ensure their own backups and reanimation in whatever form they choose at their own discretion, should they see fit to take part in any Conflict.

11. It is expressly forbidden to involve, in any way, the local civilian population in any approved Conflict unless they, as individuals, sign an approval with the Games Board, in which case they will then be deemed combatants with all the rights, remuneration and responsibilities that such a designation entails.

12. Weapons of Mass Destruction are only to be used with the express approval of the Planetary Director of the Games Board. Nuclear weapons whose timed radioactive half-life exceeds one orbit of the nearest sun to the planet on which the weapons are deployed are expressly forbidden.

13. Weapons which alter the genetic structure of any recognised biological group are expressly forbidden.

14. All air, sea and land warcraft must employ power systems that, as a main component, use a pressurised gas system to either drive turbines or act as electrical generators. Any power system that employs a flammable liquid as part of its power generation will require the

express approval of the Planetary Director of the Games Board prior to deployment. Units utilising water cracker technologies will be given the most favourable status and immediate approval. Units using systems deemed archaic, or any technology that is over 200 years old in design, will also be given favoured status. Such units are able to have no greater than a ten per cent advanced technology input unless that advanced technology is the water cracker type.

15. Orbiting weapons platforms are forbidden as are all Orbital Surveillance Systems.

16. Aircraft and drones used for battlefield surveillance must be unarmed.

17. All aircraft and flying craft of any description are speed restricted to that of the local speed of sound. Their range, on a single supply of fuel or power cell, must not exceed 1000 kilometres. Their maximum combat ceiling is restricted to 5000 metres.

18. Antigravity craft of any description and devices are approved with the acknowledged restrictions of air-, land- and watercraft.

19. Watercraft of any description are not to exceed 10,000 metric tonnes dry weight. No ship is to exceed a speed of 350 kilometres per hour, or to carry any armament of any description exceeding 300mm diameter for ammunition size. The maximum fuel allowance of any watercraft of either surface or submersible description is seven standard days at full power. Maximum depth allowable for any form of submersible is 100 standard metres.

20. Land vehicles, including armoured fighting vehicles, are not to exceed a dry weight of 100 metric tonnes, must not exceed 120 kilometres per hour speed or carry a weapon

of any description which exceeds 150mm in diameter and two metres in length. The maximum fuel endurance at full power must not exceed sixteen standard hours.

21. All communication systems for the Conflict must be by way of standard frequency modulated radio with a maximum range of 200 kilometres.

22. Capture and use of any opposition's personnel and equipment is allowed at any time. Ownership considerations will be judged at the termination of the Conflict. Personnel are to be given the opportunity to switch sides, should such occasions as a rout occur, as judged by the Conflict Marketing Unit. All ranks, pay rates and bonus considerations must remain in place. Any individual or unit which attempts to change sides without the express approval of the Conflict Marketing Unit can be judged as hostile by all sides and removed from the battlefield pending penalties.

23. No battlefield recording by video or audio is to be made by any member of the Conflict. This is the express concern of the Games Board and its production wing, the Conflict Marketing Unit. All images, recordings, surveillance images and satellite images are the property of the Conflict Marketing Unit. Once the battle timings have commenced all personnel involved in the Conflict can be recorded by the agents of the Conflict Marketing Unit at any time and in whatever circumstances the agent deems to be of marketable interest.

24. It is expressly forbidden for any member of any side of a Conflict to interfere with or hinder any recording agent of the Conflict Marketing Unit, in whatever action they are performing. All planned actions in the Conflict, at all levels, must be made available to the recording agents,

who can then record any actions of interest. All personnel involved in the Conflict are required to advise the agents of anything noteworthy or interesting of which the agents are not aware. The recording agents (with the approval of the local agent of the Games Board) can require the set battle, as notified, to be fought again if it is found some action or actions were particularly noteworthy and the recordings of such were not deemed satisfactory by the unit editor. Should such occur, the Conflict Marketing Unit is to carry the cost of weapons repairs and additional issuing of ammunitions, transportation and specific briefings of new combatants. Should any action of any members of the Conflict have caused the requirement of the re-recording, then costs will be awarded accordingly, as decided by an Adjudicator of the Games Board.

25. All members of any acknowledged Conflict are required to actively pursue, capture or, at very least, immediately report any non-sanctioned weapons ammunition, arms dump, supplier or manufacturer of non-sanctioned weapons to the nearest member or agent of the Games Board. Death of any known, non-approved arms manufacturer, supplier or dealer is sanctioned. Bounties for the proven death or capture of such individuals are immediately payable to the approved individuals concerned by the Conflict Marketing Unit.

Penalties

Members, agents and direct employees of the Games Board, and its marketing, intelligence, weapons and enforcement components, are charged under these articles to enforce the will and requirements of the Games Board at all times.

Penalties from minor monetary fines up to and including total death can be awarded by any member agent or direct employee of the Games Board, acting in conjunction with two other members of the Games Board, as long as those individuals are from different wings of the Games Board.

Right of Appeal
This right will only be awarded if there occurs a possible consideration of a difference of opinion, between at least three or more assigned members of the Games Board or its agents, at the time of any specific incident to which a penalty is about to be awarded.

Penalties are as follows:
- Deduction of individual's daily pay.
- Forfeiture of any or all specific battle bonuses.
- Forfeiture of Recognition.
- Forfeiture of Equipment.
- Forfeiture of Rank.
- Forfeiture of Battle Rights.
- Forfeiture of Freedom.
- Forfeiture of all unit assets both collectively and privately owned.
- Forfeiture of Re-Life as paid for by the Conflict Agreement Insurance.
- Forfeiture of Current Life.
- Complete and Total Death.

Acknowledgments

To my darlings: Liz, Luke and Charlotte. Also the family, Dave Wheeler, Tim Wheeler, Margaret Dine, and the Dine and Webb families.

To all my friends, my humble thanks for your faith that I could create this: Mac MacKinnon, Geoff Shepard, Aaron Huriwaka, Al Brady, Mike and Kenney Antipas, Sally Aydon, Graham Kyle, Bob Thomson, Isaac Hikaka, Dan Falconer, Anneke Bester, Gary and Jill Winter, Graham Nightingale, Greg O'Connor, Cedric and Beverly Heard, Graham Duncan, Wayne Singh, Yvette Reece, John Harvey, Mike de Rutger, Alba Garcia-Rivas, Scott Overton, Daisuke Nakabayashi, Robb and SueAnn Merrill, Jon McLeary, Roger and Sue Mortlock, Lester and Ann Polglase, Giles McCabe, Chelsea Mainwaring and family, Doug Casement, Caroline Williams, Nanette Cormack, Geoff Boxell, Linda Wills, Bill Hohepa, Bruce and Cathy Jenkins, Andrew Short, Hayden Applegarth, Peter Payne, Greg Miller, Suzie Williams, Richard Carrington, Nico Matsis, Zane Smith, Julie Wake, Willie and Nina Heatley, Annabel Graham, Andreas Bierwage, Peter Elliott, Ra Vincent, Nick Weir, Tim Abbot, Vince Hoffmann, Jim Mora, Garth Holmes, Claire Bretherton, Jerry Glynn, John Harvey, Karl Ogle, Tim Sherman, John Howe, Natalie Forsythe, Geoff Scott, Dave de

Burg, Mark Stevens, Vishav Jyani, Gordon Bankier, Curtis Boswell, Tanya Snively, Ian and Sharon Davis, and Steve and Samantha Wright.

To the sterling wordsmiths of HarperCollins, my never-ending gratitude, especially Steph Smith, Kate and Rochelle.

Special thanks to those who push me along: Mac, Al, Robb, Graham and Geoff.

A FURY OF ACES 1

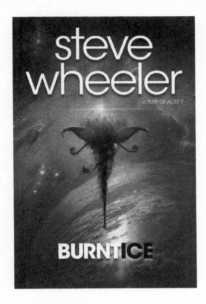

In our future worlds the Administration rules the Sphere of Humankind, the Games Board sanctions and funds wars and conflicts, and the Haulers' Collective roams the space routes like the caravanners of old.

Marko and his crew of fellow soldier-engineers are sent to investigate a largely unknown planet. When they encounter strange artefacts and an intelligent but aggressive squid species, they are forced to embark on a perilous journey far from the Sphere.

They will have to survive not only other alien encounters but also their own Administration's deadly manipulations.

Political factions and galactic media moguls vie for power … and money.

A FURY OF ACES 2

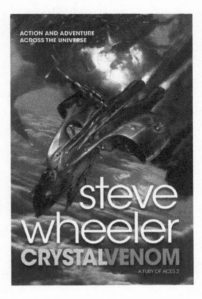

What will you do when the hand that nourishes you starts choking you? The crew of *Basalt*, the interstellar frigate, are major media heroes, famous beyond their wildest dreams. The various factions of the Administration, the Games Board, the Haulers and the corporate Gjomviks all want a piece of their action, and will go to any lengths to manipulate the famous ship and crew to make more money and gain more influence, even if it means savaging *Basalt* beyond recognition.